RACING
TO
MURDER

BY
BEN GUYATT

For Those Who Have Inspired Me

© 2006 Ben Guyatt
All Rights Reserved

ISBN # 978-1-4116-9781-2

Produced by Seldon Griffin Graphics Inc.
www.seldongriffin.com

Chapter One

Traffic flashed behind the silhouette of Randall Grange as he stumbled towards the railing of the Skyway Bridge. An orange glow illuminated his left hand and something metallic glimmered momentarily on his chest. A few drivers honked their displeasure and swerved to avoid him, but he didn't notice. "Great fucking night for it!" he said happily with a hint of intoxication.

He took a heavy drag from his joint as the paper burned fast and singed his yellowed fingers. He blew several perfect smoke rings and playfully wrote his name in the air with the ember. "Just like a sparkler," he said childishly but was suddenly embarrassed. "Thirty years old for Christ's sake!"

His glazed blue eyes gazed wondrously at the sprawling City of Hamilton across the shimmering bay. The sparkling lights of the steel industry reflected perfectly in the calm but black water as monolithic freighters loaded and unloaded their cargo in a ballet of cranes and pulleys. "Goddamn lunch bucket town! Bunch of thieving, murdering, raping fuckers!" he grumbled and spat his disdain, some of the drool defying gravity and hanging from his sandpaper chin.

He dizzily threw his head back and squinted at the light-polluted night sky. "Like you used to say, Mom, every star is the soul of a life lived... and I bet you mine falls," he said and angrily flicked the joint away. "Supposed to make a wish. I wish... I wish I had a fucking reason not to do it," he stated sombrely, watching the joint dancing in the breeze before sweeping downward.

Randall clumsily pushed aside his police badge and dug through his breast pocket until he retrieved a crumpled packet of cigarettes. Empty. He studied the warning label and the picture of a diseased heart. "Stupid fucking things promised to kill me! Beg for death and all I get is life!" he mumbled and carelessly tossed the pack away. "Well, when you want something done right, you got to do it yourself," he said, cracking his knuckles determinedly and tugging at his navy blue, wrinkled trousers with a thin red stripe on each leg. "Isn't that what you used to say, old man?"

Randall cautiously inched forward until he was leaning against the rail, his police hat suddenly sailed off his head and disappeared with the wicked updraft. "Holy Christ!" he whispered, smoothing back his blonde hair, mesmerized by the network of beams that faded and blended into a dark, muted abyss. "Jesus, it's cold!" he lamented and drew the collar of his dark short-sleeved shirt up.

He closed his eyes and breathed the smoggy air as the violent breeze howled and swirled around him. Randall barely opened one eye, spied the heavens and shook a naughty finger. "I hear you laughing at me. Always chasing me around with those guts in your hands. Was only fear that kept my little feet moving. What was that anyway, some sort of fucked-up hazing thing?" he said and sniffed at the foul air. "This place smells like those animals. Like you. Never could get that stink out of my nose. Blood, guts and booze. Can still see it on the sawdust... and me. Made my shoes all sticky," he said and chuckled. "Gave me good traction to get away from your sick fucking ass though."

Randall started to cough and gagged but managed to swallow. "Know what used to make me want to puke, other than you? That fucking chopping block. Hated everything made of wood since then and you thought I liked all that shit. Wasn't a mama's boy. She showed me compassion when she could. Something you didn't know shit about. Fuck, you weren't my real dad anyway."

Another gust of wind. Almost musical. Randall caught himself humming a song and frowned. "What the hell was that tune anyway? One Dozen Roses? Must have looked like a fucking fag sitting there singing a goddamned love song to a dead cow. Some of them were my pets... you said I could have them... then you killed them... forced me to eat them," he said with a trembling voice. "Always hoped they were just asleep," he said, lifting his lumbering head skyward again as his eyes filled. "God they were big. Big and black. You probably didn't know, shit, even if you did, you wouldn't give a fuck, but I felt sorry for them. Kind of embarrassed. I mean, they used to be powerful and majestic but," he said with a regretful sigh and a careless shrug. "You got those big, meaty fucking hands of yours on them and then they were dead. Dead and harmless."

Randall abruptly shifted on his feet and vomited. He caught his breath and spat his mouth clean. "Goddamned Tequila! Christ!" He wiped his face with his hairy forearm and noticed the plethora of razor blade scars. "See what you made me do?" he said and raised his arm. "Should have slit

CHAPTER ONE

your fucking throat when I had the chance, but I would have felt guilty. Guilty for Christ's sake!" he groused as he studied his stomach's contents splattered and dripping on the rail. "Looks just like the guts on the floor and reeks like them fucking pigs in that boiling water. And them disgusting cow heads and all them goddamn flies buzzing around," he said, annoyed, swiping at the invisible insects and then saw a june-bug struggling to free itself from a web over his head. "That was weird, seeing all them dead animals," he explained to the trapped insect. "Funny how you notice things when they're dead. Waiting for them to move and still warm." The spider fleetingly appeared and started for its meal, but Randall stood on his toes and poked the web, freeing the bug. "One victim's enough."

Below, an ear-splitting horn blast from a passing laker caused Randall to jump and clench his eyes. "That sound! That fucking sound! That axe hitting them between their eyes! They have eyes like we do! There's life in those eyes," he yelled as he thrashed his head and plugged his ears. "I hated that sound! When they hit the floor, I hated it!" Randall shouted and sobbed uncontrollably. "Why the fuck did you make me listen to that sound? Why?"

"Sir? Are you okay?" another man's timorous voice said.

Startled, Randall hastily drew out his penis and started to urinate, the current of air pushing the liquid back against his trousers. He glanced over his shoulder at the shadowy figure of Officer Tony D'Angelo, a short and stocky man of twenty-one with black hair, nervously edging towards him.

"What the fuck do you want, booger?" Randall said and turned away to wipe his eyes dry.

Tony shuffled into the light. "It was a minor fender bender, sir. No injuries. I've written it up," he said and motioned to two cars pulled off on the opposite side of the bridge. His brown eyes spotted the vomit-drenched railing. "Do you have the flu, sir?"

"Allergies."

"To what?" Tony asked, endeavouring to sound interested and to make conversation.

"Alcohol. I have one or two bottles and I puke," Randall answered sarcastically.

"Are you sure it's a good idea to urinate in the lake, sir?" Tony asked anxiously, trying to avoid staring at Randall's manhood. "I mean we are police officers."

"It's not a lake, booger, it's a bay."

"Police officers are not supposed to drink on the job, sir," Tony said, fearing the reply and biting his lip.

"Do you have any hobbies, booger?"

Tony frowned and nodded. "Yes sir. I collect police hats from around the world. I also volunteer at our church," he stated proudly. "Why?"

"Well I drink until I pass out. So you do your thing and I'll do mine," Randall replied and waved him off. "Get back to the cruiser. Be there in a minute." Tony waited, unsure whether to pursue his concerns, but then quickly walked away.

Randall's eyes fell to his bile on the pavement and noticed a few specks of blood. "I didn't want to see those executions. Didn't want to see them tied up and scared shitless, but I had to look. It's like a car accident," he said and fingered the sharp edges of his badge. "Never did like that goddamn knife you always carried. You were a sick fuck. Seems to me you enjoyed bleeding them," he said, watching a trickle of rainwater run down the beam beside him. "All that blood, steaming and going into that slimy fucking grate," Randall added, shivering and studying his badly scarred hands. "Your paws made me sick when I heard them rip off their skin. You were a fucking murderer," Randall said as a single tear rolled off his face and he watched it splash against the rail. He began to pet the imaginary head of a slain beast and whispered mournfully. "Their blood dripped like that... yours too."

Randall sniffed hard, straightened up and took a deep breath. He lifted one leg over the barrier, listed temporarily and swung the other foot over. "It's a devastating thing when you realize you've wasted your entire life," he said matter-of-factly. "Fucking regrets. Hell, don't matter much now," he added and stared at the cracked face on his watch, its band tarnished. He peeled it off and held it up. "This is about all I got from you that lasted, other than a fucked-up life."

Randall flung the timepiece and watched it glitter until it disappeared. "I got to do this thing. If I don't hurt myself, I'm going to hurt somebody else," he declared and rubbed his grotesque hands together. "Well world, before I go, I got to tell you I've learned a few things," he said and held out his arms to address the whole of humanity. "First, there is no justice, only the wicked survive," he said and began counting on his fingers. "If there is a God, and it's a big fucking if, he, she, it, or whatever the hell it is, doesn't give a shit about anything or anyone. Too goddamned selective. Always answers all prayers and the answer is always no... so you have to do it yourself. Gets all of the credit but takes none of the blame. Oh, and all women are cunts," he mused as more of an afterthought. He took a bow, stuck one foot out and closed his eyes, hovering on the brink of death. "Wonder what it's going to feel like. Seen others do it. Easy. One step. Hope they find me. Just another floater. Don't want to get all fucking bloated and brown. Fish food for Christ's sake."

CHAPTER ONE

Randall realized his penis was still dangling and stooped to look at it. "Wonder if she'll show up. Fuck no!" he said, scolding himself. "She won't care. Going to be one lonely motherfucking funeral. Just me in a box," he said as he laughed hysterically and fumbled to put his penis back in his trousers.

He suddenly turned sombre and withdrew his wallet. Randall flipped it open to a frayed photograph of a blonde baby girl, sitting on a swing. "Hope you understand someday. Hope you can forgive me... for everything," he said and kissed it before tucking it away. Another, deep breath. "I don't deserve to suffer anymore, but you, Dad, you got off easy. Be with you shortly, Mom. You too, fuck face," he said and let one hand go, the other clinging to the railing, his fingertips the only anchor between himself and the ever after. "At the count of three. One, two..."

"Sir! We got a call!" Tony yelled from the car.

"Fuck! Fuck, fuck, fuck, fuck!" Randall barked and hesitated as he debated whether to end his life. "Damnit! I'm sorry. Don't wait up for me, Mom... I'm coming home soon." He begrudgingly climbed back to the safety of the bridge and ran to the car. He jumped behind the wheel and kicked over the engine. "Where?"

"Frances Avenue. Domestic," Tony replied, connecting his seatbelt and realizing Randall wasn't in full uniform. "Sir, shouldn't you be wearing your vest?"

"Fuck... no. Might save me," Randall said, reaching for something beneath his seat.

"Maybe I should drive," Tony suggested timidly.

"Fuck you, booger," Randall answered as he threw the car into gear.

The cruiser screeched into traffic without signalling as other motorists sounded their displeasure. Unconcerned, Randall deftly steered the wheel with his knees, popped open a beer can and lit a half-burnt cigarette he found in the brimming ashtray. He shifted his attention back to the road, flicked on the siren and lights before cranking up the distorted rock music. The shrill voice of Mick Jagger vibrated through the rear speakers, causing the dust particles to dance with each twanging, thumping beat. Randall's foot depressed the gas pedal in time with the song 'Sympathy For The Devil' as the car frantically accelerated and slowed.

"You're not back on the dirt tracks, sir," Tony yelled over the din and smiled nervously. "Are you trying to get us killed?"

"No... I'll live forever, booger," Randall said. He drained the can, burped, crushed the empty against his forehead for Tony's sake and fecklessly tossed it out the window.

The cruiser exited the bridge and rounded a corner, the back end started to swerve, but Randall slammed the throttle and expertly corrected the wheel. The cruiser ran a stop sign, bolted sharply to the left, jumped the curb, smashed into a mailbox and continued on.

Tony checked his side mirror to discover envelopes fluttering in the breeze. He reluctantly peered over the dashboard and grimaced at the crumpled right front corner. "This isn't going to help you get back into homicide, sir."

"Who says I want to?"

The light ahead turned red as a prostitute held a john's hand. They stepped off the curb and made it to the middle of the street, but stopped when they heard squealing tyres.

Randall crushed the brake with both feet, causing the cruiser to lunge forward as the front bumper scraped the pavement. Finally, the vehicle came to a smoking stop, mere inches from the couple's feet.

"Crazy asshole!" the Lolita screamed as she marched towards the cruiser. Randall quickly pushed a button and his window hummed upward. Tony did the same as the irate lady of the evening pounded the hood. "Open that goddamned door! I want your badge number you son-of-a-bitch!" she shouted. The terrified john started backing away and waving off any guilt.

"Would you fuck her?" Randall asked calmly.

"No, sir. I'm engaged," Tony replied, blushing at the thought. Randall flopped his head to stare at him with an insulting look. "I... I don't think a man and woman should... you know, before they get married," Tony added, thoroughly uncomfortable.

"Look, booger, do me a favour and turn that fucking halo of yours down to dim. I read your bio. You used to be in a gang," Randall said as he watched the prostitute chastise her customer for walking away.

"I'm not very proud of that," Tony said, hanging his head in shame. "I guess we all have secrets."

"Don't sweat it, booger. I wanted to be a priest, but I hated God too much to serve."

"Why do you hate Him so much?" Tony asked, intrigued.

"Because the son-of-a-bitch abandoned me before I was even born."

"Well, I think I'm a good Christian. I'm always trying to be a better person, sir," Tony replied, explaining with his hands.

"You're wasting your time. We are what we are, booger," Randall said and caught a glimpse of himself in the rear-view mirror, "and there's not a fucking thing you can do about it," he added as he reached beneath his seat and retrieved the last can of beer from a ringed six-pack. He snapped it open and deliberately took a long sip in full view of the exasperated concubine. Randall gave her a half-hearted nod and drove off. He went to check his watch. "Shit! What time is it?"

Chapter One

"Ten thirty, sir."

"Goddamnit! I'm never going to make last call!"

Tony shifted uncomfortably in his seat and mustered his courage. "You know, sir, there's more to life than being a cop and drinking and smoking."

"I know... but she left me," Randall said full of melancholy.

Relieved that Randall didn't react to his audacity, Tony said. "The world isn't the enemy, sir. A badge can't be an officer's whole identity."

"It's all I got left, booger."

"That's another thing, sir. Do you call me booger because I'm a rookie? Green and all that?"

"You're a genius, booger. A real Sherlock fucking Holmes."

The police radio crackled. "That domestic at 103 Frances. A child's been heard screaming. Apartment 201. Better step on it guys," a female voice informed.

"Car 31. We're on it," Tony said professionally into the mike. "You really should be wearing your vest, sir."

"Why did you become a cop? Your cock not big enough?" Randall asked, patently agitated.

"To serve and protect, sir," Tony replied proudly.

Randall laughed and buried the gas pedal. "You've only been on the job for a week, booger. A year from now you won't give a fuck."

Tony turned his attention to the window. "Then why did you become a police officer?"

"Same reason you did." Randall said and saw Tony's deflated look. "But don't worry, booger, it happens to all of us."

Randall slowed the cruiser to a noiseless stop in a blackened alley and stepped out, his shoes splashing in a puddle, the cold water seeped through one of the well-worn soles. "Fuck!" he whispered as he raised one foot and shook it.

"Why don't you just order a new pair, sir?" Tony asked.

"I didn't plan on being a flatfoot this long."

Timorous, Tony slid out of the seat and immediately unsnapped his holster with quaking hands as his widened eyes scanned the murkiness. "God, I hate this!" he said, fighting to retrieve his crucifix and kissing it.

"God's got nothing to do with it," Randall said and scurried around a corner as Tony laboured to keep pace. "Look at it this way, booger, if you get iced, you'll get a free funeral."

"Are you an atheist, sir?"

"No. I have to have someone to hate and the sooner you realize God hates you, life gets a whole lot easier," Randall said, opening the door to the small lobby of a red brick, four storey building, disclosing dank, dirty walls that were partially wallpapered and covered with profane graffiti.

Tony spotted some dry dog excrement on the carpet. "These people live like pigs!" he managed to whisper in between deep breaths.

Randall eased into the dim, narrow corridor which led to the single elevator. "No they don't. Animals are smarter," he said. His head shifted to the irritating buzz of a flickering exit sign as Tony flanked him, half turned towards the lobby.

"You scared, sir?" Tony huffed as droplets of sweat beaded on his reddened face.

"Every second of every fucking day," Randall replied and opened the stairwell door. "Being a cop is ninety-nine percent boredom and one percent, pure fucking terror. Welcome to the one percent."

Both carefully ascended into the unknown as their footsteps echoed against the damp, cracked concrete. Randall withdrew his Glock, earning a questionable look from Tony. "We're not supposed to draw our weapons unless our lives are at risk, sir," Tony whispered just as a drip from an overhead pipe plopped on his nose.

"Look, booger, people in this fucking town will kill their own mothers for five bucks. If I'm going to die, it'll be on my own terms," Randall replied and removed the safety. He slowly pushed open the door to the second floor and peered around the corner. The walls were brushed, red velvet with tiled floors and cheap, burnt out chandeliers hung outside each door.

Tony followed him into the gloomy hallway. "Looks like a Spanish bordello," Tony said to ease his own fear by forcing a laugh.

"Probably is. Seems like home to me. Right there," Randall said and pointed to the door directly across from them. The numerals of unit 201 dangled askew as light seeped out from under the door.

"I don't hear anything," Tony said with a perplexed look. "Maybe they left?" he added hopefully. Randall suddenly held up a hand upon hearing the muffled cry of a child. They exchanged a quick nod and Tony stayed to the right of the frame as Randall rapped lightly on the door. A few moments went by. Another tapping, only harder. Nothing. "Now what?" Tony asked. Randall's hand carefully began turning the knob. "You can't do that, sir! We need a warrant!" Tony whispered urgently.

"Call it a hunch. Besides, we can do whatever we want if we feel there's someone in distress," Randall said, purposely methodical. "It's in the police handbook. Right?"

"I... I guess it is," Tony replied with growing angst. The door quietly clicked open and Randall carefully nudged it aside as the whimpering grew louder. Weapon pointed skyward, he edged inside with Tony in tow.

Chapter One

Garbage, empty liquor bottles, discarded Bic lighters, cigarette butts, articles of clothing, weigh scales, baggies and makeshift crack pipes were strewn about the room. A black and white television was on but muted near the open window leading to the fire escape. There was one couch, a glass coffee table with a modified asthma inhaler, a sixties style kitchen chair and a box spring and stained mattress in the filthy living room. Heavy metal music could be discerned, but it was tinny and abruptly stopped. The only light came from the single bulb in the ceiling as it swayed with the incoming breeze.

Randall peered into a dark bedroom on his left and saw little feet protruding from under an army type cot. He motioned for Tony to remain and slipped inside. The child ceased crying and scurried further under the bed leaving a red trail. Randall knelt down and lowered his head to discover the stark, white underwear of the ten-year-old boy and the unmistakable stain of blood on his bottom. Randall felt the bile rushing to the back of his throat and he swallowed hard. "It's okay. I'm a policeman," he whispered as the toddler began weeping again and curling himself into a ball. "Nobody's going to hurt you anymore. I promise." The child scrambled further away and Randall pulled himself up. He closed the door lightly behind him and tiptoed into the living room.

"Well?" Tony whispered.

"Stay here!" Randall answered tersely and focused on a closed door past the undersized, soiled kitchen. He swept across the room and kicked it open.

Inside the grotesque bathroom, Andy Lunder, a twenty-year-old man with greasy hair and an unkempt goatee, bolted upright from the toilet and ripped off his headphones. "What the fuck are you doing?"

Randall's eyes dropped to Andy's bloodied penis. "Move!" Randall commanded as his head shook with rage.

"Who the hell are you?" Andy said. Randall grabbed him by the throat and dragged him into the living room.

"Close the window!" Randall ordered Tony.

"What's going on?" Tony nervously replied.

"Do it!" Randall said. Tony swiftly acquiesced and closed the window, silencing the drone of the city. "Who's the boy?" Randall demanded.

Andy's brow furrowed as he pulled up his shoddy jeans and threw on a dirtied muscle shirt. "He's my bitch's kid. Why?"

Randall distanced himself from Andy with his gun trained. "Where is she?"

Andy rolled his eyes impatiently and reached for a pack of cigarettes on the coffee table. "We had a fight. She took off for a while," he replied, unfazed.

"Put the smokes away," Randall ordered. "Close the drapes," he said to Tony without looking. Tony yanked the tattered cloth across the window.

"Stand up," he said to Andy. "I'm Officer Randall Grange and you're under arrest." He fumbled for his laminated copy of the Charter of Rights and Freedoms in his breast pocket.

"I know it by heart, sir," Tony said.

"Then do it!" Randall snapped.

"Randall? Sounds like a faggot's name," Andy said with a smarmy smile, placing his pack of cigarettes into his breast pocket and noticing Randall wasn't wearing his cap. "Only fucking homo cops don't wear hats. Makes your head easier to grab onto while you're sucking their dick, uh?" he added and laughed stupidly.

"I said stand up! Turn around with your hands behind your back!" Randall barked as he readied his handcuffs.

"Fuck you pig," Andy said and relaxed into the sofa. "You need a warrant to be in here."

"You saw him lunge for me, right Officer D'Angelo?" Randall said straightforwardly to Tony. Incredulous, Tony could only stand there and stare dumbly at his partner. "I had to use as much force as was necessary. Right?" Randall shouted.

"We... we have to do things by the book, sir," Tony replied anxiously.

Randall angrily gesticulated for Tony to leave. "I am! The safety of the child is our first priority. Take the kid downstairs!"

"Shouldn't I call for back up?" Tony said as Andy lit a cigarette with a toothy smile and kicked his feet up, obviously enjoying the tension between the partners.

Randall wrapped a quivering finger around the trigger. He raised the gun and aimed it at Andy's head. "I said take the kid and wait downstairs!" Randall said, his voice breaking with emotion.

After a few moments, Tony disappeared into the bedroom and quickly came out, holding the whimpering boy and carrying him to the doorway. "What are you going to do, sir?" Tony said.

Randall waved Tony off with a nonchalant flick of his gun. "I'll call it in. You take care of the kid. See you shortly." Tony waited; not knowing if leaving was the right course of action but turned and closed the door behind him.

"Even your partner thinks you're fucked," Andy happily remarked and stood. "Now get the hell out of my house, asshole!"

Randall's eyes flared and his chin firmed. In a flash, he swung his gun, cracking Andy across the face, blood sprayed across the wall and the paedophile crashed through the coffee table to the floor. Dazed, he lifted his head, felt the blood pouring from a large gash above his left eye and began to whimper.

"Take it like a man," Randall said unaffected, he grinned watching Andy struggling to lift himself up.

Andy clung to the couch with one hand and managed to drag himself to his knees while trying to stem the flow of blood with the other. "I'm going to sue you... you... fucking asshole!"

"I doubt it. Hard to testify with no teeth," Randall answered and kicked him square in the mouth, causing him to sprawl backward onto the disintegrated table. Andy started to bawl when he realized several molars were missing from his bloody mouth. "Anything else to say?" Randall said, but Andy just shook his head.

Randall walked to the window, ripped the drape off and threw it at Andy for use as a towel. "This is police brutality! I have rights!" Andy cried.

Randall abruptly kicked him in the throat, sending him reeling to the floor again. The young man held his trembling hands to his neck and gasped for air.

Randall blinked away biting tears, sniffed hard and settled into the chair. His swimming eyes drifted off into space as he removed his badge from his shirt and set it on the table. "You know what I want most in this world?" he said quietly, plucking the smokes from Andy's pocket and lighting one. "A reason to live, but there isn't one. I'm losing faith in humanity by the goddamned minute and your time's up. I'm so fucking sick and tired of seeing the worst of everything. So, I don't care what happens to me. I've become everything I despise, but I sure know evil when I see it," he said as he caressed the sleek barrel of his weapon and held the cold, blue steel to his hot cheek. Sheer terror enveloped Andy's pulpy face as Randall wiped away the moisture beneath his eyes and cleared his throat. "Now, I'm a fair man. How do you want to do this thing... father?" he said and placed the revolver on the frame of the smashed coffee table.

Tony lifted the boy into the back seat of the cruiser and wrapped him in a blanket. Suddenly, a gunshot shattered the muggy air, Tony's head snapped round in disbelief. "Jesus Christ!" he said and scrambled back towards the building.

Chapter Two

"He's got such a tight butt, it's sinful," a young woman said, watching Vincenzo Azzopardi through binoculars as he hurried through an adoring crowd.

The woman handed the field glasses to her anxious friend beside her in the packed grandstand. "If there's a puddle under me, it isn't going to be from the rain," the second woman said giggling and elbowing her friend. She focused on Vincenzo as he impatiently waved aside a boy hoping for an autograph. Vincenzo then tore away a piece of paper that was taped to the door of a motor home before disappearing.

In the lavish trailer, Vincenzo studied the paper, written in Japanese. He crumpled it and gave a sorrowful glance to a Rosary adorned photograph of a middle-aged couple holding hands. He stroked the beads as their smooth texture rolled effortlessly across his moist palm. Vincenzo closed his arresting, brown eyes, blessed himself, kissed the diamond-studded crucifix hanging from his neck and hid it beneath his Boss T-shirt.

The twenty-four-year-old turned on the stereo just as Mozart's Don Giovanni began to play. He sank into the cool, black leather couch and held out his muscular, tanned hands. They were steady and nimble but began to tremble upon withdrawing a newspaper from a coffee tabletop with a racing car etched in the glass. The glaring headline stated: *Azzopardi Mourns Parents Killed In Plane Crash Five Days Ago But Will Drive In Monaco*. The by-line read: *Azzopardi Sr. Created Multi-million Dollar Real Estate & Banking Empire*.

Vincenzo closed the paper, glanced past his flawlessly manicured fingertips and studied the gold framed, life-sized cut-out of himself posing for an Italian pasta company. Dressed in full racing garb with the words *Hispania Gold* written across his chest and his helmet beneath one arm, he held a precarious forkful of spaghetti with his other hand. He flashed a dazzling smile and his thick, brown hair flowed down to his shoulders. "A

CHAPTER TWO

million dollar smile," he said blithely to cheer himself up with a distinct, Milanese accent. "Actually, two million."

He scanned the narrow room. The walls were decorated with various pictures of himself and his father, chronicling the junior's career from a four-year-old in a go-cart on a home built track to driving a racing car. Several showed him with celebrities from sports, entertainment and politics. In each photograph there was a different, beautiful woman at his side. "Made love to every one of them," he stated proudly.

A tumultuous crack of thunder startled him and his concerned eyes shifted to the window, where droplets of rain started streaking the glass as unhappy voices were heard bemoaning the weather.

He picked up the universal remote, turned on the large screen television and went to hit the play button for the VCR, but there was a knock at the door. "What?" he said patently annoyed, eyeing the blurry outline of a short man with blonde hair standing outside the door.

The door flew open with a gust of wind as the torrential rain swept inside. Ichiro Tanaka, a squat, Japanese man of thirty-eight with dyed hair and a round face behind bright blue, wire rimmed spectacles, bowed half-heartedly and stood there waiting.

"Well don't just stand there rice ball, come in," Vincenzo said. Ichiro turned to close the door but the vacuum of air slammed it for him. "I told you to stop giving me these!" he barked, holding up the crumpled paper. "I don't need your prayers!" he added and flung it across the room.

"Sorry, Azzopardi, but it is a Japanese custom," Ichiro replied.

"I don't care! Understand? So, what about it?" Vincenzo said half interested as he reached for a bottle of water on the table.

Ichiro produced a clipboard from inside his dripping, nylon, Team Jenkins jacket and strained to see through his steamed glasses. He raised a thick finger and rubbed the lenses as they squeaked clean. Hoping Vincenzo didn't see, he casually shuffled the Superman comic book he had been reading to the bottom of the stack of technical papers. "It does not look good, Azzopardi. Satellite says we can expect rain for the next six to eight hours. Sorry about that," he said with forced English and wiped aside the remaining hair plastered to his forehead.

"With the money they pay you, rice ball, you should be able to change the weather."

"I do not make that much, Azzopardi," Ichiro replied.

"And that's another thing! I told you not to call me by my last name! I don't care if it is proper in Jap land! My name is Vincenzo!"

"I can only call my friends by their first name," he replied and wiped his nose with a Kleenex.

"You're always sick, aren't you?" Vincenzo said and unscrewed the water bottle lid. He flicked it at Ichiro; it bounced off his cheek with a smart snap and left a red welt. Ichiro smiled uneasily and stared at the floor. "What do the stewards say?" Vincenzo said.

"It is a go," Ichiro answered timidly. "There is no standing water."

Vincenzo chuckled, stood up and stretched. "That figures. Not one of those morons has ever been behind the wheel." He removed his T-shirt revealing a taut, impeccably proportioned upper body and slipped off his track trousers. Ichiro tried not to look, embarrassed at Vincenzo's lack of modesty.

"There are a few things I think we should discuss," Ichiro said nervously as he pushed his glasses further up his nose.

Impatient, Vincenzo placed his hands on his hips. "I know you're the engineer, but just throw some wets on it and I'll do the rest," he said tiredly.

Ichiro's amiable face turned sour and he bit his lip. "I know you are under a lot of pressure, but if you are not going to listen to me, Azzopardi..."

"Then leave, rice ball! That fossil might own the team but I'm the boss!" he bellowed and appropriately pointed to the Boss insignia on his shirt. Vincenzo gingerly followed the corridor towards the back of the motor home and broke wind. "Get lost, rice ball. I'm taking a shower."

"But I wanted to speak to you about the car. The number four is bad luck, Azzopardi," Ichiro pleaded.

Vincenzo wheeled to confront him. "Not this shit again! Look, I like the number four! It's how old I was when I drove my first go-kart! It means something to me! It's good luck! I'm not a Jap! Superstition is for the weak! Get it? Now, get out!" he said and continued towards the shower.

Ichiro remained for a few moments and wanted to say something but thought better of it. He barely bowed and placed the clipboard back inside his jacket. He felt his sore cheek, opened the door and smiled upon seeing Teresa Legaro running towards him as her wind blown umbrella impeded her progress. The twenty-three-year-old mulatto was chased by a throng of paparazzi, snapping photos and shouting questions. "He is not very happy today," Ichiro warned, entranced by her hazel eyes.

Teresa shrugged, "He never is," she said unconcerned with a Southern US idiom as Ichiro gladly opened the door for her. "But that's none of your business. I'll handle the man, you take care of the car." Teresa added, slamming the door in his face and carelessly throwing the umbrella aside.

Chapter Two

She immediately recognized the sound of running water and shook her head as her curly, black mane fell over her shoulders. Despite the soaked appearance, Teresa was magnificent. Her skin tight T-shirt clung to her chest and highlighted her petite breasts. She peeled it off and slipped out of her jeans, revealing a lacy thong. Her long fingers pulled off her panties and exposed a wisp of tawny, pubic hair. A sexy smile broke across her face as she strolled down the hallway.

Vincenzo stood under the showerhead as the water cascaded over the back of his neck. Through the rippled glass of the shower doors he saw her approach, her slinky body gliding effortlessly. The door slid open. "Mind if I *come* in?" she asked salaciously.

"Yes," he answered sternly and rammed the door closed so hard that the shampoo bottle fell from the plastic rack. The door slowly reopened.

"I know the last few days haven't been easy for you, or me, but I'm here to help you," she said and caressed his face, but he slapped her hand away.

"I don't want you touching me anymore."

"What's wrong with you? You're not gay, are you?" she said with a light-hearted laugh, trying to ease the tension.

Vincenzo's nostrils flared and he backhanded her; she fell heavily to the floor. "Get out half-breed!" he said and casually resumed lathering.

Teresa felt her jaw as her eyes clouded over. A tiny trickle of blood spilled from one nostril and into her mouth. "See what you did?" she said and wiped it away.

"I thought I told you to stop sniffing that shit!"

Embarrassed she had been caught; Teresa tried to change the subject. "You're not the only one to ever lose their parents! At least yours loved you!" she said as she buried her head in her hands and began crying.

"That's right, go ahead and twist everything around so that you're the victim. You're pathetic," he stated, rolling his eyes. "Now I know why your mother was a drug addict too, she couldn't stand you. You're nothing but a spoiled brat."

Teresa eyed the hairdryer and for an instant, contemplated throwing the appliance into the shower. "You have to win at everything, don't you? You think it's easy being your wife?"

Vincenzo chuckled and shook his head in disbelief. "Give me a break. The toughest decision you have is whether your underwear matches your earrings."

Her angelic face hardened as she dragged herself up. "Do you have any idea how many guys would like to make love to a supermodel?"

"You might be beautiful on the outside, but you're ugly underneath and if they knew the price, they wouldn't touch you," he said and turned the hot water knob further, engulfing his body in steam.

"What the hell is that supposed to mean?"

"You're a high maintenance woman and life's been easy for you. You get whatever you want with a smile because you think your beauty should be rewarded. It's time to grow up," he said as he continued bathing.

"What about you? You've never worked a day in your life. If it wasn't for your father's money grabbing, you'd be shining shoes in Milan!" she countered.

Vincenzo pointed a threatening finger at her. "Don't you talk about him like that! He worked hard so I could race! The man had to literally pry my blistered fingers off of the wheel when I was a boy," he said, demonstrating with his hands.

"Boo-hoo," she retorted and pretended to wipe away tears. "The great Vincenzo has feelings."

"You make me sick," he said and closed the door again.

Teresa slid it open. "Then why did you marry me?"

"You're an image. Part of the team," he replied casually.

"I doubt it. When you met me, you couldn't keep your eyes off me... or your hands," she said with a simper.

Vincenzo rubbed the shampoo into his hair. "You can't stand to share the spotlight, can you? And now it's shining on me more than you. And the only reason *you* married me is because you thought it might help your career. Well guess what? Things change. You're not as desirable as you think you are."

The comments stung Teresa to the core and she bristled. "Maybe we should end this thing."

He laughed the suggestion off and rinsed his hair. "Don't be so melodramatic. Besides, you owe me."

Teresa searched for the right words, but she knew he had trumped her. "Fuck you!" she said and stormed away.

Vincenzo closed the door. "Not today," he replied as he caught a mouthful of water and playfully spouted it out.

With an African Grey Timneh parrot on his shoulder, Benny Rabowitz caught his reflection in the small, stainless steel refrigerator and smiled upon seeing his distorted figure dressed in a flowery Hawaiian shirt and underwear. He rubbed his sweaty, completely bald, fifty-year-old head and opened the freezer door. He closed his eyes, enjoying the blast of frozen air as he grabbed a red Popsicle from a full box.

CHAPTER TWO

Unwrapping the treat and letting the paper fall to the floor, he tramped across the hotel suite and, from a coffee table, took a pair of binoculars from beside a book on ornithology. He flicked on the television and slid the balcony door aside. "No bath please!" the parrot squawked, shaking itself and hoping off Benny's shoulder to the patio table. The bird hurried inside but Benny stepped out and giggled with delight as the moisture soaked carpet squished between his chubby toes.

He looked right past the edge of the building and watched the white caps crash into the breakwater and smash high into the air, churning the surf into an iridescent, frothing spectrum of turquoise, black and blue. He anxiously glanced through the field glasses and followed the gulls circling the harbour, portending the insidious storm. A few dove and plucked the hapless fish, trapped by the brief undertow as the sound of water sucked and receded. Benny's attention shifted to the extravagant yachts heaving in the harbour as the mooring lines tightened and relaxed with each ebb and flow, causing an ominous creaking. A police boat with frogmen patrolled the area near the shore to ensure a twelve-foot border away from the seawall in case the unthinkable should occur.

He ducked instinctively as vicious, spidery flashes of lightning danced beneath low, fast moving, smoky grey-blue clouds, providing a natural, brilliant display of fireworks. The following, pernicious thunder reverberated before finally dissipating within the sound of the muffled sea.

"The kind of place suitable for Oberon," Benny said enthusiastically, blowing a kiss as a piece of Popsicle broke off and rolled down his shirt, but he didn't care. "Ah Monaco. Where fantasy meets reality. If you have to inquire as to the price, you can't afford it. But I can," he added gleefully and raised his frozen treat to toast.

Benny studied the glamorous, historic streets, slick from the steady rain, the glossy pavement mirroring its own Gallic, storybook image. He looked down at the road, appearing from out of the tunnel beneath him, snaking through the tiny principality, barely visible through a ghostly, creeping fog. Palm trees swayed, rustled and bent in the stiff, humid wind.

"First staged in 1929, this competition is not just a race, it's an event and the crown jewel of motor sport. Unique, but vastly outdated vis-à-vis the design of other circuits, the Grand prix is an incumbent race, especially for the sponsors," the British television broadcaster said. "Winning Monaco is akin to a coronation and striking it rich, enshrining the victor's place in racing history while the losers only find fool's gold."

Benny noticed a topless, beautiful woman on the balcony below and slipped one hand down his underwear. "Qualifying is paramount in order to ensure a good starting position, for it is nearly impossible to pass. Patience is a formidable weapon in the armoury of a racing driver and no other race tests a man's mettle as much as Monte Carlo," the broadcaster continued.

Benny masturbated and eyed the filled grandstands, the bodies hidden beneath a sea of colourful umbrellas. Dozens held flags depicting their favourite teams and drivers that snapped wildly in the breeze. He ejaculated and rubbed the discharge into his psoriasis-covered palms.

He focused on the girl below again as she sipped champagne and sampled culinary masterpieces. Benny looked through the binoculars and observed the elite, crowded into the cover of archways and balconies, perched high above the circuit at various levels throughout the incongruous, narrow and confined tiers of architecture. "They don't care about the race," he chuckled to himself. "The only reason you're here is to be seen, admired, respected, envied and hated. The track is the real star, not you, not even the drivers."

Another streak of lightning, and the delayed boom of thunder, caused applause to erupt from the drenched spectators. Benny continued scanning the crowds. "You do know you're frowned upon. It's xenophobia, pure and simple. Mere commoners. Suitable targets of boorish ridicule safely articulated out of earshot," he said, feigning a stuffy, British accent and sucking on the Popsicle. "But you foreigners are the true racing enthusiasts. I know you love that sweet racket that rings in your ears for hours after the finish. It's an audible souvenir to be savoured and remembered. It's the heat of the battle. The intoxicating smell of racing fuel and the flecks of rubber covering you from head to toe," he added and licked the remains from the Popsicle stick. "All of this is the irresistible, sensory ingredients that amalgamate into the cocktail of the Monaco Grand Prix... and I'm going to ruin it," he said joyfully and stepped back into the suite.

"It's about gear heads. Aficionados of speed and technocrats happy to argue the intricate aspects and psychics of racing," the broadcaster said. "From around the globe, both young and old, the rich and middle-class flock to this place called Monaco to witness the ultimate race, the pinnacle of tradition and mystique. And the inclement weather is only adding to the excitement."

Benny wiped his hands off against his underwear and sat on the couch. He retrieved a metallic silver briefcase from the floor with one eye on the television. It showed trucks touring the track with jet engines mounted on the beds in a vain attempt to blow-dry the raceway. Another angle highlighted the minuscule streams of water trickling down the sides of the hilly circuit before pooling on even ground. Track workers feverishly endeavoured to sweep the large puddles away only to have nature's wrath replenish what was previously removed.

Chapter Two

Benny clicked open the case, revealing several black pieces of tubing and heard the track announcer's voice blaring over the speaker system, but it was indiscernible as crackling interference frequently interrupted his commentary. On the television, the spectators covered their ears with each shrill message. "An odd reaction considering the amazing fact that one hundred thirty decibels are about to be unleashed for ninety minutes," the broadcaster said with a laugh.

Benny ceased what he was doing and was riveted on the television, showing the twenty-two cars lined on the grid, their liveries a spectrum of colours and sponsorship. "A static exhibition of art; sleek, high-tech machines, aesthetically pleasing lines, flowing contours of aerodynamics and the magic perception of colossal speed, even though inert," the broadcaster said. The television displayed a collage of shots; technicians and mechanics making last minute adjustments, drivers talking strategy with their owners and engineers, others chatting with the circus of media and trying to appear calm, but keenly aware of the usual anxiety steeping in their stomachs, bordering on nausea. Before each racer, a beautiful woman, scantily clad beneath a clear raincoat, held a sign indicating the starting position and smiled brightly despite the downpour.

Benny resumed his work and soon had a complete rifle in his hands. He held the weapon steady and looked through the scope at the parrot, resting atop a lamp. His finger pulled the trigger. An empty click as the scaled skin on his finger split and started to ooze blood. "Damn!" he shouted and sucked on the wound.

"Damn!" the parrot echoed.

Inside his motor home, Vincenzo kissed his crucifix and zipped up his racing suit. He readied his umbrella and eyed Teresa with disdain. She was sprawled across the couch with her fingers beneath her panties, stroking her womanhood, engrossed in two lesbians in a men's magazine. "I don't know why you buy those things. They're perverted," he said, catching a glimpse of Teresa gracing the cover of several, fashion monthlies on the table.

"Most *real* men like it," she replied as she licked her thumb and flipped the page to another series of pictures.

"What if someone walked in? How would that look?"

"You're the superstar, remember? Who cares what I do?" she said and sniffed some cocaine off a tiny mirror to purposely annoy him.

Vincenzo looked at the picture of his parents, fighting to maintain his temper. "I don't need this right now, Teresa," he said quietly, taking a deep breath and still staring at the photograph. "Aren't you going to wish me luck?"

"Why should I? You're the best, right?" she answered and picked at a half-eaten plate of hors d'oeuvres beside a full bottle of Dom on the coffee table.

"I don't think a food bag is what a supermodel should look like," he said.

"I'll throw it up later," she replied flippantly and deliberately stuffed another handful into her mouth.

"Good. I don't want a fat wife," he said jokingly and went to kiss her, but she turned her face away. "Are you at least going to watch?"

"Doubt it. I think I'll go to the casino," Teresa said, grabbing the bottle of Dom and drinking greedily, the liquid splashed from the corners of her mouth.

"You know how I feel about you wasting my money in those places!"

"Don't you mean *our* money?" she replied and held up her ring finger. Teresa burped and barely wiggled her fingers to say goodbye. Vincenzo hesitated and stormed out, leaving the door banging in the wind. Teresa immediately scrambled to close it. "Asshole!" she shouted after him.

She collapsed into the couch, reached for the remote, turned on the television and skimmed through the channels until she found the race. "Welcome back to the Grand Prix of Monaco. Vincenzo Azzopardi has already won four out of the seven events so far this season, including victories in Australia, Brazil and San Marino," the British broadcaster said as a photograph of Vincenzo was displayed. "He managed a second place in Spain and a third in Austria. Starting second today is Braedon Stirling, who is of course, the defending world champion. The wily old veteran versus the young lion has made for a fierce but friendly battle within Team Jenkins," he added as Teresa instantly sat up upon seeing footage of Braedon's racer scything through a corner.

Teresa muted the television and picked up her framed wedding photograph from the end table. She stared at it for a few seconds and hoisted it above her head to smash it when she abruptly put the picture back in its place. She checked her Rolex, hurried to a closet, threw on a pair of faded denims with the knees worn away, removed her coat and hastily stepped into her black running shoes. She started for the door but stopped and felt her ring.

Teresa wavered, waiting for a signal, inherent or external, that would change her mind. Two tears streamed simultaneously down her perfect face. Resolution. A deep breath as she removed the ring and set the symbol of her marriage on the coffee table. "Eighty thousand dollars... keep it," she said and put it on her finger again.

Teresa donned a white ball cap and put on her sunglasses. She opened the door a crack and made sure there was nobody waiting. She pushed it open; the air rushed in and blew the remote just enough that it fell to the floor. She struggled to close the door and finally managed to slam it shut.

The VCR suddenly turned on revealing a grainy and jittery video. The picture cleared showing a younger Vincenzo Azzopardi with Randall Grange, arm in arm, standing proudly beside their racers next to a sign that read *Homestead Raceway, Florida*.

Members of the press instantly enveloped Vincenzo as he made his way through the pit lane. Reporters jostled for position and shouted their queries amidst photographers and television crews vying for the best shot. He restlessly motioned the assemblage aside as the mass of media divided and watched him vanish into the restricted grid area.

Vincenzo heard the familiar, irritating sound of rubber poking against pavement but kept his eyes straight ahead. "Vincent," a crusty, English voice said breathlessly. Vincenzo turned to Samuel Jenkins, a bespectacled, eighty-three-year-old with thinning, silver hair, wearing a headset and leaning on a titanium cane. His milky blue eyes and stoop masked a once stronger, dashing, young man.

"For the last time, my name is Vincenzo!"

Samuel awkwardly angled his way towards him, the old man's withered face revealed with each, closing step. He tapped his watch. "You're late as usual."

"You pay me five million pounds a year to win, not to be punctual," Vincenzo snapped.

"As a future world champion, I would think that you'd want to be as professional as possible," Samuel said and wrapped his arm around him for the benefit of the hawkish press. "Even a prima donna like you is expendable."

Vincenzo pushed Samuel's arm away and quickly descended into the cramped cockpit as Ichiro, half bowed, waited nearby. "I don't think so. I have a one year, airtight contract," he said arrogantly, "and in case you haven't noticed, I have the pole for today's race."

"Maybe so, but any fool can have an accident," Samuel said with a grandfatherly smile and gesticulated to his cane. "Just like you, I was impetuous once and thought I knew everything. World War Two changed all that."

Vincenzo rolled his eyes and pulled on his driving gloves as Ichiro and the mechanics busied themselves with the car. "I don't want to hear another one of your boring war stories."

"First of all, you'll call me Mr. Jenkins! It's a pity your parents, God bless them, didn't teach you respect for your elders, especially one that is your employer," Samuel said tersely.

"You can't fool me, old man. I know the stories about you. How ruthless you were in getting what you wanted. Like last year when I won the Formula 3000 championship in Japan. I wasn't even out of the car yet and you shoved a contract in my face."

"You signed it."

"And so did you, which just goes to prove that you're just as greedy as the rest of us," Vincenzo replied.

Samuel's eyes fluttered as he tried to contain his rage. Checking to make sure nobody was listening, he leaned forward and supported himself against the car. "I have hard work and self-discipline to thank for my success! I turned nothing into a fortune and I don't need some impertinent rookie telling me what I know!" he whispered through gritted teeth as Ichiro looked away, pretending not to listen.

Vincenzo was unfazed by Samuel's unusual display of anger and laughed. "I think you're getting too old for this business. It's a young man's sport and you're a dinosaur. Maybe you should hang it up and join your wife," he said matter-of-factly.

Samuel began to tremble. "You... you have no right to talk to me like that."

"Oh, I forgot, she died of cancer last year, didn't she?" Vincenzo responded and stared coldly at him. "I never could figure out why you married a Jap." Samuel promptly pivoted so Vincenzo couldn't see his turmoil. "Aren't you going to tap my car with your cane for good luck? You always do. Don't worry about it, old man, I'm going to win anyway," he said smiling; happy he had hurt him.

"I'm still the world champion and will be at the end of the season," an Irish voice chimed in. "Enjoy the lead because you're going to lose it at turn one. Clean and square of course," Braedon Stirling said. He meandered towards his racer, suited in a crisp, perfectly fitting uniform and with a cocksure smile. Tall for a driver and thirty years old, his physical appearance defied his age: short, jet-black hair that was slicked back, penetrating hazel eyes and youthful, sharp features. Upon seeing him, Samuel's face instantly brightened.

"Well, well, well. If it isn't the old man's favourite person in the whole world," Vincenzo said. "Why don't you just adopt him? He could be the child you never had. What was it anyway?" Vincenzo added and faked trying to recall the facts. "Oh yeah, you took a few shots in the family jewels from the Japs at a POW camp, right? Just for lighting a cigarette," he continued, shaking his head with mock disgust. "The slants can be tough, eh Ichiro?" Embarrassed and shamed, Ichiro just turned away.

"Shut your trap," Braedon said.

CHAPTER TWO

"I don't take orders from a terrorist," Vincenzo quipped, eyeing a tattoo of the word *Provo* on the back of Braedon's right hand.

"But you do from me," Samuel said to Vincenzo.

Braedon shook his head with pity. "Poor Vincenzo. Still trying to get under my skin. How childish."

"Let's keep it clean you two. Remember, we're on the same side," Samuel said and tapped the nose of Braedon's racer with his cane while purposely looking at Vincenzo. Downcast, Samuel limped off.

Concerned, Braedon watched Samuel blend into the crowd before turning to Vincenzo. "If you know what's good for you, you'll leave him alone."

"What are you going to do, mick, blow up my car?" Vincenzo said with a chuckle as he checked his hair in one of the mirrors. "I guess it runs in the family, uh?"

Braedon's steely eyes flinched and his nostrils flared. "Samuel means a lot to me and I won't stand by and watch you treat him that way. Save your anger for the track and don't take it out on him."

Another laugh from Vincenzo as he waved off Braedon's ominous remarks. "You really are starting to believe your own press, aren't you? That you're some kind of gentlemen. If people only knew the truth about you."

"I don't know what you're talking about," Braedon said with a frown.

"Yes you do," Vincenzo replied with a sly smile. "Come on, rice ball," he said to Ichiro and waved him over.

Braedon hesitated for a few seconds and offered his handshake to Vincenzo but the Italian ignored it. "Good luck," Braedon said.

"Have a nice crash," Vincenzo replied and pulled on his balaclava.

"There are some things you don't say in racing and that's one of them and you damn well know it! Take it back, Vincenzo!" Braedon demanded.

Vincenzo joyfully flipped him off as Ichiro handed him his helmet, emblazoned with the Italian flag. He wrenched it on as Ichiro connected the radio wire, drink hose, and air-conditioning tubes.

Braedon turned for his racer, looked skyward and closed his eyes. "God help me," he whispered fearfully to himself and slipped on his racing gloves, balaclava and finally his green, cloverleaf decorated helmet.

Ichiro handed Vincenzo a plastic drink bottle and he took one, last sip before carelessly throwing it at him, despite the fact that Ichiro was waiting with his hand out, ready to accept the refuse. Ichiro began coordinating the myriad of belts and secured Vincenzo with an intentionally hard yank. "Is that the best you've got, rice ball?" Vincenzo said.

"Why do you have to treat me like that?" Ichiro replied and nervously adjusted his glasses.

"Because I can. You don't seem to understand, I'm the star, and I can do and say whatever I want."

"You still need me to win races," Ichiro said as he attached the steering wheel.

"You're not that good. I could win this thing driving a tractor," Vincenzo shot back. "You'd better go, the rain is starting to make your hair dye melt," he added sarcastically.

The comment obviously hurt Ichiro and he lingered momentarily. "Good luck.... I think you are going to need it," he said slightly bowing, and then briskly walked away.

"Not likely," Vincenzo said and waited until Ichiro was far enough away before reciting the Lord's Prayer and blessing himself.

Vincenzo tilted his head to Braedon who was staring back at him. "Even He can't help you now," Braedon shouted, his voice dampened beneath his helmet. Vincenzo focused on the track ahead and promptly closed his visor just as the engines were fired all down the grid.

Manicured, maroon painted toenails staggered across the cold, marble, balcony floor as each foot left a moist trace that swiftly evaporated.

Teresa gazed at the fans scattered about the racetrack and threw out her arms. "Let them eat cake!" she shouted drunkenly and tripped back into the opulent, gambling suite. She clumsily raised her glass of champagne, drained the contents and giggled as a petite waitress filled the fine crystal again. Teresa smiled flirtatiously at her and slumped onto the stool in front of the blackjack dealer.

Teresa scanned the eloquent room with its exquisite art, French colonial furniture, gold-stemmed lamps, an intricate, massive chandelier and panoramic vista of rain-soaked Monte Carlo. "My place makes this look cheap," she said as Frank Sinatra began to play on an invisible sound system.

The dealer dealt her a four and himself a three. Another four for Teresa as she squealed with delight and playfully separated her legs. "Split them!" she said as she fumbled for some chips, knocking most of them to the floor. The waitress scrambled to pick them up as Teresa gamesomely ran one finger down her back. The waitress stacked them neatly on the table and stepped back with her hands behind her waist, but was clearly embarrassed. Teresa equalled the amount of two hundred thousand per hand.

"Good luck," the dealer said.

"The daughter of a Southern preacher don't need no luck," she replied, exaggerating her drawl. The dealer extracted a five and a six from the shoe. Joyful, she stamped her feet and quickly doubled-down. Eight hundred thousand on the line. Teresa downed her drink and it was immediately topped up. She didn't notice the dealer give her a three and a four, giving her one hand of twelve and the other of fourteen. Her attention moved back to her cards and she pouted. The dealer flipped over his card. A seven. Teresa shrugged off the potential, costly loss. The dealer's stealthy fingers seemed to slow as he slid the unknown card across the brilliant, green felt towards his other hand.

He turned it over. A ten. "Sorry," he said disingenuously and scooped away her money. Teresa checked her stakes. Two hundred thousand left.

"Would you like something to eat?" a man's French accent said. "The salmon is excellent today."

"Unless you got grits or catfish, leave me alone!" Teresa barked and began biting her nails as she studied her chips. The casino manager slipped into the room, quietly closed the door behind him and mimicked slitting his throat to the dealer, indicating Teresa be cut off from gambling further. The manager snapped his fingers and the dealer and waitress hurried into another room. "May I have a moment?" he said to Teresa.

Teresa spun around on the stool, struggled to her feet and grabbed the towel wrapped bottle of champagne. She poured too fast and the liquid spilled on the floor. "I'm sure you have someone who licks that up," she said and meandered to the couch. She crashed downward; her body's force caused the couch legs to scrape across the hardwood floor, leaving several marks.

The manager relaxed into a chair. "I believe the race is about to start," he said with a sincere smile.

"So?" she replied and kicked her feet up onto the antique, cherry wood coffee table.

"Perhaps you would like to take a break and watch."

She scoffed. "Right. All you give a damn about is whether I have enough money to continue playing in this... this... this scam!" she blurted with a sweeping gesture to the room.

He reached into his pinstripe suit, removed a piece of paper and placed it on the table. "You've lost one million, six hundred thousand," he said. "That's on top of the nearly two million you already owe us."

Teresa suddenly burst into tears and buried her face in her hands. "Can't you see that I'm upset? Why are you being so mean to me?"

"Maybe you should stop and visit us again in the future... when you've paid off your debt," he said, completely unaffected.

Teresa instantly stopped blubbering and her eyes hardened. She pulled her legs up, deliberately allowing a glimpse of her womanhood. "You must know who I am," she said salaciously. He couldn't help but watch as her fingers slid over her hardening nipples and brush between her legs.

She took the champagne bottle, teased the tip with her tongue and slowly wrapped her glossy lips around it as she gently moved her head up and down. A pleasurable, guttural moan emitted from her tender throat.

"I'm sorry, but I think you should go. The casino reserves the right to deny any player," he said with a reddened face and stood. Teresa hurled the bottle past him; it smashed against a painting of an eighteenth century warship on choppy seas.

He surveyed the damage and retrieved a pen and pad from his coat. He scribbled something and placed it back inside his jacket. "That was a five hundred thousand dollar painting, Mrs. Azzopardi. I'll add it to your bill," he said and marched to the door.

She jumped to her feet. "My husband has a line of credit here!" she shouted.

"It was him that asked us to stop it and quite frankly, he was the only reason we gave it to you in the first place," he said without breaking stride. "I'm sorry, but we cannot allow you to continue gaming," he added and went to exit, but she rushed past him and closed the door.

"With a little luck, maybe my husband will get killed and I'll collect the insurance," she said with a laugh as she dropped to her knees and unzipped his fly. Disgusted, he pushed her aside and swiftly departed.

"Faggot!" she yelled after him and swiped her glass of champagne off the table. She stumbled back onto the balcony, eyed the starting grid and focused on her husband's racer. Teresa squeezed the glass until it shattered and licked the spiralling blood from her fingers as she looked to God. "Please... make him suffer," she said with a knowing grin.

Randall's lifeless body was lying on the filthy mattress inside Andy Lunder's living room, his dry, open eyes staring unfocused on the yellowed ceiling. "Reminds me of church. Counting all those fucking candles and waiting for Jesus to show up," he said and scoffed. "Was the only thing I remember from the great Almighty," he whispered and took the last swig from a small bottle of Jack Daniel's before drawing on a half burnt cigarette. Another cursory scan of the repulsive surroundings. "I don't blame you for being poor. I was too. It just depends on whether you choose to live with it in dignity," he said and winced upon seeing a used tampon hanging over the side of a full wastebasket.

Randall heard a squeak and caught a glimpse of a mouse scurrying across the floor. "Good thing my old man isn't around to see you," he said to the rodent. "He trapped one once, but I got it out. Tried to get the wrinkles out of his little neck... but the fucker stepped on it right in front of me," he added, grimacing and covering his face with his forearm.

CHAPTER TWO

Randall peeked at Andy Lunder's dead body sprawled on the floor in a pool of blood from a bullet in his neck. "Thanks for the drink," he said and waved the bottle. "Sorry I had to end you but I play to win," he continued, studying Andy's stark white complexion and shocked mouth still agape. "I did us both a favour. Your worthless ass will wind up in a cardboard box, thanks to the taxpayers. Not everybody has that luxury. Take my old man; he was on display in the goddamn living room. Couldn't afford a funeral home," Randall said and shivered. "Scared the shit out of me just walking past him to take a piss at night. Kept waiting for him to open his eyes and look at me," he added and moved Andy's head so that the dead man was staring at him. "Got used to it though. After a while I wanted to sit with him... thought maybe he was lonely... now I can't even remember what the fuck he looked like," he said with a tired sigh.

Randall gazed into Andy's aimless eyes. "Do you know you're dead? Always wondered about that. I think dead people have secrets," he whispered and felt Andy's cold, hardening face. "Feels like wax. Like that fake fruit my mom kept in a bowl on the kitchen table. Real stuff was too expensive. Took a bite out of an apple once," he said and laughed, "and the old man was so pissed he made me eat the whole fucking thing."

The levity promptly vanished from Randall's face. "But dead is dead... and so are you," he said, tucking the empty bottle into Andy's stiffened right hand and dropping the burning cigarette into his mouth. "See you in hell," he whispered.

"What happened, Grange?" Hank Wallace's harsh voice said, shattering the moribund atmosphere.

Randall's eyes blinked and methodically moved to Tony and Hank, standing in the doorway. Randall barely raised a hand to greet them. "How's it hanging, Hank?"

Staff Sergeant Hank Wallace, a lanky man of forty-five with a receding hairline and meticulously groomed beard, peered over his glasses to soak in the squalid apartment. He stepped in, crossed his arms and drew a long breath. "Well?" he asked wearily as Tony remained in the doorway, thoroughly terrified.

Randall retrieved the packet of smokes near Andy's body and took one. Hank cleared his throat as a vocal reminder. "That's evidence, Grange," he said.

"It ain't going to bother nobody," Randall replied and sat up. "You like being a cop, chief?" he queried philosophically.

"Not when I have to deal with guys like you," Hank said, removing his glasses and rubbing his weary eyes, "and I'm not the chief."

Randall shot him a sly grin. "But you will be, eh Hank? Good thing your uncle's the mayor."

"My name is Staff Sergeant Wallace!" he said, angry at the insinuation. "Now what happened?"

Randall lazily slid off the mattress, stood and casually stretched. "I killed him," he said matter-of-factly while yawning. "He went for my sidearm and I capped the sorry prick. Right, booger? I mean, Officer D'Angelo?"

Nervous, Tony took a step forward and licked his parched lips. "Yes... yes, that's right," he said as Hank glanced over his shoulder at the rookie to sense the validity of the claim.

Randall walked to the window and lit the smoke. "Wish the stupid fuck had capped me instead," he whispered to himself.

"You do realize that there'll be an investigation. The crew is on their way," Hank said as Randall nodded, but the concept horrified Tony further. Hank leaned over Andy's body and noticed the bottle and cigarette. "You have no respect for the community, Grange," he said with disgust.

Randall chuckled and stared at the city. "Know what your problem is, Hank? You're getting too sympathetic for scum like him," he said and haphazardly gestured to Andy, "and that's the fucking problem with society today."

"It isn't that simple. The problem is that you're a dog fucker, Grange. And you need sensitivity training, but you're probably beyond even that," Hank said.

"Oh, I see. So this piece of shit fucking some kid up the ass isn't his fault, uh?" Randall replied.

"There are underlying social and medical needs that have to be addressed!" Hank said, raising his voice.

Randall edged closer to him. "What the fuck happened to you, Hank? When you were a flatfoot, you were normal, but now you're a fucking lawyer's wet dream. Those motherfuckers dictate the justice system and you don't even get pissed when some asshole like this walks!" he said, motioning to Andy.

"You're job is to enforce the law, not to write it or break it!" Hank shouted.

"Look around you, Hank! Open your fucking eyes for Christ's sake!" Randall said and gestured at Andy again; "It's mind over matter. They don't mind and we don't matter!"

"Care to tell me why you've always had a problem with authority, Grange?" Hank said, regaining his composure.

Chapter Two

Randall gave him a blank stare. "You haven't got that kind of time," he answered and tapped his cigarette ash.

"I saw the cruiser, it's the second one you've damaged since you were busted down from homicide. And then there's the drinking," Hank said.

"Is that it?" Randall said, thoroughly bored with the conversation.

Hank raised an eyebrow. "Isn't that enough?"

"Just say what you have to and fuck off," Randall replied.

Hank kicked over the sixties style chair and marched to Randall, inches from his face. Tony contemplated intervening but thought better of it. "Then here it is! You're an alcoholic and a druggie Grange! We've all got our demons, but you need professional help!" He turned away and began pacing, brimming with frustration. "Chances are we'll never know what really happened here tonight. You can thank your partner for that," he said and gave Tony a disapproving glance. "But by God I know one thing I can do!"

"I'm a good cop! I was the best suit the force ever had!" Randall yelled as Tony closed the apartment door to keep the growing number of curious tenants from hearing.

"Sure, when you were sober! But it was always by your own rules, wasn't it? The public doesn't work for you, Grange, you work for them!" Hank countered.

Randall took a few guarded steps towards him. "Are you firing me?"

"You're suspended with pay until further notice! And if I find out there was any breach of protocol, I'll see to it that your pension is revoked! If you want to save your job, swallow your pride for once and cooperate!" Hank shouted.

"I don't want any modified duty crap! It's all or nothing!" Randall remonstrated with a hint of fear.

"Then it's nothing. Consider yourself unemployed," Hank said.

"I... I think Officer Grange is entitled to legal representation and to speak to a member from the union, sir," Tony announced fearfully.

"Stay out of it, D'Angelo!" Hank said, pointing a threatening finger at him.

Tony cautiously inched closer and looked at Randall. "In cases like this, sir, you should leave the scene and get checked by a doctor. Then you get debriefed and then a lawyer and a member of the association helps you," he said anxiously.

"Shut up, D'Angelo! You're in enough trouble as it is!" Hank said.

"You have those rights, sir," Tony said to Randall.

"Thanks for your help, booger, but I'm not worthy of it. And by the way, stop calling me sir. It's fucking annoying," Randall said with a sincere smile.

"Listen to him, D'Angelo! He's not exactly a model police officer," Hank said.

"Well... sometimes the public aren't model citizens either, sir," Tony said gaining courage, causing Randall to smile again.

"Public safety comes before protecting the honour of an officer, D'Angelo. You should know that. And you, Grange, get some help. Real help," Hank said.

Randall angrily waved him off and started for the door. "Save the psychological autopsy shit! I'm not ready for the rubber gun squad!"

Hank paused, staring at Randall in disbelief and placed his hands on his hips. "Why do you abuse yourself?"

"Because I deserve it... and nobody else has the guts," he said quietly, opening the door.

"What the hell is that supposed to mean?" Hank asked.

"It's too complex for you. For anybody. Shit will go right over your fucking head like a jet," Randall said and motioned with his hand.

"I'm not going to beg you. You can't help somebody that doesn't want it. If I didn't know better, I'd say you want to be fired. That or dead," Hank said.

Randall looked over his shoulder at Hank and quipped. "You're not as dumb as you look."

"Get him out of here!" Hank yelled to Tony, just as the coroner entered.

"What killed him?" the coroner said, snapping on his latex gloves and eyeing Andy.

"Smoking and drinking," Randall replied and sauntered into the hallway.

Black running shoes hurried out of the rain and into the crowded, urbane lobby of the Grand Hotel in Monaco. Nobody at the front desk noticed as the staff's attention was directed to their customers.

The feet whisked through the network of race fans and headed for the elevators where a line of people waited for the lift. The stranger moved swiftly to the stairwell and opened the door.

Laboured breathing could be heard as the shoes jumped two stairs at a time, the wet rubber soles squeaking with each step. Suddenly, they froze upon the sound of hollow laughter from above. Two couples were descending with bottles of alcohol in hand.

The intruder hastily stepped back from view and a gloved hand held the doorknob leading to the corridor of the second floor. The voices vanished when another door was heard opening and closing. The intruder resumed the ascent, only faster than before.

Chapter Two

The door to the seventh floor was slightly ajar as the stranger's eyes scanned the deserted hallway and entered. The only noise was their feet as they padded fleetly across the carpet to the end of the corridor. Stopping at the last frame on the left, they waited and listened. A quick glance back down the hall revealed no one in sight. A hand rose and knocked lightly. After a few moments, the peephole's beam of light disappeared. The door opened a crack, revealing Benny Rabowitz with a Popsicle in his mouth. "What?" he said slightly annoyed. The stranger's hand quickly withdrew a switchblade and held it to Benny's throat and pushed him back into the room. The door gently clicked closed.

Randall missed the full ashtray and burned his fingers as he accidentally crushed out a cigarette on the wooden coffee table. Hypnotized by the television hash, he laid spread across the shabby couch, wearing only his underwear.

He brought a nearly empty bottle of Tequila to his numb lips, drank greedily and waited until the worm slowly dribbled into his mouth. His weighty head tipped to the same prostitute he almost hit earlier with the cruiser, lying naked in his bed at the end of the hall. "You look better with your clothes on," he mumbled as his bloodshot eyes partly closed and looked to the window.

The sun was rising, elucidating the soupy smog draping the city. He stumbled to his feet, swayed across the slovenly living room and stubbed his toe against an end table, causing him to drop the bottle, which smashed to the floor. He glanced over his shoulder at the bedroom and shrugged. "Never liked those tables anyway. The bitch bought them," he said as if the sleeping woman was listening.

Randall made a sweeping gesture at the well-worn and scratched, cloth couch, easy chair and loveseat. "This all used to look a lot better," he said and burped. "But the cat keeps trying to fuck my furniture." He haphazardly pointed to the only picture, hanging crooked on the wall above the sofa. It was a photograph of himself standing beside an open wheel racer with a brass plate reading- *Formula Atlantic Series*. "See that? Used to be pretty good. Could have went farther but had an accident. Look," he said, showing her his scarred hands. He cumbersomely lifted one foot and displayed his grossly wrinkled sole. "Took five surgeries. Skin grafts and all that shit. Other one's fucked too. See?" he said and went to lift his other leg, but lost his balance and crashed backward to the floor.

Randall grimaced from the pain and sighed. "That's one of the reasons why I became a cop... *was* a cop. At least I was still a part of the chase," he said and hiccupped. "But racing... God I loved it," he said passionately.

"Was the only thing I never took for granted. Made my hair stand on end. Old man used to take me to stock car races. Like that would make up for all the shit. Always felt bad about it when he was sober. Started driving when I was seven. Seven for Christ's sake! Fuck, I was good," he said proudly. "He didn't care though. Took out my anger behind the wheel. They said I was brave," he said and scoffed. "I just didn't give a shit. Had one hell of a great future ahead of me," he added mournfully. "Nothing worse than having ambition... having been important at one time... and then being nothing again."

Randall's head rolled to the side, taking in the strange view of the small, disorderly kitchen. The fridge and stove constantly hummed and the floor was a tarnished black and white tile. Once eggshell coloured cabinets were jaundiced with globules of dried paint. "Never home decorate when you're loaded," he said and spied a cockroach scurrying under the refrigerator. "You'd go faster with less down force," he said and chuckled. Randall's gaze unwillingly moved upward to a child's piece of faded artwork, held to the refrigerator with a pizza restaurant magnet. The crayon depicted the shining sun over two adults holding hands. "I miss you," he whispered. "I'm sorry, Jessica." The solemn moment was broken by the meow of a cat; Randall elevated his head to discover the feline standing in the open window with a dead bird in its mouth. "Spart! Where the hell were you all night?" he said.

The cat jumped over the rickety stereo system, dropped the bird near Randall's hand and doubled over to lick his privates. "You too, uh? You ain't the only one getting your oil changed," he said, scratching his testicles. Randall's face suddenly hardened as he picked up the bird and studied it. "Was late coming home from school... old man was drunk.... again. Mom tried to defend me. Had this starling I found injured. Was nursing it back to health... the fucker threw it at her and missed. Hit the wall... dead," he explained to the cat as he fought back the tears. "Beat the shit out of her like he always used to... then me."

Spart vocalized again and strutted into the kitchen. Randall wiped his eyes, battled to his feet and swept the cat up into his arms. He pressed his face into the feline's as Spart promptly proclaimed his displeasure. "Know why I love you? You're the only one without sin... and the only one that loves me back," Randall said as the cat strained to escape and took a half-hearted swipe at him. Randall carried him under his arm to the fridge.

The refrigerator door opened. One tin of cat food, mustard and an empty ketchup bottle. Randall grabbed the can and continued transporting Spart to the cupboard, but there were no dishes. He looked in the sink, piled high with every cup, glass, plate and piece of cutlery he owned.

Chapter Two

Randall twisted the faucet; the ancient pipes grumbled and shimmied. After a few seconds, brown water trickled out and soon, clear liquid. He held a saucer under the tap, but the encrusted food remained. He rubbed it clean on his chest and set it on the floor. Spart leapt out of his grasp and waited, typically loquacious. Randall emptied the tin and tossed it onto the counter where it spun noisily. "Enjoy it. From now on, you have to take care of yourself."

Randall sauntered into the bedroom and kicked the mattress and the woman awakened. "Good morning," she said lasciviously.

"Get out," he replied tersely and clamped her arm.

She resisted and gamely tried to cover herself. "No breakfast?"

Randall scowled and hauled her to her feet. "I said get the fuck out!"

The confused and meagrely frightened woman began clumsily gathering her clothes. "What's your problem?"

"You got your money!"

She pulled on her panties and skirt. "You're an asshole!"

"Just hurry up!"

She eased into her bra, threw on her blouse and took her time to button. "You cops are all the same. Fucking weirdoes!"

Randall seized her by the throat with his left hand, pushed her to the wall and lifted her off the floor. His right hand coiled into a fist as her fearful eyes caught a flash of his white knuckles, poised to strike. Suddenly, his grip relaxed and she slid down to the floor. He stepped back, gaping shamefully at the floor as she straightened herself, gaining confidence. "You're fucking insane!" she said and bolted out of the room.

Randall waited until he heard the door slam and shuffled into the kitchen. He opened a cabinet under the sink and withdrew another, full bottle of Tequila. Randall twisted off the top, took a slug and stumbled into the living room. The television picture was poor. He bashed the top of the set with his fist until it cleared and flicked the knob to the desired channel that was broadcasting the Grand Prix of Monaco. He dropped into the couch, set the bottle down and reached for something in the drawer of the coffee table. "The cars are just completing the formation lap and we are moments away from the start of the Grand Prix of Monaco!" the British announcer said.

Randall retrieved a small, plastic prescription bottle indicating the drug Halcion, 0.25 mg. "Take one at bedtime," he said, straining to read the fine print. He popped off the lid and spilled the entire contents into his leathery palm. He felt the dozens of smooth, tiny, football shaped, powder blue pills. "Take them all if you never need them again," he remarked in a medical tone and stuffed them into his mouth. Randall washed the pills down with a healthy swig and forced himself to look at the artwork on the fridge. "Bye baby," he whispered.

He stretched across the couch just as Spart leapt onto his lap and began cleaning himself. Randall stroked the animal's head and smiled, reaching for a packet of cigarettes on the table. "Peace at last," he murmured.

Gloved hands pulled aside the thick curtain, allowing a sliver of light to enter the darkened hotel room. The intruder barely opened the sliding doors that led to the private terrace as the ambience of Monaco flooded inside, the sheeting rain misting the air.

A cursory scan of the adjacent balconies and those beneath disclosed a rash of boisterous spectators anticipating the race. The door closed and silenced the room again. "Hello. Who are you?" the parrot said, perched on Benny Rabowitz's shoulder. Benny sat on the couch, completely terrified with his hands tied before him and a piece of duct tape across his Popsicle stained mouth.

The stranger's silhouette whisked across the suite and took the rifle. The shadowy figure moved back to the balcony with the weapon in hand and opened the door a few inches.

The scope focused and the cross hairs trained on the head of a track worker adjusting his headset.

A finger squeezed around the trigger, the room filling with the unmistakable cadence of stretching leather. The crescent shape of the metal twitched as the finger applied more pressure until it clicked, void of ammunition. The door closed again and the rifle was carefully placed against the frame.

The stranger gently removed the parrot as Benny watched with concerned eyes and shook his head in defiance. A twist of the bird's tender neck produced the sickening sound of severed cartilage. Tears welled in Benny's eyes as his breathing intensified.

The intruder unscrewed the cap on a bottle of Gin and corralled Benny's head against the wall. His chin was pushed up as the liquor was poured into his nostrils. He thrashed wildly as the bottle drained, his body convulsing and his face contorting, choking with the bitterness. Finally, mercifully, empty. Diligent, involuntary breathing.

The gloved hands withdrew a crumpled packet of *Hispania Gold* brand cigarettes and shook one free. A lighter opened and shattered the serenity for an instant with a sonorous, steel clang. The flame swirled with the flow of air, casting eerie shadows across the room and highlighting Benny's tormented, glowing face as he stared sadly at his dead pet.

The stranger inhaled, the flame drawing towards the tobacco as the paper crisped. The flame was extinguished with the flick of the wrist and the body recessed into a chair. Another inhalation. A steady, blue stream of smoke exhaled upward and floated. It was only a matter of time.

Vincenzo checked his left mirror and saw the other racers through the downpour as they fell out of line and into their starting positions. The orange, oscillating beacons atop the safety car were blurry, but became clearer as it neared the rear of the grid.

His hands were wrapped tightly around the high-tech wheel, his eyes concentrating on the slick road ahead, surrounded by a concrete canyon and a mosaic of advertising.

Vincenzo's heart rate was climbing and he could feel the rush of adrenaline as his limbs became tense with an esoteric but familiar tingling, a tingling every living organism intrinsically comprehends when they are about to be hunted.

The crowd stood in amassed, awed admiration, knowing that death was only a mistake away. Anticipation grew to the point of anxiety as pangs of excitement flowed through the spectators. Some continued to wave banners while others held their hands close to their mouths. All knew one of the greatest spectacles in racing was about to unfold.

Vincenzo's eyes trained unblinking on the first corner, scarcely visible with the pelting rain, he felt the tiny vibrations against his rainbow-coloured visor.

The speed warriors were ready and the start was in the hands of race control as forty-four eyes were focused on the horizontal arm of lights at the vanguard of the grid. An infinite amount of possibilities awaited the drivers over the next ninety minutes, piquing from boyhood dreams of glory to indescribable anguish. Underlying was the unspoken element of extreme danger, rarely seen but ever omnipresent in the darkest corridors in the minds of the men about to test their skill, fortune and courage.

The first of five lights on the starting post glowed red as an immense bolt of lightning temporarily basked the circuit in fluorescent white. Deep, angry thunder rumbled.

The second light came on. The whine of engines began to steadily rise and the gears were engaged.

The third light. The massive power plants churned a deafening symphony of combustion.

The fourth light. The motors screaming a high, ear piercing pitch.

The fifth and final light lit as twenty thousand, tormented horsepower readied to be unleashed. It seemed one more second would result in a conflagration of overtaxed technology. The lights abruptly blinked out. The vociferation of the crowd overpowered that of the machinery as the field launched from the grid. Grooved tyres pumped gallons of water leaving rooster trails of spray as the machines jockeyed for position, barrelling for the first right-hander.

Samuel was glued to a monitor in the pit lane watching Vincenzo and Braedon, side by side as they rapidly closed in on turn one. "Watch it! Watch it!" he yelled to nobody in particular. "That's millions of pounds you're playing with!"

Braedon slipped the nose of his car down the inside and lightly tapped the brakes. Vincenzo had a split second to decide whether to cut him off as both hurtled towards the corner. There wasn't room. Vincenzo backed off and promptly fell in behind as they approached the tricky Ste Devote corner while the fans erupted, praising the bold manoeuvre by the world champion.

Vincenzo strained to see the cherry glow of Braedon's rain light amidst a wall of blinding spume. The young Italian steered to the left, clearing his line of sight considerably as he ascended the Monte De Beau Rivage. Too late. The next corner caught him by surprise and he tucked in behind his team-mate again.

The Jenkins' cars were nose to tail with scarcely a foot between them. They swiftly converged upon the slow right-hander at Mirabeau at the end of the long slope. Vincenzo tried to dash up the inside but once again, Braedon slammed the door and nearly sheered off Vincenzo's front wing. "I had the corner! That son-of-a-bitch cut me off!" Vincenzo complained into his mike.

Samuel whistled at the near miss and said. "We'll have a chat with him old boy. Press on."

The duo of racers entered the slowest part of the circuit; twisty, elevation changing turns at Virage Du Portier. Vincenzo's car danced in and out of Braedon's mirrors as he looked for an opportunity to pounce.

Inside the Grand Hotel room, the tip of the rifle brushed back the curtain. A gloved hand gently opened the sliding door allowing the din of shrieking engines to burst inside, the racket reverberating off the walls.

The scope trained on the Jenkins cars as they started the sweeping right turn, heading towards the tunnel. Suddenly, Benny groaned as he endeavoured to stand up, but fell face first onto the floor. Surprised by the distraction, the assassin had no chance for a shot.

Braedon's vehicle temporarily lost traction, entering the dark passageway as Vincenzo attacked and inched up on the inside. Braedon's right and Vincenzo's left front tyres touched for an instant, causing the nose of Vincenzo's car to rise a foot in the air and violently bounce down again.

Braedon accelerated but Vincenzo had to back off as his car began to skid. The pair rocketed through the tunnel, vapour contrails searing off of their rear wings as the noise sang against the walls.

The throttles eased and the gearboxes started to grind as they shifted down. The duet paraded towards the Nouvelle Chicane and tiptoed through the fast left and right. "I think I have a puncture! Left front!" Vincenzo barked. "Must have been the contact. I'm coming in."

Irate, Samuel bashed his cane against the console. "We're not ready! We'll have a look at the telemetry. Hang on," he said and glanced at Ichiro. "Well?"

Ichiro studied the monitors. "It looks good to me."

"Everything is fine," Samuel said to Vincenzo.

"Don't give me that shit! I'm the one driving the fucking car!" Vincenzo's voice shouted, causing Samuel to pull off one side of his headset. The old man looked to Ichiro again.

"Monitors do not lie," Ichiro said.

"You may be right, Vincent. Give us a minute," Samuel said and elbowed Ichiro. "Behind the wheel they're like children. You have to pacify them."

Braedon crossed the start/finish line with Vincenzo in step. The Italian spied his racer's left front tyre and saw the water funnelling off, the Bridgestone insignia a solid streak of white. His apprehensive gaze moved to the wishbone suspension and he searched for any sign that might indicate a drop in the pressure of the nitrogen filled tire.

The assassin's finger was poised on the trigger as raindrops peppered the gun barrel and dripped off without a trace. The lead cars were heard approaching, but the wind unexpectedly picked up and forced the rifle's tip to agitate. The gloved hands swiftly secured the weapon again and waited.

Braedon's hands pulled the wheel to full lock, making the right-hander nearing the entrance to the tunnel for a second time. Vincenzo drew alongside at the apex and caught a brief glimpse of his team-mate looking back. Ireful, Vincenzo raised a shaking fist as his foot slammed the throttle.

The assassin pulled the trigger. A quiet pop.

The bullet penetrated the lower half of Vincenzo's visor and shattered the plastic. His head snapped back and tilted lazily to the right side as a rush of blood sprayed the inside of his helmet. The shock hadn't registered with his brain as his fist was still defiant in the air, but slowly, his hand relaxed and fell back into his lap as his foot weighed heavily against the gas pedal. The RPMs revved and redlined as the racer was mired in third gear.

Confused, Samuel and Ichiro studied the telemetry. "Vincent? What's going on? Broken gearbox?" Samuel said. Silence, except for the occasional crackle of the radio. "Vincenzo?" He turned to Ichiro for an answer.

Ichiro remained entranced upon the monitors and scratched his head. "I think his radio is dead. It must be a massive electrical failure."

Flashing warning lights illuminated Vincenzo's cockpit as the rest of the pack was rapidly gaining. His body convulsed, his visor obliterated by a sheen of blood.

Vincenzo's racer steered itself into the guardrail, the right, front tyre exploding on impact with a flare of orange. Billowing plumes of blue and white smoke jetted from the stressed engine as the machine hugged the length of the wall through the tunnel, creating a spectacular hail of sparks.

Track marshals immediately waved their yellow caution flags as the other competitors swung to the left to avoid the incident.

Light from the end of the tunnel was speeding towards him and in a minutia of time, his panicked brain contemplated if it was the portal to death.

Vincenzo's car broke free of the guardrail's embrace and drifted to the centre of the road as he exited the tunnel. Another competitor swiftly converged and slipped down on the inside, but their wheels touched. Suddenly, Vincenzo's view was vertical. Surreal. A menacing sky. Only the sound of the engine and air sweeping underneath. Tyres continued spinning. Peaceful. Wonder at the droplets of blood hanging in midair. Now, ground coming up.

Vincenzo's car nose-dived into the barrier, flipped upside-down and began to freefall over the edge. The machine started to cartwheel and hit another railing as the heavy engine disintegrated and broke free from the careening monocoque. Wheels flew and splinters of carbon fibre shimmered as they sailed through the air. The chassis tumbled end over end before smashing into the turbulent Mediterranean with a thunderous splash. White, foaming waves quickly enveloped the vehicle and dragged it under.

The murky water was cold as air bubbled noisily to the surface. Light from above grew dimmer with each passing moment.

An alchemy of blood and oil swirled around him in an all-encompassing blanket of mortality. Vincenzo's hands instinctively scrambled to press the belt release against the effervescing undertow. He could feel his lungs beginning to fill as the racer sank and hear his own muffled cries beneath the violent waves. The panic desisted. Acceptance. Vincenzo relaxed and felt gravity suck body and machine downward to an awaiting, watery grave.

CHAPTER TWO

The assassin forced Benny's finger around the trigger, his intoxicated body slumped on the couch. The sliding door was opened and Benny was dragged to his feet. The bindings and tape were removed and he was pushed towards the balcony. "Please... please don't," Benny muttered. The assassin grabbed him by the back of the neck and waist and heaved him over the rail.

A woman's scream was heard as Benny frantically flailed his limbs before landing in a flower garden with a sickening thud.

Chapter Three

"Like getting hit in the face with a shovel... the older you get when you're alone the more you realize that nobody loves you. Not yesterday, not today, not tomorrow... and if anyone ever did love you... fuck, they sure as hell don't now," Randall said drunkenly into the telephone. "But my ma loved me. He didn't... not the right way," he said and shook his head, scolding himself for getting off topic. "It's being alone, whether you deserve it or not... that's what haunts your ass," Randall continued with a heavy sigh. "Tired now and... and I'm sorry I put you in that position. I mean that. Thanks for covering. Should have spoken to you in person but just ain't got the guts. Bye, booger... Tony. Please take care of Spart, will you?" he added and fumbled to place the receiver back in the upright cradle on the wall.

Randall carelessly dropped his spent cigarette onto the carpet and stamped it out with his bare foot, but felt no pain. The lethal efficacy of booze and drugs was working quickly as the halcyon cocktail permeated his every cell, providing a wonderful apathy that coursed through his veins. "Too bad not everyone can check out this way," he said as he staggered across the living room and fell to the floor.

Randall eyed the upside down bottle of Tequila near the edge of the coffee table and reached for it, but he knocked it over and the liquor poured to the carpet. He frantically crawled to the gurgling elixir, rolled onto his back again and opened his mouth. Tongue sticking out, Randall caught the last few drops as the bottle emptied.

He noticed the nap of the musty carpet and ran his fingertips across the rough surface and cringed. "Rug burned my hands when you grabbed my feet and dragged me out. Fucking scared. Do anything but that. Got used to it though... even felt good sometimes. Fuck... even thought it was normal at one time," he whispered shamefully and felt an orgasmic warmth.

Chapter Three

He wet himself and tried to lift his head but couldn't. Inertia. Randall's eyes dilated and blinking decreased incrementally. Brain activity slowed. Sight withered to a blur. Sounds became especial and warped.

At first there was an aloof, dull ringing in his ears, but it mushroomed into a steady, vociferous toll, becoming the harbinger of his quietus. The muscles in his neck atrophied and his tiresome head fell to the right, dribbling coagulated saliva from his benumbed mouth. "To hell with you *step dad*," he said with disdain. "If my real father had been around he'd have kicked your fucking ass... to hell with you," he continued, his voice trailing off as he teetered on the brink of unconsciousness.

Randall eyed a tattered binder on the bottom shelf of the coffee table and clumsily pulled it out. He opened it and looked at a photograph of himself holding a plaque and shaking another police officer's hand. "Officer of the year," he scoffed and gazed at the yellowed, newspaper clipping glued to the opposite page. The headline read, *Rookie Officer Works On His Own Time & Retrieves Stolen Bike*. "That was the best thing that ever happened to me being a cop," he said with a slight smile as Spart appeared and began rubbing his mouth on the corner of the binder. "Kid had cancer," he said to the cat. "Told them I found it after I chased some kids... was bullshit. I bought it for him. Couldn't stand to see the little guy suffer any more," he added just as Spart started chewing the corner. "Hope he's still alive."

"It is with great sadness, that I must inform our viewers that Vincenzo Azzopardi has died in a tragic accident here in Monaco," the British announcer's dejected voice said on the television.

Randall wasn't sure he heard the bulletin correctly and pondered if he was dreaming or possibly experiencing a bizarre prelude to necrology. "He ain't dead," Randall said and laughed. "Little dago is unstoppable. Jesus! Guys in the paddock used to shit their pants when they heard your name, Vince. Never told you, but I was scared too. Remember those two chicks we fucked in Homestead?" he said and grinned. "That's the only reason you came over here, to screw American woman. Lucky bastard. But you're good, Vince. Really fucking good."

"To repeat, it has been confirmed that the wonder from Milan, Vincenzo Azzopardi, has been killed today in Monte Carlo. We're going to show you the accident again, but we would like to warn you, the pictures are disturbing."

Randall fought to pull himself up, but his body was limp. He looked at the television through distorted eyes and saw the water spewing wreckage of Vincenzo's car being hoisted from the Mediterranean. "Can't be," he lamented as he tried to move again but failed.

Randall rolled his head until it faced his right arm. Mustering all his strength, he forced his fingers down his throat and disgorged.

The vitriolic act temporarily rejuvenated his body; he crawled towards the telephone and managed to haul himself up to one knee. Another regurgitation. Randall grabbed hold of the drywall for support and waited for another swell of stamina. He lifted his fatigued body upward and went to take a step, but his legs were rubbery and he stumbled, smashing his forehead against the wall on the way down.

The receiver fell from the upright cradle and dangled as the cord unravelled wildly before him. It was just out of reach as his hand stretched to snatch it, but he was blinded by blood streaming into his eyes. Randall relented, stared at the ceiling and wondered if it the discoloured plaster would be the final thing he ever saw.

Benny's eyes stared upward, his mangled body lying in a pool of blood with various bones protruding through his twisted limbs.

The coroner peered over the balcony and watched a police photographer circle Benny as two workers prepared a white body bag. "From his position, this was no accident," he said, referring to his notes. "The victim has torn skin from hitting the railings on the way down, and the body is too close to the building to be a suicide. Jumpers land further away," he added matter-of-factly and waited for a response.

His eyes couldn't help but slowly drop to long, luscious legs and follow them to a shapely waist beneath a tight, red skirt. Higher to a matching jacket and healthy cleavage. Gwen Gaudet's penetrating brown eyes stared at him; her normally flowing, black hair was tied in a neat bun. The thirty-one-year-old was perfect, save a long, narrow scar from her hairline to her brow despite meticulous makeup. "Bloody migraines," she said with a French accent and popped a few pills into her mouth. "Anything else?" she added, rubbing her sore forehead as other plain clothed officers and technicians milled about Benny's hotel suite.

"I can't say for certain, but I think he had a belly full of booze. I could smell it on him. The autopsy will confirm it," he said confidently. "Once they cut open the trachea they'll notice any alcohol."

"Obviously," she replied and motioned to the empty liquor bottle on the coffee table. "I want the lungs checked too. If there's any in there, he choked, which means somebody forced him."

"The victim didn't have any chipped teeth," the coroner said frowning, checking his notes.

"I said check it. Run the blood and urine too. If those come back negative for booze then I'd say he was force-fed his cocktails, wouldn't you?" Slightly embarrassed, the coroner could only nod. Gwen studied

CHAPTER THREE

the dead parrot and the book on ornithology. "Too bad he didn't survive. I would have loved to question a parrot," she said sarcastically. "No ID on the victim?"

The coroner shook his head just as a uniformed, pregnant, female officer approached. "Inspector Gaudet?"

Gwen turned to her, smiled and patted the officer's stomach. "Congratulations," she said.

"Thank you," the officer replied proudly.

"You should be on modified duty. I know how hard it can be to breastfeed wearing a bullet-proof vest," Gwen said with a laugh. "And get yourself a briefcase. You can hide the breast pump in it. You need any help, let me know," she whispered and gave her another warm smile.

"I will," the young woman said happily. "The front desk says the victim registered as a Mr. Leonard Pinto. Paid in cash," she continued and handed Gwen a slip of paper.

Gwen crumpled it, stuffed it into her skirt pocket and eyed the high-powered rifle on the floor. "An assassin wouldn't use his real name. I want his prints and any on the gun ASAP. Let's just hope there's a match on the database," she said and turned to the small group of detectives and clapped her hands. "Listen up people. If Mr. Pinto turns out to be a real person, I want background checks," she said and began counting on her fingers. "His movements and contacts. Family and friends. Banking information. Medical. Anything and everything. Start with the people closest to the victim and expand outwards," she said and checked her watch. "Any surveillance video the hotel has, I want it. Question the staff and check if there were any meal deliveries. See if anyone saw or heard anything unusual, but do it discreetly. I don't want the whole world to know the best racing driver in the world was murdered," she said and looked to the technicians. "I want lasers in here to check for unseen fibres and hair and I want a search for ear prints. Since there was no forced entry, whoever iced Mr. Pinto probably listened at the door first. The human body leaves its mark, people. Find it," Gwen continued and gestured to the police photographer. "I want every inch of this place photographed and videotaped. Let's get to work. I have a ninety-eight percent conviction rate and I want it to stay that way." Everyone busied themselves as Gwen stepped onto the balcony and watched Benny being zipped up. "So somebody helped him off the balcony, uh?"

"I'd say so," the coroner answered timidly, standing in the doorway.

"Well, either Mr. Pinto pulled the trigger or someone else did. One thing is for sure, it was a professional hit," she said.

"How do you know for certain?"

Gwen gave him a mocking glance and motioned to the suite. "Does this look like a crime of passion to you? Besides, who else could hit a moving target at those speeds?" The coroner nodded sheepishly and walked away as Gwen sighed heavily. "Should have stayed in bed," she said to herself retrieving her cell phone and dialling. "Yes, I'd like to make an overseas call... Canada." While she waited, Gwen looked down at the trampled garden. "Such a waste of flowers," she lamented.

"Truth is, he should be dead," a man's voice said. Randall heard rubber squeaking against a waxed floor and the starchy crispness of wrinkling material. Something cold and metallic was pressed to his chest.

He opened his baggy eyes and saw the fuzzy outline of a physician scribbling on a clipboard and fleetly exiting.

Bright light projected a curious network of rays from the window and a sharp surge of pain flashed inside Randall's head. He smelled the familiar odour of disinfectant and heard the ping of the PA system. "How do you feel?" Tony said, sitting in a chair, dressed in civilian clothes and holding a bible.

"Had worse hangovers," Randall replied and licked his parched lips. "Got a smoke, booger?"

"This is a hospital, sir," Tony said sternly and opened the bible. "I'd like to read you something, sir," he continued and cleared his nervous throat. "'However, if a man deliberately attacks another, intending to kill him, drag him even from my altar, and kill him'," Tony concluded with a grievous look.

"That's why I did it," Randall said and offered him a bored glance. "Exodus, twenty-one, thirteen, right?" Tony checked the reference and his astonished eyes slowly moved upward. "I told you I wanted to be a priest," Randall continued and tried to sit up but flinched, his stomach muscles aching.

"They pumped your stomach, sir."

"Who found me?"

"I did. I got your message. I was coaching my boy's basketball team and decided to end practice early. An act of God, wouldn't you say?" Tony said and squirmed in his seat. "Suicide is a sin, sir. What the hell... heck, were you thinking?"

"I was bored. I just partied too much. That's all," Randall replied.

"This is serious, sir," Tony said unconvinced and pointed to the window.

Randall was suddenly aware of the criss-cross of wire mesh that was part of the pane. He looked at his wrists and feet, realizing he was tied to the bed. "What the fuck is all this?"

Chapter Three

"They think you're a risk... and they're right," Tony said nervously.

Randall struggled to wriggle free from the nylon straps as the veins in his hands bulged. "Get me out of this shit!"

"I can't... it's for your own good, sir," Tony said uneasily.

"Don't fucking preach to me, booger!" Randall barked and finally relented.

Tony gathered his courage and stood. "You know what your problem is, sir? You demand respect, but you don't give it back," he said and began to pace.

"What the fuck is this? What do you care about me?"

"Believe it or not... I look up to you, sir. I know about you. You were the youngest to ever make homicide. You used to be the ideal officer... but not now," Tony said sadly, avoiding Randall's angry stare.

"I'm not here to be your fucking hero, kid!"

"Good cops treat suspects with respect! With fairness! You're supposed to feel sympathy for them! Empathy! But you... you're nothing but a cynical, cold-hearted man!" Tony shouted, his voice shaking.

"Take your fucking guilt elsewhere, booger! You covered for me! Big fucking deal! You don't know me! And that fucking kiddy diddler had it coming!" Randall replied, his head trembling with rage.

"Police officers have to be politically correct, sir!"

"Oh fuck you! You wait, booger! You wait and see! It'll happen to you someday! You're going to wake up and realize that being a cop has made your personality fucking shit! That being a cop is too emotionally goddamned painful!" Randall said.

Tony returned the bible to the table drawer and turned for the door. "Goodbye, sir."

"Wait! Please, Tony... I need your help. Please," Randall pleaded as Tony hesitated with his hand on the knob. "You... you must have heard about my friend, Vincenzo," Randall said.

"I did... and I'm sorry. I know the two of you were close at one time."

Randall's head tilted to the window and he closed his eyes. "He saved my life. Did you know that? Was in the Atlantic series. Toronto, 95. You know the Princess Gate?" Randall asked, Tony nodded and returned to his chair. "Vince used to take that corner so damned fast. Had bigger balls than any of us," Randall said with a chortle, but quickly became serious again. A deep breath. "He was in the lead. I was second and chasing him. Had been since the green. Every time I got close, he'd pull away," Randall said as his boyish grin returned. "Crafty son-of-a-bitch. Was like he was baiting me, you know? Anyway, last lap we came down the straight heading for turn one at the Gate. Another guy, Belancher, I think his name was, some stupid, French-Canadian fuck," he said and looked at Tony. "The asshole decided to trade paint with me and we bumped. Don't remember much after that. Just flipping over and over and over," Randall said, recoiling at the memory. "Christ, I thought I was going to die. Sure ended my fucking career. I'll never get behind the wheel again. Wouldn't want to anyway. Lost the edge," he said and moistened his lips again. "Can I have some water?" Tony poured a cup and cradled Randall's head.

"Not too much," Tony said and took the cup away.

"Thanks. It ain't Tequila but it'll do," Randall said and managed a smile.

"What happened then, sir?" Tony said, completely enthralled with the story.

"Well, the car slammed into the gate, what was left of it anyway. Was upside-down and on fire. Shit. I didn't know. Was out cold. Thought I could hear the sirens though. Everything was loud. Felt hands pull me out," Randall said as his throat tightened and his eyes watered. "You know that crazy bastard actually saw it in his mirrors and stopped? Did a three sixty and sacrificed the win to save my sorry ass." He sniffed hard and closed his drenched eyes. "How do you thank someone for that?" he said.

"You can't, I guess," Tony replied, embarrassed at the emotion stirring in his own eyes.

"This is the second time I've been saved by a friend... thank you. You won't have to do it again. Promise."

Tony saw the conviction in Randall's eyes, but wavered momentarily. "If I let you go, what will you do?"

"Go to a funeral."

Tony shook his head, not believing what he was about to do. "If they find out I let you go, I might end up behind bars," he said, eyeing the wired window and beginning to untie the straps. The manacles were finally removed; Randall felt his wrists and rubbed the feeling back into the skin.

"There's hope for you yet, booger. Just tell them I escaped," Randall said and slapped him on the back. Tony guarded the door as Randall hurriedly withdrew his clothes from a cabinet. His stiff leg missed the trousers on the first attempt and he nearly fell over. Randall zipped up his jeans, threw on his denim coat, squeezed into his cowboy boots and heartily shook Tony's hand. "Thanks again, Tony. I'll drop you a line," Randall said and opened the door to discover Hank Wallace waiting for him.

"Going somewhere?" Hank said and offered him a bouquet. "These are for you," he added with a candy-eaten grin.

CHAPTER THREE

Exhausted, Teresa's swollen eyes blinked away her running mascara. "Why won't they let me see him?" she whimpered and sluggishly rose to her feet. Samuel gently took her hand and pulled her down again.

Both waited in a secluded lounge of the Princess Grace Hospital as a throng of boisterous reporters waited just outside the windowed doors. Two gendarmes guarded the entrance and frequently pushed the media further away.

"I can't believe he's gone... I can't," Teresa said, burying her head in Samuel's chest as he ran a gnarled hand across her hair and began to rock her.

The old man's gaze shifted from his arthritic fingers to a rattan chair in one corner of the room. "See that?" he said with a faint smile, trying to distract her. "I used to work on furniture like that with my father. He had a shop in Manchester. We lived above it," he said, but Teresa continued weeping as he held her tighter. "We all want something better, don't we? Joined the British infantry at nineteen. Father was proud but mother was furious," he said with a chuckle. "I wanted the excitement. To see the world. It was what I wanted... just like Vincent," he added and cupped her chin, forcing her to look up at him. "He did what he wanted, Teresa. What he needed to do. It's what made him happy."

"What about me?" she said with tears streaming down her angelic face. "Who's going to look after me?"

A young, black physician walked briskly towards them. "Mrs. Azzopardi. Mr. Jenkins," he said with a French accent. "I'm Doctor Savoie."

Teresa jumped to her feet. "Why won't you let me see him?"

"I'm sorry for the delay," the doctor said.

"We've been waiting for hours!" she shouted as Samuel went to take her arm, but she wrestled it away. "What are you hiding?"

"I apologize, but I can't let you see him just yet," Dr. Savoie replied.

Teresa grabbed him by the jacket. "I'm his wife! Don't you know who I am? You have no right!" she yelled and stormed past the doctor, but he quickly restrained her. The reporters flocked to the windows and started snapping pictures. "Let go of me!" she screamed.

Samuel vaulted to his feet, leaning heavily on his cane and shuffling towards her. "Teresa! Teresa!" he barked as he spied the paparazzi with concern. "Get hold of yourself!"

"You don't give a damn about any of this! All you care about is your investment! Well guess what? He's dead!" she said, glaring at Samuel.

"Perhaps I can get you a sedative," Dr. Savoie said.

"Look at you!" she yelled at the doctor, full of disgust. "Nigger thinks he's a big man! Where I come from you'd be picking cotton!" she said, shoving Samuel aside and fighting to break free from the doctor. "I want to see him!" she shouted and peered into the room. Teresa caught a glimpse of the blood spattered sheet that covered Vincenzo's body as two men stood with their backs to her on the other side of a curtain. "What are they doing in there?"

Dr. Savoie pulled her away with Samuel's assistance as the reporters shouted questions. A nurse appeared and the doctor motioned to her. "Get me a sedative!" he commanded as Teresa was manhandled to the couch. Suddenly, her eyes rolled back and she collapsed.

Inside the room next to Vincenzo's body, Friedrich Hesse, an old looking, thirty-four-year-old with greying hair and a long face, watched with alarmed, blue eyes as Dr. Savoie tried to revive Teresa. "We have to keep this quiet, Mr. Carmen," he said under his breath with a German accent. "If this gets out we're finished," he added as he loosened his tie.

"One man's tragedy is another's fortune," Julius Carmen replied unconcerned, thick with Russian parlance and a sparkle in his green eyes behind red-rimmed glasses. Dressed in skeet shooting attire and khakis, the well tanned man of thirty-five with a full beard removed a platinum flask from inside his vest, unscrewed the cap and took a healthy swig. He sighed with satisfaction and offered the vodka to Friedrich. "Care for a bite of the green snake?" he asked, but was rebuffed with a simple shake of the head. Julius meticulously picked some lint off his coat and sat down. "This just might increase ticket sales even more. People only go to races for one reason," he said and pushed away his blonde bangs, cut in a bowl style.

"A man has been murdered for God's sake!" Friedrich said and shuddered when he looked through the slit in the curtain and saw Vincenzo's blood spiralled fingers, hanging out from beneath the sheet.

Julius broke into a knowing grin. "Look Friedrich, I know you want your own racing series, but this one is mine and as long as you work for me, you'll do as I say. I also know that you tried to raise the financing to do it, and that your attempt to give it prestige by asking Vincenzo to drive was rejected. That's over now, right?" Julius said and Friedrich nodded sheepishly. The Russian greedily rubbed his hands together. "Good. Now, the first thing we should do is speak to the lawyers about merchandising." He excitedly withdrew a minute gadget and clicked a button. "Memo... Azzopardi paraphernalia in memorial," he said into the device.

"What about the police? They might have something to say about all this," Friedrich said, gesturing to Vincenzo's body.

CHAPTER THREE

"We do." Startled, Julius and Friedrich looked to Gwen leaning against the doorway. She gracefully reached into her pocket and smartly unfolded a leather wallet. "Special agent, Gwen Gaudet, Direction de la Surveillance du Territoire," she said with authority and deftly flipped it closed.

"That must be your helicopter I saw land on the roof," Julius said with a smirk.

"No, it's the French taxpayers'," she countered, remaining in the doorway.

"It's an old Russian custom, Gwen. It's bad luck to greet someone standing in a doorway," Julius said and gladly looked her over. She stepped closer as Julius offered his handshake. "I'm Julius Carmen, president and CEO of the racing series," he added and peeled off his fake beard much to her surprise. "I like to people watch because I can't enjoy privacy in public."

"You'll call me Ms. Gaudet," she replied.

"My... my name is Friedrich Hesse, Ms. Gaudet. I'm Mr. Carmen's assistant," Friedrich said nervously and awkwardly shook her hand with a sweaty palm.

Gwen swiped aside the curtain and gingerly pulled back the sheet over Vincenzo. She withdrew a pen and used it to push Vincenzo's head to one side, revealing a small entry wound under his right eye. "Good shot," she said coldly and wiped the pen against the sheet to cleanse it of invisible germs. "Who gave you gentlemen the authority to be in here?" she said, leaning down and stared unaffected at the three-inch, exit hole in the back of Vincenzo's skull, his brains dripping into a stainless steel pan. Julius smiled and lured her eyes to a plaque on the wall reading, *The Julius Carmen Wing*.

"You see, Gwen, I mean, Ms. Gaudet, I reside here in Monaco. I like to give back to the community," Julius said proudly.

Gwen examined Vincenzo's blood splattered helmet on the counter and fingered the dent on the inside. "I'm sure it doesn't hurt your taxes either," she said without looking.

"Gaudet, Gaudet," Julius said, trying to recall and tapping his chin. "You wouldn't be any relation to Jean-Paul Gaudet, France's former, public works minister, would you?" he added with a devilish grin.

"As a matter of fact, I'm his daughter," she said, closing her eyes and sniffing some flowers in a vase on a filing cabinet. She felt the velvet texture of a rose and gently plucked it from its stem.

"Terrible shame what happened to him," Julius said, melodramatically shaking his head. "Suicide, wasn't it? If memory serves me correct, he was in prison at the time for taking millions in kickbacks from contractors, wasn't he?"

"Yes," she replied quietly with a stony face as Friedrich shifted uncomfortably and further loosened his tie.

"It would seem Monaco is a tax haven for both of our families," Julius said happily.

"I'm not here to discuss my family, Mr. Carmen," she said and produced a pad from her pocket. "Where were you when this happened," she asked Julius.

Julius sat down again and crossed his legs. "On my yacht. I live on it. Perhaps you'd like to visit some time for a little skeet shooting?" he added with a seductive smile.

Gwen ignored the invitation, scribbled in her pad and turned to Friedrich. "And you?"

"He was with me," Julius said.

"Am I speaking to you?" she said to Julius, he shook his head. "Then shut up."

Friedrich cleared his throat and dug his hands into his pockets. "He's right. We were having a party."

"I don't appreciate your tone," Julius said as his face hardened.

"It's the only way to make people like you understand," Gwen answered.

"What kind of person *am* I?" Julius said with a laugh.

Gwen retrieved a pill bottle from inside her pocket, flipped off the lid and shook two tablets into her mouth. "The kind that gives me migraines because they don't think before they speak," she answered tiredly. "And wipe that stupid grin off of your face or I'll do it for you." She snapped the bottle top back on and tucked it in her pocket. "I know who she is, but what about him?" she said, pointing to Samuel and looking to Friedrich for the answer.

"That's Samuel Jenkins. He owns the team that Vincenzo drives... drove for," Friedrich said sadly.

"Who won the race?" she said, flipping through her notes.

The query temporarily flummoxed both men. "Braedon Stirling," Friedrich said.

"Who's he?" she asked.

"Vincenzo's team-mate... was, I mean," Friedrich replied, annoyed with himself for making the same mistake twice.

"No offence, Ms. Gaudet, but you don't seem to know a lot about racing," Julius said condescendingly.

"No... just murder," Gwen replied.

"Murder?" Julius wondered in a mocking tone.

"I'm sure you noticed there's an extra hole in his head, Mr. Carmen. What would you call it, an accident?" she said. "Seems you don't know a lot about racing either."

The smirk vanished from Julius' face as Friedrich suppressed a grin. Gwen opened the door. "Could you please come in here, doctor?" she said. The physician gave Teresa a comforting pat and entered. Gwen closed the door and flashed her identification at Dr. Savoie. "DST. I'll be brief, gentlemen. As far as you're concerned, Mr. Azzopardi died from the trauma of the accident, caused by suspension failure. If you tell anyone anything else, I promise you that charges will be laid. Is that understood?" she said.

"Now just a minute, the public has a right to know!" Julius said and marched for the exit. "And I intend to tell them!"

"Take one more step and the only racing series you'll see, will be the inmates lining up to be your husband!" Gwen threatened. "I have the authority, Mr. Carmen. It's your move." Julius froze and his eyes locked with hers in a pseudo game of chicken until begrudgingly, he sat down again.

"What are you going to tell them?" Dr. Savoie asked her with concern, gesturing to Teresa and Samuel.

Gwen checked herself in a mirror, straightened her jacket and fixed a strand of hair that was slightly out of place. "That's none of your business," she said and fixed the rose to her lapel.

Randall fidgeted with his clip-on tie and squirmed in his uncomfortable suit as Tony pinned a yellow rose to Randall's lapel. "I look like a fucking idiot," Randall said.

"Yellow is for hope, sir," Tony said, still trying to affix the flower, his tongue concentrated in the corner of his mouth.

Randall focused on the door beside him and ran his finger along the smooth, etched lettering of the marbled glass that read, *Special Investigation Unit*. He heard voices but was unable to understand the conversation. Overtly, Randall took a swig from a Mickey inside his jacket and arched his back in the stiff, wooden chair. "You'd think these goddamned morons could afford better furniture."

"You've been here so many times, I'd think you'd be used to it by now," Tony replied and chuckled at his own joke.

Randall gave him a smartass look and withdrew a crooked cigarette from inside his wrinkled jacket. "They drag me all the way down here to tell me I'm finished. Waste of fucking time," he said and lit the smoke.

"You don't know that for sure, sir," Tony said squinting as he checked his uniform in the reflection of the window.

Randall frowned at him and said. "That's it? You don't have some biblical, bullshit pearl of wisdom for me, booger?"

Tony mulled it over and smiled. "'And keep me from deliberate wrongs. Help me to stop doing them. Only then can I be free of guilt and innocent of some great crime.' Deuteronomy, seventeen, twelve," he recited proudly.

"Wrong, booger. Psalms, nineteen, thirteen," Randall said plainly, Tony frowned, disappointed by his error. Randall rolled his eyes when he looked at the clock on the wall. "Fuck! I'm going to miss my goddamned flight!" he said, the cigarette dangling from his mouth. He banged on the door, causing the glass to rattle. "Hurry up, fuckers! Let's get this shit over with!"

"I don't think that's going to help your case, sir" Tony said. "If you don't behave yourself, they just might put you back in the rubber room." The door suddenly swung open and two suited men and a woman brushed by Randall with a disgusted glance.

"Nice to meet you too, assholes," Randall said and purposely blew smoke at them as he withdrew the flask again. "Civilians judging cops. Fucking politics. They don't know jack shit about us."

"Get in here, Grange!" Hank Wallace barked, standing in the doorway with his arms crossed.

Randall drained the bottle, belched and handed it to Tony. "Good luck, sir," the rookie whispered.

Randall casually shuffled into the sterile boardroom and Hank yanked the cigarette from Randall's mouth. "I thought this was supposed to be an inquiry," Randall said, spying a bird building a nest on the windowsill.

"It is and it's over," Hank replied as he sat at the head of the desk and interlocked his fingers.

"Permission to sit down, sir!" Randall said militarily and delivered an overly dramatic salute.

Hank pointed a threatening finger at him. "Don't be an idiot. You're in enough trouble as it is."

Randall hooked a chair with his right foot, dragged it closer, spun it around and sat in it backwards. He pulled out the pack of smokes and withdrew one with his teeth. Hank promptly leaned forward, grabbed it out of his mouth and broke it in half. The two stared each other down, waiting for the next move. Randall jostled the packet and removed another. Hank reached to take it but Randall clamped his wrist and held it tight. "What's your fucking problem?" Randall asked.

Hank swung his other hand around, collared Randall by the neck and pulled him closer. "You are!" Hank shouted. Randall capitulated with his hands and opened his mouth, allowing the smoke to fall. "Are you ready

CHAPTER THREE

to listen?" Hank said as Randall straightened himself. "Sit in that chair like a man, not a child."

Randall leered at him, righted the chair and sat properly. "You're really pushing it, Hank."

"I can afford to and the name is Staff Sergeant Wallace," Hank replied as he swivelled in his seat and drew a big circle on a chalkboard behind him. He drew several, smaller circles inside the big one and stared at Randall.

"That's great, Hank. Maybe next week we'll start you on crayon," Randall said.

Hank fought to maintain his temper and pointed to the small circles. "These are us," he said and motioned to the big circle, "and that's the line of the law. You can approach it and even go past it, but not completely outside it. It's a fine line between order and chaos. Good versus evil. And when cops break the law, we're held to a higher standard than the criminals. Try and remember that. Understand?"

"As much as I'd like to," Randall replied, more interested in the bird.

"You crossed that line with Andy Lunder," Hank said. "The only problem is, I can't prove it."

"Tisk, tisk," Randall said and yawned.

Hank opened a drawer, retrieved a file and held it up. "Know what this is?"

"All the women that have rejected you?"

"It's a complete record of your career," Hank said, opening it and donning his reading glasses. "Entered police college at nineteen and became a constable at twenty-one. Worked through the ranks and reached sergeant by age thirty, becoming the youngest homicide detective in the force's history. A stellar record... until last year," he said and flipped the page. "Found guilty of stealing marijuana from the evidence room and drinking on duty. Crashed an unmarked while under the influence. Demoted to constable, fourth class, by me, for two years," he added and closed the file.

Randall clapped sardonically and said. "What an epic! Tell it again, Dad."

"The psyche department thinks you're certifiable and so does the SIU. I guess that explains your visit to the hospital. But I don't think you're crazy. I think you just don't give a damn, but you're not going to be my problem anymore," Hank said happily and sat back in his seat as Randall studied a collection of antique police firearms in a cabinet. "In all my years on the force, I have never drawn my weapon once."

"Christ, I hate martyrs. Who the fuck do you think you are, my father?" Randall said with a laugh.

"He obviously did a poor job."

The statement deflated Randall and his eyes lowered. "The man was murdered... you have no right to judge him."

"I'm sorry... I forgot about that," Hank said sincerely.

Randall took a few moments to gather his thoughts. "Just tell me what the three stooges had to say and we can all get on with our lives."

Hank's sympathetic stare evaporated. "If you're referring to the SIU members, they hate you almost as much as I do. God, I love a democracy," he said as Randall abruptly flung off his tie and bolted for the exit. "Where do you think you're going?"

"I've had enough of this fucking shit!"

"Sit down!" Hank shouted.

"I don't work for you any more. If you want to press criminal charges against me for offing that piece of shit, go ahead! Otherwise, fuck off!"

"There will be no charges," Hank said quietly.

"What?" Randall said, totally stunned.

"You've been transferred."

"No thanks. I don't want to be a crossing guard."

"You don't have a choice," Hank said.

"Who says?"

"Higher-ups," Hank replied and retrieved a small pamphlet from inside the file.

"You can go tell your uncle the mayor to shove it up his hairy ass!" Randall said and strolled to the door.

"It's a little higher up than that."

"What the hell are you talking about?" Randall said.

Hank slid the booklet across the desk towards him. Randall opened it to discover a plane ticket. "You leave tonight," Hank said.

"England? I don't get it."

"You're specific skills are required."

"By who?"

"I'm not at liberty to say."

"And if I say no?"

"Then you're off the force, permanently. No pension and charges will be pursued in the Lunder case," Hank said.

"I thought you said you couldn't prove what happened," Randall stated confidently.

"You never know how the courts will go, but you can count on me not to back you up. By the time they're finished with you, you won't be able to a job as a security guard. And Tony can start looking for another career too," Hank said as he eased back in the chair with his hands behind his head. "So, what's it going to be?"

    Randall studied the ticket again; his perplexed gaze then drifted to the window as the bird flew away.

Chapter Four

Fatigued eyes became hypnotized, watching the windshield wipers from the back seat of a limousine.

The black super stretch pulled off the busy London street and stopped at the curb. The chauffeur hurriedly stepped out and opened the backdoor, the point of a wobbly cane appeared. The driver offered a hand of assistance, but Samuel impatiently pushed him aside with his walking stick.

The old man popped open his umbrella and hobbled towards the monolith of glass and steel. He stopped and titled his head back; the raindrops caused his milky eyes to flicker. Samuel spied the fly-yellow, *Hispania Gold* sign above the facade and followed the shape of the edifice as it tapered upward and disappeared in the fog. "The battle begins," he whispered and entered the building.

Samuel checked himself in the highly polished, stainless steel wall of the glass elevator as the city dropped from sight and became engulfed in a cloud. He held his hands out and saw they were shaking. "Damn!" he whispered angrily to himself.

The doors noiselessly parted and he followed the plush corridor, admiring the framed portraits of regal looking men on the left. The wall of fame was a company history lesson, from the founder in 1731 to the present day CEO, save an obvious, missing portrait between the last two. Beneath each picture was a plaque with the individual's identity, all ending with the surname Suarez.

On the right, another chronology of Hispania Gold's involvement in racing with dozens of photographs depicting various cars and drivers. The last two pictures were of Braedon Stirling and Vincenzo Azzopardi with a black ribbon across one corner of the frame.

A buxom brunette was waiting for Samuel at the end of the passage and she nodded her greeting. He did the same as he reached for one of two huge, mahogany doors with brass handles. "I'm sorry Mr. Jenkins, they're not quite ready for you yet," she said.

"They never are," he replied and quietly leaned the door open.

Felipe Suarez, a suave, fit man of twenty-four with too much jewellery and a silver streak through his receding black hair, sat at the head of a long, narrow, marble slab, dressed in an immaculate, silver Armani suit with a red and yellow handkerchief. He stroked his Vandyke beard with one hand and fingered the large, diamond stud in his left ear. A dozen suited men sat around the table, each separated by several feet. "That is my final offer. Take it or leave it," Felipe said casually into the telephone with a heavy Spanish accent. "Good. I knew you'd see it my way. I'll have the paperwork to you by tomorrow," he added and hung up.

"I see you still haven't put a portrait of your father in the hall of fame," Samuel said.

Surprised, Felipe stood up with his arms outstretched. "Buenos días, Sammy. So good to see you again.

Samuel gestured to the phone and said. "Another victim?"

"I just bought the third largest tobacco company in the United States," he replied exuberantly and strolled to an impressive bar against a wall with the Spanish flag above it. "Revenge for Cuba, Puerto Rico and the Philippines," he continued with a smile, but was sincere in his statement. "Can I get you a drink?"

"No, thank you. Your father was a good man, God rest his soul," Samuel said.

Felipe tossed a couple of ice cubes in a glass. "Then you didn't know him that well," he countered.

"What you did to him was criminal," Samuel stated, much to the uneasiness of the other men.

"He was mentally unfit to run this company and I was the only one who had the courage to step in," Felipe answered with a hint of anger.

"Have you spoken to your mother lately?" Samuel purposely inquired as he eyed a wall sized photograph of Felipe behind the wheel of a Hispania sponsored racing car.

"You'll be happy to hear that she wants nothing to do with me," Felipe said, filling his glass with Scotch and watching Samuel stare at the photograph. "It's a shame I didn't get a chance to race at the highest level, but you thought Vincenzo was better than me, but I deserved the ride," he said with a chuckle, but was deadly serious.

"A lot of people didn't... including your father," Samuel shot back, unfazed by the implicit insult.

Felipe raised the lead crystal to toast. "To the King, Juan Carlos and Queen Sophia," he said and downed the liquor.

Chapter Four

"You do realize you're in England," Samuel said.

Felipe grinned and took his seat at the head of the table. "A man has to make sacrifices when his wife owns fifty-one percent of the company and wants its corporate office in her home country."

"And how is Mrs. Gold? I mean, Mrs. Suarez?" Samuel said, deliberate in his mistake.

"Busy with her first baby. Please Sammy, sit, sit," Felipe said and gesticulated the Team Jenkins czar to a chair.

"I'd prefer to stand," Samuel said, hoping they didn't see him shaking as he felt a bead of sweat trickle down his hand to the cane's bone handle. "This had better be important. You know I'm preparing for a funeral."

A pause of uneasiness. "On behalf of all of our employees here at Hispania Gold, we extend our deepest sympathies," Felipe said stiffly.

"I'm sure the loved ones of your customers say the same thing. Now, what do you want?" Samuel asked.

Slightly flustered, Felipe sat straight in the chair, the leather stretching. "Hispania Gold has been honoured to sponsor Team Jenkins over the last ten years."

"Actually, this is the eleventh," Samuel said.

"Right. Eleven. Thanks to you and the series, we've had a global presence."

"You still do."

"However, due to the recent tragedy, we do have some concerns," Felipe said.

"Vincenzo hasn't been dead forty-eight hours and you're ready to pounce! I remind you that we still have a contract until the end of the season!" Samuel said too loudly.

Felipe held up a dossier. "Our contract clearly states that our sponsorship is valid as long as Vincenzo Azzopardi and Braedon Stirling drive. We've spent quite a bit of money Sammy and our shareholders expect a return."

"Braedon is still piloting the sister machine, and he is still the defending world champion!"

"Nobody is saying we're pulling our sponsorship. As a matter of fact, anecdotal monitoring tells us that since the death of Mr. Azzopardi, sales have actually increased. It's quite remarkable," Felipe said, referring to another slip of paper.

"Then, what is it you want?" Samuel said, completely confused.

Felipe withdrew a platinum cigar box and slid it the length of the table to Samuel. "Please, have one," Felipe said. Samuel opened the container, plucked one of the Havanas and a member of the board quickly lit it with the matching lighter. "What are your plans to fill the seat? Pardon me if it sounds cold, but business is business," Felipe added.

"I... I hadn't thought that far ahead," Samuel answered. "I'm going to take a look at a few of the boys in Formula 3000... maybe CART in America. Why?"

"I'm ready to offer you a deal, but I need an answer... and soon."

"I do not bend to pressure Felipe and frankly, I am more than a little insulted."

"You should know better than anybody that sponsorship dollars are getting harder to come by," Felipe said.

"You're not the only company interested in promoting their name."

"I know Julius Carmen has some rights to Azzopardi's merchandising with their logo, but you hold the rest. Correct?" Felipe said with another grin.

"Yes... that was part of the contract I had with Vincenzo. If I resigned him after this year, he would have been entitled to half of the merchandising. Why?"

Felipe stood and studied the Spanish flag. "I think it only makes corporate sense to have two Spaniards in the seats," he said and turned to Samuel. "Here's my offer. You give me fifty percent of merchandising, I choose the replacement for Azzopardi, and I will extend my sponsorship for another four years. I also get fifty-one percent stock of the team as well as being the second driver. I'm better than Stirling anyway," he said arrogantly.

Samuel was shocked and didn't notice the heavy stare of the room. Slowly, his arid lips peeled apart. "You can't be serious... that's outrageous," he said, barely audible.

Felipe knew Samuel was dazed and edged towards him, setting him up for the coup de grace. "Racing is the most expensive sport in the world and you've invested millions, but not as much as me," he said, leaning closer to Samuel's ear. "You see, Sammy, I have a lot more control now, control that you know nothing about, but more importantly, I know what *you've* done," he whispered as Samuel's cane slipped from his nervous hand. "I'll have the paperwork ready in a few days."

Randall's hands trembled as he carried two cups of steaming coffee to Tony, sitting at a small table in the airport cafeteria. "Take one! My fucking hands are burning off!" Randall said despite the cigarette hanging from his mouth.

"You're not allowed to smoke in airports anymore, sir," Tony said and took a cup.

Chapter Four

"Fuck them," Randall said as he sat and tapped his ash onto the floor. He retrieved a tiny bottle of rye and waved it at Tony as an offer.

"No thank you, sir," Tony replied and nervously bit his lip as he watched Randall empty the bottle in his coffee. "Sir? Maybe you should stop drinking."

Randall raised an eyebrow at his partner's audacity and said. "You got a lot of balls, booger, but it's none of your fucking business. Besides, the problem isn't stopping, it's stopping from starting again," he continued and stirred the liquid. "Don't you do anything wrong?"

Tony's eyes fell away and his head lowered. "Yes... I didn't tell Wallace the truth about what happened with Lunder," he said, full of shame.

Randall leaned back in the seat and kicked his feet up onto his scratched, plastic suitcase. "What's your biggest goal, booger?"

"To be a good Christian," Tony replied without missing a beat.

"Don't give me that bullshit. What's your real dream?" Randall said, blowing the steam off his cup.

"I... I'd like to be police chief someday," Tony replied softly, slightly embarrassed as he played with his stir stick.

"Better learn to swallow," Randall said and winced from the strong drink. "You think the chief has a perfect record? We all got our dirty little secrets, booger. Some are just better at hiding them than others and some just don't give a fuck," he continued and winked.

"That still doesn't excuse what I did."

"Look, if every officer told the truth, there wouldn't be any cops at all. Sometimes the end justifies the means."

"No matter what Andy Lunder did, he was still a human being, sir," Tony said, fearful of the response.

"He knew right from wrong. Even a baby that sticks his hand on a hot stove won't do it twice."

"Don't you think it's a little more complicated than that, sir?" Tony said. "Lunder was a victim of society."

"Victim is just another term for people who are too fucking dumb or lazy to own up to their mistakes," Randall said with a nonchalant wave of his hand. "Know what my old man used to make me do? He always made me sweep the floor after dinner. The fucking place would be spotless when I was done, but the cocksucker would push crumbs on the floor just to give him an excuse to kick my ass. Telling me he didn't know right from wrong? Telling me I didn't?" Randall said void of emotion. "I'm a victim too, but my dream isn't to bugger kids."

"What is your dream, sir?" Tony asked, genuinely interested in the answer and content to change the subject.

"Don't have one," Randall answered, stifling a belch.

"You must have had one at some point," Tony said.

Randall's gaze unwillingly drifted to a father lifting his son into an arcade car ride. "To stay a professional racing driver," he said and stared longingly at the toddler as the father dropped some coins into the box, "and to have known my real dad. Always wondered what he would have been like."

"What happened to him?"

"Killed in a car accident when I was two... can't even visit him... he's buried in Montreal, where he was born," Randall said, avoiding Tony's stare and dropping the cigarette to the floor. He crushed it out with his cowboy boot. "Both dreams are dead."

"What about your mom?"

"Dead," Randall replied coldly.

"Guess I'm lucky. My folks are still around. I even still live at home," Tony announced with abashment.

"Nothing wrong with that," Randall said and lit another cigarette.

"Mom works for the phone company and pop's a janitor. Not very glamorous."

"Money's money, booger," Randall said. "My old man was more interested in his own well-being than me and my mom's."

"What did she do?"

"Housewife," Randall answered curtly.

"And your stepfather?"

"Not much," Randall said, uncomfortable with the direction of the conversation. He checked the clock on the wall and stood. "Better get going."

"Have you figured out what they want with you in England?" Tony asked as they started towards the boarding gate.

"Nope. Haven't banged any British broads so it ain't a paternity suit," Randall said sarcastically. "Sure I'll find out when I get there."

Tony stole a glance at him. "Is there anything I can do for you while you're gone, sir?"

"Look after my cat, okay? Shit, he's all I got left," Randall said, giving Tony his apartment key and handing his ticket and suitcase to the clerk.

"Sure," Tony said, tucking the key in his trousers and awkwardly wrapping his arm around him. "You going to be okay, sir?"

"What, are we fags or something?" Randall asked, spying Tony's arm.

Tony maintained his grip. "You can't fool me, sir. Like it or not, you have feelings, just like everybody else. You take care of yourself."

Randall shook his hand and gave him a slap on the back. "Is this where we kiss?"

Chapter Four

"Touch me and I'll kick your butt, sir," Tony said with a smile.

"There's hope for you yet, booger," Randall said and entered the lounge. "And keep your hands off my pussy," Randall added. Tony gave him a wave and walked away.

"You'll have to extinguish that cigarette, Mr. Grange," the clerk said, checking his ticket.

Randall dropped the cigarette in the cup, gave it to her and turned to watch Tony disappearing around a corner. "Going to miss you too, booger," he whispered.

Randall settled into a chair and perused some magazines on the table. He flipped one open and immediately focused on a liquor advertisement. "Better have one last piss," he said.

In the deserted men's room, Randall washed his hands and noticed the door opening in the reflection of the mirror. A large man in a black suit entered and leaned against the door with his arms crossed. "Air Canada flight 709 to London, now boarding at Gate 7," a female voice said via the PA system. Randall reached for some paper towels but the dispenser was empty. He dried them against his trousers, staring at the stranger.

"What the fuck are you looking at?"

"Monsieur Randall Grange?" the man said with a French accent.

"Who wants to know?"

The man's eyes looked to the speaker in the ceiling. "That isn't your flight."

Randall held up his ticket stub. "Flight 709 to England, pal."

The man stepped forward and snatched the ticket out of his hand. "You're on a different flight. Follow me."

"Like hell," Randall said and went to lunge at him, but the man sidestepped him and bent Randall's arm behind his back, pushing him to the wall. "Who the fuck are you?" Randall said with his face squished against the cold tile.

The man released him and opened the door for him. "Larry... your bodyguard."

Eyes stared at the whirring ceiling fan in the darkened room and shifted to the open window as a soft breeze swayed the lace curtain. The subtle smell of roses wafted in with the gentle sound of the warm wind as strange, lifelike shadows from tree branches danced against the bedroom wall.

Braedon Stirling studied a large painting of a pretty, petite redhead with alabaster skin and dazzling green eyes in mid-pirouette. The brass plaque read, *The Royal Academy of Ballet*.

He sat up and glanced at the alarm clock. Four-thirty a.m. He swung his feet over the side of the king-sized bed and caught a glimpse of his toned, naked body in the floor length mirror. He shuffled noiselessly to the casement window and peered out.

"Always seems bigger at night," he whispered as he gazed at his sprawling, English estate. He heard the whinny of a horse and looked down the lush, perennially gardened lane, past a homemade equestrian park and nine-hole golf course to the large, red stable. "Even you know something is wrong," he said as he strained his neck to see the full moon, its light so luminous he squinted.

His attention turned to Lisa, the woman in the painting, leaning up on one elbow, half covered by the blanket. "What is it?" she said quietly with a sleepy, English accent.

"Nothing. Go back to sleep."

She pulled the covers up to her neck and rested against the headboard as she gazed upon the painting. "I'm going to do one of you next," she said happily.

"Fine," he said, lost in thought.

"Are you going?"

"I guess," he said with a heavy sigh and sat on the edge of the bed.

"Scared?"

"It's considered bad luck."

Lisa rolled her eyes and reached for a packet of cigarettes on the night table, he shot her a disapproving glare. "I'm not in the mood," she said and lit the tobacco. "My husband drives a car at over three hundred kilometres an hour and he's worried about my health," she continued but instantly regretted the comment and crushed it out. She crawled across the bed and flung her arms around his waist, pressing her head against his lower back. "I think it's good that you go."

Braedon laid her head in his lap and stroked her hair. "It's an unwritten taboo."

"Who says?"

"The other drivers."

"It doesn't matter what they think. It's what you think. What you feel in your heart," she said and snuggled closer.

"I didn't really like him, though. I'd feel like a hypocrite."

"Going to a funeral is about respect, Braedon," she replied as he caressed her, her eyes glued to the tattoo of the word *Provo* on the back of his right hand. Her cherubic face turned to their three-month-old boy in a bassinet on her side of the bed.

"What is it?" he asked, realizing the sudden change in her demeanour.

"Nothing."

Braedon forced her to look at him. "What?"

"I just wish you'd get that removed," she said, taking his right hand.

"It's a part of my heritage. I keep it as a reminder," he said just as the infant started to whimper.

"What will you tell him about it when he's old enough?"

"That his grandfather was a hero."

"Losing his job as a miner and then robbing banks for the Provisional IRA doesn't make him a hero. It makes him a criminal," she replied and went to their son. "There's nothing noble about dying from a hunger strike in prison."

"I don't want to get into this," he said and opened an impressive, walk-in closet. Inside, dozens of silk suits hung on one side and casual wear on the other.

"Well I do," she said, cradling the sulking baby in her arms and positioning a breast. "I also want him to know that his grandmother was murdered by the IRA. That his only living grandfather sits at home with no reason to live and won't even come to see his own grandson," she added with a breaking voice.

"You haven't suffered as much as I have," he scoffed.

"Just because I'm from England doesn't mean I had it any better," she said as the boy began suckling.

"Were you born in the Belfast ghetto? Did you have to live in public housing? You had a bathroom and hot water! Did you have to rely on state benefits? Did your parents have to pay for school books, paper and pencils?" he said, raising his voice and angrily throwing a suitcase onto the bed. "You know what I remember about being a kid? Police stations! Security bases! Border patrols! Being treated like some kind of animal! I want my son to know the sacrifices of his blood!"

"Then I hope you also tell him that his father was arrested in London with explosives and was sent to prison!"

"I'm proud of that! It was a mistake, but I'm still proud of it!" he said, folding some clothes and tossing them into the suitcase. "Hell, if I hadn't done it I'd never have met Samuel."

Lisa slowly moved towards him, carrying their son as her eyes filled. "Or me. Do you love me, Braedon?"

He pulled on his underwear and trousers. "Of course," he answered impatiently.

Her free hand cupped his face. "We haven't... it's been a long time, Braedon."

"I'm a busy man," he said, engrossed with dressing.

"I know! We all know! You're the world champion!" she snapped, suddenly losing her temper.

"And that's the way it's going to stay! The only reason you know I'm the champion is because you read it in the paper!"

"Don't start that again," she said as she sat on the bed with the baby.

"You haven't been to one race! Not one! You don't mind the glory, but you won't support it!"

"We have a son, remember? I gave up a career for you!" she said, gesturing to the painting.

"Don't give me that! I never wanted children and you know it!"

"You're the one that didn't like me taking birth control pills! You listen to your priest, but not your own wife!"

"Just because you don't follow your religion doesn't mean I won't adhere to mine!" he barked.

"I don't care that you're Catholic and I'm Protestant! Can't you see? I just want us to be a happy family!" she pleaded.

"We're raising him Catholic," he stated succinctly and pulled on a shirt.

"No discussion? Your word is final and that's it?"

"You don't care about your faith, remember?" he replied and stepped into a pair of loafers.

"But I do about what kind of son I want. He needs to make up his own mind when the time is right."

"When I get back, we're getting him baptized," he said matter-of-factly and threw on a tweed jacket.

"No."

"I'm the man of the house! I'm the breadwinner!" he shouted and closed the suitcase.

"Keep your voice down! You'll scare him!"

Braedon marched for the door but suddenly stopped. "I'll be back in two days," he said and looked at her over his shoulder. "Why won't you go to any of the races?" he quietly asked.

"You know the answer to that," she said softly. "Every time you get behind that wheel, I wonder if what happened to Vincenzo will happen to you," she added and began to cry.

"It won't!"

"How can you be so sure?"

Braedon took a deep breath to temper his anger and said. "Look, you're a new mother and your emotions are all messed up. Okay? Now, be a good girl and call for the jet."

"Do it yourself."

Annoyed, he picked up the phone, pushed one button and waited momentarily. "I'll meet you at the airport in one hour. Italy," he said and hung up.

The baby finished nursing and Lisa placed a towel over her shoulder before burping him. "He was the last time we made love," she said, gently

Chapter Four

patting the infant's back as Braedon started down the hallway towards a winding staircase. "Maybe the reason I don't go is because of what I might find."

He froze. "What?"

"Is there someone else?"

"I won't dignify that," he replied with a flushed face.

"Answer me... please."

"I'll call you from Milan," he said and started down the steps.

"I may not be here when you do."

"Don't make threats you can't keep," he answered unconcerned without breaking stride.

"No...it's a promise," she whispered and held the baby closer.

Randall looked out the window, the view slightly vertical and banking as a bead of sweat rolled own his pale face. His fingers dug into the armrest as he watched the mist rocketing past, frequently revealing neat patches of land. "*Now* are you going to tell me where the hell we're going?" Randall said breathlessly to his stoic bodyguard. Stone-faced, Larry remained hidden behind a Paris newspaper. "You really should consider renting a personality," Randall added.

"I'm not here to amuse you," Larry replied and turned a page.

"You're doing a good job so far," Randall said and surveyed the plush, six-seater, executive jet as the seatbelt sign turned off. He quickly unbuckled himself and started towards the back of the aircraft.

"Where are you going?" Larry demanded.

"I was thinking about jumping. I'm getting a drink, you dumb fucking ape," Randall replied as he proceeded to the small refrigerator. He opened it to discover bottles of water and juices. "Tell the stewardess there's no goddamned booze on this flight!"

"I had explicit instructions that there be no alcohol on board."

Randall angrily flung the door closed making the glass containers rattle. He withdrew his cigarettes with quaking hands, lit one and simpered at Larry.

"Extinguish that," Larry ordered.

Randall laughed and relaxed into the leather, swivel chair again. He blew smoke rings as Larry reached for the cigarette with an extended hand. "Fuck you," Randall said as Larry lunged for it, but Randall was too quick for him. "Pretty slow for a bodyguard."

"Put it out," Gwen Gaudet's voice commanded. "I mean it."

The cigarette instantly dropped from Randall's mouth in disbelief as he focused on Gwen standing in the doorway of the cockpit. His surprised eyes soaked in her beauty as she turned to Larry. "Excuse us, please,"

Gwen said. The bodyguard fleetly disappeared to the front of the plane and closed the door behind him.

Gwen sat, slowly and deliberately crossing her legs, allowing Randall a glimpse of her black lace panties as he quickly tried to force his attention upward. He could smell the subtle scent of her perfume and felt a burning between his legs. "Nice to see you, split lips," he said with a grin and suddenly jumped in his seat. "Shit!" he shouted and removed the cigarette from his smouldering crotch.

"I said put it out. If there's a spark, we're all dead."

Randall lifted one foot and crushed it out against the sole of his cowboy boot. "What is this, some kind of fucking joke? What the hell are you doing here?" he questioned, utterly bewildered.

"Obviously, you haven't lost your flair for words or fashion. Always the rebel," she said, eyeing his faded denim.

Randall glanced around the aircraft. "I see you're spending my money well."

"Hardly. You haven't offered any."

"Is that what this is all about? Going to force me to pay at thirty thousand feet?" he said and spotted the wedding ring he had given her. "Looks like you miss me."

Gwen folded her arms, slightly embarrassed at his minor victory. "I don't want to forget the past. Two years wasn't that long ago."

"I know, living through hell lasts an eternity, doesn't it?"

"Same old Randall. Some habits never die."

Randall straightened his dungaree jacket and pulled a lever to extend the chair. He stretched out with his hands behind his head. "True, you still seem like a bitch."

"It's attitudes like that, that make me glad I left the force... and you."

"I always said feminists were bitchy because they weren't getting laid. Obviously, you're not getting any."

"You really are dysfunctional, aren't you?" she said, thoroughly enjoying the jousting.

"Hey, I don't have to blame anybody for the way I am," he said casually.

"No. Just me."

"Don't flatter yourself. I take responsibility for my own actions."

"Like Jessica?" she said, but immediately regretted the statement. Ashamed, she lowered her eyes, the high-pitched whistle of the engines suddenly deafening and overbearing. "I'm sorry... that wasn't fair."

The levity promptly vanished from his face as his sheepish eyes darted about. "No worries," he said smiling, pretending her comment didn't faze him, but it was obvious he was overwhelmed. After a few ungainly

Chapter Four

moments, he reached inside his jacket pocket and stared at the photograph of Jessica on the swing set. "Speak of the devil," he continued with a strained chuckle and waved it to show her. "How is she?" he asked nervously with his hand over his mouth.

"She's a fighter. She's with the nanny," she countered with a happy nod, trying to alleviate the onerous atmosphere.

Randall tucked the picture back in his pocket and cleared his throat. "Any change?" he said quietly, his chin in his chest.

"No," Gwen replied softly. Their eyes locked and there was an understood, silent detente. His gaze fixed out the window and saw they were over the ocean. "Still scared to fly?" she said, glad to change the subject.

"Not crazy about it," he replied and forced himself not to look out the window.

"I could never understand that. You always liked speed."

"On the ground, yes. Ain't natural having your ass in the air," he said and pulled down the shade. "How are the headaches?" he asked, spotting the bottle of pills in her breast pocket.

"I still get them," she said and felt the scar on her forehead. "The doctor says take two aspirins and don't call me in the morning," she continued sarcastically, hoping to ease his conscience, but his face remained sullen. "Look Randall, if it's any comfort, it was just as much my fault for getting in the car with you that day."

He swallowed his emotion and avoided her stare. "I dream about it sometimes, you know. Always the same. Starts in the bar. Going home and picking her up, and then you. I'd driven down that street a thousand times, right?" he said. She went to say something, but realized his words were a necessary catharsis. "Went right through that fucking stop sign, didn't I? Drunken fucking idiot!" he continued, shaking his head at the memory of his stupidity. "Still remember the look on your face just before the other car hit. Cold that day. You said something about how pretty the leaves looked," he concluded as his quivering voice faded.

"Stop it, Randall," she whispered.

He clenched his eyes and his face grimaced. "Can still hear the glass breaking. The metal. Can see her in the car seat. Head was at a funny angle afterward," he explained with his hands, "Could tell her neck was broken... blood all over your face... ain't fair that nothing happened to me, is it?" he said as his head sank. There was a few seconds of awkward silence until suddenly, the plane shook violently, startling him.

"It's okay. Just a little turbulence," she reassured.

Randall inhaled deeply, struggling to remain calm and motioning to the luxurious surroundings. "I didn't know frog homicide detectives were paid so good," he said jokingly to mitigate his own anxiety as she sauntered to the fridge, the cloth of her dress gently brushing against his skin. He pinched her shapely behind as she stooped for the handle. "Now I remember why I call you split lips," he said.

Gwen abruptly pivoted, slapped him hard on his surprised face and twisted one of his thumbs back making him cringe in pain. "Ever since I wasn't allowed in the police station because I was wearing nail polish, I knew being a cop would be an uphill battle. There used to be a cultural difference between male and female officers," she said calmly, maintaining the pressure on his digit. "And I've always had to work twice as hard because I am a split lip. But now that there's a little more equality, I don't have to take that kind of shit anymore. Barefoot and pregnant doesn't apply. Understand?"

"Got it," he winced as she released him. "I think you broke my fucking thumb!" he complained as he studied his reddened hand.

"You're lucky I didn't rip your dick off," she said and relaxed into her seat.

"Such language," he said sardonically with a grin. "What would your mother say?"

"Why don't you call her and find out?" she replied, twisting the cap off the water bottle, the air escaping loudly, embellishing her point.

"How is the old bird by the way?" he said and blew on his thumb.

"The same. She gets quite angry if I don't speak to her every day," she said and took a long sip. "Costs me a fortune in phone bills."

"I read about your dad. My sympathies," he said sincerely. She nodded her appreciation. "He'd be proud that you've done so well."

"With your talent, you could have been chief of police by now if you had a little diplomacy," she said and carefully plucked a hair off her jacket.

"I don't swallow," he answered with a simper.

"That was a nice try but you can't get under my skin anymore, Randall."

"So who *does* split lips work for now?" he said and winked.

Gwen crossed her legs and folded her arms. "Staff Sergeant Wallace tells me you killed a suspect. Is that true?" she said bluntly, popping a few pills into her mouth and washing them down with the water.

"He was a kiddy diddler," he replied, frowning at the odd question.

"Did you ever bother to find out the consequences of your actions on the boy and his mother?"

"Anything is better than where the kid was."

"Not that you care, but social services took him away and the mother is in rehab. Lucky for you the system works."

Chapter Four

"Only when it's too late. What the fuck do you care about some trailer trash anyway?" he said and squirmed in his seat, uncomfortable with the direction of the conversation.

Gwen noticed and replied. "There's no escape, Randall. You can't walk out like you used to. Why did you kill him?"

"I told you," he answered with a tinge of anger.

Gwen opened a briefcase and removed a file. "I need to know your mental state because according to Wallace, it's not so good."

He chuckled and said. "I damn near kill you and Jess, then you leave me, now I've lost my job and to top it all off, I'm going to miss the funeral of a friend. How the hell do you think I feel? I don't give a shit whether I live or die."

"Are you going to try and kill yourself again?"

"What do you care?"

"You keep swimming in that pool of self-pity and you'll drown."

Randall's face stiffened and he leaned forward, collapsing the chair to its original position. "Okay, now that our heart wrenching reunion is over, what the fuck I am doing here?"

"There's that subtlety I was taking about."

"Jesus Christ woman! Do I have to beg you?" he shouted.

Gwen reflected for a moment and answered. "*I tried that once, you kept drinking anyway.*"

Randall bolted to his feet and began pacing. "I don't know what the fuck is going on here, but you're on some kind of a power trip or something! You're more fucked-up than I am and believe me lady, that's saying something!"

"Vincenzo was murdered," she said coldly, holding up the file. "A shot was fired from the Grand Hotel in Monaco."

The rage inside him instantly evaporated and he felt his knees weaken. "What?" he mouthed completely dumbfounded and stumbled to sit in the chair beside her.

Gwen placed the folder on the table, opened it and shuffled various photographs revealing Vincenzo's bullet wound, and Benny Rabowitz lying in the garden. "The guy kissing the flower bed checked in under the name Leonard Pinto. It was an alias for Benny Rabowitz," she said, waiting for a reaction.

"So?" he said in confusion, still trying to recover from the shocking news.

"We ran the prints. Had a bit of a tough time due to his psoriasis, but we found a match. Benny Rabowitz is *The Rabbit*."

Randall's stunned face verified he knew the name. "The assassin?" he asked incredulously.

Gwen removed a printout from the file. "Benny Rabowitz, born in Galilee, Israel, 1954. Entered the military at eighteen and became a sharpshooter. Later joined the Mossad and entered the Metsada," she recited from the paper.

"What the hell is that?"

"Special Operations Division. Specialize in assassinations, paramilitary and psychological warfare. He worked collecting intelligence and counter-terrorism. Covert stuff. He was an operative in East Germany and Russia. Instrumental in getting refugees out of Iran, Syria and Ethiopia. Hell, he even did a stint at the UN," she said, referring to the notes.

"Where did you get all this?" he wondered, leafing through the photographs and wincing at the ones of Vincenzo.

"Almost every country has a file on him, including us at the DST. Do you know what this is?" she asked and he nodded. "Most of it came from MI5 and the CIA. Certainly not from the Israelis. They don't want to talk about him, let alone acknowledge he exists. He knew too many secrets. It seems the Rabbit hired himself out to the highest bidder after he defected from the Metsada. Unconfirmed reports put his finger on the trigger of at least three high profile assassinations in the mid-nineties," she said and took a sip from her water bottle. "Rabowitz made a deal with the Israeli government. They'd let him live as long as he never returned to Israel. Unusual, but they suspected he wrote down everything he knew and had it safely tucked away in some bank to be made public should anything untoward happen to him," she continued, rubbing her sore forehead as Randall listened, totally baffled by a photograph of the dead parrot. "Anyway, The Rabbit lived a quiet life on an impressive ranch in Arizona. Good climate for his psoriasis. He had enough money and actually wrote a book on birds. He retired from offering his services two years ago... until just a few days ago. We found his fingerprints on the rifle that discharged the bullet," she said and withdrew a photograph of the gun. "A German TPG-1. Fairly new weapon. .308 calibre. Full metal jacket. No other prints in the room and no eyewitnesses. We found some clothing fibres, but there's nothing to match them to. We checked the hotel and race video and nothing. No family and no friends. That's all we know. A total dead end," she concluded and summarily closed the file.

Randall stared dumbly at her, allowing the information to sink in. "So what has all this got to do with me? Sounds like you've found the killer," Randall said, completely baffled as he perused the pamphlet.

"We found an empty liquor bottle in the suite. The autopsy revealed there was alcohol in his lungs, but not in his blood or urine."

Randall's eyes slowly looked up, full of suspicion. "Someone forced him to drink?"

"Good work, detective," she said and raised her water bottle to toast his assumption. "I think The Rabbit was there to do a job, but somebody got him first. A lot of questions though," she continued and counted on her fingers. "Who was the Rabbit's target? Who killed him? Why? And why was Vincenzo murdered?"

"Jesus Christ!" he whispered in disbelief. "How come you know all this?"

"I was invited to work for the DST, the Directorate of Territiorial Security. France's version of the FBI and CIA. Internal intelligence... including assassinations. Started last year to get away from the stress on the Paris force," she said and downed a few more pills. "The workload was too much, and I wanted more time with Jessica. Looks like I made a mistake," she said. "Whether I like it or not, I've been assigned to this case."

"What about me? What the hell am I doing here?"

"Unfortunately, you're my new partner... and we're going undercover."

"What?" he replied thoroughly dumbfounded. "Says who?"

"Me and Prince Rainier. He asked me as a favour. My father knew the family," she stated and tapped the file. "And this has to be kept quiet for obvious reasons. Very quiet. We've already enlisted the support of the British government."

The announcement overwhelmed him as he searched for something to say. "Then... then where are we going?"

"To a funeral."

Chapter Five

A handful of photographers waited patiently by a gate at the Linate Airport in Milan. One pointed to a private jet, suddenly appearing from the low cloud cover, the sound of whirring cameras filled the air.

The airplane's wheels screeched with a brief skid of smoke as it touched down and taxied towards a private terminal.

Inside the aircraft, Braedon eyed the throng of reporters. "Vultures," he said and noticed the flapping, Italian flag at half-mast. "Talk about an overreaction," he added with disdain.

The jet's engines screamed and kicked up dust as it rolled closer to the terminal. The pilot powered down and the plane came to a stop with a slight dip of its nose. The door opened and an airport worker quickly secured the stairs. Braedon stepped out to an immediate barrage of clicking cameras and questions regarding his personal feelings about Vincenzo's upcoming funeral, but he simply waved to the media and hopped into a waiting Rolls Royce limousine.

Braedon instantly poured a healthy drink from the Lead Crystal decanter and splashed in a couple of ice cubes. He cooled his forehead with the cold glass, took a long sip and picked up the newspaper on the small cabinet in the middle of the floor. The bold headlines described a nation's grief, accompanied by photographs of Vincenzo and his shattered racer, attributed to suspension failure. Another by-line reported there was no visitation, only a private service at the grave. "Two-bit dago had it coming," he huffed and spat on the paper before folding it and tossing it aside. The phone rang and he lifted it from the cradle. "The Grand Hotel Brun?" the chauffeur's voice said.

"No. Open up," Braedon replied. The tinted window between them lowered and Braedon handed him a piece of paper. "Take me there."

With one eye on the road, the driver examined the directions and frowned. "Are you sure, Mr. Stirling?"

"Just do it."

CHAPTER FIVE

Thirty minutes later, the limousine pulled over on the outskirts of a sleepy hamlet, the majestic, snow-capped, Italian Alps looming in the distance.

Braedon climbed out, retrieved his wallet and withdrew some bills. "You're certain this is where you want to be?" the chauffeur said bemused as Braedon pressed the money into his sweaty hand.

"I'm sure. And next time I want a car that wasn't made in England. Understood?" Braedon said. The driver nodded in confusion. Braedon watched the limousine turn around and disappear in a cloud of dust.

The world champion removed his jacket, slung it over his shoulder and stared in awe at the rolling, resplendent, green landscape. A smile broke across his perspiring face, gazing at the quaint villas and spires, but grimaced upon seeing the ancient cemetery, illegible headstones askew, a few affluent markers of gleaming marble and eclectic sculptures with weather worn inscriptions. "Forgive me," he whispered, eyeing the church and blessing himself before donning a pair of dark sunglasses.

He started walking and focused his attention on the minions going about their business; some farming tiny tracts of land, others congregating at a cafe, many on bicycles attending to their errands.

Inside the limousine, the driver picked up a pair of binoculars and watched as Braedon trudged up a long, winding road. The chauffeur dialled his cell phone and waited. After a few seconds, he said. "It's me. Yeah... I just dropped him off. What do you want me to do? You sure? Okay."

Braedon shielded his forehead from the scorching sun and admired the magnificent, Romanesque architecture of a Fifteenth century castle. His hands became moist and could see his shirt flutter with each beat of his heart as he pressed a button outside a huge, iron gate. After a few seconds, the barrier opened with an electric buzz and he followed the pathway, surrounded by an exotic garden emitting a heavy, sweet aroma.

Braedon slowed his pace; picked a red rose, but pierced his finger with a thorn. Sucking the blood away, he saw her; hair loose, half covering her face and breasts visible through an untied, white lace blouse. His eyes lowered to her bare legs and feet.

She waited with a seductive gaze and overturned her hand, wistfully inviting him inside. Braedon moved closer, kissed her and swept Teresa off her feet before carrying her into the mansion.

"I don't know why you just didn't let the fucking bellhop carry these for Christ's sake," Randall complained breathlessly, with a cigarette dangling from his mouth he bashed open the door with one of the suitcases in his hands. "I'd carry you across the threshold, split lips, but I'm a little busy," he added sarcastically and motioned for her to enter.

"I don't want the department to have to pay for more than is necessary. Besides, if you quit smoking, you might feel better," she replied as Randall followed her inside, using his foot to close the door behind him.

He instantly dropped the baggage and whistled his admiration at the luxurious suite: marble flooring, two bedrooms, a huge bathroom, dining room, kitchenette, spacious living room with a bar and a solarium with an adjoining balcony overlooking the city of Milan. "Jesus H. Christ! These fucking grease balls sure know how to live!" he said.

Gwen carried her suitcase into the larger of the two bedrooms as Randall gleefully rubbed his hands together. He danced to the well-stocked bar and fished out some ice cubes, but suddenly stopped. "How gauche," he said sarcastically, wiping imaginary dust off his jean jacket and dropping them back into the bucket. He retrieved the tongs, daintily picked four out and plopped them into a highball glass as his fingers twitched, trying to choose a liquor. Finally, he decided on Canadian Club and clicked his heels together, blithely exclaiming. "There's no place like home." He added a dash of water and stirred with a crystal stir stick, but the ash from his cigarette dropped into the drink. A shrug. "Adds flavour."

"Put that down," Gwen's voice bellowed.

"Do you have a problem with me having a cocktail?" he replied in a deliberate, haughty voice.

"I always have," she said, watching from her bedroom. "Don't you think you should unpack?" she added in a motherly tone and hung some garments in a huge closet.

Randall kept the drink and kicked his suitcase into his room. "Give me one good reason why I shouldn't imbibe as they say," he said, taking a long, loud sip so she could hear and smacking his lips.

"Because you're working for me now, and if you don't cooperate, I'll send you back to Wallace and he'll activate the charges in the Lunder case," she said happily.

"Look, you're used to living the high life. Let me enjoy it," he replied and noticed the standard bible on the night table. He picked it up and carelessly tossed it into the wastebasket.

"What is that supposed to mean?"

Randall opened his suitcase, turned it upside down, emptied it into the top drawer of the bureau and closed it with some clothing still hanging out. "You were rich when you were a kid," he said, enamoured by the eloquent room. "But my old man wasn't exactly a good earner and any money he did have, he pissed away at the track or on a bottle," he continued and used

CHAPTER FIVE

his heels to step out of his cowboy boots. "Never was enough food or clothing," he added nonchalantly and opened the mint on the pillow.

"You never did talk about your dad that much."

Randall peered around the corner into her room and saw her unpacking her panties. "What can you say about an asshole? It speaks for itself," he said, admiring her behind as she leaned over to open a drawer.

She sensed his presence and pivoted. "I expect you to respect my privacy," she said sternly with her hands on her hips.

"It's nothing I haven't seen before," he said gamesomely.

"And never will again," she replied and closed the drawer hard for effect. She brushed past him into the bathroom and snatched the drink out of his hand. "I mean it, Randall. I catch you with the sauce and you're out. Cool it on the cigarettes and no dope either," she added, plucking the tobacco from his mouth, slightly tearing his dry lips. "I'm taking a shower," she said and slammed the door in his face.

"Fuck," he said, checking his lip for blood. "Working with your ego is going to be a problem," he added and leaned against the frame.

"As long as you don't challenge me, we'll be fine," she replied as the sound of running water was heard.

"I thought we were supposed to be partners," he said and lit another smoke.

"We are. I'm the boss and you're the employee."

"Detectives on a case need to be equal and compatible and we ain't," he said matter-of-factly and quietly nudged the door open a crack. "Too much personal conflict here," he added and watched in the mirror as she undressed.

"I can separate my professional life from my personal. Sounds to me like you're the one with the problem," she replied, seeing the door was ajar but pretending not to notice. She deliberately felt her breasts and studied herself in the steaming mirror.

Randall's eyes widened and he licked his lips. "Hard to believe I was attracted to that kind of bitchiness way back when," he said and shook his head clear of impure thoughts.

"I wake up wanting to go to work. You never did. That's not being a bitch; it's being a professional. I always went that extra mile," she stated proudly and half turned to check her buttocks.

"Yeah, well not all of us were born with a silver spoon up our ass," he said and felt an erection growing.

"Money has nothing to do with it," she replied, opening the soap.

"How many cops do you know that went on an exchange program from France to Canada because they were bored with Paris for fuck sakes?" he asked and tried to push his erection down. "How many cops do you know that could afford it, never mind the connections to pull it off? I only know one, you."

"If I hadn't, we would have never met."

"My point exactly," he said sardonically.

"What do you want from me?" she asked as she suddenly opened the door, catching him by surprise, he quickly lifted his hands away from his crotch.

"To... to admit that you're privileged and not the talented, supercop you think you are," he said, slightly flushed as his nervous eyes couldn't help but scan her silky, nude body from head to toe. "That, and that you're a cockteaser."

"That only applies when you want the man to have a chance," she said with a wicked smile, noticing the obvious bulge in his trousers and stepping into the shower. "I think you're just jealous of my success."

"Only when any fucking door opens for you just because you got coin."

"God. I'll never marry another cop again," she said melodramatically and closed the shower door.

"That makes two of us. You must have sucked the right dick to get transferred to the DST," he said, inhaling the tobacco and making a sucking sound.

A few seconds of silence as he gladly waited for her volley. The water abruptly turned off. "There were five of them," she said quietly.

"Uh?" he said, watching her distorted figure behind the glazed glass.

"I was working homicide in Paris. I was the closest to the scene that night so I went. The kids stole a car and drove through an alcohol checkpoint," she said and sighed heavily. "They hit a streetlight. Killed five of them instantly. The other two get to spend the rest of their lives in a wheelchair," she continued as Randall saw her head lean against the tile. "So I volunteer to tell the parents. You know, the thing with Jessica, I figured I could handle it... I was wrong. I got a little teary and my superiors reprimanded me for it. That's the problem with being a cop, isn't it? There's no time to adjust. Be a good little robot and move on to the next thing, right?" she said with her hands as her voice broke. "I went to a coffee shop later and some American tourist saw my badge and asked if he put a donut on his dick, would I blow him?" she said with a slight laugh. "He didn't mean any harm I guess, but I snapped and hit him. You know as well as I do that when women cops screw up, they get treated harsher. After that, I decided to take the opening in the DST."

Randall swallowed hard, struggling to find the right words. "At least you just belted yours, I killed mine," he said with a warm smile, even though she couldn't see it.

"When I became an officer, the thing that scared me the most was having to kill somebody... but when that guy said that... it was the first time I could have taken a life and not cared."

"Don't be so hard on yourself. It just means your human, whether you like it or not. Listen, you're a good cop, split lips," he said, trying to lighten her emotion. "You're honest. A good listener. Great intuition skills and you have integrity. The only fault you have is your arrogance. Don't know if that's a French thing or just you."

"You sure know how to compliment a girl," she replied and turned the water on again. "Shall we list your faults?"

"We haven't got that long," he said and sat on the bathroom counter. "Which brings me to my next question. Why do you *really* need me? It's obvious you can handle this thing on your own."

"Don't you want to catch your friend's killer?" she asked, lathering.

"Of course," he said, tapping his cigarette ash into his hand and feeling a slight tingle from the heat, but his scarred, nerveless palm rejected the pain.

"I need all the help I can get, Randall. You might be a lousy husband and a terrible father, but unfortunately, you're still one of the best homicide detectives I know."

"Talk about compliments."

"Why did you and Vincenzo drift apart?"

A shrug. "He changed. Big city. Bright lights. All that success shit. Went to his head, I guess. Either didn't have or want the time with me. Maybe both. Not really his fault though. I might have done the same thing."

"Think he had a lot of enemies?"

"There are no friends in racing," he said condescendingly and lowered his gaze to between her legs.

"I thought that was something unique only to you."

"Why don't we just cut the crap here? What is it you want from me?" he said, forcing himself to look away.

"I'm just asking you a few questions. It's basic detective work."

"You could ask any one of the main players in this thing and get more information," he said and rubbed the mirror to see himself.

"Not without raising a lot of suspicions. Besides, nobody knows it was a homicide. If this got out, all hell would break loose. That's why we're going undercover. Needless to say, the reputation of racing in Europe is at stake."

"Who *does* know?" he said, studying his physique and spying hers as he sucked in his stomach.

"A few of the gendarmes in Monaco, the attending physician and," she said, trying to recall. "Julius Carmen and Friedrich Hesse."

"Those two fucking idiots," he said with a roll of his eyes. He released his stomach muscles with a wince. "The Laurel and Hardy of racing."

"Hesse seemed okay."

"He's Carmen's cabaña boy. Too stupid to know anything else. Tried to start a new racing series but couldn't get the coin. Even tried to lure Vince into jumping ship," he said and plucked a grey hair from his head.

"I know that. I did my homework in the short time that I had."

"You do realize that sooner or later somebody will leak the truth," he said and examined the hair with a frown.

"That's why we have to move quickly. I'm hoping we'll learn more at the funeral. In the meantime, I've got my subordinates doing some digging on the principals."

"Vincenzo's wife and Team Jenkins, right?"

"We have to start somewhere."

"Still can't figure out why anybody would cap Vincenzo," he said and tried to rub away the bags under his eyes.

"Anyone is capable of anything and people only kill for emotional reasons. Greed, love, revenge, jealousy. Find the motive and…"

"Find the killer. I know. Homicide 101. At least we know it was a professional hit," he said and pulled back his lips to check his teeth.

"But why was The Rabbit done? Was it political? And why would the killer leave a slug for evidence? If he can hit a moving target in the head, he sure as hell could pick off a fuel tank full of alcohol."

"Maybe they wanted to leave their calling card," he said and stuck his tongue out to examine it.

"Still need a motive," she replied and began to shampoo.

"Perhaps it was a sponsor," he said and felt the age lines upon his face.

"They would have the most to lose, wouldn't they?"

"Not if their investment isn't paying off. A billboard moving at two hundred miles per hour might get a lot more attention standing still. What about insurance?" he said, rubbing his stubble as he studied his profile.

"Hopefully, I'll have that information by tonight. We had to wait to get Interpol's help with the warrants."

"There's another possibility… maybe The Rabbit did kill him and the lab stuff is all wrong," he said and pulled down the skin beneath his eyes.

"Don't even say that. Besides, even if that were true, we still have to find out who paid for the contract. No matter what, this case isn't going to be easy to crack," she said and rinsed her hair.

"Fuck no. At this level of motor sport, it's damn tough to get inside the bubble. Lots of secrets and they ain't going to give them up," he agreed,

CHAPTER FIVE

making sure she wasn't looking and removed his penis. An unhappy look and he tried to stretch it.

"That's your job," she said and turned the water off.

"Doing?" he replied and hurried to tuck his manhood back in his trousers. The shower door opened and he casually threw her a towel.

She wrapped herself and said. "By being my husband again. In separate bedrooms of course."

His mouth dropped open in disbelief. "What? How the fuck is that going to help?"

"Do you still have your ring?"

"Ah... no. I... I pawned it," he said completely flustered.

She walked past him into her room. "Figures. We'll get you something," she said and put on her watch. "Hells bells," she added, checking the time. "I forgot to call my mother." Gwen popped a few pills and picked up the phone. "The woman always gives me a headache."

"You're not telling me everything. Why do we have to be husband and wife?" he asked again in a panic.

She held up a finger, indicating for him to be quiet and covered the phone. "I'll tell you at dinner," she whispered and closed the door.

Randall waited for a second, listened to Gwen greet her mother and hurried to the bar. He drank straight from the bottle of rye, collapsed into a plush leather couch, crushed out his smoke and stared into space. "Bitch is up to something," he said to himself and checked her door before reaching into his jacket pocket and withdrawing his wedding ring. He studied it until his eyes drifted off again

Samuel's cloudy eyes studied a spectacular, night photograph of Tokyo on the wall. The only sound was the hypnotic, steady click of a pendulum. He looked to the grandfather clock and checked it against his own timepiece, his eyes unwillingly moved back to the picture. "Quite a snapshot, isn't it?" the British, mouth-filled voice of Jerry Thomas cheerily asked. "I took it last month when I was there for a conference."

Samuel barely glanced at the dapper, suited, young man standing in the doorway of the opulent office, noisily eating a sandwich. "I was one hundred and seventy pounds when they captured me... I came out at sixty-eight. I looked like a skeleton with the skin pulled over it," Samuel lamented and gave him a steely look. "It's disgusting."

Jerry smiled confidently, straightened his silver nametag, closed the door and strode to the magnificent, oak desk in front of a bay window, displaying a vista of London. "I mean no disrespect, but the war *is* over Mr. Jenkins," he said and sat in his huge, leather chair.

"It never will be for me," Samuel replied as Jerry swivelled in his seat to close the blinds, but stopped when Samuel added. "It was visions of home that kept me alive in that sweltering hellhole."

Jerry tossed the sandwich into the wastebasket and rubbed the crumbs from his hands. "Sorry about that. I'm eating on the go today," he said and drank from a bottle of water.

Samuel stared at the wastebasket, and then his eyes were slowly drawn to the photograph again. "For two years I had to eat rice with worms and bread with bugs in it. Even cockroaches. Yours is a wasteful generation."

Jerry retrieved the sandwich and managed a stiff smile. "Anything for a customer. I apologize. I didn't mean to upset you," he said disingenuously.

"You didn't. It's just that you should know better. Your grandfather did."

Jerry decided not to counter and looked at an oil painting of the banking patriarch. "The two of you must have been quite a handful for the Japanese. He was the one that gave you your first loan to open the car dealership after the war, wasn't he?"

"You know he did."

Jerry consulted his computer screen as his fingers danced across the keys. "You've done quite well for yourself over the years, Mr. Jenkins. Not very many self-made millionaires by the age of thirty. Let's see... started your own business and began building racing cars," he continued, referring to the monitor. "Quite impressive. So," he added and leaned back in his seat. "Twelve million pounds is a lot of money."

"Are you going to give it to me or not?" Samuel said impatiently.

"May I ask what it is for?" Jerry inquired just as there was a light tapping at the door.

Jerry's secretary poked her head inside the room. "May I get you a cup of tea, Mr. Jenkins?" the elderly woman asked with a longing look.

"No, thank you," Samuel replied without looking, she closed the door again.

"She always liked you... and she's single," Jerry said with a grin and a wink.

"There's only one woman I'll ever love and she's dead. Now, what about the money?" Samuel said matter-of-factly and banged his cane against the floor. "I do have a plane to catch."

"Is the money for business reasons?" Jerry asked with a raised eyebrow.

"It doesn't matter what it's for!"

"And what about collateral?" Jerry said, checking the computer.

CHAPTER FIVE

"What about it?"

Jerry licked some mustard off his finger and held it to the screen. "You don't have any," he said bluntly. "There's nothing to borrow against. We practically own your house and the bank considers your racing team a bad investment, especially with the tragic death of Vincenzo. Our condolences by the way. I'm sorry, Mr. Jenkins, but for us, it's a matter of risk," he concluded and turned the monitor away.

Samuel felt a chill surge throughout his body and battled to his feet. "I need this! Can't you understand?" he said and slammed the desk with his fist, causing the various pens and pencils to jump.

"I am sorry," Jerry said coldly and stared at him without emotion. "We cannot extend further credit."

Samuel swiped his cane across the desk, knocking papers, the water bottle and several writing instruments to the floor. He grasped the frame for support and held the tip of his cane to Jerry's chin. "I practically kept this place afloat! You weren't too proud to take my money back then!"

Jerry slowly pushed the cane away while feeling for a button beneath the desk. "Perhaps you should not have made so many bad investments over the years. You cannot hold us responsible for any speculative trading you've done. Now, if you'll excuse me, I do have other clients waiting."

Outside the office, the secretary noticed the flashing light on her desk and pushed a button on her phone bank.

Jerry lifted the telephone receiver and pretended his secretary was on the line. "Tell him I'll be right with him," he said and hung up.

"Please... I'm begging you," Samuel whispered. "You're my last chance."

Jerry stood and extended his hand, but Samuel ignored it. "Good day, Mr. Jenkins."

"There was a time when people showed me respect... a time when I could buy and sell the likes of you," Samuel said through clenched teeth and limped to the door.

"Money isn't everything, Mr. Jenkins," Jerry said casually and dropped the sandwich back into the wastebasket.

Samuel half-turned to him. "It is when you have nothing else," he replied sadly and shuffled out.

The stereo thundered, playing a southern choir singing the praises of Jesus as Teresa giggled and dashed up the splendid, winding, marble staircase while Braedon waited at the bottom. He looked at the wall beside the steps and saw a flood of photographs of Teresa that didn't cover brighter paint where other pictures used to hang. "A little soon, don't you think?" he said.

"This is my house now," she replied curtly. "He owed me."

He glanced over his shoulder and noticed a full box of empty frames, hastily shoved into a half-open closet. Braedon's eyes shifted to the huge living room and spied a stack of charred photographs in the smouldering fireplace. Some were curled and blackened, but they were clearly pictures of Vincenzo. "I think it's the other way around. You were nothing but an American whore when he got you off the streets," Braedon said.

Teresa grinned. "No. I was already modelling when I met him at Homestead," she said, playing with her hair. "I think you're feeling guilty."

Braedon ignored the jab and glanced down the long hallway, revealing a kitchen with garbage on the floor and counters, amidst a sea of dirty dishes. "Why don't you get the maid to clean that up?" he asked with disgust.

"We never had one. The great Vincenzo felt I had to earn my keep," she said sarcastically, examining her nails as her face promptly darkened. "He made me do dishes and cleaning... I watched my mama do that until it killed her because some white preacher knocked her up and wouldn't support us," she said with swelling anger. "I might have half my mama's blood, but that don't mean I have to do what she did," she added while vehemently shaking her head.

Braedon chuckled. "You've done pretty good for a poor, little, nigger girl from South Carolina."

"Don't call me that!" she shouted, suddenly enraged and slumping down, beginning to weep.

Braedon smiled wide and removed his jacket. "You can't fool me. A little slut like you, pimping yourself out at the age of sixteen can take it," he said and slowly ascended the steps. "Little slut was a stripper and even slept with women to get an agent," he added and began unbuttoning his shirt.

Teresa peered between the banister posts as her black mane covered her face. "Why do say those horrible things to me?" she said quietly.

"Because the little slut likes it," he answered and unbuckled his belt.

Teresa stood and couldn't help a bashful smile as she lifted her floppy blouse to tease him, her body basked in the wash of sunlight streaming through the massive window behind her. "Heaven awaits y'all," she said with a deliberate, southern drawl and invited him with her finger.

Braedon's legs weakened and his heart raced as his sweaty palms grasped the refreshing, brass railing. "I'm going to fuck your baby black ass, you dirty little slut," he said.

Teresa removed her blouse with one, expert motion, displaying hardened nipples. She balled the piece of clothing and playfully threw it at him and she ran her fingers over her breasts and touched the downy hair between her legs. She swivelled and disappeared around the corner.

Braedon reached the top step and glanced into a room on his left. Inside, dozens of trophies and ribbons were strewn about the floor with a wall-sized poster of Vincenzo torn in half. He entered her massive bedroom as Teresa sat on the edge of the bed with a seductive gaze. His eyes caught a bevy of sexual toys and exotic oils on the night table beside a small mirror of cocaine. He glanced at Vincenzo and Teresa's wedding picture on the other table. "I want you to fuck me in front of him," she whispered. Suddenly timid, Braedon went to her as her hungry fingers unsnapped his trousers and yanked them off. Teresa slid off his briefs and gently stroked him. "I missed you," she said and tried to pull him downward, but he resisted. "I want you inside me," she sighed and spread her legs.

Braedon quickly rolled off the bed and began to pace, spying the wedding picture. "I'm sorry... I don't think we should... I can't... I thought I could, but I can't," he said nervously.

Teresa slammed the photograph face down and playfully tried to grab him. "It's okay, baby. It's just you and me now. We can finally be together. We don't have to worry," she said.

"It's not appropriate," he replied, anxiously running his fingers through his hair. "I... I think we have to show some respect for him," he said and quickly pulled on his trousers.

"Fine," she said, rolling her eyes and fingering herself. "Don't fuck me. Lick me," she added with a pleading smile.

Braedon threw on his shirt. "It's wrong," he said and started to button up.

She sat up and pouted. "Why can't you pleasure me?"

"He was your husband... I just can't... he's dead," Braedon said and buckled his trousers.

"I didn't love him. He was a cruel, selfish, arrogant bastard!" she said as she embraced Braedon and covered his chest with kisses.

"You must have loved him at one time," he said and pushed her away.

"Never!" she whispered angrily.

"Then why *did* you marry him?"

"To make you jealous. Because I couldn't have you," she replied with childlike eyes.

"It was money and fame," he stated.

"I did it to stay close to you!"

"Did *what*?" he asked, full of suspicion.

Teresa avoided his inquiring eyes. "There's been nobody else! Ever! I love you Braedon. I want us to be together, always. I want us to get married," she said with soaked eyes.

"Are those real tears? It's so hard to tell anymore," he said and started to walk away. "I don't think we should see each other for a while."

"If you leave, we're finished!" she yelled.

"We never got started," he said and stepped into his shoes.

"Braedon! Please! Stay with me!" she screamed, curling into the foetal position, but he kept going. "Go on then! Leave you filthy mick! Vincenzo was a better fuck anyway!"

Braedon suddenly wheeled to confront her and pointed a threatening finger. "Don't ever call me that!"

"Irish fuck! Did you take it up the ass when they sent you to the Borstal? Did they make your sweet, little, eighteen-year-old ass bleed? I bet you liked it!" she shouted.

Braedon bolted back into the room and slammed her into the bed. "Nigger bitch!" he yelled and slapped her hard, but she only laughed.

"Big man! Big fucking mick lover!" she replied.

Braedon's eyes widened as he grabbed one of the vibrators off of the table and rammed into her mouth. Her head thrashed about, but he forced it deeper as she started to gag. "It's what you wanted, wasn't it?" he shouted as she struggled to break free. "Suck it! Suck it!" he shouted and ejaculated in his trousers. After a few moments to gain his strength, he withdrew the vibrator and lifted himself off the bed. "Stay away from me. It's over," he said calmly, tossing the sexual aid at her and strolling out.

Teresa coughed several times and suppressed the urge to vomit. "I decide when it's over! It's not up to you!" she tried to shout in between breaths as she heard his footsteps hasten down the stairs and out the door. Teresa regained her composure and wiped away the tears. She picked up the phone and dialled. "Yes, The London Times, please," she said breathlessly.

A candle flickered, the oozing, pinkish wax the same colour as the streaked horizon. Randall sat alone on the deck of the nearly deserted, hotel restaurant and gazed upon the fiery red, half-moon hanging low over Milan. The city lights glistened in the cool, dusk air, the sound of traffic distant, yet somehow comforting.

A giggle was heard and he shifted his attention to a dimpled, dark haired, six-year-old girl in a flowery dress sitting by herself at another table. Eating a plate of spaghetti, she roared with laughter every time she sucked the noodles into her mouth with a loud smack as the sauce sprayed her chubby cheeks.

CHAPTER FIVE

A smile broke across Randall's face as he watched her antics and he stood. Tentative, he slowly approached her and pulled out a chair. "Hi there," he said with another smile.

"Hi," she replied, quietly cautious.

"Can I sit down?" he asked.

Her eyes fluttered and she looked around. "I'm not supposed to talk to strangers," she said with her head down.

Randall slid into the seat. "If I tell you my name, then we're not strangers," he said and extended his hand. "My name is Randall."

She pondered his offer and carefully shook his hand without looking, leaving a trace of tomato sauce on his skin. "I'm Michele," she said shyly and bit her lip.

"Where are your parents?"

"They had to do some shopping and stuff," she said, averting her eyes and sitting on her hands.

"Who is looking after you?"

"I am," a woman's concerned, Italian voice said. Startled, Randall spun in his seat to find a middle-aged lady dressed in a hotel uniform with a tag on her blouse that read *Nanny*. "Who are you?" she asked in halting English.

"Randall Grange. I'm a guest here at the hotel," he said anxiously, surrendering with his hands. "It's okay. I have a daughter about her age."

"Yeah?" the woman said, not believing him and wiping the child's face with a napkin.

"I'm not some weirdo or anything. I'm a police officer," he said, mildly offended.

"Then you should know better," the woman said curtly and took the girl by the hand. "Come on, sweets. It's getting chilly out here."

"Can I have some chocolate ice cream?" the toddler asked as she was led away.

"I'll buy," Randall said hopefully.

"It's already paid for," the woman said and hurried the girl into the hotel. As they were about to round the corner, the toddler turned and waved to him. Randall gladly returned the gesture and watched them disappear with a saddened face.

"It seems you have that effect on a lot of women," Gwen said jokingly, standing behind him with a briefcase in her hand. He went back to his table; his jittery fingers opened a can of cola and emptied it into a glass. "Nice to see you're listening to me about the booze... for once," she said, taking her seat and putting the case down beside her, revealing a quick view of her breasts with no bra, beneath a low cut sweater. "Cute kid. Sorry I'm late. The information took longer than I thought."

"I want to see her," he said softly, gazing at the table where the girl had been.

"Uh?" Gwen replied, getting comfortable.

"Jessica... I want to see her when this is all over."

The request temporarily flummoxed Gwen as she struggled to respond. "Well, it had to come up sooner or later. Listen Randall, I don't know if that's such a good idea."

"Why not?"

"It might be too hard on you... and her," she said.

"She was only three when it happened. She probably doesn't even remember me."

"She does... and she asks about you sometimes," Gwen said awkwardly.

"What do you tell her?"

"I don't want to talk about this," she said and opened the briefcase.

"What do you tell her?" he demanded.

"What am I supposed to say to her? What reasonable explanation do I give a five-year-old child so that she understands? That her father never calls because of what? That he doesn't care? That he's an alcoholic? That he's too racked with guilt?" she whispered angrily.

"You told her I was dead... didn't you?" he asked incredulously.

"I had no choice!" she replied shamefully.

"You had no right!" he shouted, causing some of the few patrons inside the restaurant to glance over.

"You have no rights! You gave them up when you almost killed her, not to mention me!" she countered.

The comment deflated him and he shrugged. "When you're right you're right. I have no defence... but I still want to see her."

"Look, I don't want to fight about this right now. You help me with the case and do as I say and I'll think about it. God knows how I tell her you rose from the dead, but I'll come up with something. Deal?" she said and massaged her aching forehead.

Randall contemplated for a few moments and figured an escalating argument was not in his best interest. He raised his glass to accept, took a sip of the soda and his face contorted. He wiped his chin with the sleeve of his denim jacket. "I don't know how people can drink this shit. Haven't had so many of these goddamned things since I was a kid. Old man would always give me one after... swore I'd never drink it again," he said as his voice faded.

Gwen gave him an odd glance and studied the metropolis. "Beautiful isn't it?" she said with a heavy sigh; relieved they were on to another subject.

CHAPTER FIVE

"Looks like any other city to me," he said and lit a cigarette.

"I thought you were going to take it easy on those?"

"Hey, one fucking disaster at a time, okay?" he replied and drew heavily on the tobacco.

"Reminds me of when I was a little girl," she said, enthralled with the beautiful view, she turned in her seat to get a better look. "We'd always have these huge Sunday dinners and then sit on the veranda. If it was clear enough, we could see all the way to Paris," she said with melancholy eyes. "I can still smell the garden."

"How's your mom?"

"Uh?" she replied, coming back to reality and slightly embarrassed. "Oh, fine. I guess I get a little sentimental after I talk to her. It gets me to thinking about my dad. I really do miss him."

"I wouldn't know the feeling."

"I'd be so full after supper, he'd rub my stomach until I fell asleep," she said smiling, remembering happier times and watching as a waitress removed the plate from the girl's table.

"My old man used to make me rub the back of his neck after eating and if I stopped, he'd kick my fucking ass," Randall said matter-of-factly and carelessly flicked the ash from his smoke.

Gwen frowned, his harsh statement ruining her stroll down memory lane. "Why do you have to swear so much?"

"Police work will do that to you," he replied unconcerned.

"I don't talk like that."

"Ease up, split lips," he said with warning eyes.

"I know you're uptight about tomorrow," she said softly.

"A funeral's a funeral," he replied with a shrug.

"You don't have to go."

"The man saved my life. I owe him that much."

A waiter appeared. "A glass of white wine please. Wait, on second thought, I'll have what he's having," she said and reached into her pocket for some pills. "Must be the humidity."

Randall drained the cola and held up two fingers to the waiter. "Make it two," he said, crunching on the ice cubes and turning to Gwen again. "You don't have to do that."

"What?"

"I'm a big boy now. If you want a drink, have it."

"No. It would keep me up."

"Does the opposite for me," he said as a gust of wind made her shiver. Randall removed his jean jacket and gave it to her.

"Thanks. Aren't you cold?" she said, wrapping herself in the coat.

"Nope. Got enough goddamned antifreeze in these veins to keep me warm forever."

"Did you ever... you know, get help?" she asked uneasily.

"Tried AA. Didn't last long. Earned my first chip and got so fucking hammered I bet it in a poker game."

Gwen laughed, but soon became serious. "How are you Randall? Really," she said with genuine interest and covered his hand with hers.

He was taken aback by her gesture and smiled at the velvet touch of her skin. "Tired of trying to drink your memory away," he said unabashed and pinged the glass with his nail.

Gwen's hand quickly retreated and she looked off, uncomfortable with his statement. "I did what I had to," she whispered.

"I know, I know. Always kind of held out hope though... like some stupid ass schoolboy," he said with a forced chuckle. "But sometimes that's what kept me going at night. You gave me more than enough chances and I fucked it up anyway. I don't blame you," he said sheepishly just as the waiter entered with their drinks. "Phew. Saved by the bell, uh?" he added sarcastically as he withdrew a couple of bills and gave them to him.

"I think the DST can handle a couple of pops," she said, still reeling from the exchange and swallowing her medication.

Randall took a drink, crossed his legs and leaned back in the chair on two legs. "So, what about it?"

"I... I think it's better that we don't discuss our past. At least not while we're working together," she said nervously.

"That's great but I'm talking about the case. What did you find out?" he said, lifting his backside to return his wallet.

"Oh," she replied, staring dumbly at him and fumbling through her briefcase. "A few things. We haven't had that much time to work on it. To start, my people looked into the standards. You know, finances, work history, medical, all that sort of thing. We looked at the people closest to Vincenzo. Jenkins, Stirling, Teresa and Ichiro," she added, consulting her notes.

"Ichiro?"

"He was Vincenzo's race engineer. Nothing out of the ordinary with him," she said and handed him the sheet. "Same goes for Braedon."

"This is going to be like finding a needle in a fucking haystack," he said and sighed heavily.

"Maybe not," she answered with a grin and looked over her shoulder to ensure privacy. "Samuel Jenkins paid Vincenzo five million this year to drive and also had a policy on Vincenzo worth eight million. Teresa stands to gain four million in insurance benefits but get this; Vincenzo didn't leave her his family fortune. His will stated the Catholic Church gets it and she knew it."

Randall whistled his awe. "Sounds like two, very good suspects," he said, but the optimism abruptly vanished from his face. "Thing is though, if Vincenzo kept winning, he would have been worth more to everybody."

"I know. I thought of that. Money may not be the motive here, but I think it's a safe bet to say that it was for The Rabbit. By the way, his bank records show no substantial deposit so maybe he was supposed to be paid later, but it's more than likely he would have an offshore account anyway," she said and gave him some more papers to examine.

"Needle in a fucking haystack," he reiterated and extinguished his cigarette. "What else have you got?"

"That's it. As usual, we only have thirty days before we have to disclose to Jenkins and the others that we did a search. If we want more, we're going to have to get closer and we haven't got a lot of time," she said and sipped her drink.

"And we're supposed to do this posing as husband and wife?" he said dubiously and lit another smoke.

"Well, the only way to get close enough to find out what happened to Vincenzo is to infiltrate Team Jenkins and the sport itself," she said, squirming in her chair and shunning eye contact.

"That's assuming that whoever killed him is connected to the team or within the racing world itself."

"Chances are, it was an inside job. I think we have to go on that assumption," she said, busying herself with the briefcase.

"You're probably right, but if it was someone on the inside, it would have made a lot more sense if the killer had sabotaged the car," he explained with a puzzled look as he watched her rummage through some papers.

"Maybe, but the person could easily get caught, before or even after the crash. There's always a forensic examination of the car after a fatal racing accident. Maybe they couldn't take that chance?" she said and hid her face behind the case.

"What are you trying to say?" he asked, full of suspicion.

"That... that you don't have to be there to help pull the trigger," she replied, stealing a glance at him over the top of the briefcase.

He frowned at her strange behaviour and said. "It's obviously a conspiracy, but I still don't see how having us pretend we're the happy couple will catch a killer. It's hardly an all access pass."

"That's why I want you sober, healthy... and stable," she said uncomfortably.

"Whatever the hell you're trying not to say, just say it."

Gwen clasped her hands together and nervously licked her lips. "I want you to take over Vincenzo's ride," she said quietly and leaned back, expecting a heavy rebuttal.

He studied her for a few seconds with a stone face until he burst out laughing. "Fuck! You almost had me going there. Holy shit you're good! Whatever's in that cola, throw it out for Christ's sake!" he said, continuing to laugh hysterically and banging the table, but Gwen kept staring at him until his jocularity slowly diminished. "You... you can't be serious," he finally managed to say as he tried to catch his breath.

"Evidence leads to solving and we don't have any so we have to get some. It's not like we can post a reward," she said, gathering the papers and stuffing them into the case.

"Have you lost your fucking mind?" he said too loudly. Another round of odd stares from the customers.

"Keep your voice down! Look, you said I was good cop. I'm motivated to find the truth and I have good communication skills. Well, I'm communicating to you right now, you're going to drive that car," she said and snapped the briefcase shut.

"It's impossible!" he whispered, completely aghast, he leaned closer to plead his case. "I haven't driven one of those things in years!"

"Scared?" she asked, trying to bait him.

"Fucking shitless! It can't be done!" he said and held the cold glass to his suddenly perspiring face.

"It's the only way," she said, casually leafing through the menu. "The pizza looks good."

"Look, I thought I was here to help with this case. That's all!" he replied and ripped the menu out of her hands.

"Do you really believe I brought you all this way just to play cops and robbers? I don't need another gumshoe. You said so yourself," she stated and took back the menu.

"Then let somebody else do it!" he barked and snatched it away again.

"You're the only one I know that is used to driving at over two hundred miles per hour. What should I do, hire a beat cop?" she replied and went to take it back again, but he held it out of her reach.

"There has to be another way!" he said, completely flustered and going to light the cigarette in his mouth that was already burning.

"You're also the one who said racing is a closed society. I just can't walk in and start asking a lot of questions," she said and warmed her hands over the candle.

"The press will have a fucking field day with this! They'll see right through it! Everybody will! I don't even have a racing licence!" he said and realized he was charring the tobacco.

CHAPTER FIVE

"I'll worry about that. You just drive the car."

"It's not that easy, Gwen! We're talking about professional racing for fuck sakes! You can't just hop in and drive away like it's some kind of domestic appliance! I don't know any of the circuits! I've never driven one of those machines! It's way out of my fucking league!" he said and lit a new smoke.

"The next race is in Montreal. You've raced there. Besides, we should have a pretty good idea who did it by then. It's not like you have to compete for the entire season," she said and stood.

"This thing won't be solved that fast and you know it!" he answered, standing to confront her.

"I'm not asking you, Randall, I'm telling you," she indicated with her finger.

"Well, I won't do it!" he said immaturely and crossed his arms.

"I'll call Wallace," she stated bluntly.

"Gwen, listen to me, please! I can't do it! The last time I was in a car, it damn near killed me!"

"I know, you had the accident," she said, waving off his concern.

"So you should realize how dangerous it is! I lost my edge! Once it's gone, you can't ever get it back! I'm not in shape! Physically or mentally!" he said, gesturing to his body and mind.

"That's a chance we'll have to take."

Randall kicked back the chair with the heel of his boot, knocking it over. *"We?* I'd be the only one taking a goddamned chance! I'm not going to be some guinea pig so you can look good and get another fucking promotion!"

"Is that what you think this is all about?"

"This is insane! I can't do it! Jenkins will never agree!" he said and began to pace.

"I'll handle him," she replied and picked up the briefcase. "We'll talk about it again tomorrow."

Gwen turned to leave, but he clenched her arm and spun her around. "I haven't got the balls anymore! It'll never work! Think about what you're asking me to do! It's not a fucking video game! I'll probably end up killing the other drivers as well as myself! Is that what you want?"

She freed herself from his grip. "You used to tell me the European guys were overrated, remember? You said they weren't aggressive enough. Here's your chance to prove it."

"Holy shit! I wouldn't being trying to win, just survive!"

"Does that mean you'll do it?" she said with a sparkle in her eye.

"Fuck no!"

"Vincenzo was your friend. At least he used to be. You said you owed him. I would think that you would want to help find his killer. Try thinking about someone else for a change. Now if you don't mind, I have to call home and check on Jessica. Get some sleep, Randall. We have a funeral to go to tomorrow and it's time to get to work."

Randall watched her stroll away. "I'll go to the service but after that I'm fucking gone! I'll take my chances with Wallace! And I'll get the courts to allow me access to my daughter! I mean it! Find yourself another coffin pilot because I'm not doing it!" he shouted after her as the waiter appeared again. "Give me a triple Jack Daniel's and keep them coming!" Randall said to him and withdrew yet another cigarette with trembling hands. He lit it and discovered he was already smoking one. "Fuck!" he whispered, putting one out and slumping into the chair. "Absolutely no fucking way!" he added and began to hyperventilate.

Chapter Six

Samuel sat in his pine study listening to Mozart playing softly on an old fashioned phonograph. A bundled baby in his arms, he gently rocked the child as he stared longingly at an ornate trophy cabinet displaying awards for racing. "Who knew it would end like this?" he said quietly. "I had to fight to stay alive as a prisoner... and now I have no reason to live as a free man... except for you," he added and kissed the infant's forehead.

His tired eyes focused on another wall with yellowed, faded photographs of himself in the British Army Special Forces, posing happily with his former comrades. "Most of them are dead now," he whispered to the baby. "Some just couldn't take it," he said and studied some pale snapshots showing him alone, staid and aiming a rifle. "I was a pretty good shot. Won plenty of cigarettes," he added with a smile and lightly poked the child's chest. "But don't you ever smoke. Right?"

Samuel suddenly shuddered at the sound of the howling wind and glanced at the tree branches scratching against the pane. He carefully carried the child to the window and admired the breathtaking view illuminated by the moon, vibrant, green grass sloping downward to a cliff, overlooking misty whitecaps on the English Channel. "Did I ever tell you about that trip?" he whispered. "They shipped us in a twenty by twenty hold with a hundred and fifty prisoners. The Yanks fired a torpedo and split the boat in two. Sank right in the harbour, but I managed to swim ashore," he said as his eyes drifted back in time. "I remember seeing all those bows and sterns and masts in the water... like a giant graveyard. After that it took twenty-three days to get to the camp. There were two thousand POWs there. That's where I met your mother. She was a nurse for the Japanese army," he said and smiled. "She took good care of me and I fell in love. It caused quite a stir back home when we married. She taught me to forgive... but I'll never forget," he said as his face hardened. "The Japs made us move one pile of rocks to another, day after day. Nothing to read. Not much to eat. Some soup. We had to boil the water," he said and adjusted his glasses. "The lack of vitamins ruined my vision," he added and tickled the baby's stomach. "But I can still see you."

Samuel placed the toddler in its wicker bassinet and hobbled to the fireplace. He grimaced as he bent over to retrieve a fire iron to separate the burning embers. He returned the utensil to its stand just as an antique, grandfather clock chimed once. He checked his timepiece. "I guess the driver will be here soon," he said with a tired sigh and limped into the hallway.

He opened a sliding paper door and stepped into an alcove, the tatami floor crackling beneath his feet as he stared at a large Buddha sitting on a throne with lions at the base. Samuel's gaze moved to a hanging scroll and an array of fine pottery. Finally, his eyes rested upon an oil painting of a beautiful young Japanese woman. "I gave Scott a few days off, Aki. I have to go away for a while," he said and gently touched her cheek, the canvass dark and smooth where his fingers had touched a thousand times before. "I love you," he whispered and closed the door.

Samuel continued down the eloquent corridor, he unwillingly eyed a dust covered, handicap scooter parked near the front door before painfully beginning to ascend the twisting staircase, despite an electric lift. "Sorry, Aki. I know you want me to use them, but it means giving up," he said and continued upward.

Outside the wrought-iron gate surrounding the massive property, black gloves withdrew wire cutters from inside a long black trench coat. The pliers opened and quickly snipped the power conduit dangling from a small, metal box. Hands easily slid the gate aside and a shadowy figure scurried inside.

Upstairs, Samuel gripped the towel rack for support and carefully leaned into the shower. He turned the gold-plated faucet, felt for the right temperature and disrobed. His withered, frail body stepped into the streaming cubicle.

Outside the front door, the gloved hands tried the knob, but it was locked. A silencer appeared, fired quietly and blew the mechanism apart. The door was noiselessly pushed open and the intruder stepped inside. The silhouette stood silently, listening to the sound of spraying water from above and the familiar sound of Mozart's *Eine kleine Nachtmusik*. The person glided across the foyer into the study and casually lifted the needle off the record. The ghostly outline of the individual sat in Samuel's leather chair and polished the silencer with a Kleenex, taken from a gold box on a nearby table.

Samuel was about to lather his thinning hair but stopped and turned the water off. He waited, thinking he heard something and was promptly annoyed at the amplified drips from the shower nozzle. He gently opened

Chapter Six

the door and listened. He heard it. The sound of Tchaikovsky, echoing from below. Samuel frowned, stepped out and quickly dried himself.

In the study, the music pounded, causing the windows to vibrate and the pictures to lightly dance, knocking them askew. The intruder's hand poured a generous glass of Napoleon brandy and swilled it. A dainty sampling and a sigh of satisfaction. The drink was set down on the small table and the person edged towards the baby.

Samuel wrapped himself in his robe and carefully surveyed the hallway. He looked to an alarm sensor in one corner of the ceiling to find it wasn't breached, and limped expeditiously into the enormous, master bedroom where he opened the drawer of the nightstand. Samuel withdrew a pistol and checked the chamber. Full. He moved cautiously into the long corridor again, his hand steadying his body against the oak railing. Samuel stopped at the edge of the stairs and listened. Suddenly, he noticed the magnificent chandelier above the foyer, its crystals jingling and the front door ajar, the sound of air sweeping inside. His face turned to horror as he spied the baby on the floor below, its head decapitated. "Sweet Jesus," he cried softly as he went to take a fearful step, but a hand grabbed him by the back of the neck, causing him to drop the gun. The assailant pushed him to the rail as Samuel tried to break free. "What do you want?" Samuel managed to yelp, thoroughly terrified as his body was easily lifted over the banister.

"Only a senile old man plays with a baby doll," Karl's Russian voice said. Samuel remained silent, too petrified to respond. "You probably have sex with your little doll," Karl added mockingly.

The Russian spun him around and clenched Samuel's throat with one hand as the old man's feet dangled. "I... I couldn't have children of my own," Samuel said with a choking voice.

"Perhaps you're too senile to pay off your debts too."

"I swear I have it... it's just going to take a few days... it's the insurance money," Samuel replied, fighting to breathe.

"Mr. Vladin has been very patient," Karl said. The burly Russian's arm began to quiver as the weight of Samuel's body strained his muscles. "I can't hold you forever."

Samuel's horrified eyes glanced downward as his slippers fell off and slapped hard against the marble floor. "Please... don't," he said as his face bloated and reddened.

"We said something bad would happen. We didn't want to hurt you," Karl said, his glove beginning to slip as Samuel's eyes started to roll back and his body relaxed. "You don't have it, do you? We warned you Mr. Jenkins! We warned you!"

Samuel felt a tingling throughout his being and a rush of heat. Dizziness. His bowels and bladder emptied. Urine gushed down his legs and dripped to the floor. He struggled to remain conscious, but his brain finally yielded. Blackness.

"No fucking way," Randall mumbled as he staggered down the poorly lit steps of the restaurant patio, which led to a gardened pathway. He tripped but managed to awkwardly sit on a step. He titled back his glass of bourbon with his teeth, sucked the last few drops and brought it down, noticing the distorted outline of a caterpillar inching along. "Can you believe, split lips?" he said drunkenly into the empty glass as his voice echoed. "I'm waking up just to survive and she wants me to go kill myself in a racecar. No fucking way."

Randall set the glass down and picked up the caterpillar as his eyes crossed, staring closely. "You got the life, eh? You can change into something else. Not me though. I'm stuck being a loser," he said and eyed a marble statue of Mary holding Jesus overlooking a fountain further down the lane. "Know I wanted to be a priest? Is true. But God and I have a love-hate relationship," he said, slurring his words and explaining with his clumsy hands "He don't love me and I really fucking hate Him... because He never even tried to stop it... seems He only helps when things are good." A long, loud burp. "I used to have ethics. Don't know where the hell they went. Weight of the world crushed them, I guess," Randall said and delicately petted the insect. "You though, you're totally without sin, aren't you? Maybe I should have been a bug. You ain't got no worries. No pressures. Don't ever be a cop, though," he slurred and waved a warning finger at it. "I wanted to save the world once, but it didn't want to be saved. Got to be nice to be a pig, but the public tells you to fuck off anyway. I got to see the dark side. Kind of fascinated me there for a while and then it turned into disgust," he said and saw a young couple holding hands, strolling along. "I used to be like them once. In love... probably still am, but she don't feel the same way. How could she?" he grinned, watching the man and woman kissing. "Gwen was a whore in bed, though. All prim and proper in public, but fucked like a tiger! Good cop, too. Better than me... and that sure as fuck didn't help," he said and stretched out on the grass, putting the caterpillar on his chest as it tried to escape. "I don't blame you for not liking me. Lot of people don't like me... fuck, I don't even like me," he added and fumbled through his denim jacket for a cigarette. Randall fished out the empty packet, crumpled it and tossed it away. "Shit. Got to go and get smokes," he said to the caterpillar and hiccupped. "Been nice talking to you, fuzzy."

Chapter Six

Randall carefully set the insect on the grass and heaved himself up. He lurched up the stairs, meandered into the dimly lit lounge and bashed the bar with his fist. "Bartender! Get me a bottle of Jack Daniel's and a pack of Marlboros!" he bellowed and squinted, noticing a slightly overweight but pretty, shorthaired brunette sitting alone at a table in the corner, writing. The unimpressed barkeep gave him the bottle and smokes; Randall carelessly dropped a few bills on the counter and lugged the liquor towards her. "Mind if I sit with you?" he said winking and spying her large breasts beneath a top with no bra. "What's your name?" he asked as he unwrapped the packet of cigarettes and pulled one out with his teeth before lighting the wrong end. The bitter taste of tobacco caused him to spit and he righted the smoke.

The twenty-four-year-old looked him up and down with disgust. "Candice Goldenstein and yes, I do mind," she replied, noisily moving her chair so her back was to him and continuing to write.

He extended a leathery hand. "Randall Grange. Nice to meet you," he said, lighting the cigarette properly this time.

"Excuse you," she said without looking, neglecting his handshake and dramatically waving away the smoke. "I value my health." Randall rocked on his feet, shuffled around her and helped himself to a chair much to her chagrin. "I'm not one of those woman that likes aggressive drunks," she said.

He noticed her glass was almost empty and leaned across the table, knocking the decorative vase with flowers aside. Randall turned her glass upside down, spilled the contents onto the table, righted it and filled it with bourbon. He topped up his glass and raised it to toast.

"To new friends," he said happily.

Candice smiled sensuously and poured her glass over his head; the liquor burned his eyes and doused his cigarette. "I don't drink, and let's stay strangers," she replied, shoving her chair back and hurrying to the bar.

"Tough ones are always worth it," he said to himself with a grin, blinking wildly and chasing after her. Candice took a seat on one of the stools; Randall sat beside her and snapped his fingers at the bartender. "Garcon, I'll have whatever she's having," he said. The barkeep nodded and looked to Candice.

"Hemlock, please," she said.

Randall laughed as he hooked the rung of her stool with his cowboy boot and pulled it closer. "We'll die together, just like Romeo and Juliet," he said as she hopped onto another chair, further away. Randall leaned on the bar with his elbow and held his heavy chin in his palm. "You're Jewish, right?"

"Nothing gets by you," she said and motioned to the barkeep. "Ginger ale, please."

"I could tell by the attitude," he said and dug his hand into a bowl of peanuts, spilling most of them.

"And what is that supposed to mean?"

"What are you doing in Milan? Vacation?" he asked and tossed some nuts into his mouth, but a few missed.

"Not that it's any of your business, but I'm on assignment," she replied and accepted the soda from the bartender.

"Let me guess, international spy, right?" he said and grasped her hand, forcing her to wait for a toast. "I'm Canadian and you're Jewish, so let's drink to hockey and... and... what are you guys famous for?"

"Saying goodbye. Shalom," she said impatiently as she tucked her things into her purse and started to walk away.

Randall nearly fell off the stool and followed her with the bottle dangling from his hand. "So you're a writer, eh?"

"I'm a journalist," she said, mildly offended as she quickened her pace to the lobby. "I'm here to cover a funeral. Unfortunately, it's not yours," she added and pushed the elevator button to open the doors.

"That's why I'm here too... an old friend of mine died in an accident," he said, abruptly downcast.

"Sorry to hear that," she said disingenuously, quickly entering the lift, the doors closing as Randall leaned against the wall for support. After a few moments, the doors pinged open and she poked her head out. "Just a hunch... but who was your friend?"

"Uh? Oh, you probably never heard of him. He was a bug eater. I mean, a racing driver," Randall replied and wandered back towards the bar.

Candice exited the elevator and chased after him. "You're talking about Vincenzo Azzopardi, aren't you?" she said excitedly, withdrawing the pen and pad from her purse. "What's your name again?"

"Why?"

"I'm with *Open Wheel Magazine*, I'm here to do a piece on Azzopardi. Wait a second! Now I remember you! You used to run in the Formula Atlantic series, right?" she said, pleased with her memory.

Randall turned back for the elevator and nearly bumped into her. "I have to go," he remarked, desperately trying to end the conversation.

Candice pursued him as she jabbed her pen into her cheek, recollecting. "You were supposed to be pretty good. 'King of the wet', that's what they used to call you. A bitch to pass. Aggressive. Maybe too much. They had you pegged for stardom but... but... I can't remember what happened to you."

Chapter Six

"I ran out of gas," he said and pushed the elevator button several times.

"I know! You had that big accident in Toronto. Azzopardi gave up the win, right?"

"I really don't want to talk about this," he said as he impatiently continued pushing the button and trying another.

"Are you still racing?" she inquired, poised with her pen, ready for his answer.

"I have to get some sleep," he said as the doors opened and he stumbled inside.

"If you're not racing, what are you doing now?" she asked and followed him as the doors quickly closed and banged hard into her shoulder.

"I'm unemployed," he replied and backed into the corner, avoiding her stare.

"That explains the clothes," she said, rubbing her sore arm. "Married?" she added with a tinge of sexuality.

"Is that a proposition or a question?" he said, eyeing the elevator light flashing through the floors.

"Whatever you want it to be," she said and blushed, obviously uncomfortable with her own display of flirtation.

"You're new at this, aren't you?" he said knowingly.

"What do you mean?" she replied nervously.

"I remember your type in the pit lane. Green writers looking for a story, any story that would launch a career," he remarked and took a drink from the bottle.

"I *am* qualified," she said, straightening herself up to enhance her claim.

Randall scanned her from head to toe. "I bet you are. There's no story. Vince is dead and that's it," he said. Candice pushed the emergency button and the lift suddenly stopped as warning bells started ringing. "That's just fucking great! What the hell did you do that for?" he barked.

"Give me a break, Grange. I'm a new reporter and I need a story. I could use this," she pleaded.

Randall frantically pushed all the buttons, but to no avail. He sank to the floor and lit a cigarette, the smoke curling upward. "There's nothing I can tell you that you don't already know."

"It's hard enough getting a straight answer in this business, but you knew the man. I promise I'll write a great piece! Sensitive, warm, honest. Please, I just want a few minutes of your time," she said and awkwardly sat down beside him.

"No comment," he said as he rested his head against the wall.

"I'll do a piece on your career," she offered as she wrote his name on the pad and underlined it.

"I don't have that kind of ego anymore," he said and blew some smoke rings.

"Forget about the interview. How about just talking?" she said, tucking the pad into her purse and the pen into her healthy cleavage. "I'll start. I've always been a bit of a tomboy. You know, into sports and all that. Absolutely love racing. I would do it myself but it's a man's game. Pretty sexist if you ask me," she recited, but Randall could only stare at her fast moving lips, thoroughly bored. "Let's see, I was born in Israel and served in the military. Mandatory you know. I can kick most men's asses. I guess you could say I'm a feminist. Not over the top, though," she said with a shrug. "Oh, you'll find this interesting, I almost got killed in an explosion at a cafe when I was little so my mom decided to move us to South Africa. My uncle owns a publishing company there. I went to the University of Witterand for journalism and he gave me a job as soon as I got out," she said as Randall continued to study her, amazed she rarely took a breath. "Love movies. My dream is to eventually work for the New York Times and win the Pulitzer for fiction. Murder mystery, actually," she said with an embarrassed smile. "Never knew my father and my mom never talks about him. I live with her in South Africa. Phew," she said with a heavy breath and a forced smile. "Some say I talk too much. So, what's your story?"

Randall maintained his perplexed stare, guzzled some more bourbon and simply stated. "Dead parents. That's it."

"What did they do?"

"Housewife and an asshole. Shouldn't you be writing that down?" he said sarcastically.

"I take it you didn't love your father?"

"I did... I just didn't like him," he said, stifling a belch and staring at the ceiling with glazed eyes. "Don't like bells... cow bells... church bells... sounds of death," he said quietly.

"Uh?"

"Nothing."

"Any siblings?" she asked.

"Not that I know of."

"Where are you from?"

"Hamilton, Canada," he replied, coughing up some phlegm and spitting it on the floor, making her cringe.

"Married?"

"You already asked me that," he said and wiped the drool from his mouth with his sleeve.

Chapter Six

"You never gave me an answer."

He took a moment and said. "Used to be."

"What happened?"

"What difference does it make?" he said as his eyes fell to her chest.

Candice crossed her arms to cover her breasts, cognizant of his leer. "Any children?"

"A daughter. Never see her though. Is like a dream... a nice dream," he said with a long blink.

"I hope to have one someday."

Randall crushed out his cigarette on the floor and inched closer, his eyes still trained on her cleavage. "They'll never go hungry, that's for sure," he said and licked his lips.

Embarrassed, Candice jumped to her feet and pushed all of the buttons. "What's taking so long?" she demanded.

"You're the one that got us into this fucking mess. Got a boyfriend?"

"Several," she said but was hardly convincingly.

"You're a virgin, aren't you?" he replied with a smile, and removed his denim jacket.

"What are you doing?" she said fearfully and fumbled through her purse.

"It's getting hot in here."

Panicked, Candice found a tiny, aerosol container and held it up. "I have pepper spray!" she warned.

"Great. Should come in handy the next time you're attacked by a salad. Relax. I'm not going to touch you," he said, balling his jacket and using it as a pillow against the wall.

"Why... don't you think I'm attractive? I mean... I know I'm a little overweight but I can't help it... I have big bones," she said, suddenly offended.

Randall stared at her with a bewildered expression. "I don't think weight is your problem."

"Uh?"

"Have a belt," he said as he wiped the lip of the bottle with his sleeve and handed it to her.

"Classy. I told you I don't drink."

"Are you on some kind of weirdo medication or something? Have a drink for Christ's sake."

"No thanks. I don't like the taste."

Randall took a healthy swig and winced. "After two or three, you can't tell."

"Are you an alcoholic?"

"Raging. Just like Ma and Pa Kettle," he stated unashamed. "Although for her it was a necessity," he added sombrely.

"Why?" she said, retrieving her pen and pad and beginning to scribble notes.

"Just the way life worked out... and now I'm just killing time," he said and guzzled again before closing his weary eyes.

Candice knelt down and sat beside him. "Sometimes, talking to strangers is the best medicine," she said sympathetically.

Randall opened one eye and gave her a dubious glance. "What the fuck's the matter with you?"

"Nothing. I was just trying to help. I thought maybe you needed someone to talk to," she said disconcerted.

"A reporter? You're the last person I need," he scoffed and ripped the paper from her pad.

"Sounds like you don't trust me."

"Hell, I don't even know you, except for your life story and that you have big bones," he said and crumpled the paper before lighting it, filling the elevator with smoke.

Candice swiped the bottle from his hand, swallowed a mouthful and shivered. "Okay? Now can we talk?" she said with a scowl.

"Have another," he said and titled the bottom of the bottle for her.

"I'm not going to sleep with you," she said uneasily.

"That's what they all say," he replied with a devilish grin, watching her choke back another shot as the sprinkler system activated.

"Oh shit," she murmured.

Dressed in skintight jeans and a flimsy blouse, Gwen yanked the curtain aside, flooding the room with blinding sunshine despite the spotty rain. "Get up!" she said as Randall grunted and rolled over in a cocoon of cotton. Gwen eyed the empty bottle of Jack Daniel's and beer cans strewn about the floor and huffed. She picked up his jean jacket, felt the soft, threadbare material and grimaced. "Was there ever a time you didn't wear denim?"

"Twice. Our wedding and my old man's funeral," he replied, his voice dampened by the blankets.

"The tux was a rental. Do you even own a suit?" she said and flung the coat away.

"Why are you in here?" he grumbled.

"The service is in a couple of hours," she said and ripped back the sheet, revealing his nudity. Embarrassed, she quickly looked away. "I... I'm sorry."

Chapter Six

Randall flopped onto his back, placed his hands behind his head and proudly gazed upon his erection. "What's the matter, split lips, haven't seen one of these in a while?"

Gwen's eyes fell to his crotch. "Not one that small, no."

He crawled out of bed, moaned from the hangover and shuffled across the room into the bathroom. "Well, not many of us can fill a cathedral," he said, worriedly scrutinizing his manhood in the mirror and pulling it to make it longer.

"You never were a happy drunk, were you? I guess that's why you're still single," she said and began to gather up the cans.

"What's your excuse?" he countered, turning his head in her direction as he accidentally urinated on the floor.

"I value my career more than my emotions. I'm a product of your environment," she said and brushed the cigarette ash off the nightstand into her palm.

Randall poked his head around the corner. "Maybe that's why I don't like you."

"I'm not here to be admired by you," she replied and dusted her hands off in the ashtray.

"You're in the right place," he muttered, sauntering back into the room and slipping under the covers again.

A drowsy woman was heard awakening and Candice's head suddenly popped up from beneath the sheets. She rubbed the vision back into her eyes and spotted Gwen. "What's going on? Who are you?" she said to her with a gravely voice.

Shocked, Gwen's mouth opened but the words wouldn't come. Finally, she managed to say. "I'm his wife!"

Wearing only a bra and panties, Candice bolted out of the bed and cumbersomely began gathering her clothes. "He said he wasn't married!" she pleaded and turned to Randall. "You lied to me!" she shouted angrily.

"Just get your fat ass out of here!" Gwen snapped and motioned to the door.

Candice wheeled to confront her and Randall raised a curious eyebrow. "She has big bones," he said, thoroughly enjoying the potential catfight.

"Now just a minute you little bitch!" Candice said to Gwen. "I can handle myself pretty good! I can bench two hundred so watch your mouth!"

Gwen rolled up the sleeves of her blouse and inched closer to her. "I don't care if you can lift a cow, you have no idea who you're dealing with! I'm going to give you five seconds to haul your ass out of here or I'll do it for you!" she whispered in a menacing tone.

Candice considered the offer, swallowed hard and started for the door. "He wasn't that good anyway," she said and scrambled out of the room carrying her clothes as Randall stole a boyish peek at Gwen.

"What the hell do you think you're doing?" Gwen asked with folded arms and a reddened face.

"Holding auditions for your side of the bed. What business is it of yours?" he casually replied and leaned up on one elbow.

"It *is* my business if your drinking problem affects this case!" she said, grabbing the Jack Daniel's bottle and hurling it at him, cracking him on the knees.

"Jesus!" he yelped, rubbing his sore leg. "How the fuck would you know if I had a drinking problem?" he said and reached for his cigarettes.

"Because you made love to a bottle more than you did to me," she shot back and threw an empty beer can at him, bouncing it off his head.

"Stop it for Christ's sake!" he said and felt his forehead. "I think you're jealous," he added and lit the smoke.

"I don't care who you sleep with as long as it isn't me," she said and whipped another can at him, but he deflected this one.

"For someone who doesn't mind, you sure are making a fuss about it."

"Who was the slut anyway?"

"Some reporter from a racing magazine. Met her at the bar last night. What the hell are you getting so worked up about?" he said, scratching his testicles.

"What? Are you out of your mind?" she asked incredulously.

"Don't worry, I didn't tell her anything," he replied, waving off her concern.

"You may have jeopardized this whole investigation!" she said and scrambled to dig out the pills in her pocket.

"Relax, she was looking for a story about Vincenzo," he said and sat on the edge of the bed.

"Did she know you?"

"Intimately," he said with a grin and drank from a half empty beer can.

"I meant about your racing days!" she said and swallowed her medication.

"Yeah. I gave her some boring facts and figures that she could look up on her computer if she wanted to. Trust me, she doesn't have a clue about you," he said and gargled the liquid.

"As an officer on this case, you should know better than to do something stupid like this!" she said, shaking her head in disbelief.

"I'm not on the case, remember?" he said and belched.

"Oh yes you are! I called Wallace and told him that you were being uncooperative. You'll be arrested the moment you step off the plane," she said and snapped her fingers to emphasize the point.

"I don't care," he said and deliberately flicked the ash from his cigarette at her feet.

"That's not what Tony will say."

Randall's cavalier attitude promptly vanished. "What is that supposed to mean?" he said with a steely glare.

"Wallace said that aside from you losing your job *and* your pension, he'll press charges against Tony for aiding and abetting. He'll end up just like you."

"You wouldn't," he said and stood.

"Watch me."

"You're a real cunt, you know that?" he said, taking a step towards her.

"Just how selfish are you Randall? Are you willing to drag a friend down with you for something he had nothing to do with?"

Randall's eyes flared and he reached for his underwear. "Don't you lay that crap on me!" he said.

"Truth hurts, doesn't it?" she responded and pointed to a floor length mirror. "Take a good look at yourself! Is there any shame in there?"

Randall avoided his reflection and pulled on the garment. "Leave me alone," he said quietly.

"Do you know what I see? A coward. A man that has a chance to redeem himself but refuses to do it," she said and withdrew the tattered photograph of Jessica from his wallet. "I wonder what she would think?"

"That's not fair," he whispered as he snatched the picture from her with a trembling hand.

"She's in a wheelchair for life, but she still fights. You used to tell me that you'd be a better father than the one you had. You're no different than he was," she said with disgust and started for the door.

"Fuck you!" he shouted. "I have a conscience! I have the fucking nightmares to prove it!"

"And Jessica and I don't?" she replied without breaking stride. "All you care about is yourself."

"Do you know why? Because nobody ever fucking cared about me!" he yelled.

"I used to."

Randall slumped down onto the bed with his head in his hands. "You're never cured... you just try cope," he said with a breaking voice and studying his scarred arms. "You take the anger out on yourself... when you're young it's razor blades and when you're older it's drugs and booze... you just don't know what it was like for me."

Gwen pivoted, but was unaffected by his emotional confession. "That's right, I don't. You know why? Because you never shared it with me. I have a pretty good idea what happened, but you shut me out!"

"It was my right!" he said.

"And that's what makes you so selfish, Randall!"

"I'm scared, goddamnit! Is that what you want to hear? I can't help you, Gwen! I guess I'm not as brave as you!" he said with a hint of sarcasm.

"Come down off your crucifix! You don't have a right to be scared! You don't have anyone depending on you! I do," she said, pointing to herself. "When Jessica was born my biggest fear was that I'd get killed in the line of duty and it still is!"

"That's your choice, not mine! You want to be a fucking hero, go right ahead!"

"I give up," she said, capitulating with her hands. "Go home! It's my fault anyway! I should have known you were too messed up to help! Get yourself a good lawyer! You're going to need it!" she said and opened the door.

"How is she today?" he asked softly without taking his eyes off the picture.

Gwen stopped in the doorway and took a moment. "She has the sniffles, but she'll be alright," she said and turned to face him. "And as far as Jessica and I are concerned, do yourself a favour and forget us!" she added and slammed the door hard behind her.

Randall weighed her words and caught a glimpse of himself in the mirror. "I don't want hear it," he said shamefully.

At first, Gwen thought they were birds as they swung in low and circled, faint in sound and distant to the eye.

Standing beneath the canopy of trees atop a hill, she looked through her binoculars and saw the distinctive outline and heard the deep, thumping din of helicopter blades punching through the dense air.

Gwen lowered the field glasses and massaged the pain between her eyes. She downed a couple of pills and focused on the locals in the valley below as they ceased their activities and craned their necks, sourly looking skyward at the onslaught of airborne media.

She watched as the police cordoned off the confined, dirt road that led to the cemetery juxtaposed to a rustic, stone church and spied the ocean of reporters and photographers standing behind the temporary barricades, fanning themselves with sweat soaked hats.

A procession of limousines suddenly appeared over the horizon and the cameras started flashing, splashing the speeding vehicles in a gleam of

CHAPTER SIX

intense white light. The officers hurried to pull back the provisional gates as the parade of cars entered and quickly disappeared over a ridge in a cloud of dust.

"Bird watching are we, split lips?"

Startled, Gwen turned to discover Randall holding a bouquet of flowers. "What are you doing here?" she said with disdain.

"A peace offering," he said and held out the flowers, admiring the sundress sticking to her sweaty body.

"Keep them. If they didn't work when you used to come home drunk, they won't work now."

He motioned to the smart black suit he was wearing, despite the poorly knotted tie. "Pretty good, eh?" he said just as some bird droppings landed on his shoulder.

Unimpressed, she focused on the church again. "Did you buy it or steal it?"

"I'll take that as a compliment," he replied and cocked his head to study the excrement. "Even going to try and quit the smokes and the booze... Scout's honour," he added uneasily and held up the wrong fingers to swear the oath.

"Shouldn't you be down there?" she replied tersely without looking.

He sat on the ground with his back against a tree and set the bouquet aside. "You know me, always wearing my heart on my sleeve. I'd probably start bawling," he said and spat on his handkerchief before cleaning away the bird mess.

"I doubt it. You're incapable of feeling the pain of others," she said and wiped the perspiration from her brow with her forearm.

A heavy sigh as he balled the handkerchief and tucked it inside his breast pocket. "You're not going to make this easy, are you?" he said and popped a cigarette in his mouth, but didn't light it.

"Why should I?"

A moment of hesitation as he ran his fingers through the moist grass. "I'm sorry about this morning. Nothing happened. She passed out before anything could... not so sure I would have anyway."

"Doesn't matter to me. You're not the first man to think with his penis."

Randall waited for a few seconds before secretly withdrawing a flask, he went to take a slug, but realized she was looking. He smiled innocently and poured it on the ground. "See?" he said as she turned away in disgust. "Listen Gwen, racing is some pretty serious shit."

"So is murder," she replied matter-of-factly.

He went to light the cigarette, caught himself, but left it in his mouth and put the lighter away. "Driving can't be scruffy. Have to be smooth.

Head down and mouth shut," he said, speaking with his hands. "Make a mistake and you're easy meat. I've been there. Shit. Those guys are all over you like a fucking rash," he added and anxiously watched a bead of sweat roll down her bare back and disappear, leaving a small, wet circle.

"What is this, a lecture in racing clichés?"

Randall heard the squawking of birds above him and he looked up. "Got in a hell of a lot of fights when I was in school. Kids used to tease me about my old man. Said that he was a stinking drunk. I had to defend him even though I knew they were right," he said as his eyes clouded over. "I was never proud of my father. It's a fucking lousy feeling to live with," he said through gritted teeth as Gwen stole a glance at him. "I want Jessica to be proud of me one day... and you... and I need a reason to keep on living... and you've given me one... so I'll do it. I'll drive."

"How do I know you're not going to bail out on me again?" she said, unconvinced.

"You have my word," he replied, offended by her remark and surprised at her indifference.

"It doesn't mean much, Randall. Remember, I know you."

"What do you want from he?" he asked angrily and stood.

"A commitment."

"I'm giving you one!" he answered, raising his voice. "What the hell else can I do?" he added and dusted off his behind.

Gwen turned to face him. "My father always used to say that a person's word was the only, one, true thing they had to prove their worth."

"Did he tell you that before or after he went to prison?" he said with a simper, picking a blade of grass and putting it in his mouth.

"My father was a good man! It was her that pushed him! She... she had to have the finer things," Gwen said, suddenly demonstrative. "He loved her so much... he just made a mistake... we all do sometimes," she said with her head down.

"You're not immune to having a fucked-up family. Everybody's got one," he said and leaned against the tree. "At least I admit it."

"You don't know what you're talking about," she said, fighting back the tears and starting to walk away.

Randall followed. "What's it like to know your dad was probably forced to suck cock? I guess he knew what it must have been like for your mother."

Gwen pivoted and slapped him hard across the face with a shaking hand. "Fuck you!"

"What's this, a display of emotion? Maybe you're not the cold-hearted bitch I thought you were." Gwen went to slap him again but he caught her

CHAPTER SIX

hand and held it tight. "Come down off your fucking high horse woman. Do you want my help or not?"

"I hate you!" she whispered, staring into his blue eyes.

"Good. At least we have one thing in common. Yes or no?" he asked, still clutching her hand.

Gwen continued eyeing him for a few seconds and finally whispered. "Yes!"

"Fine. I'll probably hit everything but the goddamn lottery," he said as he released her and felt his jaw. "A simple thank you would have sufficed."

"For what? Coming to your senses?" she said and rubbed her sore wrist.

"You can do better," he replied, giving her a fatherly look.

Gwen waited and studied the welt on his face. She cupped his cheek and kissed it softly. "Thank you," she said, slightly embarrassed. "You do look good by the way."

Equally disconcerted, Randall gestured for the binoculars and she gave them to him. "So, what's the next move?" he said, watching the mourners congregate outside the church.

"First, I'll have a chat with Julius Carmen to get you cleared for a racing licence."

"How do you know you can trust him?" he said as he loosened his tie.

"He'll keep his mouth shut, believe me," she said. "Then I'll get a press kit together, but I think it's best you avoid the reporters as much as possible."

"They're hounds. Whatever they can't dig up, they make up," he said and handed her the glasses.

"And you need to stay away from the pit bunnies. You're supposed to be my faithful husband."

Randall rolled his eyes and crossed his heart in a mocking manner. "Yes dear. When are you going to convince Jenkins I'm the man for the job?"

"As soon as the service is over."

"Now for the big question, how are you going to tell him?"

"I haven't figured that out yet. If I tell him who we really are, it could tip off the killer."

"I don't think the old man did it."

"I can't take a chance like that," she replied and placed the binoculars in her purse.

"As your partner on this case, I think you should tell him. If he does know who did it, that kind of pressure just might force the guilty party to the surface," he said and fanned himself with his tie.

"Maybe, but I'm calling the shots and I say we don't. We just can't barge in and start asking a lot of questions."

He removed his jacket, sat down again, stretched out and glanced at his watch. "It's eleven a.m. You'd better start thinking pretty fast. The clock's ticking," he said and lit the cigarette.

"I thought you were quitting those?"

"I am... right after this one... maybe," he said and inhaled deeply. "Besides, if I'm going to get killed in a racecar, I may as well enjoy this," he added sarcastically.

At the cemetery outside the ancient chapel, Teresa stood alone before Vincenzo's closed, gold and silver casket, decorated with cherubs at each corner and a crucifix in the centre. One end of the coffin was adorned with a small Italian flag and a replica of his helmet was on the other. The only sound was the distant chirping of birds and the wind, gently flapping the tarpaulin overhead.

Clothed in a tight black dress and veil, Teresa was sensuous, even in grief. Lips trembling and fists clenched, she pretended to kiss the casket but spit instead. "Rot in hell!" she whispered and didn't look when she heard footsteps echoing off the weathered, stone pathway.

Braedon knelt before the coffin and blessed himself, his eyes open and one corner of his mouth curling into a sinister smile. He turned to Teresa with his head cowed. "Would you like me to sit with you for a minute?" he said timidly. "The others will be here soon."

"He didn't like you... and neither do I," she said quietly, mesmerized by her drool, rolling off the polished metal of the coffin. Hidden from view, Teresa reached into her purse, opened an intricate snuffbox and quickly snorted some cocaine.

"For God's sake, Teresa, show some respect!" he said, nervously eyeing the area to ensure nobody saw her.

She stroked the crucifix as her head tilted girlishly. "I wonder what it would have been like to fuck Jesus," she said.

Braedon grabbed her hand and pulled it away. "Stop it!" he said angrily and blessed himself again.

"Don't you dare preach to me? My mother had sex with whites *and* blacks, niggers to you! Some of them even raped me, including a man of God! A man who turned out to be my father!" she said, glaring at him.

Braedon remained unaffected by her outburst, surveying the modest surroundings and sitting in one of a dozen folding chairs. "The least you could have done was given him a proper funeral. His fans deserved a chance to say goodbye. It was selfish of you not to agree to a state funeral."

CHAPTER SIX

"This was his church when he was a boy. Besides, he had enough glory when he was alive," she replied flippantly and took a seat. "Glory that he took away from you. You're probably happy he's dead," she added and checked her look in a compact mirror.

Braedon took a deep breath and waited, choosing his words carefully. "When my father died, I said some awful things to my mother when she sent me to London," he said and studied the tattoo on his hand. "But she just wanted me away from the violence. She wanted me to have a better life."

"This isn't about you. It's about me," she said and snapped the compact closed.

"No, it's about your husband," he replied and reluctantly gazed upon the casket again. Teresa discreetly slid her hand between her legs and withdrew the same vibrator he had forced into her mouth at her home. She covertly pressed the dampened sexual aid into his hand. "I knew you'd come. Miss me?" she asked sarcastically.

"You're sick!" he said with disgust and hurriedly gave it back to her.

A sudden burst of tears. "Why can't you love me?" she demanded.

"You're a fake! You don't care about Vincenzo or me! It's all about money!" he said, trying not to shout.

Teresa slipped her hand between his legs. "I love you," she whimpered.

"Don't!" he replied and removed her hand.

Teresa's face stiffened and the tears abruptly stopped. "Then you leave me no choice."

"What are you talking about?" he asked, straightening his jacket.

"I have a certain lifestyle, Braedon. One that Vincenzo's insurance cannot cover. I'm getting older and modelling won't last forever," she said, perusing her nails.

"And?" he questioned, full of suspicion as he stood.

"Having been your lover, I *am* entitled to compensation. I've already made a call to the London Times. I told them I have a great story. The kind that pays, but I wanted to give you a chance to be reasonable," she said and wiped away a trickle of blood from her nose.

"I'll just deny it," he said and felt the nausea brewing inside his stomach. She withdrew an envelope from her purse and presented it to him. Braedon opened it with tremulous hands to discover a tiny cassette and frowned his puzzlement. "That's my insurance policy. It's amazing where you can hide a video camera, isn't it?" she said and waved the vibrator so only he could see. "I wonder what the people will think when they see you shoving this down my throat. I wonder what your wife will think. Sexual assault? Maybe even rape," she added with a gleam in her eye.

The colour rapidly drained from his face as his muscular legs became warm and weak.

Braedon fumbled for a chair and hesitated until he found the strength to speak. "How... how much?" he managed to whisper, suddenly winded.

"I'll let you know," she replied with a smirk as he quickly stuffed the tape into his jacket just as a cane was heard scraping along the stones.

"Teresa, Braedon," Samuel said with a hoarse and nervous voice, wearing an ascot to hide the welts inflicted by Karl. The old man shuffled to the casket, his shoulders heaving slightly. He retrieved the handkerchief from his breast pocket and dabbed away a tear with an arthritic hand. "I'm sorry Vincent... I know you didn't like me calling you that... sorry Vincenzo," he whispered. Samuel waited until he regained his composure before turning and taking Teresa by the hand. "It's quite a circus back there," he said with a stilted smile, hoping to alleviate the obvious tension and kissing her hand. "How are you?"

"I'm surprised you could pry yourself away from the press," Teresa said, taking her hand back and silently beginning to sob again.

There were a few seconds of uncomfortable silence until Braedon wrapped his arm around Samuel and escorted him a few feet away. "Are you okay?" Braedon said, noticing the old man's grey colour.

"Just a little flu bug," Samuel replied and patted his moist forehead.

"How are things going for Montreal?" Braedon asked.

"Fine, fine. We'll have that testing session at Silverstone in a few days. I trust you'll be ready."

Braedon nodded. "Have you thought about another driver?"

"I'm looking, but I was thinking perhaps I'd just run your car for the remainder of the season... out of respect for Vincenzo," Samuel said uneasily.

"What? We need two cars! I'm going to need some help out there!" Braedon said too loudly.

Teresa jumped to her feet. "I don't believe you two! My husband is dead and all you can do is talk about replacing him!" she said and continued weeping.

"I'm sorry. You're right. This is not the time nor the place," Samuel said and saw a group of mourners approaching as he placed his hand on her trembling shoulder. "Please accept my apology," he said as Braedon watched with disgust. The world champion took a seat in the second row as Ichiro appeared, followed by other crewmembers, Julius Carmen, Friedrich Hesse and Felipe Suarez. One by one the men offered Teresa their condolences and took their seats.

CHAPTER SIX

Samuel hobbled over to Felipe and grasped the back of a chair for support as he leaned in. "What in God's name are you doing here?" Samuel said angrily under his breath.

Felipe felt his finely groomed, Vandyke beard and fluffed his red and yellow handkerchief. "Did you know I was a missionary at one time? I *am* a human being, Sammy, despite the fact that my investment is lying up there," he said and rolled his wristwatch, admiring its diamonds glistening in the sun.

Samuel chuckled. "The only reason you were a missionary is because you're wife was. Pretending to be a man of compassion helped you steal her family's tobacco empire. You haven't worked an honest day in your whole, spoiled life."

Felipe held his hands out and happily gazed upon his many gold, platinum and diamond rings. "When I was seventeen my father forced me to work on one of his filthy tobacco plantations in the Philippines. He said it would build character and help me gain a better understanding of the business. To appreciate what the average worker had to endure," he said and shook his head with a mocking smile. "The only thing I learned is that there is always an easier way."

"I earned my empire," Samuel said proudly.

"Speaking of which, have you had time to consider my offer?"

"It was more like an ultimatum," Samuel said and noticed the priest coming towards the congregation.

"Call it what you will, but I want an answer. And I want it now," Felipe replied, polishing his sunglasses and putting them on.

"In your office, you said you knew what I had done... I still don't know what you're talking about," Samuel said nervously and caught a glimpse of his angst ridden face in the reflection of Felipe's sunglasses.

A quick chortle. "Come, come, Sammy. People talk, especially to powerful men like myself. But, if you're a gambling man, then go ahead and refuse me," he said with a careless shrug. "However, I guarantee you won't be in business very long. By the way, when you were a prisoner in the war, what was your biggest fear?"

"What? I... I guess being sent to an extermination camp. Why?" Samuel said, totally bewildered.

Felipe picked up a dead leaf and felt its rough surface. "That's what prison would be like for you now, I'd say. I mean, you survived it once, but you were a young man back then. This time around, you'd probably die quite quickly," he said and closed his hand over the crackling leaf, shattering it into a dozen pieces.

"I... I still don't understand what you're saying but... but I am a businessman... and I guess we can talk," Samuel replied, trying to sound nonchalant but knowing full well Felipe's inference as the tobacco czar allowed the pieces to fall from his hand and be swept away with the breeze.

Felipe slapped him on the back with a knowing grin. "I knew you'd see it my way. As a matter of fact, why don't I take you out for dinner and we can talk about it?"

"No, thank you," Samuel said and went to walk away.

Felipe grabbed Samuel's frail arm and prevented him from taking another step. "I'm not asking you, Sammy, I'm telling you," Felipe said and tapped his diamond encrusted Rolex. "Eight o'clock then in the hotel dining room. Pleasure doing business with you," he added as the priest took his place at the lectern.

Inside the humble chapel, Gwen squinted through the blazing sunshine, watching the ceremony out of a small, stained-glass window as Randall sat in a pew, staring at the modest altar. His steely eyes slowly journeyed upward to the crucifix. "It's been a long time," he said quietly, withdrawing a cigarette and lighting it.

"I don't think you should smoke in here," Gwen whispered nervously.

"You still believe in God like a good little Catholic girl should?" he asked and stretched out on the pew, the warped, ancient pine creaking beneath him.

"That's a personal question."

"Hey, I've seen you naked. The man's waiting and you're in His house," he said and haphazardly motioned to the heavens.

Gwen shunned looking at him and bashfully replied. "Yes... I guess... maybe. I don't know. I think God's your conscience... I don't really think there's a heaven and hell. I think we have to respect one another... love our children... be humble... be gentle with people... all that kind of thing."

"Jesus! Where the hell did that come from?" he asked with a frown.

"You asked," she said with embarrassment.

"Know what I think? I think that if this great deity exists, he jerks off while he watches people suffer," Randall countered without taking his eyes off the ceiling and scratching his testicles. "There can't be no God. There's too many fuck-ups. Life's just a bunch of random shit. Some of it sticks to you and some of it don't." He turned his head to gauge her reaction as globules of sweat rolled off his face, plopping onto the wooden floor and absorbing quickly. "Fuck, it's hot. Reminds me of the day we planted my father. Did I ever tell you about that?" Gwen shook her head and returned her attention to the service. "Shit. Got halfway to the cemetery and the goddamned hearse quit. Had to walk five fucking miles to get help. Must have been a hundred degrees," he said and scraped away some encrusted dirt on the bottom of his shoe with his lighter. "So fucking hot the tar bubbled. Got shit from my mom for wrecking my new shoes. What a day. What a rotten, fucking day that was," he said and studied the blue smoke from his cigarette wafting upward to the wooden beams. "Almost as hot as the day we got hitched. Remember?" he asked with a smile and looking at her playfully, upside down.

"How could I forget?"

He flicked his ash carelessly onto the floor, earning a reprimanding glance from Gwen. "Hey, if the place catches fire, let Him put it out," he said and gestured to the crucifix. "You make it sound like our wedding was a bad thing."

"Any time the groom shows up bombed out of his mind and two hours late, it isn't a good sign."

"You'll never let me forget that, will you?" he said, flipping through a tattered hymnbook.

"It's the forgiving part that I've always had a problem with," she replied and deliberately felt the scar on her forehead.

"I guess that's why you left me, eh split lips?"

"Let's get something straight before we go any further. I don't like being called split lips. I wanted to be a police officer since I was twelve and I put up with a lot of crap to get where I am. I earned respect and I expect it from you."

Randall defiantly blew a smoke circle at her. "I wanted to be a cop so I could catch assholes like my father, and because I fucking hate criminals, and all I've learned is that people never change."

"I can see that," she said, giving him a quick once-over.

"Must be nice to have no flaws."

"Just one. You."

"So now you're perfect, uh? I'm just here to be used and then tossed away? Seems like a habit with you," he said.

Gwen closed the window and turned to him. "Look, there's no future for us. You're going to have to deal with any guilt you might have about Jessica and me. Any reasonably sane person would have done the same thing in my position!" she said and rubbed her aching forehead. "God, you're giving me a migraine," she added and popped a few pills into her mouth.

"Hey, I understand why you did what you did. There isn't a fucking second that goes by that I don't regret what happened to Jessica," he said and gazed upon the altar again. "I wished I'd been killed that day. Would have saved you both a lot of trouble... and me. But at least I'm trying to accept it. Sounds to me like you're the one with a conscience problem."

"I used to have one but thanks to you, I don't anymore. Come on, the service is almost over."

"You sure get pissed when you try and hide the truth," he said gamesomely and dragged himself up.

"How you get your head through doors with that ego is beyond me. We're here to do a job. Period," she explained with her hands.

"Think you can be around me without getting emotionally involved?"

Gwen chuckled and said. "Just drive the car and try not to kill yourself."

He held his hand over his heart, faking love sickness and picked a daisy from a vase on the sill. He closed his eyes and plucked the petals. "She loves me, she loves me-,"

"Not!" she interrupted, yanking the flower from his hand and tossing it aside. "Let's go to work," she said and watched as Randall withdrew his wedding ring from his pocket. "I thought you sold it?" she asked with surprise.

"Couldn't get enough for it," he said, slightly embarrassed. He took her hand, interlocked his fingers with hers and led her to the door as Gwen gave him a questionable glance. Randall felt the weight of her stare and said. "If we're going to do this thing, let's do it right. You never know who could be watching."

"Fine. But this time, see if you can behave like a good husband should," she said and removed the cigarette from his mouth.

"Yes dear," he said sarcastically as they exited the building, but he suddenly stopped and focused on the gleaming casket. He swallowed hard and felt a burning in his eyes, causing him to look away. The only sounds were the priest's voice inviting the congregation to recite the Lord's Prayer, the faint drone of helicopters and the heat induced racket of the crickets. Randall lowered his head in worship, much to Gwen's surprise. He blinked back his emotion and saw her watching him. "Fucking sweat," he said with an awkward smile as his chin trembled. His childlike vulnerability made her heart stir and she wrapped her arm around his shoulder. "Fucking hate funerals," he whispered with a breaking voice and fumbled for his handkerchief.

Gwen reached into her purse, found some Kleenex and dried his eyes. "Bird poop, remember?" she said with a heartening smile.

Their eyes locked and they unconsciously inched closer together. Randall caught a whiff of her perfume and fought the urge to embrace her as his hand slowly rose to caress her face. Gwen whetted her tingling lips and was about to kiss him, but suddenly dropped her purse, spilling its contents, her bottle of tablets scattering on the ground. She hastily knelt down and gathered them up as he froze upon catching a peek of her breasts

Chapter Six

beneath her translucent sundress. Randall further loosened his tie and shook his head clear. "I could use a drink," he said, completely flummoxed and eyed the church doors. "Maybe I'll slip in and grab some of that sacramental wine."

Gwen continued stuffing the pills back into the bottle, popping one into her mouth for good measure as Randall bent down to help her. "It is getting hot, isn't it?" she said with a flushed face.

They stood at the same time and bumped heads as Randall anxiously frisked himself for a cigarette. "Do ah... did you say you had people patrolling the perimeter?" he said, trying to make conversation. "Sometimes the killer likes to see the fruits of his labour."

"I have people stationed all over the place recording anything that moves, but gut instinct tells me that's where the answer lies," she replied, pointing to the gravesite and fixing her hair.

"What makes you so sure?" he said and found his smokes, only to discover the packet was empty.

"I can't explain it. It's just one of those hunches, you know?"

"I spent most of my career listening to my heart instead of my head," he said and laughed stupidly.

"Except when it comes to women," she said with an equally dumb chuckle.

He looked her over and said. "Touché."

Disconcerted, Gwen took his hand. "Let's go," she said.

The priest concluded the service and closed his bible. The mourners disbanded, offering condolences to Teresa as they departed. Samuel limped to her and said. "Do you want me to stay with you for a while?"

"No, thank you. I think I need some rest," she replied and dabbed at invisible tears.

"Is there anything you need?" the old man asked.

"It might sound strange but... I'd like to keep travelling with the team. I'd feel like I was close to him," she said, staring at the casket again before spying Braedon, quickly walking towards his limousine.

"Absolutely," Samuel replied and hugged her. Teresa gave him a peck on the cheek and sauntered away, leaving Samuel alone at the casket.

"Mr. Jenkins?" Gwen said. Startled, Samuel pivoted to find Gwen and Randall behind him. "I'm Gwen Grange and this is my husband, Randall."

An exchange of handshakes. "Randall Grange.... Randall Grange," the old man said, trying to recall. "Vincenzo's team-mate in the Atlantic series, right?"

"Yes sir," Randall replied proudly, thoroughly star struck. "It really is an honour to meet you."

"If memory serves me, he saved your life in Montreal, I believe."

"Toronto, actually," Randall said, nervously correcting him.

An uncomfortable smile from Samuel. "He was quite a man. Truly one of the best," he said as an uneasy silence ensued. "Well, I should be going."

"Um... could we talk to you for a minute?" Gwen asked.

"I am quite busy," Samuel replied.

"It'll only take a few minutes," she said.

"Very well. What can I do for you?" Samuel said and sat with great difficulty.

"I realize that this is not the best time to discuss this but... but I represent Randall as a driver now," Gwen said.

Samuel instantly battled to his feet. "I should have known! You ought to be ashamed of yourselves!"

"Nice one," Randall whispered to her.

"I meant no disrespect, Mr. Jenkins. Could I arrange for a meeting with you later on?" Gwen said, but Samuel was already hobbling away as she looked to Randall with panic in her eyes.

"Mr. Jenkins... Vincenzo was murdered," Randall blurted.

Samuel stopped and looked over his shoulder. "What?" he replied, completely shocked. Stunned, Gwen glared at Randall and whispered. "What the hell do you think you're doing?"

Samuel's face reddened with rage. "What kind of a man are you?"

"Dedicated," Randall said and strolled to the casket. "Want to take a look?"

Gwen followed and grabbed Randall's arm. "I do not approve of your tactics!" she whispered angrily.

Randall broke free of her grip. "If it was somebody you knew that was six feet under, wouldn't the end justify the means to you?"

"No! This isn't some crack deal gone bad!" she said.

"Murder victims don't care about social class or diplomacy, only justice," Randall said.

Samuel pointed a shaky finger. "Whatever sick game you're playing, I'll see to it that you're both behind bars! Suspension failure killed him!" he said with desperation.

Gwen reached into her purse, retrieved her identification and held it up. "We're with the DST, Mr. Jenkins."

"For all I know that could be a fake! You're probably some damned reporter!" Samuel said with a quaking voice.

Randall removed Vincenzo's helmet from atop the casket and pulled off the Italian flag, the smooth nylon flapping with the breeze. "Forgive me Vince," he whispered as his trembling hands released a bolt. He lifted the lid, disclosing Vincenzo's turgescent face. Randall stood there, his eyes transfixed and moistening. "Dad," he whispered and touched Vincenzo's rigid, cold skin. After a few seconds, Randall gained control of his feelings, cleared his throat and said, "See for yourself." The old man reluctantly edged closer to the coffin, but refused to look despite Randall pointing to the bullet wound. "Someone shot him."

"My God... why?" Samuel said, becoming light-headed and dropping his cane.

"That's why we're here," Gwen said, picking up the walking stick and pressing it into his withered hand.

"Murdered?" Samuel mumbled in disbelief, but he wasn't convincing.

Randall and Gwen exchanged a brief glance; both sensing something was amiss. "Do you have any idea who might have done this?" Randall asked in an insinuating tone and closed the casket.

Samuel gave him a wicked stare. "What is that supposed to mean?"

"My partner meant no disrespect," Gwen said, immediately assuming the role of good cop versus Randall's bad cop.

"Do you think I had something to do with it?" the old man demanded.

"Did you?" Randall said matter-of-factly.

"How dare you?" Samuel shot back, visibly shaken and faltering as Gwen assisted him to a chair.

"That's enough, Randall," she said and tried to comfort Samuel with her hand.

Randall gave her a quick wink and pulled out a chair. He spun it around, sat in it backwards and leaned closer to him, mere inches away. "We know you stand to collect eight million dollars in insurance money. You're up to your elbows in this shit," he said with an intimidating grin.

"If you're trying to scare me, you're not," Samuel said, but was beginning to perspire. "If you peruse this, you can speak to my attorney!"

"You know, the kind of pressure homicide detectives can apply is pretty fucking nasty," Randall casually said. "Can really screw up your life. I mean you can't sleep, can't eat, can't relax. Just waiting to see when we're coming to arrest your ass because like it or not, you're the prime suspect."

"He's had enough, Randall," Gwen said. "We're sorry we bothered you, Mr. Jenkins. We'll be in touch."

Samuel went to stand up, but Randall gently pushed him down again and looked to Gwen. "May as well tell him."

"I don't know," Gwen said.

"The man that killed Vincenzo told us you were the one that hired him. He's already going to jail for the rest of his life so he has no reason to lie.

He says he can prove it. If there was ever a time to come clean and make it easier on yourself, it's now, Mr. Jenkins," Randall said.

Samuel's dread-filled eyes pleaded with Gwen. "I didn't hire anyone! I didn't! You have to believe me!"

"Not good enough, Mr. Jenkins," Randall said as he stood and pretended to reach into his jacket pocket. "Stand up and put your hands behind your back." The old man wavered, debating his response and burying his head in his hands. "I said stand up!" Randall shouted, causing Samuel to jump in his seat.

Gwen gently took the old man by the arm and started to lift him up. "You'd better do as he says, Mr. Jenkins," she said.

"God... I didn't think they would do it... I thought they were just trying to nick me for more money," Samuel whispered and began sobbing uncontrollably.

The revelation astounded Randall and Gwen; they looked at each other with surprise. "Who's 'they'?" she said, quickly withdrawing a pad and pencil.

Samuel took a heavy breath and ashamedly said in between sniffles. "About a month ago I received a letter... it was the second one... both were on Team Jenkins stationary. They demanded another twenty million pounds or... or else they would kill one of my drivers."

"You said another letter. What happened with the first one?" Randall said.

"A year ago, the first note came and demanded twenty million pounds... they threatened to kill my wife... I had to pay it," Samuel said, shaking his head to alleviate the painful memory.

"Why didn't you call the police?" Gwen asked in a soft tone.

"I couldn't... I was too scared... they told me that if I did, they would kill her... after I wired the money... she died anyway... cancer," Samuel said, his weak voice trailing away.

"Money does drive crime doesn't it?" Randall whispered to Gwen. "Nothing worse than an assassin branching out into high finance."

"Where did you send the money?" she said, slightly annoyed at Randall's commentary.

"A numbered account in the Cayman Islands... I tried to trace it, but couldn't."

Randall looked to Gwen. "Well?"

"I'll try and see if a warrant from Interpol will work, but those accounts are designed to protect the very thing we'd be looking for. It's probably been laundered," she replied. "Did you keep the letters, Mr. Jenkins?"

"No... I know I should have, but I couldn't bear to have them," he said and wiped his nose with his handkerchief.

CHAPTER SIX

"Do you know where they were sent from? Did you check the stamp?" Gwen asked, a nuance of anger in her voice.

"No return address, but they were mailed from England. It's my fault Vincent's gone... I just didn't have the money," Samuel said and hung his head in disgrace.

"I want you to give me the account number, and if you hear from them again, you don't make a move until I say so. Is that understood?" Gwen said impatiently.

Samuel's face promptly became dour as he gathered his courage. "Fine, but stay out of my way! I have a business to run!"

"And we have a murder to solve! We expect your cooperation," she replied, surprised by Samuel's sudden demeanour.

"Racing is a multi-million dollar business! I don't have time to play cops and robbers!" Samuel said and struggled to his feet and forcefully jamming the handkerchief into his breast pocket.

"Are you listening to yourself? Just how much are you willing to risk to save your empire?" Randall said and gestured to the casket.

"Everything," Samuel replied icily.

"Then you won't mind when I tell you that Randall is going to take over Vincenzo's ride, and I'm going to pose as his wife. Obviously, it's someone involved with your team," Gwen said.

Flabbergasted, Samuel banged his cane against the ground in contempt. "Absolutely not!"

"I *am* experienced. I've driven open wheel and stock," Randall said defensively.

"Always turning left on some country bumpkin track on a Saturday night with a bunch of inbred hicks, hardly qualifies you to pilot one of *my* machines!" Samuel said through gritted teeth.

"How do you think people will react, not to mention your sponsors, if I take this thing public? It would ruin you. Besides, this is a homicide investigation. You have no choices here," Gwen said and continued scribbling some notes.

"What about Braedon?" Samuel inquired. "He has to know what's going on."

"You don't say anything to him or anybody else," she replied.

"He's a sitting duck!" Samuel decried.

"And a potential suspect. Everybody is... including you. It's my way or you close up shop altogether. Make a decision. Now," Gwen answered.

"What about Carmen and Hesse? He needs a racing licence," Samuel said, hoping his suggestion would be a barrier to her plan.

"They know who I am. I'll arrange things, and I don't want you talking to them about any of this," she said. "Well?"

Subjugated, Samuel leaned heavily against his cane. "If I agree... what happens next?" he asked begrudgingly.

Gwen handed him her card. "If you remember anything or they contact you again, I want you to call me."

"When's your next testing session?" Randall asked.

"The day after tomorrow. Silverstone," Samuel said sternly, looking at him with disgust.

"We'll be there. I'll let you know what and when you'll inform the press," Gwen said. "In the meantime, I'll have twenty-four hour security on you and we'll tap your phone just in case." Samuel waited and eyed both of them, still trying to grasp the situation. Finding no words, he nodded and finally hobbled towards his limousine.

"You were right about that hunch," Randall said to her once the old man was out of earshot.

"Don't you ever do that again," she replied, watching Samuel steal a brief glimpse of her as he ducked into his car.

"What?" he said, although he knew what she meant.

"Take a stupid chance like opening the casket. You were lucky Jenkins folded," she said and put away her pad.

"Jealous?"

"This is my case and you will follow by my rules!" she said and clicked her pen to make her point.

"You always did like it on top," he replied playfully.

"Joke if you want, but doesn't shitting your pants at over two hundred miles per hour scare the hell out of you?"

"Not as much as you scare me," he said with a mischievous smile.

"You're smarter than you look. Come on," she said and walked away just as her cell phone rang.

Randall whistled and fanned himself. "Bitchy and sexy... that's why I married you in the first place." He promptly stopped waving, felt the scorched skin of his palms and went to the coffin. He placed one hand on top. "Hey Vince... thanks for... you know... I'm going to get whoever did this to you... I promise." He turned to find Gwen standing behind him and breathless with an excited look upon her face. "What?" he asked.

Gwen took a deep breath and sat as she indicated with her phone. "Things just got a whole lot more interesting. Everybody knows Julius Carmen owns forty-nine percent of the series and that another forty-nine percent is publicly traded, but guess who owns the other two percent?" she asked, Randall shrugged. "Vincenzo's father. We had to get a warrant to find that out."

"He was killed in a plane crash, right?" Randall said, stunned by the revelation.

"Right, and the accident board is still investigating. When those results come out, it just might lead to a criminal inquiry and make things even more complicated," she said and popped a pill into her mouth.

"So with Azzopardi Senior dead, who was the benefactor?" he asked. Gwen simply pointed to the casket. "Jesus H. Christ!" he whispered and sat beside her.

"And now that he's gone, that two percent belongs to Carmen... which now makes him majority owner. Apparently, he and Vincenzo's father had done some banking business in the past and the two percent was used as collateral."

Randall leaned back in the chair. "I think our list of suspects just expanded," he said with a heavy sigh as he motioned to her. "Give me one of those pills... I think I'm getting a migraine.

Chapter Seven

Samuel sat alone in a dimly lit booth, mesmerized by the flickering candle as the jittery shadows highlighted his gaunt appearance. "No need to look into your future, Sammy, I already know what it is," Felipe said with an evil grin and slid into the seat. Samuel quickly busied himself with the menu, but Felipe lowered it. "Business before pleasure, Sammy."

"I've found a driver so I don't need to look at your offer," he stated matter-of-factly.

Intrigued and amused, Felipe sat back and took a breadstick from the basket. He popped one end into his mouth, crunched loudly and said. "Who is he?"

"Randall Grange. He used to run in the Formula Atlantic series in North America a few years ago. He was pretty good," Samuel replied uneasily without taking his eyes from the menu.

"Was?"

"He still is," Samuel said forcefully.

"I thought we agreed that I would pick the driver," Felipe said, dusting some crumbs from his beard and checking his look in the dinner plate.

"That was your idea. I never endorsed it. As a matter of fact, I haven't agreed to anything," Samuel said and flipped a page.

"Where did you find him?" Felipe asked with an impatient roll of his eyes and picked his teeth with his finger.

Samuel put down the menu and poured himself a glass of water with shaking hands. "I made some calls. The best in North America are a little too expensive. Besides, they've already started their season and it would be impossible to get them out of their rides right now," Samuel said, and drank to cool his parched throat.

After another bite of the breadstick, Felipe haphazardly gestured to a handsome man of twenty-one with long, black hair sitting at another table, surrounded by four gorgeous, adoring women. "I'm sure you know who that is," Felipe said with a mouthful.

"Alberto Americo? He's on another team," Samuel said with contempt.

"He wants out of his contract and I'm willing to pay the penalty. He wants to drive for us and I think he's the best. He will make an excellent team-mate for me," Felipe said.

"Just because he's Spanish doesn't make it so," Samuel replied.

"I'm going to make him change his last name. Americo sounds too Yankee for me," Felipe said with another grin. "There's nothing I hate more than Americans and Frenchmen."

"I want Grange," Samuel said sternly.

"Why, because he's cheap?" Felipe said and dipped his finger into the soft butter and loudly sucked it off.

"I know racing and I know talent when I see it! You don't!" Samuel snapped.

"I don't believe you're in any position to dictate anything to me," Felipe said and leaned across the table, his dark eyes staring into Samuel's. "I'm like a tiger. I can see right through you. I know all of your secrets and all of your weaknesses."

"Why do you want my team? You have enough money to start your own, or buy another one," Samuel said, trying to change the subject.

"You know Carmen won't allow any more teams into the series and none are for sale, but guess," Felipe said gamesomely.

"It's revenge, isn't it? Because I wouldn't hire you as a driver. Because Vincenzo was better than you."

"That was a nice try. Would you like to hear the truth now?" Felipe said and noticed a fly near the centre of the table. Samuel gestured with his hands, confidently inviting the response. Felipe's brown eyes followed the erratic insect until he snatched it out of the air and held it in his closed fist. "Money is the most important thing in life. Wouldn't you agree?" he asked as the sound of buzzing emitted from his hand.

"I always thought love was," Samuel replied coolly and took another drink of his water.

Felipe chuckled and spied the trapped insect with wonder. "Old timers like you always say that, but we all know the truth. Power should be held by a few. People like me," he said and held the fly by its wings. "You see, Sammy, you're trapped," Felipe said as Samuel shifted nervously in his seat and adjusted his ascot. "Was she worth it?" Felipe added, noticing the welts on Samuel's neck.

"It's just a little rash... an allergy," Samuel replied.

A sinister smile. "I control your fate, Sammy. Do what I say or the world finds out about you," Felipe said and ripped one wing from the fly.

"I'm getting a little tired of these threats. I'm calling your bluff."

"What was it like, bringing home a Japanese bride after the war?" Felipe asked, setting the fly down and laughing as it spun helplessly in a circle.

"Don't talk about her! I loved her!" Samuel replied, angry at the reference.

"It must have been hell, walking around with her in public. I can't imagine the shame you felt," Felipe said, enjoying the angst he was causing.

"The woman saved my life! She was just a nurse, not a soldier!" Samuel barked as his face turned crimson.

Felipe pushed his finger into the butter again and swirled it around. "Feels like pussy and tastes just as sweet. Tell me, are Oriental woman different down there?" he asked sarcastically.

"Your father was right. You're a cruel, selfish man!" Samuel said.

"The only thing he was good for was his money. And now it's mine, but there's never enough, is there?" he said with a smile. Felipe retrieved a cell phone from inside his coat and deftly flicked it open with a shake of his wrist. "If you think you were a pariah back then for marrying a gook, wait until I tell the people what I know. I'll give you one last chance... or I make the call."

"To?" Samuel asked unconcerned.

"The police. They should be able to get the ball rolling," Felipe said, waving the phone in Samuel's face.

Samuel steadied his cane and squirmed out of the seat. "Go to hell!" he whispered.

Felipe shrugged, punched the keys and waited. "Yes, Scotland Yard, please," he said, but Samuel suddenly snatched the device out of his hand and turned it off. "I knew you'd come to your senses," Felipe said and toyed with the fly with the point of his steak knife.

"I'll sign a contract after Grange tests at Silverstone, no matter how he does. If you don't like what you see, then you and Americo are in. Fair enough?" Samuel said and offered his hand to consummate the deal.

"Why the stall, Sammy?" Felipe said and removed the other wing from the fly.

"Grange is good," Samuel said, avoiding looking at the tortured bug. "You might like him better than Braedon and Alberto... and... and he might be a good team-mate for you... you would probably outshine him."

"I'll think about it," Felipe said, happy at the thought and suddenly sliced the fly in half with the knife. "But if you're playing games with me, I will put you out of your misery... permanently."

Chapter Seven

Through a telescopic lens, cross hairs trained on Julius Carmen. Wearing sunglasses and a tall glass of vodka with ice in hand, he sat at a patio table in a much too small Speedo by the pool at the Brun Hotel in Milan. His full, false beard glistened with sweat in the sweltering sun and he frequently flicked his head, causing a spray of perspiration. He moved a chess piece on the board and motioned to Friedrich Hesse, sitting beside him, dressed in a sweat soaked suit. "Check," Julius said, thoroughly bored.

"I'd like to change, Mr. Carmen. I'm feeling a little faint," Friedrich said and tried to cool his red face with a glass of already warm water.

"I thought you liked the great outdoors?" Julius said condescendingly. "You're the one who goes on and on about the environment."

"I like cycling, Mr. Carmen, but this is not healthy," Friedrich replied and rubbed his face with a rapidly melting ice cube.

"As my subordinate, you need to look as professional as possible, even in this heat," Julius happily replied and stirred his drink.

"If I may be so bold, Mr. Carmen, why aren't you in a suit then?" Friedrich asked and studied the board.

"I'm your superior and you don't question my authority, Friedrich. I'll ignore it this time because I know you're German, and your type has a tendency not to think before they speak. The last kraut that tried to beat a Russian was crushed. Remember that," Julius said tersely and handed him the sun tan lotion. "My back," he ordered, Friedrich hesitated.

"I didn't earn a MBA at Cologne University to be a servant," Friedrich replied nervously and moved his king piece.

Surprised by Friedrich's defiance, Julius removed his sunglasses and lazily tilted his head to look at him. "Do you still want your own racing series someday?" Julius said and moved his queen without looking. "Check."

"Yes," Friedrich answered awkwardly.

"Would you like to have my job in the future if your dream doesn't come true?"

Friedrich resumed examining the board and shifted uneasily in his seat. "If the opportunity came up... I would consider it," he said and moved his king again.

"Do you own your own bank in Zurich? Do you own a shipping empire? Are you an oil tycoon?" Julius said smugly and moved again. "Check."

"No," Friedrich replied softly and moved his king yet again.

"So you don't have enough money to ever own your own series, and the only way you'll ever get my job is if I give it to you. Perhaps if your father was more than a factory worker in a filthy brewery and your mother was more than a librarian, you'd have a better future, but they aren't," Julius said and moved his rook. "Checkmate," he added and handed Friedrich the lotion.

Friedrich reluctantly popped open the bottle and began rubbing the liquid onto Julius just as Gwen approached, wearing another sundress. "Still in disguise, I see," she said, referring to Julius' beard. "Mind if I sit down?" she added as Friedrich stood to honour her presence, but Julius remained seated.

"It's always a pleasure to welcome a beautiful woman, MIlaya moyaA," Julius said, putting on his sunglasses again and eying her figure as she sat.

Gwen found her pills and swallowed several. "I'm not your sweet and yes, I understand Russian," she said and snapped the lid closed.

Julius bowed, thoroughly impressed. "Still having headaches, I see. Do you know that in Russia, they say love making is the best elixir for those," he said with a sly smile.

"In France we cure them with a glass of wine and an aspirin," she countered.

The scope slowly searched the eloquent grounds and focused on Randall, leaning against a wall with his arms crossed, intensely watching the trio. Wearing a pair of cheap flip-flops, tattered denim shorts and a dingy, maple leaf T-shirt with a dirtied Toronto Blue Jays baseball cap, he spat and scratched his testicles, amidst the regular bourgeoisie.

Julius checked his watch. "I'm a busy man, Ms. Gaudet and my yacht is waiting to take me back to Monaco. Please, make it quick," he said and stared longingly between her thighs.

Gwen fanned herself with the drink menu and crossed her legs, aware Julius was watching. "I have some important matters to discuss with you."

He watched a bead of sweat roll down her throat and disappear between her breasts. "Perhaps you should have a cold drink before we begin," he said seductively and deliberately spread his legs, providing her with a clear view of his bulging thong.

"No, thank you. I need a racing licence," she said, ignoring his physical gesture and trying not to stare at his well-endowed manhood.

Julius gazed at a gorgeous brunette strolling by, smiling seductively at him. "Who is it for?"

"The driver that's replacing Azzopardi. His name is Randall Grange," Gwen said.

"Never heard of him," Julius replied whilst watching another beauty on a lounge turning over to tan her bare breasts.

CHAPTER SEVEN

"He's my husband and a police officer," she said, motioning to Randall, sifting through an ashtray at an empty table. He found a long enough butt, surreptitiously lit it and managed to take a few drags.

"Classy fellow. He doesn't even look like he could pass the physical. I can't do it." Julius said sharply and took a sip of his drink.

"Can't or won't?" Gwen asked.

"I assume this has something to do with your investigation," Julius said with a hint of impatience, and held out his arms for Friedrich to lotion.

"I'm not at liberty to get into details, but yes," she said and watched with bewilderment as Friedrich obliged.

"Does he have any experience?" Friedrich chimed in.

"That's enough, Friedrich!" Julius barked.

"He used to drive in the Atlantic series in North America," she said to Friedrich.

"That's Mickey Mouse racing. He'd get killed over here," Julius replied with a laugh.

"We can do this the hard way or the easy way. It's your choice," she said.

Another chortle from Julius. "I don't think you really know who you're dealing with."

"I think I do," Gwen said confidently and retrieved a small notepad from her purse. "Julius Carmen, born 1968 in Baku, Azerbaijan. Attended the Plekhanov Russian Academy of Economics. Family has been in the oil business since 1882 and you inherited the fortune after your father's death from a heart attack. Mother died eight days later," she said and turned a page. "You made even more money upon the break up of the Soviet Union by purchasing state owned companies, including shipping and oil. No siblings. Joined the Russian military and served time in Chechnya," she continued and raised a curious eyebrow. "Sharpshooter credited with killing dozens of Muslim insurgents and even worked for a time in the KGB. Loves skeet shooting, the ballet and racing. So much so that you bought forty-nine percent of the shares in this racing series. You're all about money, Mr. Carmen," she concluded and expertly flipped the pad closed.

Julius raised his glass to toast. "Very impressive, Ms. Gaudet, but at least my family came by our money honestly, not on the backs of the taxpayers."

Gwen's upper lip trembled with rage as she suppressed the urge to fight back. "But there's one more thing not a lot of people know. Even though you own forty-nine percent of the series, Vincenzo Azzopardi's father owned two percent, which reverts back to you, doesn't it? Vincenzo would have inherited that, but now he's dead."

"Are you suggesting I had Vincenzo's father killed and then killed Vincenzo?" Julius said while laughing as Friedrich eyed his boss with suspicion.

"I didn't say that, but it's a good question," she shot back.

Julius smiled and drained his glass. "I think you've been reading too many spy novels," he said and stood. "Do svidAniya," he added and gestured Friedrich along.

"I didn't say you could leave," Gwen said.

Julius removed his sunglasses and hung them from the gold chain around his sweaty neck as he gazed into the distance and saw dark clouds rapidly approaching. "The forces of nature can be deadly," he said and glanced at her. "One should always be careful of powers greater than they are."

"That sounds like a threat," she replied.

"Just looking out for your safety," Julius said with a smile and began to stride off.

"Get back here," Gwen commanded.

Julius stopped and turned to her. "Look *Mrs. Bond*, I didn't like you the first time I met you and I like you even less now. So, why don't you take that junior G-man badge of yours and shove it up your pretty little ass. I'm not going to give you that licence and if you make trouble for me, I'll see to it that you'll be handing out parking tickets for the rest of your life. Is that clear?" He went to walk away but suddenly, a hand grabbed him by the scruff of the neck and another twisted his left arm behind his back. Julius was marched to the pool's edge and thrown in. He thrashed around, found his bearings and surfaced, coughing and spitting with his saturated, fake beard dangling in a sticky mess. Friedrich laughed hysterically and clapped his hands, but quickly desisted upon his superior's scolding glance as other patrons at the pool suddenly recognized Julius, causing a wave of whispers.

"That's no way to talk to my wife," Randall said, waving a naughty finger at him.

"What the hell are you doing?" Gwen whispered angrily to Randall.

"Protecting the honour of my woman," he replied whimsically.

"Do you ever think before you act?" she said, shoving Randall aside and kneeling down to assist Julius out of the water. "I apologize for my husband's actions, Mr. Carmen, but it is imperative that you give him the licence," she said with an outstretched hand, keeping her voice down.

"Get away from me!" Julius said and swam to the ladder as he struggled to right his beard.

"Mr. Carmen, I don't want to, but I can force you to do this. It's official police business," she whispered so others wouldn't hear.

CHAPTER SEVEN

Julius dragged himself out of the pool. "You'll be hearing from my lawyer!" he said and snapped his fingers, Friedrich immediately jumped to his feet, ready with a towel. Gwen and Randall watched as they hastily retreated into the hotel.

"What an asshole," Randall stated with a shake of his head.

Gwen just stared at him completely enraged and pushed him into the pool. She started to march off, but Randall quickly clamped her leg and pulled her into the water. Other guests delighted in the impromptu comedy sketch as Gwen popped up with her hair plastered to her face, mascara running and her sundress ballooning with air. Randall began laughing as she desperately tried to straighten her clothes. "I'm sending you back to Wallace! Then we'll see who's laughing!" she said.

Randall leaned back and began to do the backstroke while spouting water from his mouth. "You can't split lips. You need me, and you can't get better than the best."

"Go home, Randall!" she said and waded for the ladder.

Randall's smile quickly vanished as he swam to her and took her hand. "I'm sorry," he said with sincerity.

She ripped her hand away and kept going. "Leave me alone!"

Randall tackled her into the water, much to the joy of the spectators. After a few seconds, they both surfaced with Randall gripping her by the shoulders. "What the fuck happened to you, uh? I don't even know you anymore! You walk around with that fucking righteous attitude of yours! You're no better than anybody else, so take that goddamn pickle out of your ass!" he said and couldn't help eye her perfectly shaped breasts showing through her wet summer dress. "I think you went back to Paris because you think you belong there with all those snotty, uptight fuckers, and the only reason you became a cop was because of your fucking ego!"

Gwen pushed him away. "What do you want me to be, a no-good drunk like you? A person who can't go five minutes without bitching about his pathetic childhood and his screwed up father? A person so racked with guilt that he hasn't got the guts to confront his own mistakes? No, I'll stay the way I am!" she said and reached for the ladder. "You'll always be a low class loser!"

Enraged, Randall clenched her arm as Gwen spun around and swung at him, but he grabbed both her hands and forced her to the wall with a heavy splash. "You're nothing but a fucking bitch! Maybe I didn't come from money, but at least my family did the best they could!"

"Your family's best will never be good enough," she replied matter-of-factly and wriggled free of his grip.

Randall clenched a handful of her dress and tore it off with one yank. Embarrassed, Gwen quickly sank to her knees and covered her breasts as Randall slammed her to the wall again. "I admit my old man was a fuck-up and my mother was a drunk, but I did what I could to pull myself out of that shit!" he said as his eyes watered. "Did you have to deliver fucking newspapers and goddamn pizzas just so you and your mother could eat? No, you wouldn't know anything about that! You and daddy were too busy deciding whether to have the fucking lobster or steak and what fucking part of the world to have it in!" he said sarcastically.

"You're just jealous that I was close to my father! That he took care of me!" she said.

"All he did was make you a miserable cunt!" he said, equally surprised as she was at his choice of words. Both stared each other down until he warily kissed her moist lips. The onlookers erupted into applause and craned to see the détente. Randall's firm jaw relaxed and his eyes softened. "Reminds me of when we conceived Jessica. Remember? We jumped the fence at the park," he said. Gwen smiled warmly as he loosened his grip on her shoulders, but she abruptly lifted her knee into his crotch. The male spectators gave a collective groan as Randall hunched over in agony.

"You're fired! Do you understand that? I don't want you around. Ever!" she said, climbing the ladder and hurrying away as she covered herself with a nearby towel.

Randall gagged, endeavouring to pull himself up and wandered aimlessly until he grasped the coping and noticed all eyes were upon him. A stupid smile. "Just a little foreplay before the honeymoon," he managed to say with a slightly higher voice.

Chapter Eight

Gwen looked out the tiny window of the sleepy, 18th century English bed and breakfast and gazed upon a line of pear trees at the edge of a small valley. The early morning dew sparkled beneath a low, lingering fog. It cleared for an instant revealing a deer, but it was swiftly obliterated again.

Wearing jeans, a sweatshirt, running shoes and her hair in a ponytail, she checked her look in an antique, floor length mirror and nodded her approval. A slight smile broke across her face as she happily closed her eyes and breathed deep, her olfactory senses heightened with the stuffy smell of breakfast cooking. She grabbed her purse, entered the narrow hallway and noticed the bathroom door was closed at the end of the corridor, steam escaping from the bottom.

The stairs creaking beneath her, she descended into the quaint living room, decorated with more antiquities and the owner's obvious passion for horses. Gwen rounded the corner into the dining room and noticed three place settings. "How are you this morning?" a stout, middle-aged English woman named Mrs. Wickens asked. Wearing an apron, she worked at the stove with her back to Gwen.

"Fine, thank you," Gwen said and sat, eyeing the other plates. "I thought I was the only one here," she added with concern.

Ruddy faced, Mrs. Wickens placed a glass of orange juice before Gwen and a bowl of fruit. A box of cereal was added along with milk, yoghurt, scones, tea and coffee. "A young man came in late last night," she replied and happily resumed cooking bacon, eggs and sausages. "His name is Duncan."

"Oh," Gwen said with relief and surveyed the plethora of food. "I really think you're cooking too much for just three people."

"My late husband ate like a horse. Cooking plenty is a habit I guess. Besides, I want to make sure my customers have a lot of choice," she said proudly and busied herself with some toast. "Now, would you like me to tell you about the things to see around here?"

"I won't have time, actually," Gwen said regretfully. "I'm here to work."

"I won't ask. It's none of my business. If my husband were here, he'd be asking you everything under the sun. He was a nosey man, but a good one," Mrs. Wickens said and barely looked over her shoulder. "Married, dear?"

"Divorced, but I'm seeing someone now. He's Swedish," Gwen said fondly.

"Polite and patient those Swedes," Mrs. Wickens stated casually and fanned herself. "Lord, I wish I had air-conditioning. This house is over two hundred years old. Would you like a broiled tomato?"

"No, thank you," Gwen replied and smiled, admiring the surroundings. "I miss living in the country."

"What part of France are you from?" Mrs. Wickens said and placed a plate of fried potatoes, toast and mushrooms on the table.

"I live in Monaco now, but I'm originally from Paris," Gwen said and studied an array of homemade jams.

"Good morning all," Randall said cheerily, standing in the doorway.

Gwen turned to him, completely surprised as Mrs. Wickens gestured him to the table. "Good morning, Duncan. Breakfast is all ready. Sleep well?"

Randall pulled up a chair and eagerly rubbed his hands together, spying the mountain of food. "Great! Don't get rest like that in the city," he said and filled his plate with fruit and yoghurt.

"Duncan?" Gwen asked perplexed.

"If I'd used my real name, you would have left," he said and bit into a pear.

"You're damn right! What the hell are you doing here?" she whispered.

"Helping my partner," he replied and drank his orange juice.

"Have some bacon and eggs, Duncan," Mrs. Wickens said as she went to load his plate.

"I'd love to but I can't," he said and elbowed Gwen. "Can't drive a racecar with a heavy gut, uh?"

"Do you know each other?" Mrs. Wickens asked with a frown.

"Not anymore!" Gwen said and stormed out.

Randall chased after, pear in hand as Mrs. Wickens just stood there totally bewildered. "Funny, he doesn't sound Swedish," she said to herself.

Chapter Eight

Gwen hurried out of the house and followed the gravel driveway to a black Mercedes 500SL with Randall behind her. "Hell of a car, split lips. Rental?" he asked casually with a mouthful of pear.

Gwen clicked the fob, unlocked the doors and hopped in. "Get away from me!" she said, but Randall ignored her request and climbed into the passenger seat. "Get out!" she barked.

"Nope," he said with a calm smile and took another bite.

"I don't want you around!" she said and inserted the ignition key.

"You need me," he replied as bits of the fruit sprayed from his mouth.

"I never needed you! How the hell did you find me?" she asked.

"I followed you all the way from Milan. Was even on the same flight, but I couldn't afford first class," he said and finished the pear. He wiped his hands clean and buckled himself in. "Ready to go?"

"Where?" she said, completely stunned.

"Five miles from here. Don't bullshit me, split lips... I mean, Gwen. You're going to Silverstone to do some digging during the test session," he said and turned the car on. "These things only work when you start them by the way," he added sarcastically.

"I don't want you involved in this case! Do you understand that?" she said and turned the car off.

A playful roll of his eyes. "Did you tell Jenkins I wasn't going to be testing today?"

Gwen hesitated and finally said. "No... I hadn't figured out how to tell him. But I will! Now get out!"

A knowing grin from Randall. "That means you expected me to show up, which proves you know you need me," he said and turned the engine on again.

Gwen shut it down once more, stepped out, marched to his door and opened it. "Are you going to get out or do I have to drag you out?" she said and rolled up her sleeves.

"Look, I'm sorry about what happened with Carmen, okay?" he said with apologetic eyes.

"That's all you ever say! You screwed up with the reporter, the funeral and at the pool!" she said, counting on her fingers. "Just how many chances am I supposed to give you?" she continued just as a gunshot was heard, the bullet missing Gwen and lodging itself in the door. Both of them turned to see a black BMW with no plates and tinted windows racing towards them.

"Get in!" Randall yelled as he unbuckled himself and slid behind the wheel. Gwen jumped into the passenger seat as another shot shattered the window and sprayed her with glass. Randall hesitated, unaccustomed to the stick shift on the left but quickly slammed the Mercedes into gear and rocketed away as bits of gravel flew in a cloud of dust. "You okay?" he asked, fighting the wheel as he checked the rear-view mirror to discover the BMW was giving chase.

"I think so. You?" she replied and swept away the shards from her body.

"Yeah! Get down!" he ordered. She sunk into the seat just as another blast blew out the back window. "Jesus jumped up Christ!" Randall bellowed and buried the throttle. "How's Jessica's cold?" he asked with his eyes glued to the road.

An odd glance from Gwen. "I don't think this is the time to discuss our daughter!" she replied.

"How is she?" he said angrily and geared up again as the BMW tried to pull alongside, but Randall veered to cut it off.

"Fine! She's fine!" she countered with equal angst.

"There's something I need to tell you," he said and stole a glance at the BMW as it swung to Gwen's side. "My stepfather... did things to me... sexually... until I was thirteen. Keep down!"

Gwen curled into the seat and frowned at the odd confession. "I know," she said.

"I still loved him though... hard to understand why he did what he did... I'd like to hug him one more time, you know? And then I'd like to kick his fucking ass," Randall said and finally buckled himself in. "I think my mom knew... but she was in denial... explains the booze, I guess. Is probably why she worked so hard to help me with the racing after he was murdered."

"Why are you telling me all this now?" she said and attached her own seat belt.

"To let you know that there are reasons... reasons for the way I am... felt guilt... shame... like maybe it was my fault... I was so fucking scared of him... telling you in case we don't make it," he replied sheepishly just as another bullet penetrated the dash.

Gwen bit her lip and considered what to say. "I'm seeing someone. His name is Peter Pettersson," she said awkwardly.

"I know. Swedish, right?" he said calmly and turned down another road, but the BMW continued the chase.

"How did you know that?" she asked with surprise and peeked at her side mirror to see the BMW weaving from side to side, looking for a chance to get closer.

"I heard you tell Mrs. Wickens. Love him?" he asked, barely looking at her. Gwen stared at him for a moment and turned away. "Well?" he added.

"I think so... yes," she said with a tinge of guilt.

Chapter Eight

"Is he good with Jessica? Does she like him?" he said methodically as bullets ripped through the trunk.

"Yes... they get along great," she replied, albeit reluctantly.

"Good... that's good," he said nodding; trying to convince himself as he felt the heat from another bullet as it narrowly missed his head. "Fuck this! I'm starting to get pissed!" he said and steered the Mercedes off the dirt road and smashed through a rotted, wooden fence, entering a wheat field, but the sedan followed anyway. "Where's you fucking gun?" he shouted as he struggled to see in an overwhelming storm of dust and chaff, the sound of crackling shoots almost deafening.

"Uh? Oh, right, right. I'm on it!" she replied, still dazed by the conversation and withdrew the weapon from her purse just as Randall swung the vehicle wildly, causing her to drop it. It bounced and slid under her seat. Her fingers tried to wrest it free but couldn't. "It's stuck!" she cried as another bullet ripped into his headrest.

"Hang on! This might help!" he said and steered hard to the right, the wheels spinning on the moist ground but finally finding traction, spewing earth and wheat shafts.

Gwen struggled to grab the gun, but to no avail. The BMW spun out, but quickly righted itself and followed. "I can't get it!" she complained.

"Where's your goddamned backup?" he shouted as another shot pierced the rear-view window, causing it to explode.

"At the circuit! What the hell do I need protection for?" she replied, continuing to grapple with the trapped weapon.

"Well, you're a fucking target now! Brace yourself!" he said and slammed on the brakes, the Mercedes sliding sideways on the slippery wheat, freeing the pistol.

"Got it!" she yelled and pivoted in her seat to take aim as Randall buried the pedal again. Gwen fired several shots, peppering the BMW's hood.

Randall eyed the warning light, indicating the radiator was sucking in too much debris and sped up a small hill, causing the car to become airborne for an instant before slamming onto a paved road. "There's no fucking place to hide out here!" he groused as he surveyed the countryside for an escape while the BMW gained ground.

Another round blew apart her side-view mirror. "You're the bloody racing driver! Do something!" she shouted as the BMW tagged the Mercedes' rear end.

Randall gave her a surprised look and rammed the car into top gear. "Hold on!" he said with determination as the Mercedes pulled away. Suddenly, Randall jammed the brakes and expertly wheeled the car to the left as the BMW shot past.

"What are you doing?" she asked worriedly as Randall raced towards the BMW and lowered his window.

"Playing a little game of chicken!" he replied as the BMW performed a perfect three sixty and sped towards the Mercedes.

"What?" she said, thoroughly incredulous.

"Get ready! I'm going to pass them on my side!" he yelled as the vehicles rapidly closed the distance.

"Pass on my side! My side!" she said and steadied herself against her door, ready for a shot.

A mere ten feet apart. "Now!" he ordered and drove hard to the right. Gwen fired, blowing out the BMW's rear passenger side window.

Randall checked the rear-view mirror and saw the BMW disappear down the road in a haze of dust as he pulled over to the shoulder. "Did you see anyone?" he asked breathlessly and searched himself for a cigarette.

"No," she replied with a heavy sigh and frantically dug through her purse for her pills. "That was close," she added and held her hands out, but they weren't shaking.

"If they wanted us dead, we would be. They're just trying to scare us," he said and popped a smoke into his mouth with a trembling hand.

"They're doing a good job," she said. They stared at one another for a moment until, simultaneously, Gwen swallowed a few pills and Randall lit the cigarette.

"Who knows we're cops?" he asked and took a heavy drag.

"Carmen, Hesse and Jenkins," she said, fingering a neat bullet hole in the dashboard. "The car rental company is going to be pretty upset. Oh, and the doctor in Monaco," she said as her phone rang. She flipped it open. "Yes? Hi... what did you find out? How much? Really. Anything else? Okay. Keep me posted," she said and hung up.

"I think we can rule the doctor out," Randall replied and stepped out of the car. "What about Carmen and Hesse?"

"Aside from you pissing him off at the pool, he now has majority ownership of the series. As for Hesse, he wanted to start a new series and tried to get Vincenzo to star in it," she said and got out of the car.

"I don't know if that's a strong enough reason," he said, studying the myriad of bullet holes throughout the Mercedes. "Carmen's in first place. Who else have we got?"

"Jenkins and Teresa. Both get insurance money, and I just found out Teresa owes the casino in Monaco about four million dollars and Vincenzo stopped her line of credit, but then again, she doesn't know who we are," Gwen said and knelt to survey the damage to the door.

CHAPTER EIGHT

"And those are just the possible suspects we know about," he said and sat on the hood. "That's why I should keep working with you."

"Don't sit on there," she said in a motherly tone and waved him off.

"Do you really think it's going to make a difference?" he replied and gestured to the many gunshot holes. "Any news on the Caymans or Vincenzo's father's plane crash?"

Gwen shrugged, joined him on the hood and stole a glance at him. "Nothing yet... um... I'm sorry about your stepfather and what happened," she said sincerely.

A nod of appreciation. "Where did you meet him?" he asked quietly without looking at her.

"A party... he's a good man," she said uneasily.

Randall jumped off the hood and tossed her the keys. "He'd better be. Let's go to the track," he said and climbed into the car. Gwen stood there for a second, knowing she had hurt him and slid behind the wheel.

Chapter Nine

The sun hung low in the east, half its sphere hidden behind smeared, crimson clouds. A light mist sprinkled the infield grass and a few hares wandered about aimlessly. Inscrutable fog rolled relentlessly, swirling, rising and descending in an eccentric dance. Silverstone, the home of British motor sport in Northamptonshire, built on a WWII bomber airfield. Stillness. Anticipating a throw back to glory, as a Lancaster should suddenly blast through the heavy air.

Dark, empty grandstands, save the silhouette of a person high in the last row across from the start/finish line. A scope focused on the windows above the pit lane and zoomed in on Gwen entering a room.

Inside one of the luxury suites, a suited Friedrich Hesse poured a cup of black tea and handed it to Julius Carmen, sitting on a couch, wearing faded jeans and a T-shirt, but without the fake beard. "What are you doing here?" Julius asked Gwen with disdain and deliberately sipped his tea too loudly.

"I could ask you the same thing," she replied and strolled to the windows.

"As majority owner in the series, I take great interest in all aspects of the sport," Julius said and snapped his fingers at Friedrich. The German retrieved a plate of various buns, fruit and bagels and held it before Julius as the Russian pondered what to choose. "Actually, I'm also here to do a little skeet shooting with some friends," Julius continued and plucked a bagel from the platter.

"Would you like one?" Friedrich said to Gwen, motioning to the tray.

"If she wants one, let her get it herself!" Julius barked, chewing noisily.

"No, thank you," she said to Friedrich. "Mr. Carmen, I wanted to apologize again for my husband's actions at the pool... and to talk to you about the racing licence."

"Apology not accepted. More sugar," he said to Friedrich and handed him the cup. "You should know Ms. Gaudet, that I spoke to my attorney about this, and he says I don't have to help you at all."

"I told you that this investigation is not to be discussed with anyone!" she replied angrily.

Friedrich gave the cup back to Julius. "Wonderful art, don't you think?" Julius said to Gwen and pointed to a painting of a Lancaster bomber. "I love weaponry. That plane carried sixty-four percent of all the tonnage of the RAF and the RCAF. .303 calibre machine guns. Could rip you in half," he said to her with a menacing smile.

Gwen relaxed into a sofa and crossed her legs. "My father had a lot friends, Mr. Carmen, many in the former Soviet Union. He especially liked Mr. Sydoruk," she said casually. Julius' smirk suddenly vanished. "I'm sure you've heard of him. Former head of the KGB... and your former boss when you were there. Dad would have him to our country estate. I still stay in touch with him. Did you know he has a new job? Seems he probes tax cheats now," she said and helped herself to a cup of tea.

"How is Jessica?" Julius countered. "Just like you, I do my homework, Ms. Gaudet. How is life in Paris? Going to finest clubs and restaurants. Mingling with the rich and famous. Not a bad life for a police officer," he said and spread a healthy dose of cream cheese on his bagel.

"You would be wise to stay out of my personal life," Gwen said quietly with a threatening tone.

"Do you have any idea how much I'm worth, Ms. Gaudet? Over ten billion and I came by it honestly. So I'm not that concerned about threats made by some pompous gendarme," Julius said casually and bit off a large piece.

"Mr. Hesse, would you excuse us please?" Gwen said with a smile.

Nervous, Friedrich hesitated and looked to Julius who waved him out. "It's okay, Friedrich. This won't take very long," Julius said. Friedrich nodded politely to Gwen and tripped over his own feet as he hurriedly left the room. Julius took another bite and daintily dabbed his mouth with a napkin. "You'll have to excuse Friedrich. Poor man has never been with a woman. I think he might be homosexual, actually," he said to her, totally unconcerned as he sat back and drank his tea.

Gwen rubbed her aching forehead. "You're giving me a migraine. Please, just do us all a favour and give me the licence," she said, slowly sauntering towards him and downing a couple of pills.

"If this is your lame attempt at police brutality or coercion, I'll have your badge," he replied confidently and stuffed the last piece of the bagel into his mouth.

Gwen promptly leaned down, grabbed him by the testicles and squeezed, causing him to stand. "I'm only going to ask you one more time, are you going to give me the licence?" she asked calmly and twisted his scrotum as Julius winced. He clenched his teeth as bits of bagel oozed from his mouth and he vigorously nodded his approval. "Pleasure doing business with you," she said and released him. He collapsed to his knees. "If anyone asks, Jenkins wanted the licence, and if you're thinking of giving him a hard time, don't. He knows who I am and he's been instructed to tell me everything," she said and opened the door. "And one more thing, if you tell anyone else what's going on, I'll see to it that you're a permanent soprano. Understood?" Another nod and Gwen casually walked out of the room.

Friedrich cautiously entered and assisted Julius to his feet. "We need her out of the way!" Julius said angrily and limped to the couch.

Inside another opulent suite, decorated with numerous photographs of racing cars and WWII aircraft, Randall stood staring at a pair of crisp, white, Team Jenkins racing overalls, hanging in a clear plastic bag on the door. He slowly raised one hand, barely touched it and stepped back. He felt his jugular and found himself breathing harder as sweat began to form upon his forehead. "When she comes in, just tell her you're too fucking scared... no... just tell her you don't feel well. Shit! Tell her the truth... you just don't think you're good enough," he quietly said and ran his fingers through his perspiration soaked hair.

He withdrew the tattered photograph of Jessica and kissed it. "I never got to teach you much, but be careful what you ask for Jess... you just might get it," he said and tucked the picture back inside his denim pocket. Randall suddenly opened the bag and his fingers felt the tight weave of the Hispania Gold emblem on the front before stroking the uniform's epaulettes. "Remember these, Vince? Last time I saw them they were smouldering... but your hands pulled me out of that hell... makes you wonder what the fuck I'm doing here, doesn't it?" he whispered and suppressed a gag. "I haven't got the guts anymore... old man used to say I was a pussy. Hell of a thing to say to a kid, but maybe he was right. Ain't got the skill.... getting old fucks up your courage. Damnit! I need a smoke!" he said and fumbled through his coat until he found the packet. Empty.

Randall angrily threw it aside as his nervous eyes spotted a vending machine at the end of the corridor. He scrambled through his jeans and found some change, but it wasn't enough. Randall hastily pulled away the cushions on a couch and loveseat and found some coins. A satisfied smile. "Never fails," he said and hurried down the hall, his cowboy boots echoing

Chapter Nine

off the tiled floor. He inserted the coins, but realized he was still short. "Son-of-a-bitch!" he said too loudly and looked around to ensure he was alone. Randall smashed the glass with his elbow and grabbed a packet as the money dispenser released and spilled change into the tray. After quick deliberation, he swiped the coins, took another pack and swept the shards under the machine with his foot.

He entered the suite again, closed the door and locked it. He opened one of the packs and tried to light one, but his hands were shaking badly and he accidentally snapped the tobacco in half. "I could use a drink!" he barked and caught a glimpse of a liquor cabinet with various bottles. Randall opened the door and grabbed a bottle of scotch. He twisted the cap off and brought the bottle to his trembling lips, but stopped. "Sorry Gwen... sorry Jessica... sorry Vince," he whispered and took a swig as he gazed out the window at the pit lane below. "Used to be a stone cold bastard! Drove with balls! Loved to scare the shit out of the other guys," he said and grinned, remembering. "Christ, they were terrified. Could see it in their eyes," he said and studied his reflection in the glass. "But now... I'd just be out there making noise... body's been too abused... not enough sleep... too much booze... dead heart... and hooked on sin," he lamented and took another gulp, the cure-all spilling out the corners of his mouth. A heavy sigh of appeasement and he wiped his mouth with his sleeve.

Randall's eyes dropped to examine his shaking, scarred hands and he closed his eyes. "Can still smell my own skin melting," he said as his stomach churned and he swallowed, trying not to vomit. "You know what you're more scared of, Randall? Looking like a fucking idiot!" he said and felt his mouth beginning to fill with saliva as his heart rate doubled.

He dropped the bottle, scrambled into the bathroom, knelt down and violently regurgitated into the toilet. Mustering strength, he dragged himself up and turned on the coldwater tap. "Goddamnit!" he complained as he splashed the water across his hot face. There was a light knocking at the door.

"Randall, are you okay?" Gwen's soft voice asked.

"Fine, fine. Just taking one last piss," he replied nervously and cleaned his mouth. Randall flushed the toilet, checked himself once more and opened the suite door for her.

"You look pale. Are you sure you're all right?" she said and felt his forehead, noticing the spilled bottle of scotch lying on the carpet.

"Feel great," he said with a dumb smile.

Gwen pointed to the photograph of Jessica inside his breast pocket. "She would have been proud of you... and I would have been proud of you," she said, kicking at the bottle and eying the shattered vending machine. "But you'll never change," she said in a monotone voice and marched for the door.

"Fuck!" he whispered, scolding himself for not hiding the scotch. "Getting shot at today was easier than this," he mumbled to himself. "I threw it up anyway," he pleaded with a nervous chuckle, but he kept going. "I'm sorry, Gwen, but I can't do it... I haven't got the balls. I thought I did but I don't."

"That's the first thing you've said that's true," she replied.

Offended, Randall rushed ahead of her, slammed the door and blocked her path. "I'm sorry, okay?"

"Fine," she replied with a careless shrug. "Could you please get out of the way?"

"Why no argument?" he asked, full of curiosity.

"Because I don't care anymore. I knew you'd back out. You're all talk Randall and I'm sick and tired of doing this with you," she said and opened the door.

"What about Jessica?" he said.

"If you want to see her, that's fine. I won't call Wallace. You're off the hook," she said as she started down the hall.

"I don't want to see her... I never wanted to see her," he said, replete with shame as Gwen stopped and turned to him, a confused look upon her face. Randall leaned against the doorframe with his head down. "My old man was an alcoholic... and so am I... they say that kind of abuse goes from one generation to the next," he said quietly, thoroughly embarrassed.

"You're not the type," she replied confidently. "I was never concerned about that."

Irate, Randall slammed his fist against the wall. "Goddamnit! Quit being so fucking understanding! The least you could do is yell at me! I let you down!" he shouted.

"I've kept tabs on you since we were divorced, you know," she said and inched towards him. "Do you know why I got you involved in all this? It wasn't just because I needed your help; I was also hoping to *help* you... give you a reason to live. I thought it might lead you back to your daughter," she said.

"And to you?" he asked hopefully and abashed.

"There is no *us*, Randall. I love him and that's all there is to it. You're just going to have to accept that," she said.

"What does this Peter guy do?" he asked.

"He's a yacht designer."

"I guess he's perfect," he said with an air of jealousy. "Must be nice to be a man without fear," Randall said sardonically and disappeared around the corner into the suite. He began to gather his things when she suddenly appeared in the doorway.

"He's afraid of the water. Can't swim," she said.

Randall hesitated. "Really?" he said, surprised by the confession. "At least the man's smart enough to listen to his fears."

"Tell me something, what used to be the best thing about being a cop for you?" she inquired. Randall crashed down onto the sofa and took a moment as Gwen stepped inside the suite and closed the door. "It's just us, Randall. Be honest."

"Sounds fucked up but... there was a sense of satisfaction... being able to enforce the law... protect people... doing something good in this fucked world," he said shyly.

"You can still do all those things," she said and sat beside him.

"If I do this... what happens when it's all over? I mean... about you and me," he asked, avoiding her stare.

"You go back to doing what you do best, being a police officer and so do I. And you do that with the knowledge that your daughter loves you and you will always get to see her whenever you want," she replied and took his hand. "It's an offer you can't refuse," she added with a smile and gave him a pat on the back.

Randall exhaled deeply. "You got your people around the perimeter of this place, right?"

"Don't worry, I've got you covered. We even have some extra sets of eyes. Jenkins always videotapes his test sessions so if something happens, we'll catch it. By the way, Carmen's giving you the licence," she said, happy Randall had changed his mind.

"Let me guess, you grabbed him by the balls," he said sarcastically.

"I don't work that way," she replied with a simper and checked her watch. "Come on, get dressed. We're late."

Randall watched her as she was about to close the door and said. "Hey, split lips? If something does happen... my cat... would you?" he said uncomfortably, she simply nodded. "When you go through my stuff, there's some letters... letters I wrote to my old man after he was gone... put them with me."

"I will," she said softly.

"Anything else of value is for you and Jessica. Make sure you guys get the pension and insurance. It's not much, but I want you to have it," he said with his head lowered.

Gwen nodded again. "I'll be in the hall when you're ready," she said and closed the door behind her.

Randall stood and glanced out the window. "Feel like I'm waiting for a fucking stay of execution... blindfold and last cigarette," he said with a jittery laugh and cracked his knuckles. "Ready to join the world's fastest soap opera?" he asked himself as he coolly tried to snap his fingers but, his skin was too moist from nerves. Another weighty sigh and he began to undress.

Leaning heavily against his cane, Samuel plodded along the empty pit lane and constantly glanced over his shoulder at the closed, garage doors as he held a cell phone tight to his ear. "Please.... you have to understand... I... I'm not trying to," Samuel pleaded and looked behind him again to ensure privacy. "I realize... yes sir... but I'll get it... I... I just need a little more time... please, I'm begging you... please... Mr. Vladin? Mr. Vladin? Hello?" Samuel said and listened to the line go dead. He reluctantly tucked the phone away.

"Oh God... oh God," he mumbled, shaking his head in despair and carefully sitting on the guardrail as his milky eyes found their way skyward. "Can you hear me, Aki?" he whispered in a breaking voice. "I... I need your help... I hope you can forgive me for what I did," he said as tears spilled from his eyes. "I just couldn't watch you suffer anymore... it was the only way to set you free from the hurt... and me," he said and sniffed as he wiped his eyes with his sleeve. "Remember you used to tell me that suffering has a cause... that we suffer because we're struggling to survive?" he said quietly and licked his arid lips as he rested his weary head against the top of the cane. "I'm scared Aki... I don't know if I can go on... if you can help me in any way," he said and suddenly sensed he was not alone.

"Seems the empire of the sun is setting, isn't it Sammy?" Felipe said with a smirk, standing against the garage wall with a Cuban dangling from his mouth. He removed his red handkerchief and pretended to dab some tears. "It's always touching when the elderly finally realize their own mortality... whether they're helped into the great beyond or not," he said with a wink, placing one foot on the rail and spit-polishing his leather shoe with the silk. "You know Sammy, when I was at Salamanca University, that's where I met Laurie," he said condescendingly and began working on the other foot. "I could never understand why she studied world religions. People know deep down why they're better than others, and yet we're supposed to treat everyone equally. Never made sense to me," he said with a shrug and stuffed the handkerchief into his breast pocket. "Doesn't matter what God you pray to, religion only upsets the natural balance of things. The strongest will always survive. That's why Laurie Gold needed to marry me, so I could take control of her life. It was good advice then and it is now."

CHAPTER NINE

Samuel battled to his feet. "It's my team and it's going to stay that way!" he barked, snatching the cigar out of Felipe's mouth and tossing it aside. "There's no smoking in the pit lane!"

Felipe suddenly kicked the cane out from under him and Samuel stumbled to one knee. Felipe stooped to help him for the benefit of anyone watching, but actually prevented him from rising. "You're a weak man, Sammy. I don't care what you did to your wife. I'm only concerned with what you've done with the living... and I'll give you twelve million reasons," he said and bent Samuel's fingers back making the old man wince. "I suggest you get used to taking orders, not giving them. I'm sure it's hard to cope with losing, but it's over," Felipe whispered with a menacing grin and suddenly hauled Samuel to his feet. "So, where is this racing prodigy?" Felipe said and dusted the old man off.

"He... he'll be here," Samuel replied, void of breath and visibly shaken by Felipe's actions and words. Samuel quickly hobbled back towards the garage. "Excuse me... I... I have some work to do."

Felipe followed and wrapped his arm around him, eyeing their deserted surroundings. "Life is like racing, Sammy, you either give the pressure or you're getting it and eventually, people don't care anymore and the race of life is over," he said, gesturing to the dark grandstands.

"I... I said I'd sign, but after you see how Grange tests," Samuel said as he spied Felipe's hand with its plethora of diamond rings.

"My wealth entitles me to say and do whatever I choose, Sammy. You'd do well to remember that," Felipe said and dug his nails hard into Samuel's shoulder, causing the old man to grimace. "It's going to be my team soon and you're just a relic with nothing but dreams."

Samuel stopped and turned to him. "Felipe... please," he said with rheumy eyes.

"You'll call me Mr. Suarez," Felipe replied coldly as he buffed his rings against Samuel's jacket.

Samuel shifted with his cane and frowned at the sudden demand of formality. "Mr. Suarez... you have to understand... if I lose this team, I'll have nothing to do... it's everything to me... it gives me a reason to live," Samuel whispered, replete with emotion as his eyes filled again.

Felipe withdrew the same handkerchief and dried Samuel's eyes. "Scared to die, Sammy? Don't worry, I'm sure we can find a janitor's job for you," Felipe said and slapped him on the back just as Julius and Friedrich appeared from around the corner. "Gentlemen, what are you doing here?" Felipe asked with surprise, happily shaking their hands as Samuel tried to compose himself.

"Zdravstvuite," Julius said with a mild salute. "Mr. Jenkins wants this Randall Grange character, but he has to prove he's worthy of a licence and

I'm here to make sure this dog can hunt," he said sarcastically, pretending to shoot a rifle.

Wanting to change the subject, Samuel cleared his throat and motioned to the luxury suites above the pit lane. "Gentlemen, the session's being taped so you can watch it from up there... I'm sure you'd be much more comfortable and I've arranged for some champagne with your brunch," he said with a forced smile.

"Thank you Mr. Jenkins, but Mr. Carmen has already had a bagel," Friedrich said with a grin.

"Friedrich, what have I said to you about being seen and not heard?" Julius snapped, giving his subordinate a scolding glance. "It's like dealing with a boy," he said to the others.

"I am not a child Mr. Carmen!" Friedrich shouted.

"Then stop acting like one!" Julius said. Embarrassed, he turned to Felipe and Samuel. "You'll have to excuse Friedrich, he was raised in a poor family with two brothers and three sisters so he's used to speaking out of turn. I guess he needs the attention," he said with a chuckle.

"Speaking up is common in a democracy, but you wouldn't know that, would you? Not all of us were born Marxists," Friedrich shot back, his face flushed and his fists clenched.

Surprised by the outburst, Julius leaned towards Friedrich and whispered. "That will be enough!"

"The only reason you bought into the series was to bring a race to Russia. To show the poor what the rich can do at their expense! Well those of us that didn't come from money have as much pride, if not more, than the likes of you!" Friedrich said and marched off.

"Don't worry about him, he just needs to find a good man," Julius said laughing, and demonstrated with a weak wrist, but was clearly concerned with his second in command's diatribe.

There were a few moments of uneasy silence until Felipe motioned to the stairs. "Shall we?" he said. The men pivoted and started up the steps. Felipe looked to Samuel and tapped his half million-dollar watch. "The clock never lies Sammy, he better be something special. On second thought, I don't care how well he does. I want Alberto Americo and that's all there is to it."

"But what about Grange?" Samuel said, completely panic stricken.

"That's another good thing about money, it allows me to change my mind," Felipe said and stifled a yawn as he ascended the steps. "But let him test. It'll give me something to watch while I drink your cheap champagne."

Samuel waited until he was gone, looked to the heavens again and closed his eyes. "Please Aki... my entire career... my life depends upon

Chapter Nine

Grange... please, make him good," he said as the garage door opened. Ichiro and the mechanics began setting up their gear beside two covered racers until they heard the sound of thumping blades, causing all eyes to turn upward as Braedon's private helicopter descended upon the infield.

Randall and Gwen followed a darkened corridor with light beaming from one end, leading to the pit lane. Shuffling along, he became hypnotized by the sound of her running shoes, squeaking against the polished floor. His wide eyes trained on the dozens of photographs of racing cars, dating back to the early sixties. A few pictures revealed smiling champions; Ayrton Senna, Michael Schumacher and Jacques Villeneuve. Other photos depicted drivers in the throe of battle; wheel to wheel approaching a corner, some line-astern in a blur of speed, others spinning off in the wet and several making contact as shards of debris exploded into the air.

Randall felt his heart palpitate as they passed a door with a red cross on it, indicating the infirmary. He stopped and stared. "Are you okay?" she asked after noticing he wasn't keeping pace. Randall clutched his chest and began to hyperventilate as Gwen tried to open the hospital door, but it was locked. She immediately scrambled through her purse; found a credit card and jimmied it open.

Inside, she frantically searched through the various cupboards and cabinets until she found a white paper bag and carelessly spilled the contents onto the counter. She handed it to Randall and he loosely covered his nose and mouth. "Breath in and out ten times!" she said anxiously as he complied. Gwen helped him to a stool and rubbed his back as his breathing slowly returned to normal. "It's okay, it's okay," she whispered. "How do you feel?" she asked after a few seconds.

"Like a fucking amateur... sorry," he managed to say and tiredly hung his head. "Shit! Haven't had that feeling in a while... is like staring death in the face every time you get behind the wheel of one of those goddamn things," he said and lazily gestured to a racing car photo on the wall. "Dancing with the devil... sooner or later he's going to beat your ass."

"Try to think about something else," she said, turning to a small sink and filling a paper cup with water.

Randall thought for a moment as Gwen handed him the drink. "Was eight the first time I ever hyperventilated. Old man told me to get him a beer... slipped on the hardwood floor and dropped it... seemed so loud when it smashed... beat the fucking shit out of me," he said with a chortle. "And then... you know," he said as his face darkened with shame and he looked away. "I think that's the very moment I wanted to be a cop. Your dad ever hit you?" he asked. She shook her head even though he wasn't looking. "Good people have bad sides, Gwen... but evil people... fuck... there's only one side and it's all black," he whispered knowingly as his eyes drifted off. "No hope for those bastards... fascinating though... maybe that's the real reason we're cops... not all that serve and protect bullshit."

"I'm learning more about you now than I did when we were married," she said with a light smile to mitigate his troubled stroll down memory lane.

"Had a lot more to lose back then... lost it anyway, didn't I?" he said.

"Listen Randall, what we're doing is noble whether you want to admit it or not," she said and soaked a cloth with cold water. "We've all had our battles to get where we are. When I signed up, there weren't too many female officers around. The chances of getting promoted were slim. Most of them quit. Even the media was biased against us. But it was important to me to be a part of the solution... and that applies to you too," she said and pressed the cold compress against his burning forehead.

Studious, Randall stared at her until he made a clicking noise as he sucked his teeth. "How big is he?" he asked.

"Who?" she said with a frown.

"Peter," he replied and drank with nervous hands.

"I don't know... about six four," she replied and titled his head back so the pad would stay.

"His dick. How big is his dick?" Randall asked impatiently and drained the cup.

"What? Why the hell do you want to know that?" she said, beginning to blush and busying herself by wiping the sink with a paper towel.

"You told me to think about something else. How big is he?" he said and unzipped the upper half of his sweaty uniform and tied the ends around his waist.

"Try again," she said and stole a glance at him. "Politics or something."

"He must be big," Randall said to himself with a jealous shrug. "Why politics?"

"I don't know... I've actually thought I might run for office someday... maybe make up for what my father did. You know, kind of clear the family name," she said and popped a few pills in her mouth. "Are you okay now?"

Randall rolled his head to limber his neck muscles, causing a crackling sound. "Feel like a gladiator going into the ring. You're better as a cop than a politician," he said.

"How would you know?" she asked, mildly offended.

Chapter Nine

"You're full of shit, split lips, but not that full of shit," he casually remarked and stood.

Gwen pushed him back down onto the stool. "Now wait just a second. I think I'd make a pretty good public servant!"

"According to you, that's what we do now," he said, spying a bottle of rubbing alcohol in the cabinet and licking his lips. "But don't get your panties in a knot over it."

"Cops enforce the law, but in office I can write the law and even change it for the better. People complain about it, but don't want to be involved!" she barked.

"What the fuck is this, your campaign speech?" he asked sarcastically and rose again. "I'm about to go get myself killed in a racing car, and you're on your soapbox."

"You're just like everybody else! You don't give a damn, and when someone wants to make things better, you just put them down!" she said and stormed past him into the hallway.

Perplexed, Randall followed and closed the door behind him. "What the hell's the matter with you? Is this that whole 'my father fucked up' thing again?"

Gwen pivoted to confront him, but suddenly resumed her march. "You should talk! Forget it!" she said.

"There's no shame in wanting power. You're a cop. All cops like the rush," he said.

"You don't get it, do you?"

"Hey, we're all going to end up in the same place. Dead. Hopefully it won't be for me in the next little while," he said and glanced at a clock on the wall over the doors leading to the pits. "Don't matter what you do on the way," he said. "As long as you have a good time and don't fuck up too much."

"Then I guess you've done it half right," she countered as she reached for the door handle.

Randall ignored the comment and held her back. "What are you going to be doing while I'm out there getting killed?" he asked sardonically.

A tired sigh. "Playing the concerned wife and keeping a sharp eye on everybody. I know what to look for."

"And that is?"

"Anything out of the ordinary," she said and went to open the door, but he closed it.

"I think you'll make a great politician and I think your pop would be proud of you," he said.

She couldn't help but smile. "I know you're lying, but thanks... and I... well... I want you to know that I appreciate what you're doing... and... and... you know," she said, promptly embarrassed.

"Don't worry, I'll be careful," he said knowingly.

Gwen leaned forward and planted a kiss on his forehead, her warm lips electric to the touch. "That one's from Jessica," she said and kissed him again, "and that one's from me."

"Got a smoke?" he said. She smiled once more and shook her head. "Then how about a drink?" Gwen opened the door and playfully pushed him through as she took his hand and they stepped into the garage.

The mechanics instantly stopped working and eyed him with ridicule, followed by a few unkind whispers. Ichiro Tanaka just stared at them without expression before adjusting his blue-rimmed glasses and consulting his clipboard.

High in the grandstand, the scope followed Randall and Gwen as they drew closer to Samuel.

"Where the hell have you been?" Samuel complained as he stamped his cane, causing more chortling from the crew.

Randall focused on the mechanics. "Since you guys are too fucking ugly to get laid, I assume you're good at one thing. When I tell you what's wrong with the car, I expect you to shut up and listen. Got it?" he said as the mechanics' faces sobered and they returned to their duties.

Gwen nudged Randall, surprised by his brief outburst. "What are you doing?" she whispered. "Remember, flies and sugar."

"This ain't the time for practicing your politics," he said quietly out the corner of his mouth. "I know how these fucking computer geeks think. They're smart but like cattle. Besides, if I piss the right one off, we just might find the killer. Be cool and follow my lead. It's time to stir up the shit."

"I don't like my drivers to be abrasive, Mr. Grange. It's bad for team spirit," Samuel said, hobbling closer.

"Just earning their respect," Randall shot back with a salute.

"By chastising them?" Samuel said and indicated to Randall's untidy racing overalls. "And I want my drivers to look professional at all times. That goes for language too," he said as the crew tried to stifle their laughter.

"I don't take any bullshit, *sir*," Randall said as Gwen rolled her eyes, full of embarrassment. "They might prepare the car, but I'm the one driving it," Randall countered and slipped into the uniform.

Samuel motioned Randall closer and zipped up his uniform for him. "I was raised in a middle class family. I grew up with the most foul-mouthed

Chapter Nine

people on earth, but my mother ensured that I spoke with civility and restraint. You'll do the same."

Ichiro was uncomfortable with the standoff and buried himself in a comic book as the rest of the mechanics happily looked on. After a long sigh, Randall placed his hands on his hips. "Well, my old lady was usually too pissed out of her head to care and some nights I went to bed with an empty fucking stomach. I even ate pages from the good book just to stop from puking, so don't tell me about manners."

Disconcerted, Samuel eyed Gwen and the crew before taking a moment to gain his composure. "All I'm saying is that racing is a team sport, and you must work hard and cooperate to get what you want," Samuel said and gestured to the team members. "Take the cover off." The men obliged and pulled off one of the silk, team coloured tarps.

Randall's eyes immediately lit up and he could feel the hairs upon his body suddenly stand up as a chill flashed through his bones. The gold and white, rakish vehicle wasn't just a marvel of engineering; it was a work of art. Illusion. A sleeping monster. Lightning fast though still.

Randall slowly circled the machine in utter awe, delicately stroking the sleek carbon fibre of the rear wing and smiling boyishly. "Jesus," he whispered beneath his breath and felt his throat tighten, close to joyful tears. "Beautiful... absolutely goddamned beautiful."

"Almost nine hundred horsepower packed into a three litre, V10 engine. At two hundred miles per hour, it covers one of your football fields in one second," Braedon said, suddenly appearing from the shadows. "Mess with this machine and it will definitely mess with you. Braedon Stirling," he added, half-heartedly extending his hand to Randall.

"I... I'm Randall Grange," Randall said, trying to pretend he wasn't star struck and caught a brief glance of the 'Provo' tattoo on the champion's right hand.

"I know who you are. Mr. Jenkins just told me he thinks you're worthy of a test. I disagree, but I'm not the one signing the paycheques, am I? Follow me," Braedon said curtly as the crew snickered. Deflated, Randall gave a perplexed look to Gwen and followed.

In the grandstand, the scope steadied on Braedon as he led Randall around the corner of the building. "Bang! You're dead," an indistinguishable voice whispered.

"Protestant or Catholic?" Braedon asked while surveying some heavy clouds in the distance.

"Catholic, but I don't give a shit," Randall said casually and curiously spied the sky.

"Why not?" Braedon asked with concern.

"What is this, fucking Sunday school? It's none of your goddamn business," Randall replied.

"A no name like you must have some powerful connections to get a ride. God works in mysterious ways," Braedon said and leaned against the wall with crossed arms. "Let's get something straight right off the top, coffin pilots have to earn their seats. There's about twenty-five men in other series that probably have more talent in their willies than you do in your entire body. So the question is, who did you blow to get this chance?"

"What do you care how I got the reigns?" Randall said, scratched his testicles and spat.

Braedon strolled to Randall and jabbed a finger into his chest, nearly knocking him off balance. "I do care when some snot-nosed rookie could ruin my reputation and I'm not about to throw it away on some moving chicane. If you want to drive Vincenzo's car, that's between you and Samuel, but stay out of my way!"

Randall pushed Braedon's hand aside. "Just like with Vince, you're afraid of a little competition. But me, I'm like the girl with curl. I'm really fucking good when I'm good and I'm terrible when someone pisses me off," he said with a cocksure smile and a glimmer in his eyes as he snapped his fingers.

Braedon laughed and shook his head in disbelief. "Typical American. Big mouth but nothing to back it up."

"First of all, I'm a Canadian you dumb fuck, and I'll do my talking on the track," Randall said, poking his finger into Braedon's chest and meandering away. "Better get used to looking at the back of my ass, potato-head."

Braedon's grin evaporated and his face soured. "Hey, rookie," he said. Randall pivoted to face him. "I'm the best driver in the world and the team revolves around me," he said, pointing to himself. "You're just a satellite and all I'm here to do is teach you the basics of the car and bring you up to speed, not to pamper your green hole. I don't give a damn whether you put it in the hedge or not," he said and gesticulated to the crew. "By the way, the boys are taking bets on how soon your brain cramps and you put it in the kitty litter. Personally, my money is on your first lap," Braedon added and purposely bumped into him as he walked towards the garage.

"I noticed the tattoo," Randall said as he dug a finger in one ear. "What are you, a wannabe terrorist?"

Braedon froze and looked over his shoulder. "What did you say?" he asked in a threatening tone.

Randall inched towards him. "I suppose racing a car is better than blowing one up, eh?"

Braedon's lips trembled with rage and his eyes fluttered. "You don't know a thing about my life! About my family! My politics! Our fight! My father died a noble death at the hands of the British!"

"Mine was murdered, but you don't see me painting shit all over my body. Get over it," Randall said coldly.

Braedon took a step closer. "Apologize!" he whispered through gritted teeth.

"Fuck you, IRA boy," Randall replied coolly. "Let me guess, you were an asshole when you were a kid but you excuse it with religion, oppression and all that other meaningless shit. Well guess what? You're still an asshole, but now you don't have a reason."

"And how did your old man die?" Braedon asked condescendingly, trying to maintain his temper.

"Someone shot him in the back. Dead before he hit the floor," Randall answered uninterested.

"Mine died from hunger," Braedon stated proudly. "He refused to eat to protest against the British bastards! Sacrificing one's life for a belief is honourable."

"That's a real tearjerker," Randall said sarcastically and sniffed, pretending he was crying. He went to walk away but Braedon grabbed his arm and spun him around.

"Men like you have no idea what it's like to suffer!" Braedon said and clamped Randall's hands. "Soft skin, Grange. It says a lot. What's your story anyway? Racing is just a hobby to guys like you. Are you bringing money to the ride?" he asked, full of suspicion.

Randall laughed and broke his hands free from Braedon's grip. "The only coin I got is in my street clothes. I got a wife and kid to feed and this is a chance to step up. I plan on making the most of it," Randall said. "Even a clover fucker like you should be able to understand that."

"You don't know anything about these machines, do you?" Braedon said with a disparaging laugh.

"I know enough to make you look bad," Randall said and breathed on his fingers before polishing them against his chest. "I'm a nobody, remember? But you're the world champ. Wouldn't look too good if I was better than you, eh? Man, you could go from hero to zero pretty fucking quick," he continued and laughed.

"I'm not worried," Braedon replied confidently, but was obviously weighing the dire ramifications of Randall's words. "I've been around engines since I was a boy. I went on a co-op at Jenkins' dealership and learned everything there is to know before I was sixteen. I've earned this ride with guts and brains," Braedon said vainly. "I doubt you did."

"Old man bought me a go-kart when I was seven," Randall said, uncomfortable at the recollection. "He bought it for the wrong reasons... but I drove it anyway." Braedon frowned at the odd answer and Randall noticed. "One question, superstar," Randall said, changing the subject for his own benefit. "If you hate the British so much, what the fuck is an Irishman doing driving for one?"

"Samuel may be a Saxon, but he's a decent man. And it doesn't hurt that he needs an Irishman to prove it. Come on rookie, let's see if your old man's money was well spent," Braedon answered and swaggered off.

"Guy's asshole is tighter than a snare drum," Randall said to himself and followed.

Samuel glanced impatiently at his watch as Randall and Braedon reappeared. "I was late by less than a minute once at the POW camp for role call. I was given a boiling colonic. Punctuality, gentlemen. It's the cornerstone of any good business," Samuel said as everyone gave him a confused look. "Now, if the two of you are finished, I'd like to get started. This track time isn't free and we only have it for today," he said and leaned closer to Gwen. "I would think I should be reimbursed for some, if not all of the money for this expense."

Gwen stared at him for a second with furrowed brow and took him aside. "I know you're nervous Mr. Jenkins, but can I make a suggestion?" she whispered, Samuel invited her idea with his eyes. "You need a woman on this crew. Seriously, it would help the tension. That's why female police officers are some of the best. We draw on life experience. We're more nurturing, and we set a good example for the male ego," she said to Samuel's astonishment.

"I run my operation the way I see fit. Male or female, nothing in life is for free and the fairer sex deserves no more or less respect than the other. Now, as for the money this track time is costing, will you reimburse me?" Samuel said and banged his cane against the ground.

Gwen didn't bother looking at him, still stinging by his remarks and replied. "You said yourself this was a previously scheduled testing session. But look at it this way, at least you don't have to pay Randall."

"What if he wrecks the car? Who pays for that?" Samuel groused and tapped the racer's tyre with his cane.

"I might be able to arrange something, but on one condition, you cooperate fully. Understood?" she said. "Push me too far and the deal's off."

"Fair enough," Samuel said and turned to the crew as he clapped his hands together. "All right everybody, let's get busy. We have a lot of work to do this morning."

Randall pulled on his balaclava. "I don't have a helmet," he said sheepishly.

"Give him yours," Samuel said to Braedon.

"What?" Braedon answered dumbfounded and whisked Samuel aside. "You know that's taboo!" he whispered.

"For God's sake Braedon, the man doesn't have lice! It's just for this session," Samuel barked.

Braedon pursed his lips in anger, walked into the garage and retrieved his helmet. He shoved it into Randall's stomach. "This is worth more than you've probably made in your entire life. Be careful." Randall wrenched it on and instantly felt cumbersome, as his neck muscles weren't as strong as they used to be. He waited until he gained ballast and lifted a leg into the cockpit, but tripped over the chassis. "Bloody great! He's already had an accident," Braedon said deliberately loud as members of the crew began to laugh.

Gwen glared at the men. "At least he's got the guts to get in it!" she snapped, the mechanics collectively looked away.

Randall smiled at her and winked. "That's my split lips," he said, thankful nobody could see his flushed face beneath the headgear as he stepped into the seat with both feet and slid into the cramped compartment. He immediately wriggled around, trying to get comfortable. "Goddamn tight!" he whispered to himself.

"Don't worry about the seat right now. We'll have a new one custom made for the contours of your body. For the moment, we just want to see what you can do. Belts please," Samuel said to Ichiro with a wave of his cane.

Ichiro hesitated, leaned over Randall and firmly pulled the shoulder, lap and leg belts, all meeting in a buckle. "Can you breathe, Grange?" Ichiro asked shyly.

Randall winced; his body locked into place and felt the straps digging into his uniform. "Barely," he said and offered his awkward handshake. "Call me Randall."

Ichiro ignored the physical platitude and bowed slightly. "I am Ichiro Tanaka. I am... I was Vincenzo's engineer," he said.

"Nice to meet you," Randall said, still struggling to breathe and studying the diminutive Asian's, blonde hair. "What's with the do?" he asked. Embarrassed, Ichiro pushed his glasses up and lowered his eyes. "No worries bud. Looks good on you, but don't try too hard to fit in with those fuckers," Randall said and pointed to the mechanics, earning a smile from Ichiro. "You like to drink?" Randall asked, pulling on his racing gloves with suede palms for grip as Ichiro nodded. "Right on. We'll be great friends," he said, bowed his head and offered him his handshake again. "Now will you call me Randall?" he said.

Another broad smile from Ichiro and he heartily shook Randall's hand. "Yes, Randall," Ichiro said happily.

"Good. By the way, I knew what Vince was like. Not much of a people person, but you obviously did a good job with him. Takes a great race engineer to make a driver better," Randall said.

"Azzopardi was a difficult man to work with... but he was a gifted athlete," Ichiro replied uncomfortably as his comic book fell from beneath his clipboard into Randall's lap.

Randall examined the Superman comic and casually flipped through the pages. "You like this stuff, eh? I used to steal them when I was a kid. Couldn't afford to buy them. You poor when you were little?"

"I do not think so. My father was a fisherman. We always had food on the table," Ichiro said with pride.

"I bet you worked on your dad's boat, eh?" Randall asked knowingly.

"I did. How did you know that?" Ichiro replied curiously.

"You're a race engineer. You must have had an interest in mechanical things," Randall said as Ichiro realized the obvious deduction. "First time I jerked off was to Lois Lane," Randall said with a grin and pointed to her before turning the page. "I'd love to be him. Imagine how powerful your cock would be," he said and handed the magazine back to him. "Could cum right through concrete." Embarrassed, Ichiro hastily replaced the booklet beneath his other papers as Randall stretched his fingers, one by one. "Do you believe in karma?" he asked.

Ichiro frowned at the odd question and shrugged. "Just because I am Japanese, does not mean I practice Buddhism," he replied, overly defensive.

"I do. Vince could be a real asshole. Pissed off a lot of people, including me. Son-of-a-bitch cut me off more than a few times. You know the old saying, what goes around, comes around. Hate to admit it, but maybe he got what he deserved," Randall said and rolled his head.

"It was just an accident. Those things happen in racing," Ichiro said, scribbling some notes on his clipboard, trying to seem busy.

"Everything happens for a reason Itchy... Ich... what the fuck's your name again?" Randall said.

"Ichiro!" he replied with a hint of anger. Randall shot him a crisp salute just as Samuel drew near.

"Before we go any further, I need you to sign something, Randall," Samuel said and withdrew a piece of paper.

Gwen quickly stepped forward. "What is that?"

Samuel handed her the document. "It's a contract stating Randall will not divulge information about the car when the session is completed. It's standard procedure," he said. She scanned the two-page missive and handed it to Randall with a pen. Randall scratched his name and Samuel folded it before placing it back inside his jacket. "He's all yours," Samuel said to Braedon and looked to Randall again. "Try and remember that this is a million-dollar piece of equipment you're driving and mistakes can cost you your life," Samuel added.

Gwen knelt down to Randall and offered a nervous smile. "You look good in that uniform. I never told you this but I used to look at your old racing photographs. Believe it or not, they used to turn me on," she said with a girlish smile.

"I used to bang you in your sleep. But this isn't the time to give me a hard-on. There's no fucking room," he replied boastfully and returned the smile.

"Be careful and good luck," she said and kissed her finger before pressing it against where his mouth was beneath the helmet.

Randall winked, eyeing the faces of Felipe Suarez, Julius Carmen and Friedrich Hesse watching intently from above in the luxury suite. "You too," he replied and watched her accompany Samuel into the building.

Braedon sat on the monocoque. "It's not often the wives hang around at a testing session," he said suspiciously. "I never allow my wife to attend. A bug eater has to remain focused at all times."

"What's your problem, not getting your dink wet?" Randall replied. "I can see why Mrs. Stirling doesn't come, that dazzling personality of yours is just too fucking much."

"As a good Catholic, I don't appreciate your choice of words," Braedon said angrily and blessed himself.

"Well, I'm a bad Catholic so go fuck yourself," Randall said and held up his fingers. "And while you're at it, peel this."

"I attend church on a regular basis! The least you could do is respect my beliefs!" Braedon said, completely flustered. "A gentleman would!"

"Tell me something, were you an altar boy?" Randall inquired calmly.

"Yes! Why?" Braedon responded, aware his face was beginning to glow in anger.

Randall leaned his head closer and waved Braedon near. "I used to go. Only thing I remember is how many fucking ceiling tiles there were. Counted them every goddamned week. Bet you have lots of memories. You can tell me, did the good Father ever feel you up? You know, give you a little wine and a poke in the bum? Did you like it?" he whispered gleefully.

Braedon broke into a broad smile. "I know what you're trying to do. Drivers that haven't got the courage or the talent usually bark the loudest. You can't beat me Grange, but I know you'll beat yourself," he said.

"I've watched you. You play too nice with the curbs. That's why Vince was better than you and would have become champion. If he was still bending the wheel, you would have been nothing but an 'also ran'," Randall said with piercing eyes.

"We'll never know, will we? I know he saved you in Toronto, but the man's dead. If I were you, I'd be concerned with who'll save you now," Braedon replied with a sinister glance. "Only your race craft and God will decide... maybe."

Randall stared at him for a moment, searching for any hint of complicity in Vincenzo's demise. "Now that we've exchanged pleasantries, are you going to tell me about this thing or waste more time chatting about pussy and talent?" Randall asked.

"I admire your family jewels, just don't beach them on the curbs," Braedon said and attached the steering wheel. "Remember, the maximum steering lock of this is reached in a half-turn. The wheel is the heart of the car. It's your friend, not your enemy."

"I do have *some* experience," Randall shot back.

"Let me tell you something, driving this thing through a chicane is like trying to thread a needle at two hundred miles per hour. Listen to me and you just might survive. Now, I know you drove in the Atlantic series, but there's a few things you haven't experienced before," Braedon said and indicated to the tyres. "This machine has traction control so you can go deeper into the corners, but the brakes are carbon fibre and they stop the car quicker than you're used to. They heat up to one thousand degrees Celsius pretty fast so be careful she doesn't snap out under braking. These things can rip the spine right out of you," he said and pointed to the various buttons and toggle switches. "This one is the fuel mixture, this adjusts programs on the display panel, this one is the throttle switch, the gearbox in neutral button, drink button, flashing gear shifting lights, pit lane speed limiter, main battery switch and rear warning light for rain," Braedon said purposely fast to confuse and intimidate. "That's gear program, clutch program, electronic brake balance, electronic limited-slip differential, power steering adjustment, function selector and this one is error, revs, speed, gear, lap time and temperature display," Braedon said as Randall eyes fluttered, trying to grasp the puzzle of buttons. "That's radio, this paddle on the left is for down changing gears and the paddle on the right is for changing up. There's the hand clutch control and the skip info display. Remember, the *N* button marks the site of the electrical outlet. It switches off all the electrical systems preventing a spark from igniting. The *E* indicates the fire extinguisher. Push that and it discharges into the cockpit and the engine. There's more but we'll cover it later. Got it?" Braedon said. Bewildered, Randall stared at the maze of technology, his eyes slowly moved to the *E* button.

"Remember pushing that fucking thing in Toronto... fire was too much... hoped I never had to see that again," Randall said, lost in thought.

Another wide grin from Braedon. "I know. I reviewed that tape. That's what you get for cutting people off," he said with a sneer.

A sharp glance from Randall. "Like you did with Vince in Monaco? Tell me you never had an accident."

"I haven't. Ever," Braedon replied full of pride and made a zero with his fingers.

"Then you're not driving hard enough," Randall countered.

"If you don't believe in the car, you won't drive it to the max. I know when to push and when to back off. That's the difference between you and me. That's why I'm the world champion and you never will be," Braedon said and waited for a response, but none was forthcoming. "Now, if our little pissing contest is over, I'd like to talk about the car set-up," he added, impersonating Randall's earlier attitude.

"The floor is yours, superstar," Randall replied, staring straight ahead, knowing he was trumped and dabbed some burning sweat from the bridge of his nose.

"Overheating already, are we?" Braedon asked deliberately.

"Just get on with it!" Randall snapped.

"Good. We've put in more down force than usual for this circuit so you can get accustomed to the vehicle. We don't want you to overdrive this thing," Braedon said, explaining with his hands and stood.

"Dial it out," Randall said casually, haphazardly motioning with his fingers.

"What?" Braedon replied, thoroughly surprised.

"I want it in race trim," Randall said, checking the positioning of the mirrors.

"Use your head and leave some meat on the tyres. Just do an exploration lap," Braedon suggested.

"Do you want this to be a fair test or not? Look, I was known for having fast hands, okay? If they can keep my wife satisfied, they can sure as hell handle this pig," Randall said confidently.

Braedon waited, privately debating Randall's request and scoffed before gesturing to the crew to start making the necessary changes.

"Feeling racy, are we? Well, if you want to lay on your sword, that's your business... and funeral," Braedon said.

In the luxury suite, Gwen watched Randall and Braedon from the window as the others picked at the trays of food. Despite the bartender, Felipe uncorked a bottle of champagne, startling Gwen. He sauntered to her with a glass, filled it and gave it to her. "It concerns me to see such a beautiful woman worrying about her husband. My name is Felipe Suarez. I'm the sponsor," he said with lascivious eyes.

"Gwen Grange," she said and smiled politely.

Felipe sat on the capacious windowsill and crossed his legs, eyeing Randall. "Do you think he's talented enough? I've always said women inherently know the truth... the question is, will they speak it?"

Gwen downed the entire glass and held it out for a refill. "Only when they're happy with the man they're with," she replied with a wink.

Intrigued, he gladly replenished her glass and purposely spilled some on her breasts. She had to catch her breath, taken aback by the sudden cold liquid, seeping through her clothes. "I'm so sorry," he said disingenuously. "May I?" he asked, withdrawing his red handkerchief to soak it up. Gwen gave him a flirtatious nod and he delicately sponged it away. "So, *are* you happy with the man you're with?" he asked and topped up his own glass.

"You have a wife and baby, don't you?" she said with a coquettish look.

"Yes, but that doesn't mean a man's life is over. Perhaps your husband feels the same," he said gamesomely and slid closer to her.

"Maybe you should find another hobby. One that keeps your fidelity intact," she said and shifted a few inches away from him.

"I have many. History for example. Especially, Spanish history," he replied and moved closer still.

"Anything else?" she asked and went to slide further away, but realized the wall was in her way.

"Taking what isn't mine," he said with a salacious smile. "And your hobbies are?"

"I collect fine art and I like gardening," she said and took another sip. Felipe immediately filled her crystal again.

"Who is your favourite painter?" he asked and seductively ran his finger around the rim of his glass.

"Robert Bateman," she said and stood.

"Very good. It shows you like the wild, untamed side of life," he said and rose to demonstrate his chivalry.

"It's been nice chatting with you," she said endearingly, looking over her shoulder at him and strutting away as he licked his lips.

CHAPTER NINE

"Perhaps you should focus your energy on the right Grange," Samuel said, promptly appearing behind him.

Felipe remained entranced by Gwen as she conversed with Julius and Friedrich. "What do you know about Mrs. Grange?" Felipe said with a hint of suspicion without taking his eyes off her.

"That's she married... which ought to be enough," Samuel said and grunted as he sat on the windowsill.

"I'm never full and she's next," Felipe replied with a sneer and took a healthy sip before scowling. "Cheap champagne, Sammy, very cheap."

"I wasn't born into wealth, Felipe. One learns to make do with what one has," Samuel said and gazed out the window. "I'll wager you never had to wear the shoes of man that died of hunger in front of you."

"Your war stories are getting tiring, Sammy," Felipe said with a bored sigh. "I think you've received all the sympathy you'll ever get. Besides, you've done pretty well for yourself. Although not as well as me," he said and stroked his beard. "But if it makes you feel any better, my mother told me she never loved me. She was nothing but a high priced whore. I'm sure yours wasn't like that."

"If that's true, it doesn't seem to affect you. By the way, I always liked your mother," he said to deliberately agitate him, steadied himself against his cane and stood.

"You were the only one," Felipe answered with disgust and quickly walked away.

The crew finished their adjustments and drew back, except Ichiro. Braedon circled a finger in the air and the Asian fired the engine. Randall felt the rumble dissipate throughout his body and found himself wearing a candy-eaten grin. "Damn fine," he whispered to himself. "Fucking art in motion."

Braedon hurried into the garage and stood before a row of computer screens, including a video feed. He attached a headset. "Can you hear me?" he asked.

Randall scanned the buttons, found the radio and pushed it. "Five by Five."

"Well that's one thing he's done right," Braedon said to the sanguine mechanics. "Okay rookie, the car is basically set up for actual qualifying conditions. It's fuelled for your out lap, hot lap, and in lap. Bombs away," he said and withdrew his wallet from inside his tweed jacket. He gleefully opened it and retrieved a few notes. Braedon waved them in the air, enticing the men. "Ten pounds says he eats the wall before the end of pit lane."

Randall slanted his head to Braedon and saw the mocking wager and flipped him the finger. He dropped the clutch and slammed the throttle. The wheels screamed, creating a gigantic cloud of smoke that swallowed the crew. The car temporarily remained static until the engine's momentum kicked in and the racer noisily departed in a staccato racket. Randall grinned checking his right mirror, watching the team members cough and wave their hands to clear the choking haze.

Randall geared up and felt the back end twitch. "Easy girl, easy," he whispered to the machine. Another gear. The car hugged the curve exiting pit lane and entered the circuit as Braedon raised an eyebrow, impressed Randall didn't spin out.

The racer neared the challenging, high-speed curves leading to Maggotts and Becketts as Randall changed up another gear. He felt the machine flinch, the rear wanting to wash away again, but he corrected and geared up once more.

Randall rocketed down the Hangar Straight, the G-forces pushing his head; muscles distending, hands tight on the wheel and an increased heart rate. Despite the vibration, his eyes focused on the bobbling horizon as the ribbon of asphalt slipped away, approaching the swift, right-hander at Stowe's Corner.

Braedon watched the video monitor closely. "Stowe's usually separates the men from the boys. The first time I did it, I actually soiled my knickers," he mused as the crew laughed.

Randall down shifted, crashed the curb and hastily straightened the car as it sped towards the slow left-hander at Club Corner. "Fuck you, Dad! I made it to the big leagues!" Randall whispered proudly through gritted teeth. Incredibly hard on the brakes as the sweat flew off his face and splattered his visor. "Holy Christ!" he managed to say. "Asshole was right! This fucking thing stops on a dime!" he said, feeling the blood rushing to his forehead, making him dizzy.

The racer flashed through the chicane with slight wheel spin, but the grinding sound of the traction control activated and the machine glided smoothly onto the next straight, heading for the tricky lefts at Priory. "No fear! No fear!" he advised himself as his innate skills to control mechanical mayhem came flooding back. "Attack the pavement! Attack the pavement!" he chanted to himself with bated breath, his lightning fast reflexes in perfect symmetry with his eyes as his head moved with the turn.

Gwen stood at the back of the room with Samuel and withdrew a small radio. "Okay everyone. Keep your eyes open," she whispered to her spotters.

Chapter Nine

"He's old style, brakes late and early at the apex," Samuel said proudly and loud enough for the others to hear. "Haven't seen anyone adapt so quickly since we were POWs."

"Not bad... so far," Felipe replied with a twinkle in his eyes, his attention glued to the monitor. "The last time I saw a sure thing, his business crumbled. Right, Sammy?" he said, looking over his shoulder at Samuel as the old man's overindulgence quickly disappeared.

Gwen stared briefly at Samuel trying to interpret the odd remark from Felipe and stepped forward. "What do you think now, Mr. Carmen?" Gwen said happily.

"Decent, but hardly convincing. The lap isn't done yet," Julius said. Gwen glanced at Friedrich who nodded his approval of Randall's performance and indicated his disgust with his superior by rolling his eyes.

In the pit lane, Braedon studied Randall on the monitor as he manoeuvred through the twisty bits at Luffield. "I'll be damned," he whispered and looked at the equally impressed crew, "Beginner's luck," he said to dampen their enthusiasm. "The right-hander at Copse is fast and lethal. He'll get too greedy with the curve and it'll catch him out. You wait, the back end is about to become the front end," he said and forced a smile, trying to reassure himself, more than the others.

In the grandstand, the scope followed Randall as he piloted the car past the start/finish line, the dust and sparks flying from the plank beneath the car. "An accident waiting to happen," the voice whispered.

Inside the cockpit, Randall felt the wicked bumps and heard the slamming of the undercarriage. The hot lap began. "Fucking clock is the enemy!" Randall shouted to himself. "I'm back!"

The slight incline at Copse; a blind apex and fourth gear turn at one hundred forty miles per hour nearly caught him off guard and he found himself holding his breath, but his hands expertly snatched the wheel as the car bounced over the curb, literally rattling his fillings. Back on the black stuff again, heading for the fast, second and third gear, left and right at Maggotts and Becketts again.

Braedon looked to the myriad of monitors and stared in disbelief. "That can't be right," he said completely stupefied. "There must be something wrong with the transponder."

"His first sector is only a tenth off last year's pole... your pole," Ichiro said, not believing it himself, but was delighted to say. "It did not take him long to find the sweet spot."

Braedon could feel his face redden but he was too amazed. "God this guy is fast... too fast," he lamented with a hint of jealousy.

Down the Hangar Straight again. Sixth gear. One hundred eighty-five miles per hour. The force pushed Randall's helmet against the headrest as the lap belts flapped wildly in the breeze. Randall shifted down to third approaching Stowe's for a second time. The car slid over the rumble strips as he slammed it into fourth and neared one hundred miles per hour, accelerating towards Club Corner. Tunnel vision. His peripheral sight smeared as grass, buildings and sky flashed by in a blur of speed.

Smoke billowed from the rear tyres as Randall slammed on the anchors, the red-hot brakes glowing as he down shifted to second. The car jumped the serrated curve and touched the road again, pointing for the one hundred ninety mile per hour, Farm Straight.

"Make nice with the corners Randall or you'll flat spot the tyres. Those things are black gold," Braedon said and turned to Ichiro. "I knew this guy would be all over the place like a rally car," he added smugly.

"Second sector is just two, one thousands of a second slower than last year. He is within spitting distance of your record lap time," Ichiro said, spying the monitor with a raised eyebrow.

Braedon could hardly believe his ears and fought to keep himself from displaying his wonderment. "This rookie is either the greatest career that never was or he's a complete maniac. And maniacs usually end up in pieces."

It happened. The rear wing sheared off and sailed through the air until gravity sucked it hard into the pavement and it exploded into pieces. Randall didn't realize it for a few seconds, but it was too late. The back end started to wiggle and he pressed the brakes with all his might as the car became snaky and uncontrollable. The wheels locked, but the racer was still launching itself down the road at one hundred seventy miles per hour. Steering was recalcitrant and shimmied. Randall was suddenly aware his fingers were clenching the wheel with every bit of strength he could muster and his breathing became laboured as he desperately shifted down. The abrupt bleeding of velocity forced the machine into a violent three hundred sixty degree spin. He wanted to close his eyes but dared not as he tried to pilot the missile away from the rapidly oncoming Bridge at the end of the Farm Straight. Time slowed. The world became mute, save his own, frantic greed for oxygen.

Engulfed in a cloud of dust and smoke, Randall's racer continued its death spin and careened towards the concrete underpass. Instinct kicked in as he fought the wheel to at least hit the wall backwards and save his legs. Time was up. Like all racing drivers, he let go of the steering wheel and crossed his hands across his chest and tucked his head down, a universal manoeuvre to spare a man's vital organs in an imminent crash. A mere passenger. The machine barely caught the left side of the Bridge and there was a huge bang. The normally tethered wheels flew off and the car severed into two pieces. The cockpit forward remained intact but began to roll, violently twisting and coiling as it bounced along the road.

Randall closed his eyes and waited for the insane ride to end or the ultimate funereal, price to pay. The heavy rear of the car scrapped along for a few hundred feet, but subsided as fluids and debris scattered in a fiery trail behind it.

Gwen watched the monitor with horror filled eyes. Her hands lifted to her mouth and she bolted out of the room.

Samuel sank into a nearby couch and lowered his head, resting it against the handle of his cane. Felipe casually strolled by and sampled some of the pastries on the table. "Looks like an early shower for him, doesn't it?" he said to Samuel with a mouthful of food. "There's no room in a racing car for the mind to wander," he added and began to chuckle.

Suddenly, Samuel jumped to his feet and slammed his cane across Felipe's throat, pressing him to the wall. "The man could be dead, damn you!" Samuel shouted, saliva spraying from his tremulous mouth as Julius and Friedrich looked on in stunned silence. "You don't know what it's like to see a man perish in front of you, do you? Well I saw hundreds!" he yelled as Felipe tried to wrestle free, his face reddening. Samuel forced Felipe's head to the television screen. "Take a good look! That's what death looks like! At least have the courage to see it!"

Julius and Friedrich pulled Samuel away as Felipe gasped for air until he gained his faculties. "Well, that was a waste of time," Felipe said, surprisingly calmly, and straightened himself. "I'm having a dinner party tonight Sammy, but drop by around nine and we'll discuss me and Alberto taking over the seats. It's obviously not going to be Mr. Grange and if you're thinking of fighting me on it, I have two witnesses," he whispered and indicated to Julius and Friedrich. "By the way Sammy, my mother used to hit me harder than that," he said with a grin and hurried out.

"Are you okay?" Friedrich asked and helped Samuel to the couch. Samuel nodded and patted his damp forehead.

"I have a few words of wisdom for you Samuel," Julius said. "When I finished my schooling, firms around the world wanted my talents, but I remained disciplined and stayed loyal to my country and my family," he boasted. "It was that kind of self-control that helped me get to where I am today. Remember that if you can," he said and slapped Samuel hard on the back. "I hope your man's all right. I really do." Julius snapped his fingers. Friedrich immediately opened the door for him and they both disappeared.

Seconds later, Friedrich poked his head back inside the room. "For what it's worth, Mr. Jenkins... I would have done the same thing."

"You would?" Samuel inquired wearily, although not really interested in the response.

Friedrich slipped inside and nervously peered out the door. "I know everyone believes I'm weak and mild. It's because I like nature and playing the violin and things like that," he said with an abashed smile, "but I always stand up for what I believe in. You did right."

"Friedrich!" Julius' voice bellowed from down the hall. Friedrich waved to Samuel and closed the door behind him.

Ichiro shifted his gaze from the screen to the floor, knowing something internecine had happened, familiar with the sickening feeling of helplessness when a driver fights to maintain his vehicle and his life. He flipped open his comic book to see Superman about to be crushed by a villain and clutched his stomach as Braedon noticed.

"Something you ate?" Braedon said removing his headset, knowing Ichiro was upset.

"The stomach is the centre of emotion," Ichiro said, suddenly saddened. "I hope Randall is okay."

"*Randall*? I thought you only called your friends by their first name?" Braedon said with a hint of jealousy.

"He *is* my friend," Ichiro replied and polished his glasses against his shirt. "People do not need a lifetime. It can take only a second."

Braedon rolled his eyes, shrugged, checked his watch and yawned. "What did I tell you? Pieces," he said and motioned to the carnage on the monitor to purposely aggravate him. "My work here is done. Scrap him off the road. I have some serious testing to do."

"Does it not bother you?" Ichiro asked, lamenting the accident on the screen.

"I'm the most important person in my life and as long as it isn't my intestines on the track, I can't care," Braedon said nonchalantly and sauntered away. "Sure looks like the old man's boy bit off more than he could chew, uh? Talk about a baptism by fire," Braedon added happily.

Randall forced himself to open his eyes and bristled, realizing he was upside down and slanted to the left. "Hurry... please hurry... don't let me burn... hurry," he mumbled and heard sirens in the distance. He could smell the rich mixture of oil and fuel, but more insidious, he detected smoke. Nearing unconsciousness, Randall saw a sliver of green earth and

CHAPTER NINE

noticed a dazed, baby hare caught in a mesh of carbon fibre. He used all his strength as he tore at the debris to free the screeching animal. "Know what it's like to be in a bad place... old man used to lock me in a closet... and then fuck me over," he said breathlessly and finally managed to untangle the rabbit. It moved closer and pressed its nose against his glove. "You're welcome," Randall groaned. "Now get the fuck out of here before your ass burns." The creature promptly turned and scampered away.

Randall's trembling fingers unzipped the upper half of his uniform as the photograph of Jessica fell out. He struggled to reach it but couldn't, its edges beginning to smoulder and curl. Randall gazed upward. Blackness. "No pain... not yet... in shock I guess," he said to himself and felt a burning in his throat. He pressed the belt release, but remained trapped. "Don't panic... just don't panic," he said tiredly as his eyes began to roll back. The acrid smoke grew larger and darker as his thoughts revolved around drowning in a sea of flames, the encroaching crackling of fire was now clearly audible. "I can't hang on Gwen... I can't," he whispered and slipped away.

In the grandstand, the silhouette of someone hastily gathered a bag and ran for the exit.

Chapter Ten

The sun beamed through the fine, lace curtains and flooded the small room with visible rays of light. A few people whispered off to the side, the carpeted floor creaking beneath their best shoes. Sorrowful organ music played softly in the background and the frequent ting of a bell indicated another visitor. Several, uniformed police officers slowly entered and nodded to the others they recognized. Tony D'Angelo sat in the corner weeping and reading the bible as he rocked and chanted quietly to himself. Conversing with another officer, Staff Sergeant Hank Wallace gave Randall's open casket a disparaging glance, rolled his eyes in a mocking manner and shook his head with disgust.

Gwen stood a few feet away, sickened by the overarching aroma of flowers, permeating the cool air. Dressed in black, she held Jessica's tiny hand as they both stared at Randall. Gwen gave her a motherly smile and pushed her wheelchair closer to the coffin. They both blessed themselves before silently speaking a prayer. Gwen leaned over, kissed Randall on the forehead and escorted Jessica away as the child strained to look over her shoulder, trying to freeze the moment in her memory.

At the far end of the room, another man, wearing a dark, wool suit with a neat hole in the back and a plain tie, stood scowling at the coffin. He lumbered apace towards the casket, his stark, white face with black circles beneath extreme bloodshot eyes coming into focus. As he marched nearer, he smiled wide revealing stained teeth and began to giggle, blood spilling from his cruel mouth. Randall's stepfather's glare moved to the right and he suddenly grabbed Randall's crotch.

"Fuck!" Randall shouted and sat bolt upright on the gurney inside Silverstone's hospital room. He glanced around and saw a stout but muscular, balding man of forty-five with thick glasses looking over him as Gwen nervously sat on the edge of a chair.

Chapter Ten

"Well, he's not paralysed," Doctor Grammond said to nobody in particular. "How do you feel?" he asked and immediately used a penlight to examine Randall's eyes.

"Dead," Randall replied with a groan and slowly rested back down again. "How long was I out?"

"A couple of minutes," Doctor Grammond said and tucked the light in the pocket of his jacket.

"Shit, Tequila's done worse than that," Randall said boldly to alleviate his own anxiety and cracked his knuckles. "After a couple of shots it's the best feeling in the world. Makes you forget all the bad stuff," he said, looking at his leathery hands and suddenly became sombre as he slowly turned to Gwen. "But it makes you forget the good stuff too."

"How many?" Doctor Grammond asked, thoroughly disinterested in Randall's words and holding two fingers in the air.

"Two," Randall answered tiredly.

"Do you know what day it is?" the physician inquired, covering the date on the face of his watch.

"Saturday," Randall said as the doctor attached his stethoscope and listened to Randall's heart.

"Be still, please," Doctor Grammond ordered as his eyes rose to the ceiling. "Do you remember what happened?" he asked and proceeded to check Randall's blood pressure.

"Gee, I was trying to change the radio station. What the fuck do you think happened? I crashed," Randall said and checked his emotions after Gwen gave him an unfavourable glance. "Felt like the rear wing came off... tried to control it... then I was upside down," Randall said and saw Gwen's concerned face. "Holy shit that was a close one, eh? Goddamned tank-slapper," he said with a laugh to ease her frazzled nerves as she popped a few pills before taking his hand and squeezing it. "It's okay... I'm still here," Randall said reassuringly to her.

"Well, no broken bones and a slight concussion," Doctor Grammond said dutifully, writing in his clipboard. "Chest sounds a little heavy. Do you smoke?"

"Only to excess," Randall said wryly and winced at the arrows of pain piercing through his body.

"Blood pressure's a little high too, but I'm sure your little accident has a lot to do with that. Take it easy for a few days. If you start getting headaches, feel dizzy, nauseous or start slurring, you get to a hospital right away. All in all, you're a very lucky man," Doctor Grammond said and placed the paper he was writing on in a file folder.

Wearing only his briefs, Randall swung his feet over the side of the table and grimaced. "I don't feel too fucking lucky."

"I see you have quite a bit of scar tissue on your hands," Doctor Grammond said and opened a filing cabinet.

"That's what you get for playing with fire," Randall jokingly remarked, but realized nobody thought it was funny. "Was a racing accident," he said with a bored sigh.

"I noticed the abrasions on your forearms too," the doctor said. "They look like razor blade scars," he said, continuing to flip through the manila folders.

"They are. Courtesy of my stepfather," Randall said and blew a kiss to his memory. "He was a hell of a guy."

"He did that to you?" Doctor Grammond said with surprise and turned to him, peering over his glasses.

"No, I did it, but then again, doctors don't really give a fuck about shit like that, do they?" Randall said and stifled a yawn.

"Randall!" Gwen said, shaking her head to stop him and holding a finger to her mouth.

"I'm afraid I don't understand," Doctor Grammond said after giving her a brief glance. He put the folder in the cabinet and let it roll closed before sitting on a stool, enthralled with what Randall would say. "Tell me about it."

"Don't get too comfortable, doc. I don't care much for your kind...or these kinds of rooms," Randall said, surveying the medical equipment. He flinched, reaching for his denim jacket.

"Why not? We only want to help," Doctor Grammond replied, thoroughly confused.

Randall paused for a second and rolled his eyes impatiently. "I used to get hurt on purpose to try and convince our doctor that I was... that things were happening. Fucker never believed me. Said it was self-inflicted to get attention. Believed my piece of shit old man before he'd believe me," Randall said casually and withdrew his cigarettes.

"There's no smoking in here," Doctor Grammond said, totally intrigued by the conversation and crossed his arms.

Randall lit the tobacco and threw the active match at him. "Fuck you," he said as the physician barely dodged it.

Doctor Grammond swallowed hard and nervously rose to his feet. "Um... there's help available out there if you want it... I know some excellent people," he said, removing his glasses and looking to Gwen for her support. "My brother is a very good psychiatrist."

"Sibling rivalry's a bitch, eh doc? Consider yourself blessed; you're not as fucked up as he is. Shrinks," Randall said to himself in disgust and shook his head. "More screwed up than the patients," he said and purposely blew smoke at Dr. Grammond. "Is that it, medicine man?"

CHAPTER TEN

"Um... I... I guess. Just soak in a nice hot bath and get some rest," Doctor Grammond said uncomfortably and turned to Gwen. "Keep an eye on him and wake him up every few hours tonight. He's going to be pretty sore for a few days, but he should be okay. Give him some of these muscle relaxants if he needs them," he said and gave her a bottle of pills from inside his coat. "And I wouldn't race for a while if I were you, Mr. Grange."

"Is that an order or an opinion?" Randall questioned and spat some bits of tobacco from his mouth.

"It shouldn't matter," Gwen said sternly, stepping forward.

"It's not an order. You can do whatever you wish but... but it would be best if you didn't for a week or two. Well... good luck," Doctor Grammond said timidly, still dislocated and quickly stepping out of the room as Randall gritted his teeth, struggling to slip his shirt on over his lightly bruised chest.

"A little over the top, Randall. You didn't have to take it out on him," Gwen said and helped him with the garment. "He was only trying to help."

"Bullshit. To them we're nothing but fucking guinea pigs. When they can't diagnose you or fuck you up with drugs, they send you to a shrink. Never been and never going to," he said and fought to button his shirt as she helped him.

"Maybe you should... you know, see a specialist," Gwen suggested awkwardly as a distant crack of thunder echoed.

"A little late for that, don't you think? If you're fucked up past twenty, there ain't no cure," he said and grabbed his dungarees. "Permanently damaged goods," he added as more of an afterthought.

Gwen gazed out the window and nervously cleared her throat. "I did... after the accident. I never told you because... because," she said with a deep breath, "because it's hard to love and hate someone at the same time... but it helped me... with you, with Jessica... with what my father had done."

Randall was taken aback by her confession and whistled his astonishment. "Well I'll be goddamned, split lips," he said with a snicker and grunted as he stepped into one trouser leg. "You brought out the best in me, but I brought out the worst in you and you're the one that was heading for the bubble wrap. Didn't show."

"You never took the time to notice," she said and followed a raindrop down the window with her finger.

"Let's not start this shit again. I've had enough trouble for one day," he said and stuck the other leg in.

173

"I think we should end this thing," she said as a wicked streak of lightning flashed and temporarily flickered the lights.

"What do you mean?" he replied, slightly winded as he struggled to yank on one cowboy boot.

Gwen closed her eyes, rested her head against the glass and tugged at her moist hands. "I'm going to be honest with you... I had feelings today that I haven't had in a long time... ones that I thought I'd forgotten... it was like in the beginning when we were together... even though I was a cop too... I always wondered if you'd come home."

"Hey, I'm alive," he said, waving his hand before pulling on the other boot with the cigarette dangling from his mouth.

"If something happens to you because of all this... it would be my fault... and I can't live with that, Randall," she said and turned to him. "So I'm giving you a chance to get out."

"I'm in too deep now. Whoever iced Vince has to answer for it and today is a pretty good indication that I'm not wanted... and that's precisely why I'm going to stay," he said, crushing out the smoke in a plastic kidney tray and sitting on the stretcher again.

"I thought it was just a mechanical failure," she said with a raised eyebrow.

"It was no accident," he said with determination and lit another cigarette.

"How do you know?" she asked inquisitively and leaned against the counter.

"The worst things that can happen in a racing car are pretty rare. One, the throttle sticks, two, no brakes, or three, a wing comes off," he said, counting on his fingers. "I got door number three."

"We must be getting close," she said and handed him the blackened picture of Jessica from inside her jacket.

"It also means it was someone with access to the car," he said and tried to clean the charred photograph.

"True, but it doesn't explain The Rabbit," she said and went to zip up his open fly, but promptly became flustered, realizing her actions and stopped. "By the way, we turned up nothing about Rabowitz's banking, friends or family and the Israelis aren't talking. Who knows, maybe he did the hit for free, if it was even him."

"We said it was probably a conspiracy," he said as he zipped up. "Maybe whoever hired him capped his ass to keep him quiet."

"Possible, but there has to be more to this than nicking Jenkins for money," she replied.

"Would be enough for me. Maybe it is that simple," he said and coughed. "Didn't your people see anything?" She shook her head. "Then

CHAPTER TEN

what the fuck were they doing out there, chasing bunnies?" he asked angrily.

"They were trying! Why are you so mad?" she asked.

"I usually am when people try to kill me!" he barked and scowled at the sudden, sharp ache in his back and sank down onto the gurney again. "And I'm going to nail the fucker!"

"I appreciate that, but I can't let you do it. It's too risky," she replied as another boom of thunder was heard, followed by leaden rain.

"You've been willing to risk my life all along and now you're punting me off? What's the real reason?" he said and turned up the tattered collar on his coat.

"I don't want to be responsible for your death!" she shouted and slammed her fist atop a stainless steel table, causing the instruments to clang.

"It's no crime to admit that you still love me," he said with a smirk, blowing a smoke circle and touching it at the top, forming a brief heart shape before it dissipated.

"It's not what you think! It's not what you want it to be! Damnit Randall, I'm not in love with you anymore, but that doesn't mean I don't care about you! It's selfish as hell but when you crashed today, all I could think about was the guilt I'd be burdened with for the rest of my life!" she yelled and sat again with her head in her hands.

"It was just a little shunt," he said, stung by her honesty.

"You could have been killed!" she quickly replied, staring at him.

"When you push a car to the limits, there's bound to be some mistakes... it's a part of the game," he said unconvincingly and waved away her concerns. "If you don't crash, spin out or fuck up once in a while, you're not trying hard enough."

"You're the one who thinks it was sabotaged and they'll do it again. No... I have to work this alone," she said, nodding to persuade herself.

"What about that black BMW this morning? Do you think they're going to give up? You need help for Christ's sake," he said and lifted himself off the table with obvious pain.

"I'll call in reinforcements. I might even ask to be removed from the case... for Jessica's sake... and I know you can't argue with that," she said and stood.

Randall exhaled some smoke and watched it drift upward. "You're right... but I'm going to be selfish too. You don't know what it's like to be told you're nothing but a piece of shit when you were a kid... he never had anything good to say about me... and if you hear it enough times, you start to believe it," he said, hypnotized by the cigarette. "Hell, it even gets to the point where you wake up every day just to exist... and the phone doesn't ring because nobody gives a fuck about you... to know that you're not worth anything... to walk around like... like a zombie," he said, easing to the window and barely catching his rain-blurred reflection. "Putting in time... so you end up looking at life through the bottom of a glass," he said shamefully. "Vince's death made me appreciate life again... and if you stop now... I *am* nothing again... please, don't do that to me."

"Do you hear yourself? This isn't even about a murder case for you anymore! It's about fulfilling your dreams of competing at this level! Chasing dreams of glory, and you can't! You said so yourself... and I'm sorry I forced you to," she said and marched for the door.

"I was wrong! I'm still fast and I proved it out there today, and I can help you at the same time," he said in desperation.

"Maybe so, but the price is too high... I'm sorry," Gwen said and opened the door to discover Samuel and Braedon.

"How is he?" Samuel asked and hobbled into the room, despite Gwen trying to block his path.

"He'll be okay," Gwen said as Braedon remained brooding in the doorway.

"Up until the crash, he knocked a thousandth of a second off Braedon's time from last year," Samuel said excitedly and stared at Randall in awe.

"He's a daredevil and reckless as hell. Dangerous in fact, and racing is dangerous enough as it is," Braedon countered, glaring at Randall. "And you owe me a new helmet," he said, holding the paint-scraped headgear.

Randall dug into his trousers and threw a fistful of change at Braedon. It bounced off his chest and rained noisily to the floor. "There you go Mr. Terrorist. Put it towards some dynamite, potato-head," Randall said.

Braedon went to charge at him. Instinctively, Gwen reached inside her jacket for her revolver, but caught herself as Samuel stepped in Braedon's way and corralled the champion's hands behind his back. "A little manoeuvre they taught us in basic," Samuel said short of breath, struggling to hold Braedon back.

Randall sniffed at the air. "Mmm... I smell racecar driver burning."

"Now, now, boys will be boys. Braedon, what if you had someone of Randall's calibre as a team-mate?" Samuel asked.

The world champion inherently understood the implicit remark and could hardly believe his ears as his mouth dropped open in stunned silence. "My mother forced me to go to school with Protestants so I could learn to live with them! Understand them!" Braedon whispered, easily freeing himself from the old man's grip as his upper lip trembled with rage. "My father was against it! He said you were all the same! I thought you were different, Samuel... I really did... I was wrong!" Braedon said angrily and stormed out of the room, slamming the door behind him.

CHAPTER TEN

"What was that all about?" Gwen asked, completely confused.

"He'll get over it," Samuel replied with a carefree wave of his cane. "Competition between drivers makes them go faster," he said.

"Competition?" she asked suspiciously.

"You were pretty impressive out there today, Randall. How did you like it?" Samuel asked, still leering at him with reverence in his tired eyes.

"Brought back a lot of memories," Randall said as he fought to hold back a smile. "Driving those things makes you forget to breathe."

"Tell me something, is it all bravery or do you use your brains behind the wheel of a racecar?" Samuel said and gestured to Randall's head with his cane.

"I make the car do the work," Randall answered confidently and puffed harder on the smoke.

"You know, when I was a prisoner, the Japanese commander used to torture me on a weekly basis. I could have fought back, but probably would have been killed. I was patient and after the war was over, I was at his trial and witnessed his hanging," Samuel said and pointed to a photograph of Michael Schumacher. "The driver is the last link in the chain, so he has to be cerebral. He has to think. Be patient. Choose his moments wisely, like I did. Engineers can't help if the man driving the machine can't explain what's wrong with it," the old man said. "So, are you really that quick or just lucky?"

"I'm fast. That was no fucking magic show out there, but what difference does it make it now?" Randall replied, staring longingly at the picture of the German champion.

"I'm prepared to offer you a one race contract without pay. After all, you can't put a price on a dream. However, I'm willing to offer an extension on that contract based upon your performance during another test session in traffic. In other words, racing against Braedon and then the racing in Montreal. After that, we'll talk money. I'm sure you've dreamt about a moment like this since you were a kid," Samuel said with a grandfatherly smile.

Stunned, the cigarette fell from Randall's mouth and he looked to Gwen, who was equally surprised. "If... if this is some kind of bad joke... I mean, I didn't even finish one lap," Randall said with wide eyes.

"I do not kid about racing. But be warned Randall, the eyes of the world would be upon you. Racing is a small crucible and is a law unto itself. The pressures are incredibly tense, especially from me. I don't cosset my drivers," Samuel said curtly and tapped his cane against the steel frame of the gurney to make his point.

"Could it be that hiring Randall amounts to nothing more than a publicity stunt? Something to get your name in the papers? Something to help you get another sponsor? A Canadian sponsor?" Gwen said mistrustfully and folded her arms, bringing Randall back from his elation to a harsh reality.

"You really do sound like his agent," Samuel shot back without looking at her, his attention focused on Randall.

"No. Just concerned," she replied and stepped between them.

"Randall's participation would be of great public interest. And public interest translates into dollars, something everyone in the sport understands. I'm a businessman and there's no shame in making money," Samuel said and leaned past her to see Randall. "Well, Randall? Only a handful of men would ever get such a chance, and I need an answer right now," he said and extended his frail hand. Randall licked his dry lips and felt his heart pounding. He began to pace as he chewed his fingernails and looked pleadingly to Gwen, as did Samuel.

"I've taken Randall off the case. He's a big boy, he can do what he wants," Gwen said disheartened and reluctantly moved aside.

Randall's sober expression transformed into a beaming smile. "Oh, what the fuck! I can't believe it! I'm back in the saddle!" Randall said eagerly and vigorously shook Samuel's hand with a boyish grin.

"Good," Samuel said and hauled himself up. "I'll draw up the papers. I want you back here in three days so you can test with Braedon under race conditions. We haven't got much time, the Canadian Grand Prix is in one week," Samuel said and prodded out Randall's smouldering cigarette on the floor with his cane. "I told you once and I'm not going to tell you again, I want my drivers healthy and concentrating on driving, not murder investigations," he added as he looked at Gwen and quickly limped for the exit.

"What about the car? Was it mechanical failure?" Gwen inquired, withdrawing her pen and pad as Samuel was about to open the door.

"Preliminary checks haven't told us anything," Samuel said, glancing over his shoulder at her.

"I'll be confiscating the debris and sending it to our lab for analysis," she said and loudly clicked her pen several times, "as well as the video from the session."

"Fine, but there's not much left to look at. It was probably just a faulty rear wing. Unfortunately, it happens sometimes," Samuel replied and went to take a step, but Gwen closed the door on him.

"Who had access to the car before the session?" she said and scribbled some notes.

"The entire crew," the old man said, becoming annoyed at the conversation and placing a hand on the knob.

"Including you?" she asked.

Chapter Ten

"I wouldn't sabotage my own car. I just lost one million dollars of equipment, and that makes it quite improbable, don't you think?" Samuel said and opened the door.

"You are insured though, right?" she countered and closed it again.

Samuel gave her a sly smile. "You know the insurance policy I held on Vincenzo, but you would also know that he was worth more to me behind the wheel than in a pine box."

"I'm not trying to offend you. It's just standard police work," she said and swung the door open for him. "I'll be in touch."

"I'm sure you will," Samuel replied tersely and looked at Randall. "Get your rest, son," he said and hobbled out.

Astounded, Randall resumed pacing with his hands on his head. "Wow! Can you fucking believe it?" he said with an amazed laugh.

"I think you've made a rash decision. Do I have to remind you that Vincenzo was murdered?" she said and stood with her back against the door. "This could be part of a plot and I'm not sure you know what you're doing."

"Maybe... but it's a chance I'll never have again," Randall said and lit another cigarette.

"Let me get this straight, when I asked you to drive, you didn't want to, but when someone else does, you're all for it," Gwen said and put away her pen and pad.

"I know, but he wants me for my ability and that's different. I really felt I could have gone even faster!" he replied with youthful enthusiasm and continued ambling. "I always wondered if I was good enough to be with the big boys, and now I'll find out."

"Maybe Jenkins really wants you for something else... like a target. You might be sleeping with the devil here," she said and rubbed her sore forehead.

Randall ceased his pacing. "Look, either way, it can only help with the case, right?" he said, explaining with his hands as Gwen stared at him full of doubt and sighing heavily. "Racing's in my blood... I can't shed my skin... I am what I am. It's strange... you never want something completely... and that's what keeps you wanting it. Maybe this will finally stop my dreams of racing," he said and waited for her reaction. Well?" he asked impatiently.

"I'm never going to get rid of you, am I?" she replied. He smiled and shook his head. "Come on," she said in a motherly tone and wrapped her arm around him. "Let's get you home and into that hot bath," she concluded as Randall raised a curious eyebrow.

The kettle whistled and jetted a line of steam as Lisa Stirling checked her look in its chrome cover and adjusted her lacy lingerie. After a quick hand through her flowing, red mane, she filled the teapot and carefully picked it up. She carried the gold plated, Union Jack decorated service through the cavernous kitchen, filled with stainless steel appliances and granite countertops, into the massive, baroque living room with its soaring ceiling. "I'm glad we gave her the day off. It's nice we have an evening with just the two of us. Baby's asleep too," she said happily, setting the tray down and settling into a large scale, velvety sofa beside Braedon.

He barely acknowledged her, engrossed in a videotape of Randall's test session on a wall-sized television and fumbling for an envelope on a coffee table made from a racing slick. "Why don't you go mail this for me?" he said impatiently and handed it to her.

"I'll do it tomorrow," she replied as Braedon stopped the tape, rewound it and leaned closer, watching Randall scything through a corner. Lisa filled the cups and noticed the angst upon his face. "Is he *that* good?" she said, but was hardly interested and flicked off the Tiffany lamp.

"If he is, I could be in serious trouble," he said, watching the same snippet again. "Turn that on again."

"Who is he?" she asked wearily as she turned the lamp on and plopped a few sugar cubes into her cup as he noticed.

"Sugar's fattening, and I told you not to buy it!" he replied, his eyes glued to the screen.

"Why, because your folks couldn't afford it when you were young? You're a multimillionaire now," she said and added more of the sweetener.

Braedon grabbed her hand and forced her to drop the cubes. "You don't talk about my parents! Ever!"

"Fine. You'd never know your mother was a social worker," she whispered under her breath, stirring her tea.

"What?" he asked angrily and paused the cassette.

"I said, what's his name?" she answered, pointing to Randall.

"Oh... name's Randall Grange. A Canadian. Churlish sort. Samuel thinks he's got promise," he said and started the tape again.

"Obviously, he does," she said and mixed in some cream as her eyes dropped to his bare legs beneath a cashmere robe.

"How would you know?" he answered and moved the sugar bowl away just as she was about to take some more.

"You're the one sitting there watching him. You must be worried. Why don't you forget about that for a while?" she said and snuggled closer to him.

"The guy didn't even bleed off any speed," he said, lost in thought.

Chapter Ten

Lisa parted his robe and ran her hands between his legs. "He probably just got lucky."

"On a green track? Those Canucks have a history of being tough to slow down. Could be another Villeneuve," he said, frowning at her close proximity and lifting her hand off.

"Why would you want to slow him down?" she asked pouting and sitting back with crossed arms.

"It wouldn't look too good for the reigning world champion to be upstaged by a no-name. That's the kind of thing that can end a career," he said, snapping his fingers and haphazardly gesturing to the service.

"I don't think you have much to worry about," she said with a hint of anger and filled his cup.

"What if Samuel actually signs him for the rest of the season? Racing is a very fickle business, especially the owners," he said and began biting at his fingernails.

She pulled his hand away from his mouth, cupped his chin and forced him to stare at her. "Listen to me. You're like a son to Samuel. He's stuck by you in the past, and there's no reason to believe that he won't do the same now. Don't forget, he was the one that gave you your start after the Borstal."

"I know but... but what if this Randall character is better... better than me?" he whispered fearfully.

"You said he crashed it, but what if he is? Who cares? You have a wife and family to think about. Racing can't last forever," she replied as the phone rang. "Don't answer it," she pleaded.

"It might be important," he said and removed the telephone from its cradle.

"It always is," she said full of disgust, and reached for her tea.

"Hello? Evening Samuel. Fine, fine. I beg your pardon... yes... I guess he was impressive this afternoon," Braedon said, rolling his eyes, but suddenly sitting up. "Are you sure that's a wise decision? No, no... if you insist... I'll be there. Good night," he said and hung up.

"What is it?" she inquired, but didn't care and sipped at her drink.

"Samuel *is* signing him and wants me to test with him in a few days," he said and jumped to his feet. He began pacing the Persian rug atop a flagstone floor.

"So?" she said, stealing more sugar cubes when he wasn't looking.

"I knew you wouldn't understand!" he said and studied the tape again.

"Samuel is just doing business. It doesn't mean the end of the universe," she huffed and retrieved a packet of cigarettes from the end table.

Braedon grabbed them out of her hand and crumpled them. "I don't want you smoking in my house!" he shouted.

"What am I then, a tenant?" Lisa replied and recovered an unbroken smoke from the floor. She was about to light it, but Braedon knocked it out of her mouth and accidentally slapped her in the process. She felt her already swelling lip and saw the spot of blood on her fingers.

"Serves you right for having that filthy habit," he said and returned his attention to the VCR. "And you *are* a tenant! I'm the breadwinner around here!"

Lisa meandered across the spacious living room to a photograph of the Canadian ballet star, Karen Kain. "I wish I was still dancing," she whispered to herself. "I had control... I was loved," she said as her sad eyes shifted to a custom cabinet, bursting with Braedon's trophies and ribbons. "How much is enough?" she said softly, but he didn't hear her as he was still enamoured with the tape. "I want you to quit, Braedon... I want it to be the way it used to be."

"Go to bed Lisa. You're tired," he said without looking as the phone rang again. "Get that," he commanded.

"What's happened to you? It's like you've lost your perspective," she said as she looked down a hall to her walnut-panelled, painting studio. A half-finished canvass revealed the two of them holding hands. "Remember we met at that dance? You were so kind... so gentlemanly... I used to love you so much," she whispered.

"Answer it!" he yelled.

"There's always going to be somebody faster... like Vincenzo was... you have to accept it," she said and opened a liquor cabinet.

Braedon lifted the entire service, hurled it at her, but missed and it smashed the cabinet. "Don't you ever mention that name again!" he shouted.

"Why, because he was talented? The man's dead and all you can do is worry that he was better!" she said and bent down, picking at the pieces of shattered china. "My mother gave me this... it was her favourite set," she said mournfully.

"Answer it!" he yelled and stormed towards her. "When I tell you to do something, you damn well do it!"

"Where is the man that was so sweet... so attentive... so much in love with me?" she whimpered, her green eyes tearing up as she stared at the broken shards in her palm. "She worked so hard to buy this... owned it a week before... before the bomb... a bomb from your people!"

"I said, answer the damn phone!" he screamed and clenched her arm. "And I don't want any more British crap in my house! Understand?" he said and deliberately crushed an intact cup with his foot.

CHAPTER TEN

"To hell with you!" she bellowed and broke free. She tore the envelope he had given her in two and threw the pieces into the stone fireplace. "And I don't want you mailing any more bloody checks to the IRA!"

Braedon grabbed her by the hair and forced her to the phone as she yelped in pain. "It's my money, and I'll do with it what I want! Now answer it!" he said, slamming her face into the table and releasing her.

She glared at him and picked up the receiver with a shaking hand. "Hello?" she said in a quavering voice. "Just a minute, please," she said and handed him the receiver.

Braedon waved her off and focused on Randall attacking the curbs. "Take a message."

"Can I take a message please?" she said, fixing her hair, but her face rapidly drained of colour as her eyes inched towards Braedon. Lisa clumsily hung up the phone, but it fell from the cradle to the floor and she started to gag.

"Well, who was it?" he groused.

"Your lover... Teresa's pregnant," she said, her crying voice trailed off and she bolted up one of two, majestic staircases.

Barbara Suarez nursed her six-month-old son as a dozen, surfeit women, feigned admiration. On the other side of the elegant, thick stucco-walled room with stone archways, the men congregated around a large wet bar decorated with silver and gold filigree, clothed in tuxedos and swilling brandy. Several, pretty servants in petite outfits offered glasses of champagne and lit cigarettes.

Outside on the darkened patio, amidst a haze of flowering trees and a network of cobblestone paths lined with artistic ceramics, Felipe Suarez watched a naked, trim, Alberto Americo frolicking in the shimmering pool with the Spanish flag painted on the bottom and an intricate, lavish bullfighter fountain in the centre. "You know Sammy, I started building my empire when I was twelve," Felipe said and smiled, remembering. "In order for the maids to keep their jobs, I used to make them have sex with me. I knew I'd inherit the family fortune sooner or later, and so did they. Money is power, Sammy and you don't have any," he said, withdrawing the cherry from his drink and tossing it in the pool.

"Money doesn't make for good judgment when it comes to drivers," Samuel responded, toddled to a chair and sat.

"This so called racing prodigy, Randall Grange is a joke. I've made my decision and that's final," Felipe said. "And when I invite you to a dinner party, I expect you to be on time, not two hours late," he said as Alberto playfully plucked the cherry from the water and teased it with his tongue, earning a disapproving scowl from Samuel.

"What's the matter Sammy? Never played for the other team?" Felipe said and laughed. "Don't try and tell me that when you were a prisoner, you never made love to another man... whether you wanted to or not."

"I did not!" Samuel barked, slamming his cane against the ground. "I'm a civilized man!"

"Did you go to college, Sammy?" Felipe asked and withdrew a cigar.

"You know I didn't... my parents couldn't afford it," Samuel replied ashamedly.

"What did your mother do again?" Felipe asked, despite knowing the answer as he unwrapped the tobacco.

"She... she was a housewife... she wanted to be a teacher," he said hopefully, "but my grandparents didn't have the money to send her," Samuel said and began cleaning his glasses to distract himself from his own watery eyes.

"That is why you're not civilized, Sammy. Poverty and no social standing goes from one generation to the next in your family, but most of the world is like that, isn't it?" Felipe said, scratched his Vandyke and frowned upon hearing his baby son cry. He gazed hungrily at Alberto. "I guess that's a sound you'll never get to hear, unless it's a doll, right Sammy? Shame about your sterility," he said to purposely hurt Samuel. The old man shuttered, realizing Felipe knew one of his most intimate secrets and continued to blink back his emotion. "But don't worry about it, breastfeeding makes women ugly," Felipe said as Alberto seductively sucked the cheery from its stem and dove beneath the generously lit water.

"I don't want... I don't think Alberto and you should be in the seats, Felipe.... Mr. Suarez," Samuel said, leaning on his cane with both hands, still trying to recover from the revelations.

"Unlike my cheap and cowardly father, I'm a conquistador, Sammy," Felipe said heartily. "My ancestors hungered for gold, silver and power, and I yearn for the same things," he said and motioned to the 18th century-styled, palatial mansion and its sophisticated surroundings. "I built this Churrigueresque estate much to the displeasure of my stuffy, English neighbours, but I conquered them and their attorneys... and I will conquer this series, and I will conquer you. There are several potential Spanish sponsors lined up. You're going to sign the contract," Felipe said sternly as he purposely licked the length of the cigar, much to the delight of Alberto. Felipe lit it and sucked heavily as Alberto slipped his hand beneath the water and began masturbating.

"As far as I'm concerned, we don't have a contract," Samuel replied uncomfortably, keeping his eyes to the ground.

CHAPTER TEN

"Sammy, Sammy, Sammy, you verbally agreed to the agreement. Any first year law student knows that it's binding. You just can't opt out," Felipe said and started to disrobe.

"There were no witnesses to what I said. I'll fight it in court in I have to," Samuel said and stood.

"You don't have the money," Felipe said and stripped off his silk briefs. He sat on the edge of the pool and gamesomely fluttered his red handkerchief at Alberto who was eagerly swimming to him.

"I'll find it," the old man said and began limping away.

"There isn't one bank in all of Europe that will lend you money. You're a terrible risk. What was it Sammy, bad investments, gambling, women?" Felipe said gleefully as Alberto pretended to be a bull with his fingers as horns while Felipe teased him with the handkerchief.

Samuel stopped and turned to him, gaining confidence. "I thought you said you knew."

"I'm not an idiot, Sammy. When it comes to my investments, I keep on an eye on who is spending my money... whether they know about it or not," Felipe said breathlessly with his head back and eyes closed as Alberto began performing fellatio, his long, black, wet hair cloaking Felipe's lap.

Thoroughly humiliated by the sexual act, Samuel looked away. "Perhaps you should tell me what you think you know," he said, his heart beginning to throb as he felt a trickle of sweat roll down his back.

"The only reason your withered carcass is still alive and not at the bottom of some lake is because of me," Felipe said, placing his hands on Alberto's head and pumped his mouth harder.

"I... I don't know what you're talking about," Samuel said, sickened by Alberto's slurping noises and laboured breathing.

"It's a good thing Karl has strong hands, wouldn't you say?" Felipe said with a sinister smile, digging his fingers harder into Alberto's hair as his muscles clenched and back arched.

Samuel felt his knees wobble and he tried to swallow, but his mouth was cotton dry. "How... how did you know?" he managed to whisper.

"Mr. Vladin and I have known each other for quite some time. It's amazing who you can meet in the world's finer restaurants. That is where you initially met him, in Stockholm, correct?" Felipe said, pulling Alberto off and ejaculating across his face.

"Then... then why didn't Karl kill me?" Samuel said, stunned by Felipe's announcement.

"A dead debtor isn't much good. What did you do with the twelve million pounds you borrowed from the Russian Mafia, Sammy?" Felipe said, moaning in ecstasy as Alberto wiped the semen from his face and licked it off his fingers.

Samuel edged backward and leaned on his cane for support. "They were going to kill my wife... I didn't have the money... my investments went sour... it was the only place I could get it."

"Who was going to kill your wife?" Felipe said and encouraged Alberto to lap up the remaining sperm from the tip of his glistening penis.

"I... I don't know... they said they'd kill one of my drivers," Samuel said and struggled to keep from vomiting.

"Is that what really happened to Vincenzo?" Felipe asked and slipped into the pool. Alberto instantly pushed his erection into Felipe's backside.

"No... it was just an accident," Samuel replied nervously, his head spinning from the disturbing events unfolding before him.

"Did you tell the police about the threats?" Felipe wondered as Alberto thrust harder.

"No... nobody knows," Samuel said and looked away, knowing he was telling a lie and completely disgusted.

"That's a good thing... because I bought the debt today. The rules have changed, Sammy. From this point on, I own the team, the merchandising rights, everything. My lawyers tell me the paperwork is almost finished, and you're going to sign it tomorrow. I don't think I have to tell you what will happen if you refuse," Felipe said as Alberto groaned and climaxed.

"What... what about the threats? What if they keep coming? What about me?" Samuel said, totally shocked.

"Once the public knows I'm the new owner and driver, the problems will stop. As far as you're concerned, I haven't decided yet. Maybe you should go into a retirement home. They could take good care of you... or maybe I could keep you on to run things. I suppose you do know what you're doing," Felipe said and tiredly dragged himself out of the pool.

"But... but I offered Grange a contract," Samuel said and loosened his ascot.

"Withdraw it. Alberto and I are taking the seats," Felipe said, annoyed and towelled himself off.

"But I asked him to test with Braedon tomorrow," Samuel replied.

"Then call him and tell him to forget it!" Felipe said and threw on a robe.

"But I really think he's good enough... you saw yourself... he was quicker than Braedon's time from last year... it might be good publicity... maybe pick up a Canadian sponsor," Samuel said, a distinct sense of panic in his voice.

Chapter Ten

"The answer is no! I've kept my guests waiting long enough. I think you know your way out," he said as he removed his gold encrusted watch and tossed it to Alberto. "Nice," he said as Alberto gladly accepted the largesse. "You see Sammy, we need a young man who takes orders without questions. A man who wants to please his employer. A man who is strong and is willing to take chances."

"Please, Mr. Suarez," Samuel pleaded and grabbed Felipe's arm.

Felipe suddenly clenched Samuel by the back of the head and forced him down to the ground. "Listen to me, Sammy! I'm above the law. I'm better than everyone else and I've had enough of this cat and mouse game," he said and snapped his fingers at Alberto. "I will see you in my office tomorrow morning at eight to sign the agreement, or I tell the world about your Russian amigos. So have a drink and relax," Felipe said and chuckled as Alberto rammed his manhood into Samuel's gagging mouth. "Good night, Sammy," Felipe said as the old man fought to push Alberto away. Samuel finally broke free; his false teeth fell to the concrete and shattered, causing Alberto to laugh hysterically. "Get used to tasting my ass, Sammy. It's my team now," Felipe said with a grin.

Samuel regurgitated slightly and spat his mouth clean. He looked around in desperation and spotted Felipe's wife inside the house. "You bastard! Do you think she would approve of your perversion?" Samuel said chokingly.

"It doesn't matter what she thinks. It's what I want that counts, and the sooner you understand that, the better off you're going to be," Felipe said and strolled towards the house.

"You do this and... and I might just reveal your little secret," Samuel said and gestured with disgust at Alberto.

Felipe laughed and continued sauntering along. "Go ahead. Who do you think they will believe, one of the richest men in Europe, or a washed up old man who borrowed millions from the Mafia?" Samuel realized he was beaten and sulked away as Felipe faded into the bushes, snapping his fingers again and a Spanish-costumed mariachi trio began to play inside a wrought-iron bandstand.

Chapter Eleven

Restrained, classical music filtered through the speaker system as Randall peered out the window of the descending, Government of France helicopter and saw the hazy outline of Paris in the distance. His disbelieving eyes stared in astonishment at the twenty-five hectares of magnificent, rolling, verdant hills, woodlands, and an imposing, 17th century house, sitting on a rise beside a stone barn. Further away, there was a guesthouse, an exact, smaller version of the manor. "Holy shit," Randall said. "This is what it's like to win the fucking lottery. Why the hell do you even bother to keep working?"

"Why do you keep racing? Because it's in your blood. You always told me racers have to race. You're compelled to do so. Same thing with me and police work," Gwen said, sitting beside him and studying a file.

"Fuck. It's more than that. I have to work just to eat," he said, entranced by the Marne River, abutting the property. "Money sure changes things."

"Not necessarily. Just because I'm wealthy doesn't mean I don't care. I want to make a difference," she said, patently offended and tucking the pamphlet in her case.

The helicopter rotated slowly as Randall saw a swing set beneath a glade, close to the house. "Is she here?" he asked timidly.

"No. The nanny's got her at her place," she said as they touched down.

"I still don't think coming to your house was a great idea. If they found us in England, they'll sure as hell find us in France," he said as he unbuckled himself, his eyes still glued to the swing set.

"There're agents surrounding the property," she replied and pointed to the suited men, stationed at various points inside the high-fenced estate. "If anything happens, those guys will move pretty fast."

Randall opened the door and they stepped onto the finely manicured lawn just as a horse was heard to whinny. "You bought her a pony?" he asked incredulously.

Chapter Eleven

"A horse, actually. Don't worry, we're always careful. The animal seems to know she's... you know," Gwen said, starting for the house and straightening her long, black hair.

"Jesus... I can't compete with all this," he said with a shake of his head and reluctantly moved towards the swing set.

"Nobody's asking you to," she said, finding her keys. "Don't worry about our bags. They'll bring them in."

"Remember when I tried to put one of these things together?" he asked with a nervous laugh, gesturing to the swing set.

"You never were good with directions. It helps if you're sober too," she said and unlocked the huge double doors, but soon realized he wasn't coming with her.

Randall unwillingly touched the candy-stripped metal of the swing set, its surface rough from rust and peeling paint. "You were my heartbeat... pain of losing you from my life... makes me hold my breath sometimes," he whispered.

"Come on, I'll give you the dime tour," she said, waving him along.

Randall followed the cobblestone path and slowly shuffled into the large foyer with stairs on the left, leading down to a heated, indoor pool with a bridge, surrounded by glass walls and an indoor tennis court further beyond. His head turned right to an incredibly large living room with a mezzanine, full of the latest exercise equipment. Randall's feet echoed off the ceramic floor as he poked his head into the lavish living room and saw a large fireplace with dozens of Robert Bateman paintings of big cats adorning every wall. "Bet those fucking prints cost a bundle," he said and whistled.

"They're originals," she stated proudly and removed her coat before hanging it in a massive closet with a bench. "Take your boots off. They'll scratch the floor."

Randall kicked off his cowboy boots, revealing several holes in his socks, earning a disapproving glance from Gwen. "I don't make much, but I earn it," he said slyly.

"This is the kitchen," she said and led him into the mammoth, sunlit room with a breakfast bar.

He stared at the dozens of copper pots and pans hanging from the ceiling and saw the two skylights. "I suppose you have a personal chef," he said sarcastically and gritted his teeth, checking their reflection in the double door, stainless steel fridge.

"Macy looks after most of it," Gwen said and opened some sliding doors, leading to a roomy solarium full of padded patio furniture with iron accents and a plethora of plants.

"Macy?"

"She's the nanny," Gwen said and sprayed some water onto her ferns. "She takes her when I need some time alone."

Randall absorbed the magnificent ambience and gazed upon the guesthouse. "Fuck. How much *did* your father leave you?"

"None of your business," she said, continuing to water the fauna. "If you want a drink, there's some stuff in the fridge."

Randall opened it and found a beer. He pulled back the tab and drank, but soon grimaced. "Fucking foreign suds," he said and sauntered into the gigantic, formal dining room with a stone fireplace with a crucifix above it and a photograph of Jessica atop the horse on the mantle. "Never walk again," he whispered sadly to himself.

"What?"

"I said faith can be blinding," he replied too loudly. "Where's your God now?" he said, staring at his daughter as Gwen stood in the doorway.

"A lack of faith can also be deceiving. Look at it this way, it can't hurt," she said and motioned him along. "Come on, I'll show you the upstairs."

Randall followed her into the foyer and beneath a wide staircase to another room. "Oh and this is the library," she said as more of an afterthought and watched as Randall entered, obviously impressed by the plentiful books, reading desk and giant globe. The phone rang and Gwen hustled out of the room. "Make yourself at home. Go upstairs if you like and try the hot tub."

Randall perused the many volumes and found a section low to the ground with children's books. A light smile broke across his face and his fingers glided down the well-worn spine of a collection of fairy tales. "Maybe I'll get to read it to you one day... one day," he whispered mournfully before slowly entering the foyer again where he curiously studied the lift for Jessica before ascending the steps.

At the top, he glanced down the long, hardwood corridor and ran a few feet before sliding across the well-waxed floor to a set of French doors. Randall opened them to discover a huge master bedroom with its own fireplace and stone terrace with a vista of the river. The king-sized, canopied bed was dwarfed by the generous space, and each wall was decorated with various photographs of Jessica. Randall opened another door to find a full bathroom with an adjoining powder room. Another door disclosed an enormous closet with hundreds of garments, hats and shoes. "Jesus Christ," he said. "Fucking closet is bigger than my apartment."

Randall meandered into the hall again and saw another impressive bathroom with another balcony, gold spigots, marble flooring and small, granite statues. "Sure could get used to this," he said and turned on the

CHAPTER ELEVEN

taps to fill the spacious hot tub. "I'll be back," he said happily to the bubbling water and strolled into the hall again.

Randall opened another door, revealing a pine study with a red leather chair, maple wood desk and other typical sundries; a banker's lamp, telephone, fax machine and a large filing cabinet in one corner. He snuck in and tried to open it, but it was locked. "Probably the state secret to pea soup for fuck sakes," he said with disappointment and glanced at the mundane papers on her desk: phone, taxes, utilities and other bills. He continued to the next two doors. Both were more guest rooms with their own en suites. "Split lips has got green," he said, scratching his stubble, but suddenly froze upon spying the last door at the end of the hallway with Jessica's name, crudely etched into the wood. Randall suddenly heard his breathing intensify as he took a cautious step, but his legs were suddenly heavy and his face grew flustered. He heard the phone ring again, did a quick about-face and scurried into the bathroom, closing the door behind him.

Randall quickly disrobed, placed a toe into the steaming tub and caught his breath. Gradually, he sank his bruised body into the water, releasing a satisfied sigh. He looked up, saw his foggy reflection in the condensation covered, mirrored ceiling and winced at the tender, red and purple welts on his arms. "Maybe she was right... the old man just wants you as a publicity stunt... like some kind of fucking circus act," he said, staring at his privates, floating with the roiling water before gazing at the ceiling again. "You got the balls though... got the insanity it takes to drive those things... drivers are a different breed... got to stare death in the face to appreciate life. All it is, is controlled mayhem... calculated chaos," he said with his hands to reassure himself. "But what about three days from now?" he whispered and stared at the rays of light flooding the room. Diffidently, he closed his sheepish eyes and nervously bit his lip. "You and I ain't on the best of terms big guy but... but I could use a little divine intervention," he said, feeling his sore shoulder and sighing heavily as there was a light knock at the door.

"Are you decent?" Gwen said as he covered his crotch with a washcloth.

"Never have been. Come on in," he replied. Gwen nudged the door open, holding a tray with a bottle of champagne and two glasses, and a file under one arm.

"Comfortable?" she asked, surprised by his gumption.

"You said make yourself at home," he said and watched as she set the tray down on the edge of the tub and pulled a vanity chair closer. "What's the matter, split lips, somebody die?" he asked as she sat and filled the glasses.

"You... maybe, if you keep driving," she replied half-serious and handed him his glass, "I just wanted to congratulate you on your deal with Jenkins and I know you hate French beer," she said and toasted him.

"Thanks," he said and drained the glass. "How come you're not riding my ass about the booze and smokes now?"

"You can't get blood from a stone," she said as he dangled the glass for a refill. "How do you like the place?" she asked, obliging his request.

"It's a goddamn dump, but it's okay. Who uses the guest house?" he said and haphazardly pointed in its direction.

"Um... it's usually empty," she said, thoroughly uncomfortable. "Peter uses it when he stays here... you know... for Jessica's sake. You'll be staying in there," she said, clearing her throat and rushing to the balcony where she swung the doors open. "Stuffy in here, isn't it?"

Randall immediately sat up with a concerned look upon his face. "What the fuck? How can you do that?" he shouted.

"I don't need your permission to live my life," she shot back with her hands on her hips.

"What kind of an example is that to set?" he asked, completely flummoxed. "Jess will grow up thinking it's okay to fuck around without being married!"

"Her father does!"

"She doesn't live with me!" he countered and splashed the water, pointing to himself.

"Thank God."

"Speaking of which, what do you think the great almighty would say?" he said and embraced the heavens, feeling he had scored a moral victory. "And another thing, why the hell would you have the poor girl's bedroom upstairs?"

"I want her to learn that one day she'll have to do things for herself! I'm not always going to be around and she has to become independent!" she said angrily and marched for the door.

"She's just a kid for fuck sakes! Cut her some slack!"

"Don't tell me how to raise my daughter!" she yelled and pointed at him. "I'm the one taking care of her, and I know what's best! Look, I'm not discussing this with you any further! It's none of your business!" she said, opening the door.

"Jesus!" he said and searched for something to say to continue the debate. "You've got two other bedrooms in this joint, and I'm staying out there?" he said and lit a cigarette from a pack inside his denim jacket by the tub.

"Three other bedrooms. You didn't look in Jessica's, did you?" she asked knowingly.

CHAPTER ELEVEN

Subjugated, Randall shifted in the tub and hesitated before speaking. "I'm more of a shower man myself," he said, resting his head back and closing his eyes. "I guess you know what you're doing. Come on, have a drink."

Gwen took a moment and returned to her chair. "How do you feel?" she said as a peace offering.

"Stiff, but getting better... you always liked taking a bath, didn't you?" he asked to cool the conversation and filled her glass.

Gwen's stern expression slowly melted away. "I love them. My father used to wash me when I was little and sing to me," she said with a distant smile.

"Me too... only he did a little more than washing," Randall said and sipped his champagne. "Actually, I don't know what was worse... him or getting a bath after the burns from the accident in Toronto."

"How could the accident have been worse?"

"I remember lying in that fucking bed with my feet and hands bandaged... pain was so bad it made me puke. Vince used to visit me and we'd rank which nurses we wanted to bang," he said with a chortle. "But to answer your question, it ain't easy getting a sponge bath with a hard-on."

"Jessica likes bath time," she beamed. "Loves to pass wind in the water."

"Sure sounds like my daughter," he said and kicked back the champagne. "How's her cold?"

"Gone."

He nodded his relief. "So you talked to your mother today?" he questioned and poured himself another glass.

"Of course," she replied and frowned at the odd inquiry. "That was her on the phone. She's going on a cruise next week. Thank God, maybe she'll leave me alone for a few days."

"Don't knock it. I wish I could talk to my old lady," he said and became hypnotized by the bubbles in his glass. "Funny, the moment you grow up is when you realize your folks are vulnerable, and then you know you're not invincible... and one day you wake up and you're an orphan," he said as his eyes drifted off. "Why did you bring me here, Gwen? Why didn't we just stay at the bed and breakfast?"

"Gee, I don't know, maybe I don't feel like being shot when I sleep," she answered sarcastically. "There wasn't enough security there."

"Is that the only reason? I thought we were supposed to be targets," he asked suspiciously and dragged heavily on the smoke.

"We are, but it would be nice to stop it before it happens, or at least see it coming," she said and fished out a couple of pills. "Don't read anything into this, Randall. I thought you might like to relax before the test session, that's all."

"Migraine?" he asked mildly disappointed, and carelessly tapped his ash into the water.

"No, but one's coming. I just heard back from the lab. Vincenzo's father's plane crash results were inconclusive. So it's impossible to squarely point the blame at Carmen," she said and swallowed the medication, "and Vincenzo's car was mechanically sound the report shows."

"Batting zero, uh?" he said and took another drink.

Gwen leaned back and crossed her legs. "Whoever is doing all this read the manual. The most efficient accident, or simple assassination, is a fall of seventy-five feet or more onto a hard surface, and it is usually necessary to drug or stun the subject before dropping him or her," she said rigidly, reciting from her memory of instruction.

"Benny Rabowitz, right? But then again, maybe Rabowitz's killer was just sloppy or wanted us to know the fall was a set-up."

She nodded and shrugged. "And no assassination instructions should ever be written or recorded. Decision and instructions should be confined to an absolute minimum of persons," she said and frowned, trying to recall. "For secret assassination, the contrived accident is the most effective technique. When successfully executed, it causes little excitement and is only casually investigated."

"Vincenzo's father," Randall said and she nodded again. "But that doesn't explain Vincenzo's murder or the money they want from Jenkins."

"True, unless it's a ruse, in which case Carmen looks more and more like the prime suspect," she said and filled her glass again.

"Pretty impressive all that shit you just rhymed off. You like working with all that cloak and dagger stuff in the DST?" he said and blew a few smoke circles.

"I did up until last year," she replied with a slight smile. "Then something happened that makes me wish I had stayed in Paris solving simple murders," she said, staring off into space.

"Well?" he inquired impatiently and splashed her.

"Actually, it had to do with water," she said. "I asked to join the DSGE, that's the Directorate of Territorial Security. They deal with external intelligence. Clandestine operations, homicide, abductions, observation, that kind of thing. I thought it might be better than working the internal stuff, so I volunteered for a mission," she said and shook her head regrettably. "The French government was doing some underground testing of nuclear weapons near the Muroroa Atoll, you know, French Polynesia? Anyway, Greenpeace found out about it, and our job was to stop them," she said and stood with her hands in her pockets. "I helped sink their ship in Auckland... watched one of their photographers drown trying to fetch his equipment... police officers are supposed to preserve life, not take it away," she said sadly. "The guy had a wife and kid... and I helped take away a father and husband."

"You need another drink," he said sullenly and topped up her glass. "Don't feel too bad. Last year I was doing a routine patrol... saw this guy swerving in and out of traffic. Figured he was loaded, so I lit it up and hit the wailer. Pulled him over and he steps out. Dumb fuck staggers right into oncoming and gets killed instantly," he said and shrugged. "Blamed myself for a long time... maybe if I hadn't stopped him, he might have lived... or maybe he would have killed somebody else. Who knows? Point is, people have to accept the consequences... we're not the cause. You're a cop Gwen and you're supposed to have strong values... and sometimes it gets ugly, but it's for the greater good."

"You don't really believe that, do you?"

"I have to, or the shit we go through is for nothing," he said and crushed out his cigarette on the side of the tub. "So what's in the file?"

Gwen opened it and placed it on the side of the tub. "Everything we know so far," she said and sat back with her hands behind her head, "and it isn't very much."

"Well, let's take it step by step and look at the motives," he said and lit another smoke. "It's time for show and tell."

Gwen took a drink, exhaled heavily and held up a photograph of Felipe Suarez. "Okay. Vince's folks are killed in a plane crash, but we don't know if it was an accident. Vince inherits the family banking fortune and two percent of the racing series. If Vince dies, Carmen gets that two percent," she said and put the photograph aside.

"Great motive, but like you said, a bitch to prove," he replied and motioned for another picture.

Gwen withdrew a photograph of Braedon Stirling. "World champion and wants it to stay that way. Is obviously sympathetic to the IRA and maybe there's a connection in that, but we don't know what it is," she said and tucked the photograph away.

"Possible, but pretty fucking thin. Next."

"Teresa. Had a four-million-dollar life insurance policy on Vince. Probably angry that he left his fortune to the Catholic Church, and she owes the casino four point one million. Plus the fact that Vince stopped her line of credit at the casino," she said and stood.

"Hell hath no fury," he said. "She's tied for first with the spic."

Gwen began pacing the room and removed another photograph. "Samuel Jenkins. Had an eight-million-dollar insurance policy on Vince.

Paid twenty million after the first threatening letter, but didn't pay twenty million the second time and Vince is killed. Both letters were written on the team's stationary and the money was sent to an account in the Cayman Islands which we haven't yet traced and probably won't," she said and raised an eyebrow, waiting for this thoughts.

"Not likely. The old man seems real," he mused and poured another drink.

"Friedrich Hesse?" she asked, showing his photo.

"I doubt it. Even if he wants his own racing series or to run the series, offing Vince ain't going to help him that much unless he's a vengeful nut," Randall said and burped.

"That's it," she said and sat again with her feet on the tub. "If it's not one of them for monetary reasons or some other reason, it's somebody with a pretty big grudge."

"Like Ictch... Ichiro or another crew member," he said, but suddenly shook his head at his own deduction. "No. They could just fuck with the car and not hire a pro."

"Which brings us to Rabowitz and his killer. Either Benny knew something that got him killed, or somebody wanted it to look like Benny was the assassin," she said and squinted as she rubbed her tired eyes.

"Just got to keep that bull's-eye on my head and see who moves," he said with a grunt and hauled himself out of the water. "And all you have to do now is figure out what to say when the world discovers that the newest driver for Team Jenkins was a cop. Somebody will dig it up," he said and stepped out of the tub.

Gwen glanced at his privates when he reached for a towel and grimaced upon seeing the bruises on his body. "So what? The public thinks Vince died from suspension failure. Besides, you were a racing driver, and they'll also find out that you and Vince were friends at one time. It can only make things legitimate."

"What about our history? What if they uncover that shit? What if they figure out we're working together on this case?" he said and wrapped a towel around his waist.

"Only three people know we're cops and if it leaks, we know who to go after," she replied and gathered the photographs.

"What is the meaning of this?" an angry, Swedish accent asked. Gwen and Randall turned to find Peter Pettersson, dressed in a completely white suit and holding a bouquet of flowers. Forty-eight years of age, at six foot five inches, he was an intimidating man, save his blonde but balding hair, fair complexion and deep blue eyes.

Nervously, Gwen gave him a quick hug and kiss. "Peter... this is... is..."

Chapter Eleven

Randall stepped forward, allowing the towel to drop and extending his hand. "Randall Grange. I'm her ex, but apparently not as big as you," he said with a wink and gestured between his own legs.

Peter reluctantly shook Randall's hand and looked to Gwen. "This is the Randall you told me about?"

Face flushed, Gwen tried to smile. "Randall's here on a case... with me. It's not what you think... I can explain it to you later," she said and forced a laugh.

"Don't sweat it," Randall said, smacking him on the back and saying. "I'll be using the guest house."

Peter gave her a stunned look and Gwen offered another dumb laugh. "Randall's just kidding. He's staying at a hotel in Paris," she said and pleaded with her eyes to Randall.

"Uh? Oh... right. Just a little Canadian humour," Randall said and continued dressing. "Actually, I'm staying at the cheapest motel closest to here. Tight budget."

"You're back from Tampa early," Gwen said, trying to change the subject and quickly handing Randall his jacket.

"I wanted to surprise you," Peter said and presented the flowers to her.

"You sure as fuck did," Randall said with a hearty chuckle, but soon stopped. "Nothing happened here... honestly."

Unconcerned, Peter didn't even look at Randall. "I know. I trust her, and now that I have met you, I see that I am totally correct," he said and gave her a long kiss on the mouth. "The opening of the new office took less time than I thought," Peter said with his hands on her shoulders.

"How'd an older guy like you get past the security?" Randall replied, clearly stung by the Swede's words, throwing on his denim coat and withdrawing another cigarette.

Gwen closed her eyes and swallowed hard. "I have a key," Peter said and held it up to purposely annoy him. "I met a few of the men that are outside at her office Christmas party. By the way, this is a smoke-free home."

Seething, Randall's blue eyes flared and he debated whether to charge him, but finished dressing and wandered to the door. "Maybe you two should get married," he said sarcastically and lit the smoke. "You're perfect for each other."

"You didn't tell him?" Peter asked Gwen and wrapped his arm tight around her.

"I... I haven't had the chance," she practically whispered, avoiding Randall's glare.

"Perhaps you will join us at the ceremony, Randall. It's in September. It was nice meeting you," he said and curtly offered his handshake just as

Gwen's cell phone rang. "And don't worry, I'll take good care of Jessica." Too deflated to retaliate, Randall simply turned and shuffled off.

Irritated, Gwen flipped the phone open. "Hello? Yes Mr. Jenkins. What can I do for you?" she said half-interested and sadly watched as Randall disappeared around the corner.

"Tell me you'll stay," Braedon said hopefully, sitting on the edge of the bed and holding Lisa's hand as she reluctantly stood before him. "I need you... please say you will... I'm sorry," he said and gently stroked her bruised throat. "I'll never hit you again... I promise," he said as a distant rumble of thunder sounded.

She hesitated, staring deep into his eyes as he anxiously waited for her reply. "When I was a little girl, I used to watch my father drive his lorry off to work... and then my mother would walk me to the bus stop before she went to the bank," she said with an expressionless face, "and as we went along, we could sometimes hear the men and women arguing from different houses... it was a poorer neighbourhood than ours... my mother told me that we were lucky, but others didn't have enough money... that the stress was too much for some," she said and flinched. "I remember this one time... she whisked me along when we saw a man hitting his wife in front of his children on the steps... she told me people that really love each other would never do that... she would tell me to show her the dance steps I had just been taught the weekend before to make me forget," she said and wiped away a solitary tear. "We have money... and I don't want to dance to forget... to dance for the wrong reasons."

"You won't have to," he replied and kissed her hand.

"I want to have another baby... because I know what it was like to be an only child. I want you to stop racing after this season... I want our son to have his father around... and when the time is right, I want to return to dancing... maybe even teach one day," she said softly.

"You want an awful lot," he said with a hint of temper despite his smile and avoided her glare. "We can discuss it later."

"Promise me you will stay away from Teresa," she said and cupped his chin. "Tell me the truth about what happened... I mean it Braedon."

"I promise you she's lying! We've never been together! I don't know why she's doing this... money I guess," he said with a shrug. "She always wanted me, but I rejected her.... but you can't ask me to stop what I love... and having another child will only complicate things," he said timidly and stood. "My father didn't like the fact that my mother worked and I don't like it either. Your place is here, in the home to look after the baby.

"Then I can't stay," she said, composing herself and marching into the large, walk-in closet. She emerged with a suitcase and threw it on the bed

CHAPTER ELEVEN

as a bolt of lightning flashed through the room, followed by a hellish crack of thunder.

"You don't have to leave! I've told you the truth!" he barked. Lisa swiped some clothes off the hangers. They spun on the dowel for an instant and crashed to the floor in a tangled mess. She stuffed the case without regard and Braedon grasped her by the shoulders. She winced upon his nails digging into her skin. "Listen to me! Teresa and I never did! You must believe me!"

Lisa stepped away from him. "When two people don't make love for... I can't even remember the last time!" she said and closed the suitcase with some of her clothing was still hanging out the sides. "I pretty well knew what was going on even before Vincenzo was killed! I was a fool in denial!" she said and hurried into the hallway. "I'll send for my other things later."

"I'm telling you the truth about this!" he said, following her into the nursery, but she ignored him and wrapped the sleeping baby with a blanket. Lisa gathered him up and held him close with one arm. "I won't let you take my child!" he shouted.

"You've never been a father to this boy, and it's too late to start now!" she said and shoved past him as another streak of lightning doused the lights. She carefully bent down, picked up the luggage and cautiously descended the winding staircase.

"I said you're not taking my son!" he yelled and chased after her. Lisa hastened her pace and reached the bottom. She set the suitcase down and opened the door and a stiff breeze swept in, causing the baby to whimper. Braedon slammed the door closed and plucked the boy from her arms. Lisa tried to take him back, but to no avail.

"Give him to me!" she shouted. "You don't love him! You don't love me! I want more children but you don't! So give me my son!" she demanded, holding her arms out.

Braedon lifted his crying, wriggling son to gaze upon him as nature's fury frequently basked the infant in blinding light. "He's going to be an Irishman... a proud Irishman," he said in a chant-like tone. "He'll live in a house with his grandparents like I did... he'll learn to speak the language like I did... he'll be God fearing like me... and he'll fight for the cause and never surrender," he said with flaring eyes and turned to Lisa, suddenly appearing from the kitchen as another smear of lightning illuminated her hand, clutching a butcher's knife.

"Give me my son!" she shouted with the blade pointed at Braedon.

"Stop acting like a child!" he said and deliberately held the baby in front of him. "You'll have to go through him to get to me! We're as one!"

"Cowardly Irish shit!" she screamed, boiling with rage. Her frightened eyes scanned the darkness until another flash showed her the way. Lisa ran to his trophy cabinet and with trembling hands, grasped the sides and pulled it forward. The glass structure smashed to the floor with a huge crash. She picked up a lamp and hurled it at the crucifix, knocking it off the wall. "To hell with you and your God!"

"Fucking bitch!" he yelled, setting the child on the sofa before storming towards her. Lisa cowered and raised the weapon, but he easily yanked it from her hand and shoved her to the floor. Her terrified eyes looked into his seething glare as her chest heaved with each breath. "He's my son and he stays with me! You're not going anywhere! Try to leave me and I'll kill you! Do you understand?" he whispered through clenched teeth as the front door burst open with a gust of wind.

Lisa's fear promptly vanished as the baby screamed louder. "Is that what you want? A son that grows up to be like you? Full of hate? No respect for women... no respect for anybody that disagrees with you? You're gutless! A fraud!" she said hatefully.

Enraged, Braedon cut her blouse away with the knife and held the tip to one of her nipples. She gasped slightly, the sound of pelting rain against the foyer floor overwhelming. "I should cut them off! I don't want your British poison in his blood!" he said and lightly sliced her breast, spilling a line of blood. Lisa began sobbing as another flash temporarily lit the room, his eyes catching a brief glimpse of her painting studio, its walls adorned with ballet pictures. He suddenly grabbed her leg and held the cold steel against her calf. "Hard to make money dancing with severed tendons!" he said menacingly. "Money from a mother who would have my son surrounded by... by sodomites!"

"Please... don't," she pleaded as her hand felt across the smooth floor, searching for any kind of weapon.

"It's for your own good! For the good of my son! Our son!" he said and jabbed the point of the knife into her flesh.

Lisa's frantic hand finally found an iron, horse-shaped doorstop as she screamed wildly upon Braedon beginning a slow slice across her skin. She struggled to lift the object, but managed to raise it and struck Braedon on the side of the head. He groaned and fell to the floor. Lisa grabbed the knife and saw a trickle of blood oozing from his skull during another gleam of lightning. She quickly limped to her baby and picked him up.

"Lisa... I'm sorry... I love you... please... please don't go," Braedon mumbled as he struggled to stand.

"No more apologies... it never changes... you always blame me... well it's not my fault! It never was!" she cried and painfully started for the door.

CHAPTER ELEVEN

"I'll give you anything you want," he replied in desperation and crawled towards her. "I love you... please don't go... he's my flesh and blood too," he said with an outstretched hand.

Lisa hesitated in the doorway with the rain slashing against her face. "How long have you been seeing her?" she asked in a monotone voice.

Braedon's body was too limp to continue and he collapsed. His eyes shifted nervously as he debated whether to admit to the affair and save his marriage, or maintain the facade and hope for the same. "What?" he said, stalling for time.

"How long?" she shouted, making the baby shriek louder.

"I've never been with her Lisa... it's the God's honest truth," he said as he grimaced, feeling the gash on his head and hauling himself up to one knee.

"I saw the video of you and Teresa. I found it in your closet," she said succinctly. Braedon was suddenly winded as the numbing warmth returned to his legs. Lisa continued. "I just wanted to see if you would tell me... I just wanted to see what kind of a man I was dealing with... whether you would choose between me or your career and that... that slut... and now I know. Get yourself a good lawyer because I'm going for all I can get. I earned it," she said and hastily exited, leaving the door banging in the wind.

Braedon's legs gave way and he stumbled again. He felt a tightening of his stomach muscles and he vomited profusely. "God... oh God," he whispered, but the anger soon began pulsating throughout his being when he saw the destruction of his racing trophies. He fought to stand, knocked over a table and dizzily staggered up the staircase, but fell halfway. He dragged himself to his feet, meandered upward and found his way into the master bedroom. Braedon tripped his way through the darkness to his closet and blindly reached for a shoebox on a shelf. He carried it to the bed and flicked off the lid. A bloodied hand raised a revolver against the light of the window and he opened the chamber. His other hand scrambled through a box of ammunition, the sound of steel bullets clanging together. Braedon meticulously loaded, dropping several, but finally finished loading and snapped the chamber closed with an angry slap of his bloody hand just as the telephone rang. He picked up the receiver. "Hello? Where are you? I'll be there," he said breathlessly.

Chapter Twelve

Shivering, Gwen stood at the precipice, mesmerized by the thundering waves of the English Channel as the wind whipped her black hair and sucked the oxygen from her lungs. Behind her, the idling helicopter waited, its slowing blades thumping through the damp air. She twisted the top off a pill bottle, poured three tablets into her hand and swallowed the medicine before reaching into her jacket and withdrawing the wedding ring Randall had given her. A plain, gold band. "This has to stop, Randall," she said as her eyes shifted to the lavish engagement ring from Peter on her finger with its sparkling diamonds. "I have to take myself off this case... and away from you... it's better for both of us," she whispered, closing her eyes and reluctantly letting Randall's ring roll off her palm. After a few moments she looked down at the swirling surf, the cool mist rising and sprinkling her face.

She heard the sound of tyres on gravel and turned to see Samuel's limousine park. The old man stepped out and tiredly shuffled towards her as he drew up the collar of his smartly pressed trench coat. "This had better be important," she said and dug her hands into her pockets for warmth. "Please make it quick. This storm might ground my flight back."

"Beautiful, isn't it?" Samuel said uncomfortably and sat awkwardly, propping himself against a small berm of rocks.

Gwen pivoted back to the majestic scenery. "What do you want?"

"If I had my way, I would have stayed in England and fought the Nazis," he said, staring off into the channel. "Somehow it seemed more important to defend the country on home soil."

"You didn't call me here to discuss your war memories," she said and thought how Samuel seemed older since the last time she saw him. "It's just as well I'm here though... I'm going to have another agent take over the investigation."

Surprised by her announcement, Samuel could only return his gaze to the choppy water. "When I was a POW, they used sleep deprivation on

Chapter Twelve

me. I never talked though. Sometimes I wasn't sure if I was dreaming... and the only way I knew was, was when I'd wake up screaming," he said and slowly looked at her. "I didn't see myself in a mirror for two years," he said with a laugh, but his jocularity quickly dissipated. "But when I finally did... I didn't even recognize myself. I had these deep lines on my face and a dark beard," he said, gesturing with his hands, "There was silver in it from the shock of being holed up like an animal I guess...sagging skin... I was an old man," he said and proudly stood, "but I survived... and I can't lose now... not after all I've fought for," he said and limped closer to her. "Why are you leaving this case?"

"I have my reasons," she said without looking at him.

"A lot of men came out of that camp completely different people. Insane perhaps, but I managed to hang on," he said and buttoned the top of his coat after a strong gust of wind. "That's the secret you know, learning to adapt."

"People change every day, Mr. Jenkins."

"Not love. It's the only constant and your feelings for Randall shouldn't sway your professional life, but they will," he said and placed a hand on her shoulder. "Just accept it and your job will become easier."

A polite smile from Gwen. "You're a very smart man, Mr. Jenkins. Someone will be in touch," she said and hurried for the helicopter.

"I met your father once," Samuel said. Gwen stopped and turned to him with doubt in her eyes. "It's true. We met at Magny-Cours," he said and withdrew a folded piece of newspaper. He handed it to her and she opened it to find a photograph of her father shaking hands with Samuel. "I found it in my scrapbook. Your father was there on government business. I can't remember for what exactly. I knew who you were the moment you introduced yourself." .

"Why didn't you say something?" she said, her attention focused on the yellowed paper.

"I didn't want to make you uncomfortable. I know what happened with him. It must have been hard on you and your mother," he said and smiled again. "Oddly enough, I do remember him talking about you the whole time though."

"What did he say?" she asked as her demeanour softened.

"Just that he thought you'd be the best police officer in France. How you used to cry when you were a little girl because you thought all gendarmes had to be men. He was obviously very proud of you," Samuel said with another warm smile and pointed at the newspaper. "Keep it."

"Thank you," she said and started for the helicopter again.

Dismayed his gesture didn't take, Samuel pondered for a second before nervously scratching his thinning hair and clearing his throat. "Suarez doesn't want Randall in the car."

"That's not my problem anymore. I'm not going to force Suarez, and Randall can do whatever he wants," she said and continued on.

"Your husband has great potential," he shouted.

"Ex-husband," she said too forcefully.

"Seems to me you still love him. I can see it in your eyes... my wife had the same look."

Gwen pivoted back to him. "I was supposed to act like the worried wife. I guess my acting is better than I thought."

"You can't fool me. We can lie about a lot of things, but not that," he said with a shake of his head.

"If you want me to force Suarez to accept Randall as the second driver, I can't do it," she said, slightly embarrassed by the veracity of his comments. "Goodbye, Mr. Jenkins."

"But you wanted him in the beginning."

"It's over," she said and impatiently checked her watch. "I have to go."

"Would you not agree that having Randall behind the wheel would help with your investigation?" he asked with a smirk.

"I didn't realize it at the time, but asking Randall to risk his life to find the killer is... well, it's just not the right thing to do," she said and circled a finger in the air, directing the pilot to prepare for lift-off.

"It's because you still love him," he said and hobbled towards her.

"Not that it's any of your business, but I don't love him!"

Samuel's face hardened as he drew closer to her. "I need him to drive, Ms. Gaudet. I don't have enough payroll to hire another driver, and it's the only way I can keep the team independent," he said as he wiped away the silver hair from his face, but it returned with another rush of wind.

"That doesn't concern me. I told you Randall can drive if he wants to," she said curtly and walked apace to the helicopter.

"There's something you need to know... Suarez is trying to force me to partner with him. He's trying to take control of the team... my team. He wants Alberto Americo and himself as the drivers," he strained to say.

"That's between you and him," she replied without breaking stride as the helicopter's pitch grew louder, the blades becoming one.

"I paid to save my wife from being murdered! I spent everything to keep her from harm, but she died anyway and Vincenzo is dead! Dead because I couldn't pay!" he shouted over the din as Gwen slowed. "Suarez knows something about me... something that will ruin me."

"Which is?" she said, facing him.

Chapter Twelve

"I had to find money... I loved her so much... I couldn't tell her, she was so sick... so I... I went to some people... I borrowed ten million from the Russian Mafia... they've already threatened to kill me... I tried to borrow from the bank to pay them off, but I couldn't get it," he said full of shame and hung his head, "The man's name is Vladin... and now Suarez has bought the debt."

"Why didn't you tell me this before?"

"I thought I could fix it... but I can't," he said as he inched towards her.

"How does Suarez know all this?" she said and scribbled some notes in a pad.

"He met Vladin at a restaurant... if Suarez goes public... everything I've worked for... my name... her memory... it would all be for nothing," he said as the cold wind bit at his ruddy face.

"Do you think Suarez killed Vincenzo to gain control of the team?" she said, her interest piqued.

"Nothing Suarez does surprises me. He hated Vincenzo because he was a better driver, and I gave the ride to him instead of Suarez. Please... you have to help me. I need Randall! The rules say I need two drivers. If I don't, Carmen will surely ban me. It's the only way to save my team... and maybe find Vincenzo's killer at the same time," he said hopefully and extended his hand to firm the deal. "Please?"

After a few seconds and a heavy sigh, Gwen shook his hand. "Set up a meeting with Suarez the morning of the test session. Let him choose the location, but in a public place " she said tiredly.

"Why?"

"So it doesn't look suspicious," she said, growing agitated.

"Can't you just confront him about the Russian mafia? It is a crime, isn't it?"

"Suarez is a suspect and I don't want to tip him off. Besides, it's too hard to prove when it's your word against his, and there wouldn't be a paper trail," she said as she wrote some more notes before looking up at him, a serious look upon her face. "We'll have you wear a wire. Then you get him to talk about the Russians, but don't make it obvious."

"Could... couldn't you just plant a bug in his office?" he asked, growing anxious.

"No doubt Suarez is as afraid of industrial espionage as any other businessman. He probably has monitoring equipment to pick it up. I wouldn't want to take that chance because it's not safe. Don't worry, we'll be listening in and be close by," she said and tucked her pen and pad away.

"What... what if he won't talk? What if he suspects?" Samuel said, clearly uncomfortable and staring at the ground as he nervously rubbed his chin.

"He won't suspect. You're as guilty as he is regarding the Russians and I'm sure he doesn't want the press to find out, as you don't. It's your future Mr. Jenkins. Think about it for a while. I'll call you tonight," she said and gave him a comforting pat on the back. "It'll be alright."

"Thank-you," he said and limped for the limousine, but promptly stopped. "When this is all over, you should take the time to listen to your heart... to listen to the truth. I don't know what happened between you and Randall, but my wife told me something once that might help... forget your anger and hurt because it destroys the container it's stored in," he said and managed a fatherly smile as he motioned farewell with an imaginary tip of his hat. Gwen waited until the limousine disappeared and pulled Peter's ring off her finger. She tucked it in her trouser pocket and stared regretfully at the foaming water, but a glimmer caught her eye. It was Randall's ring, resting on a flat rock a few feet below, its progress halted by a mere twig. She felt another shiver ripple through her spine, pondering the forces of fate as she carefully leaned over and scooped it up.

Braedon slowed his white Ferrari, touring through the teeming, London nightlife and the city reflected in the slick streets. He craned his neck and saw the neon lights depicting the *Club Ruse*. There was a huge line-up of Rolls Royce automobiles and other exotics parked in a queue near the roped off entrance.

Braedon pulled to a stop behind a Bentley, turned off the rumbling engine and carefully observed the area. He opened the glove box, retrieved his revolver with quaking hands, placed it inside his jacket and hastened out of the car. "I better find this thing exactly as it is now," he said to the young valet, handing him the keys and several pound coins.

"Yes sir, Mr. Stirling!" the man replied excitedly.

Braedon barely took two steps and heard the shrieks of women, calling his name. They scrambled towards him as well as the men. Braedon watched the throng converge with their pens ready and cameras flashing. He smiled and waved to the frenzy of fans as a bulky doorman pushed the spectators aside and escorted him through the maze of faces to the entrance.

Inside, the music blasted, the deep base pounding, causing the floor beneath Braedon's feet to pulsate. He felt the vibration in his chest as he hurried towards the bar in a rainbow shower of strobe lights and the stare of awestruck patrons. "It's a pleasure to have you here tonight, Mr.

Chapter Twelve

Stirling. What can I get you?" the bartender asked as he straightened his bow tie.

"Irish whiskey, straight up. Make it a double," Braedon yelled above the racket.

The barkeep expertly poured the drink and placed it on a napkin. "It's on the house."

"Thank you," Braedon said and took a healthy swig.

The barkeep motioned to the VIP lounge with small tables, booths and overstuffed chairs. "She's in there," he said with a discreet wink. Braedon peered inside and scanned the much quieter room. Suddenly, he felt a tap on his shoulder and turned to find Teresa, clumsily holding a martini, scantily dressed in a miniskirt and flimsy blouse. Her face was pale and she was visibly thinner. "So glad you could come," she said, slurring her words and hiccupping before laughing stupidly. Teresa grabbed his hand and danced her way to a booth as she began singing a hymn. "Did I ever tell you I used to be in the choir at my church? I even wanted to be a Baptist minister like my father," she said, but soon became surly. "They wouldn't let me... because he fucked my mother," she said menacingly and leered at him with cold eyes. "There's a price for pleasures of the flesh, isn't there?"

"Can't we go somewhere quiet?" he said, his nervous eyes searching the room as she flopped down on the cushioned bench.

"What did you want to do when you were a kid?" she asked quietly, her glassy eyes looking off into space.

"What do you want?" he asked angrily.

"Answer me!" she screamed and pounded her fist on the table as some nearby patrons looked on.

Braedon felt his chest tightening and held his hands up, surrendering to her request. "Okay, okay... I don't know... I was good at fixing things. A mechanic, I guess... or a racing driver," he said with a confused shrug.

"None of my dreams have come true... it's not fair, it's not fair," she said as her eyes filled and she buried her weighty head in her crossed arms.

"I really do think we should go somewhere else," he said and sipped his drink.

"This is my game. My rules. Sit down," she replied, promptly composed and sniffed some cocaine from a small box. Teresa banged her martini against his glass, drained her drink and snapped her fingers at a nearby waiter, signalling for a refill. "So, how have you been?" she asked blithely and pinched her nose until the tickling of the drug subsided.

"What are you doing in England?" he said and reluctantly sat across from her.

"Samuel said I could travel with the team," she replied in a childish voice as she played with her unkempt hair.

"I didn't appreciate you calling my home!"

Teresa giggled again and rubbed her belly. "Do you think it's a boy or a girl?"

"You're lying! I'm not paying you a cent!" he said and swept away some cocaine powder on the table.

"How much do you want to bet?" she asked gamesomely and offered a hand to seal the wager.

"How much?" he asked knowingly, slapping it away.

The waiter arrived with Teresa's drink and she stuffed a few bills down the front of his trousers. "Do you miss me?" she said to Braedon with a girlish pout.

"I'm married!"

Teresa quickly became sullen. "I know. The whole world knows!" she said too loudly with an all-embracing wave of her hands.

Braedon shifted uncomfortably in his seat and took another sip. "How much?"

She puffed out her lips as her exhausted eyes wandered to the arching lights above. "I'm not sure I want your money now," she said with a whimper.

Braedon checked his watch. "Teresa, I have a test session coming up. I need my rest."

"You know, you sexually assaulted me back in Milan," she said, waving a naughty finger at him.

"I... I've been under a lot of stress lately," he said, avoiding her glare.

"And I haven't? My husband is dead and now you... I loved you, Braedon," she said and suddenly started to cry.

Braedon checked to make sure nobody was watching and took her hands. "Listen to me, please. Just tell me what you want."

"You," she said through tear-soaked eyes.

"Teresa, I can't... we did what we did, and that's all there is to it. I have a wife and son... I have my career to think about."

"What about me? I have nothing!" she shouted, causing a few patrons to glance over again, much to his chagrin. "That fucking bastard left all the money to the church, but I'll contest it! All I get is a lousy four million from his life insurance! He deserves to rot!"

"If it's my baby, I'll take care of things," he whispered.

"It *is* your baby!" she screamed and the other customers stared once more.

Braedon hurried to her side of the booth and wrapped his arm around her. "Okay, okay, relax. What about an abortion?"

Chapter Twelve

"What would your precious God think of that? Seems your religion only works when it suits you! No! I want this child! It's all I have left from you," she said, looking into his hazel eyes.

"Come on, let's go for a drive," he said and began pulling her away.

"I might be half a nigger, but I'm not stupid, Braedon! Unlike you, I was good in school! I have a brain! No, we're staying here!" she said, flicking herself free and gulping her martini.

"Look, I know this has been tough on you... I want to help," he said, struggling to control his temper.

"No you don't... you just want me to go away... I was like a toy for you... and now you're bored with me," she said and continued sobbing uncontrollably.

"I love my wife... I know you don't want to hear that, but it's the truth."

She raised a hand and caressed his cheek. "We can be happy together! I know we can! Please, just give it a chance," she said with desperation, but Braedon backed away as her face hardened. "Ten million pounds," she said bluntly and sniffed hard.

"WHAT?"

Teresa counted impatiently on each of her fingers. "One, two, three, four, five, six, seven, eight, nine, ten million pounds. God knows I've been patient with you. I've tried to be reasonable. That will buy my silence."

"I... I don't have that kind of money!" he barked and sat opposite her again.

"Don't lie to me! You make three times that a year!"

"This is blackmail!" he said, leaning across the table, trying to keep his voice down.

"Call it what you want, but that's the price," she said nonchalantly, checking her look in a compact mirror and using a tissue to wipe away her tears.

"And if I refuse to pay?"

She sighed and snapped the compact closed. "We've been through this before. Do you think I was dumb enough to make only one copy of the tape?" she said, patting her stomach. "And now I have this."

"I want proof!" he said through gritted teeth.

"Fine. In the meantime, I'll show the press our little home movie and tell them about the baby. I wonder how much Mrs. Stirling can get out of you after that?"

Braedon stood and was about to storm off, but unwillingly returned to the booth. "If I pay, how do I know you won't do this again? How do I know you won't go to the press anyway?"

"You'll just have to trust me," she said with a chortle as she cupped her chin in her hands.

"That's not good enough!"

"Tough. I'm number one and that's the price for screwing me," she said and lifted her blouse to tease him with her bare breasts. A small piece of paper fell out. "Beauty costs, doesn't it?"

Braedon's lip curled and his fists clenched. "I'll have an agreement drawn up and you're going to sign it or there's no deal!"

"I want this done by the end of tomorrow," she said and covered her chest again.

"For God's sake be reasonable! I don't have access to that much money right now!"

"I'm sure a man as famous and important as you can call up your bank manager just about any time and he'd blow you," she said and licked the rim of her glass.

"Teresa, the money is not in England! Tax reasons! You should know that! It's going to take a couple of business days!"

"You have forty-eight hours," she replied and pushed the paper across the table. "That is the account number where you will deposit the money. It's in the Cayman Islands."

Braedon stared helplessly at the note, picked it up and tucked it inside his jacket. "Is that it?"

"No. I want you to give me a lift back to my hotel... and make love to me," she said with sincerity and brushed her hand over his crotch as she fingered herself beneath her skirt.

"I'll pick you up a few blocks away. By the park."

A devilish smile from Teresa. "Are you still driving that beautiful Ferrari?"

"Why?"

"Because that's part of the deal too. I want it," she said as Braedon promptly scurried off. Teresa began gathering her things just as the waiter was walking by. "One more for the road," she said and sat back, full of content.

Braedon rushed out of the club, ignoring the pleas of autograph seekers and photographers. Flashbulbs popped as he frenetically took the keys from the valet. He climbed in, threw the automobile into gear and sped off. Braedon opened his coat and eyed the pistol. His gaze shifted to the rear-view mirror and noticed it was shaking. His hand tried to steady it, but he realized it was him that was trembling.

Braedon pulled the car to the curb, adjacent to a small park with only one streetlight. He turned off the engine and glanced in all directions. The only sign of life was a young couple, strolling along the stone sidewalk

Chapter Twelve

and crossing the street. Braedon was suddenly cognizant of his deep breathing as condensation was beginning to form upon the windows. His jittery eyes checked the rear-view mirror again and spotted a dark figure sauntering towards the car. It was Teresa, meandering along, happily swinging her purse in a circle as her footsteps echoed off the wet pavement. He felt his throat drying and was rapidly becoming light-headed. Braedon loosened his shirt and took a few, deep breaths as he heard her humming another hymn.

"Open up, sweets," Teresa's voice bellowed as she tapped the passenger window. Braedon unlocked the door and she slid into the cold, slippery leather seat. "I'm surprised you're here. I figured you'd run off to Mrs. Stirling."

Braedon's head bowed. "She left me... thanks to you."

Teresa laughed and shrugged unconcerned. "Fucking other women will do that."

"Don't you even care?"

"Why should I? Nobody forced you to have an affair with me. Your marriage problems are none of my concern," she said and tried fixing her hair in the visor's mirror.

"Why are you doing this, Teresa?"

"Because I can," she replied, drawing a British pound sign on the steamy window, followed by the number ten million.

Braedon hastily leaned over and smudged it off. "Stop it!"

"Scared of losing a little money?"

"What if I tell the press about your blackmail scheme? Or the police?" he said tersely.

"You have more to lose than I do, and you know it," she said confidently.

Defeated, Braedon shifted the car into first gear. "Where are you staying?" he said angrily.

"The Hilton," she replied. Braedon pulled away from the curb and did a sharp U-turn, causing the wheels to shriek. Teresa grabbed the stick shift and began stroking the knob. "If she's gone, let's go over to your house and you can fuck me in your bed."

Braedon abruptly hit the brakes, making the vehicle skid to a stop. He clutched her by the neck and rammed her head against the window. "Listen to me! Do you know how easy it is to kill somebody and get away with it? I'm going to pay you what you want and that's it! I don't want to ever see you again and I swear to God I'll end you if you ever bother me again! Understand?" he said and finally released her.

"You haven't got the guts," she said with a laugh as Braedon leaned over and opened her door before shoving her out. "What are you going to do, send a couple of your IRA boys after me?" she shouted as he slammed the door closed. "Aren't you forgetting something? This is my Ferrari now!" she yelled, but Braedon raced off. Teresa pulled her jacket a little tighter against the dank, night air and vanished into the shadows. Suddenly, a shot rang out and her silhouette fell to the sidewalk.

Chapter Thirteen

A gunshot blasted. Randall sat bolt upright in bed, knocking aside the numerous, empty airline bottles of liquor and realized a western movie was playing on the grainy, black and white television. He rubbed his bloodshot eyes, watching the gunfighter stagger and fall with a gaping, bloody wound. "He'll be lonely enough... now that he's dead," another character coldly remarked as the scene cut to the victim lying vertical in a coffin outside a saloon, the new widow weeping beside her toddler. "I'm lonely and I'm still alive... but not if I stay," Randall said and struggled to lift the remote off the nightstand, but suddenly remembered it was fastened. He angrily slammed his fist on it, shattering the plastic as the television turned off. He slumped back down and eyed the alarm clock. Five-thirty a.m. "Only asleep for thirty fucking minutes and a test session today? No goddamned way," he grumbled. He lit a cigarette and watched the smoke float to the plaster-cracked and nicotine-stained ceiling before his eyes lowered to his erection. "Get over it. You ain't seeing any more of split lips... that's the meatball's territory now," he lamented and glanced at Jessica's photograph on the nightstand, propped up against the lamp in front of a farewell letter to Gwen. "Swedish meatball better goddamn take care of you. Should have kicked his arrogant, fucking ass! Don't even know the man, but I hate his guts Jess... 'cause he's going to be your new pop," he said to her picture and stroked her face. "You're just like me, aren't you? I had to be a little adult at your age... that's what happens when your father is a fuck up," he said and brought the faded photograph closer. "Don't love him more than me though, okay? Don't ever forget me... I haven't forgotten my old man... impossible... the fucking asshole... but I forgive him... 'cause I want to be forgiven," he said and kissed her before returning the picture to its place.

Randall leaned up on one elbow, coughed up some phlegm and spat it in the metal wastebasket, full of unfinished versions of his goodbye missive to Gwen. He examined the cigarette between his yellow fingers and spotted the Gideon bible. "My body is a temple... and it's a fucking disaster area," he said with a sigh and studied his hands. "You wouldn't have the same reflexes today anyway. Been too long since you had to deal with another coffin pilot... and what if you couldn't do it again? You'd be a one hit wonder... a fucking pig with lipstick... see me for the fraud I am," he said with distain and gently touched the tender bruises on his chest. He moved slightly and grimaced at his rigidity. "Feel like fucking concrete. Too old for this shit... body and mind ain't sound."

Randall slid his stiff legs off the bed and planted them firmly on the filthy, shag-carpeted floor. "Fucked a lot of women in places like this. Arrested some of them too," he said fondly, scanned the tiny motel room and squinted, noticing a discoloured and crooked painting of a sunset, bolted to one wall. "Too fucking ugly to get stolen... looks like home," he said, dragging himself to his feet and stretching, the usual cracking of bones clearly audible as a cockroach scurried over his toes. Randall fleetly snatched it up and studied the bug. "My old man used to call me a cockroach... ran away from home once to a motel and took my pop bottle money to pay for it... he caught up to me though... beat the shit out of me as usual... remember looking at one of you guys while he did," he said and gently placed the insect on the windowsill.

He turned on the lamp and gingerly gathered his clothes, strewn about the floor and stuffed them into his suitcase. He started to peel off his underwear, wandering to the small bathroom, but stopped. "Fuck that! Might give me time to change my mind!" he said, sniffing his armpits and grabbing his deodorant. He gave a hasty swipe beneath each arm and squeezed too much toothpaste, causing the tube to spew all over the mirror. "Shit!" he said and stared at the spotty glass. "I ain't jealous and I ain't no coward! And to hell with guilt!" he said and smeared the paste around until his reflection was obliterated. He quickly brushed his teeth with his fingers, rinsed, spat and gave his face a fast wash. He moistened his comb and ran it through his matted, blonde hair. "Good enough," he groused and crammed the toiletries into the case. Randall pulled on his dungarees, cowboy boots and T-shirt, closed the suitcase and stuffed his wallet in his back pocket. "Good luck with the meatball," he said, giving one last glance at the letter to Gwen. "Bye baby," he said sadly to Jessica's picture, blowing her a kiss and opening the door, only to find Gwen. Her eyes slowly dropped and focused on his baggage.

"As usual, it looks like someone is feeling sorry for himself... and quitting, yet again. Funny how the victim always manages to forgive, but the guilty can't forgive themselves," she said and leaned against the frame with crossed arms, her attention glued to Jessica's photograph. "Professionals call it private speech. Children do it mostly. Jessica does it when she's doing a jigsaw puzzle... but I guess adults talk to themselves too when they have a problem. I heard everything you said."

"I never said I was sane. I'm supposed to be crazy, remember?" he said with a reddening face.

"I don't think so. You're just lonely, a little jealous and a little scared. I think that means you're normal," she said and stepped past him into the room.

"How the hell did you find me?" he asked, thoroughly embarrassed.

"It's the cheapest and closet motel to my place, remember?" she replied and noticed the letter. Gwen picked it up and read as Randall shuffled nervously. "Short but sweet. I can't believe you'd let Peter stand in the way of finding Vincenzo's killer," she said and crumpled the paper.

"Seeing the meatball was tougher than I thought, okay? So I'm jealous! Big fucking deal! How would you feel if I was banging some other broad and Jessica was with me?" he said without looking at her.

"It would only make a difference if I was still in love with you," she said softly as Randall could only stare at the floor, understanding the message in her implicit comment. She handed him Jessica's picture. "You should keep this."

"Why? So I can remember what used to be mine?" he whispered and shoved her hand away.

"Look, I... I'm sorry about Peter. I should have told you about our plans," she said sincerely.

"I don't give a shit what you do," he replied with a careless shrug and reached for his denim jacket just as a spray of automatic gunfire shattered the window and peppered the wall. Both dove for cover as Gwen withdrew her sidearm and Randall covered his head.

"Here we go again! Goddamnit I wish I had a fucking gun!" he said. Gwen hurriedly pulled up one pant leg and produced a small revolver. She tossed it to him as another deafening fusillade exploded, raining bits of plaster upon them as several bullets tore through Randall's coat, hanging in the alcove. "Jesus H. Christ! Hanging around you is going to get me killed!" he said.

"I don't like you calling Peter a meatball! He's a decent man!"

"Hey, if the name fits," he replied, readying his weapon.

"And I don't know if you purposely haven't mentioned it or not, but you never did sign our divorce papers," she said and stole a glance at his astonished face as they crawled beneath the window. "When this is all over, I'd like you to sign them... please," she said, withdrawing the legal document from her pocket and placing it before him. "Ready?" she said. He nodded as both inched upward and peered out to discover a tan Audi. They fired several rounds, blowing out the windows and destroying the grill, but ducked again as another orange blast of fire ripped through the room.

"Whoever is taking shots at us sure likes expensive cars," he said and surveyed the damage. "The maid's going to be pissed," he said as the sunset painting disintegrated. "No loss there," he added and pulled the phone cable until the cradle and receiver crashed to the floor. "I ain't signing them," he said and slid the paperwork back to her.

"Why not? I've never asked you, until now... I felt bad enough leaving you!" she said with a touch of shame. "Guilt isn't exclusive to you, you know... you weren't the only victim that day in the car!"

"I just don't think the meatball is right for you... or Jess," he said and watched more slugs crack the drywall and ricochet, one blowing apart the television. "Fuck me! Where the hell's your backup?"

"I don't have any!" she yelled. "How dare you judge the man I love? You're blinded by jealousy!" she barked and pushed the papers towards him again.

"Why the hell don't you have any backup?" he asked incredulously and dialled 17 as per the emergency instructions on the telephone.

"I wasn't sure I wanted to stay on the case!" she said and checked her gun's magazine. "I came here for personal reasons," she said, sliding the divorce decree back to him as he stared at her in stunned silence. "Okay, I should have had some backup! So sue me!"

"Jesus woman! Why didn't you just call me and ask?" he shouted and scrambled for something else to say. "Look, make an executive fucking decision, will you? Do you want me on this goddamn case or not?"

"You're the one that wanted to drive for ego reasons!" she said and watched as more bullets laced the ceiling. "The question really is; do *you* want to be on this case?"

"Answer my question first!" he yelled and crouched further down.

"Look, are you a cop or a racing driver or both or nothing?" she asked impatiently. He searched for an answer. Silence again. They jumped up, aimed and fired, the sound of bullets tearing through the car's steel. Another return battery as they retreated. "Well?" she asked.

"This ain't the time to discuss this," he said, brushing the papers aside and noticing her glare. "Alright, alright. Once a cop, always a cop," he reluctantly admitted as she continued staring at him with raised eyebrows, waiting for him to continue. "Yeah, yeah, yeah. I'm still on the fucking case for the right reasons... I guess."

"Not good enough, Randall. I'm sick and tired of this cat and mouse game. Swear it on your daughter," she said as Randall stared soberly at her, promptly realizing the severity of the impending oath and taking a moment.

Chapter Thirteen

"I... I guess if Jess has the guts to keep fighting... so do I," he said and crossed his heart. "I swear. What about you?"

"What?" she replied, blushing slightly.

"Jesus! Do you want me on this investigation or don't you?"

"Yes... as long as your emotions don't get in the way... or mine. Okay?" she said and he nodded. "Good. By the way, I have some news." Another break as they stood, fired and ducked after another volley from the sedan. The wood frame of the window blew apart, splinters showering and a few bullets shredding the pillows and mattress. The vibrations caused the remaining airline liquor bottles to roll off the night table.

"To hell with it! If I'm dying here then I'm doing it with a buzz!" he said and grabbed a Jack Daniel's. "What is it?" he asked, unscrewing the lid and gulping it down. "Breakfast of champions," he said and grimaced.

"Teresa's been shot. It hit her in the shoulder," she replied and took the other bottle. She uncapped it, drank and coughed, much to his surprise.

"So will you if you don't keep your goddamn head down!" he shouted and pulled her closer to the floor. "How do you know she's been shot?" he said.

"Jenkins called me this morning. He told me something else too. Suarez doesn't want you in the seat."

"Why not?" he replied as there was another lull in the shooting. They stood and fired.

"Jenkins borrowed from the Russian Mafia to pay off the blackmailer, and Suarez bought the debt. He's threatening to go public and trying to force Jenkins to give up fifty-one percent of the team, and then put himself in as a driver," she shouted over the racket of another barrage from the sedan.

"I guess that clears the old man as a suspect and shines more light on the spic again," he said and picked up the telephone receiver, but stopped when he heard screeching tyres and saw the sedan disappear in a storm of smoke. Randall leaned against the wall and tried to catch his breath, as did Gwen.

"This is some serious shit! Somebody sure wants to remind us we're not welcome. I said it before, but I'll say it again, if they wanted us dead, we would be," he said, dusting himself off and lighting a smoke, but Gwen reached over and took it from him. "No pills?" he said sarcastically and lit another as panicked voices from other motel patrons were heard congregating. Randall surveyed the destroyed room as feathers wafted. "Hope the DST's got a credit card. Who shot her?"

"Teresa says she doesn't know, but rumour has it she was spotted with Braedon at a club before she was hit," she said, picking bits of debris out of her hair. "She won't admit that she was out with him for obvious reasons. It would ruin her image as the grieving widow."

"Sounds like she's protecting someone. Maybe it is Braedon, but why?" he asked and tapped the bottle to get the last, few drops. "Going to talk to them?"

"I can't. It would blow our cover if we start snooping around and asking a lot of questions. I've seen the police report. There were no witnesses. I told the locals to stay out of the way. The DST cleared it with the British. We're telling the press it was a random shooting," she said and spat some dust from her mouth. "Remember, the fewer the people that know about us, the better chance we have of making an arrest. Besides, the higher-ups want this done discreetly. We'll just have to wait and see how this all plays out."

"For Christ's sake! Do they know how hard it is to solve a murder with your arms tied behind your back?" he said and shook his head in frustration. "Alright, aside from the Suarez thing, maybe Braedon was fucking Teresa and one of them decided to break it off," he said and opened another bottle.

"And maybe the one that didn't want it to end had Vincenzo killed," she said, taking another swig and wincing.

"More motives and more suspects. Shit! Nothing's ever easy. Still doesn't explain the Rabbit," he said and belched.

"I know. That's the only part I can't figure out," she said as they struggled to their feet.

The innkeeper, a bald man with flannel pyjamas and a soggy cigar crushed in one corner of his mouth poked his head into the room. "What in God's name is going on here?" he said with a heavy French accent. "You two will stay here! The police are on their way!" he added, threatening them with a stapler.

"Hey froggie, relax. I left the window open," Randall said casually to him and pressed the room key into the manager's sweaty hand. "I'll be checking out now," he said and grabbed his suitcase.

"Who is going to pay for all this?" the innkeeper said with outstretched arms and tobacco juice flying from his mouth.

Gwen flashed him her badge as sirens were heard approaching. "The gendarmes will be here shortly sir. They'll take care of everything," she said and went to follow Randall out the door as two police cars screeched to a halt. The officers ran towards them with weapons drawn as Gwen presented her identification again. "DST gentlemen. We have the cooperation of the government. Check with your commanding officer. Just secure the area and wait for the techs," she said and turned to Randall. "I'll have my people check the ballistics in the motel room. It's a safe bet

Chapter Thirteen

they're from the same gun in the BMW," she said, fingering a warm slug in the door before exiting. After a few steps, Gwen slowed, a distant look upon her face. "Randall?" she asked. He stopped and faced her. "Please sign the papers," she pleaded and held them out for him. "You probably think our marriage was a waste of time, but I have some good memories... and sooner or later that's all you've got left, but I need some more though... some new ones. I... I don't have a lot of friends," she said sheepishly, "but I'm happy the way I am... and a man loves me and I love him... whatever you think of me... I'm a human being first and a cop second."

"I'm just a cop... and I'm not even sure of that anymore," he said, seeing her serious glower and sighing heavily. "Tell you what, as long as I'm on this case, and I promise I'm in it until the end," he said, offering the Boy Scout's symbol of honour. "I ain't signing them... but when it's over, okay," he said and offered his hand. "Deal?" Gwen gladly shook his leathery hand and kissed his forehead. "I'll be dead anyway," he said sardonically as she opened the door of her brown, rented sedan with darkened windows. "What happened to the Mercedes?" he asked, frowning at the plain automobile.

"The DST bought it. The rental company didn't care much for the bullet holes. I thought I'd better get a cheaper model," she said as a strange look came over her face. "Randall? Did... did you... you know... did you ever cheat on me?" she said, afraid of the answer and popped the trunk for his suitcase.

"Why?" he replied with a frown, carelessly tossing the baggage into the compartment and closing it. "What does it matter now?"

"My father cheated on my mother once and she found out... they never spoke about it, but I knew it bothered her. I guess it made her feel like less of a woman... I just wanted to know... I need to know... it's a chick thing as you would say," she said with a nervous laugh and rubbed her forehead.

"That little dent in your melon is kind of sexy," he said and pointed at it, but she wasn't amused. "No... that's one thing I never did to you," he said and gestured to the cigarette in her hand. "And since when do you smoke?"

"I have to work with you, don't I? Come on, we have a flight to catch across the channel," she said with a smile, pleasantly surprised by his admission.

"Uh?" he said, completely puzzled.

"I'll tell you on the way," she said as he gave her another quizzical glance. "Incidentally, how come you never did sign the papers?"

"I couldn't find a pen," he replied and rolled his eyes. "What do you think?"

"I'm flattered... I really am."

Randall slid the gun she had given him across the roof. "Piece of shit. You couldn't hit the side of a fucking mountain with that peashooter."

"Your aim always was lousy," she said playfully and climbed in. "Maybe you need glasses. You *are* getting older."

"Watch it, split lips," he said and opened his door. "Or I'll change my mind again."

"Maybe I... maybe we should change our thinking on this," Samuel said, nervously examining the pen in his jacket pocket in the back of Gwen's newest rental car as a light rain sprinkled. "I really don't want to do this," he said and suddenly jumped, startled at some kids in uniform kicking a soccer ball through the puddles on the sidewalk.

"We need to get Suarez on tape admitting to the mafia deal, but don't make it obvious. Then you can use it against him to get Randall in the seat. It might even be leverage for us to force a confession out of him if he had anything to do with Vincenzo, but don't ask him directly about it," she said and stopped at a corner, waiting for the morning rush of people to cross the street. "Suarez may be innocent and we don't need him to know that Vincenzo was murdered. If he's guilty of the killing, we don't want to tip him off that we think he's involved. If it gets ugly, sign the contract. We'll deal with it later. Remember, we can't go in there."

"Don't worry, he'll never suspect the pen is a bug. The spic isn't going to think of that," Randall said as Gwen turned onto another road with heavy, but orderly traffic. "There it is. Holy shit, looks pretty swanky," Randall said, pointing to an old but exquisite, large, red brick building with an engraved brass plaque reading, *Waterloo Grove Men's Club* above huge doors, centred between a row of buildings.

Gwen drove past the entrance and parked a few hundred yards away. "You should have tried to get him to meet somewhere else," Gwen said with a hint of anger.

"He insisted... what was I supposed to do? This was such short notice," Samuel said and licked his parched lips as he buttoned his coat with shaking fingers. "I still think we shouldn't do this. What happens if he finds it?"

"I told you, we can't go in there. We can't even plant an undercover. It's a private club," Gwen said, thoroughly annoyed and looked at Randall as she brushed back her black hair and rubbed her aching forehead.

"He can't harm you in a public place," Randall said and surveyed the mirrors to ensure they weren't followed. "You must have lied to the Japs when you were a prisoner with those fucking cowards. Just act natural."

Chapter Thirteen

"They're not Japs, they're Japanese! My wife was Japanese!" Samuel said curtly and opened the door. "Her parents died at Nagasaki, but she never called the Americans *damn Yankees*! The Japanese are not cowards! I am not a coward! And I'd appreciate it if you'd remember that!" he said and slammed the door.

"Insult a man's grapes and no matter how old they are, they'll try and prove they got guts. He's a testy old turd, but I feel for him. My heart's pounding and I ain't even the one going in," Randall said and scanned the narrow avenue, packed with pedestrians. "Not a lot of room in this town, eh?"

"Don't get soft on me Randall. Jenkins got himself into this mess," she said coldly and inspected her firearm beneath her jacket. "Check yours," she added.

Randall flipped open his denim coat and showed her the gun she had given him. "Loaded with water and ready to go," he said sarcastically and studied the limousines parked at the curb in front of the club. "That's the kind of snobby place you should be a member at... if they allowed split lips in there."

"Why are you always trying to start a fight with me?" she said as her eyes darted from mirror to mirror, checking for suspicious activity.

"Face it, your kind meets in those places so you can get away from everyday slobs like me and discuss your vision of what society should be like," he said, motioning to the minions of London. "God forbid the blue-collar trash actually have a say in what type of world we live in," he said and searched himself for his cigarettes.

"Is this a jealousy thing? I can't help the fact that your family didn't have money," she countered, obviously insulted.

"I never said we didn't have money. The fuck just pissed it away on the ponies and booze. Always put himself first," he said and found his smokes.

"Just like you."

Randall stared at her with anger mounting in his blood, but he bit his lip and faked a smile. "Are you on the rag or something? Fuck, lighten up, split lips," he said and pulled a cigarette out with his teeth.

"I don't want to get into another discussion about our families, alright? You're the one in a bad mood because you're having withdrawal symptoms. Have as many cigarettes and shots as you like and we'll both be happy," she said and folded her arms.

"Ha ha," he replied sardonically and felt a chill ripple through his body. "Goddamn. Hope nothing happens because I ain't getting out of this fucking car," he said, watching the rain slash against the windshield as he deliberately snapped the cigarette in half and lit it. "I hate this waiting shit."

"Why did you break it?" she asked and downed a few pills.

"Trying to quit. Tired of coughing up my lungs," he replied, longingly spying a pub across the bustling street. "You should cool it on those pills too. They're making you more bitchy."

"You're the last person who should lecture me on health and attitude," she said and began preparing her headset. "Let's just end this conversation before we regret it."

Randall extended his seat back and threw his hands behind his head. "Can't believe I'm sitting here on a fucking stakeout and in less than four hours I'll be driving a racing car," he said, he opened the glove compartment and began rifling through it. "At least I won't be shot at... hopefully."

"Now what are you doing?" she asked, becoming agitated and adjusting the bug's receiver.

"Looking for something to eat. There must be some DST mints in here somewhere. Taking me to McDonald's wasn't exactly the breakfast I had in mind," he replied, closing the compartment again with a disappointed sigh and restively began tapping his fingers atop the dashboard. "Was on this stakeout once. Fucking boring as usual. Sitting in a van full of stale farts and drinking freezing coffee. Was waiting for this asshole suspect to leave his apartment so we could follow him in case he was going to toss the murder weapon," he said and started to laugh. "These three, dumb fucking kids tried to steal the van while we were still in it. Actually shit themselves when they saw us and found out we were cops," he said and promptly became interested in a black, stray cat, scrounging in a narrow alley as the rain fell harder. "I don't know how these people put up with this shitty weather. A wonder Jack the Ripper even bothered to go out."

"You always did complain too much. This is paradise," she said, listening to Samuel breathe via the radio. "I once sat in a park in a snowstorm in Belgium for six hours, waiting to make contact with an agent from Iraq. We were meeting to talk about selling nuclear technology to them."

"What happened?" he asked, barely interested as he continued watching the feline huddle in a corner, the rain pelting its soaked head.

"I killed her," she said matter-of-factly and straightened her headset.

"What? Her?" he asked in disbelief. "Why?"

"We didn't want the world to know. The UN frowns upon that sort of thing. The woman was threatening to go public with the deal unless she was paid. We couldn't trust her so I was ordered to expire her. I shot her in the stomach... stole her wallet... forced the gun into her vagina after she was dead... until she bled," she said as her face contorted with the recollection. "Made it look like a random robbery... rape... can still see her lying there... bleeding to death."

Randall took a moment as his eyes drifted. "I know what you mean... Jesus... that's heavy shit you did."

"How many elites have to do that... how many get their hands dirty?" she asked quietly as the memory knifed through her soul.

"You got a lot of secrets, don't you?" he said, she reluctantly nodded. "I have one... it's the only thing that keeps me hanging on from one second to the next," he said, drawing an odd glance from Gwen. "How many people *have* you killed?"

"Enough that I'm not proud of it... enough to keep me awake at night... and enough that I give Jessica too many hugs and kisses... but it does get easier, as sick as that sounds... you get used to it... like handing out parking tickets... you just have to remember why you're doing it... for the greater good," she said and managed a slight smile. "It's the only way to keep sane... you have to choose a side... it's the lesser of two evils."

Randall leaned over and kissed her forehead, much to her surprise. "I owe you one of those too. Sorry you had to go through that shit... sorry I brought it up," he said and forced himself to focus on the cat again as he withdrew his wallet and opened his door a crack.

"Where are you going? I might need you."

"Getting something for that cat," he said, but discovered he didn't have any money. "Besides, I thought you said we couldn't go in the club."

"The old man is still a suspect and I want to see if he speaks freely, but if he's in danger, we move, even though it would reveal our identity to Suarez," she said and gestured to the partly open door. "Close that and stay in here."

"For Christ's sake woman, there's a store right there," he said and pointed before holding out his palm. "I'll be back in a minute."

Gwen sighed, rolled her eyes and gave him some bills. "Just hurry. What is it about you and animals anyway?"

"They never mask their true intentions. Can trust them. Straight shooters just like me... that's why I have so many enemies," he said with a grin and opened his door, the rain lashing in.

"What you see is what you get is not always a good thing," she said and turned on the heater.

"I know... it sure as hell didn't seem to work with you, did it?" he said with a wink and closed the door before running to the small convenience store.

"Yes it did," she whispered to herself as she watched him go.

Wearing only shorts and a pair of running shoes, Felipe Suarez admired his sweat-soaked, tanned, lean body, running on a treadmill before a mirrored wall in the deserted, colossal gym. The other velvet walls were crowded with paintings and photographs, dating back four hundred years of elite and famous clientele.

The door opened and Samuel slowly entered as Felipe felt the hairs upon his arms rising when a fob vibrated inside his pocket. "Come on in Sammy," Felipe said warmly and increased the treadmill's speed, creating a slight racket.

"Sorry I'm a little late," Samuel nervously replied.

"Don't worry about it," Felipe said and motioned to the juice bar. "Have a drink." Suspicious of Felipe's unusual hospitality, Samuel limped to the bar, the immaculate hardwood floor creaking beneath his feet. He poured himself a glass of water, sat on a stool and surveyed the luxurious surroundings. "I've been a member here since I was twenty. My father was a member too. Maybe you should join Sammy. We have quite a few activities; arts, business and socio-political discussions," he said condescendingly and raised the machine's speed again. "We have servants, waiting staff, grounds people and of course, on-site medical service," he said with a smile. "No women are allowed. We all know they're only good for one thing, right Sammy?"

"I... I guess," Samuel said, feeling his heart pounding with a slight ache in his chest.

"Would you like me to put your name in for a membership?" Felipe asked and moved the treadmill's speed to its highest level.

"No... no, thank you," Samuel said and drank.

"Don't tell me you're one of those men that believes in so-called core values of equality, due process and political openness," Felipe said sarcastically and shook his head, spraying sweat on the floor.

Samuel drank greedily until the liquid was gone and nodded heavily. "I do, yes," he said and checked his watch. "I would like Randall Grange to drive the other car... I'd like him to test again today... the other session... you know... sometimes poor rehearsal makes for good performance."

"Please tell me why you think he should be the driver," Felipe said calmly as Samuel stared dumbly at him, puzzled by the Spaniard's pleasant demeanour.

"Well... I know you've always wanted Hispania Gold to have a presence in North America... and now that you do... having a Canadian driver might be a good way to introduce your product into that market... especially since the Grand Prix in Montreal is less than a week away," Samuel said as a mild sweat appeared upon his forehead.

CHAPTER THIRTEEN

"You may be right," Felipe said, turning off the treadmill and wrapping a towel around his glistening neck. "I'm going to be away for the weekend, but I'll give you a number you can reach me at. Give me a call and let me know how Mr. Grange did today, alright?"

"Certainly," Samuel replied, still taken aback by Felipe's behaviour and filling his glass again.

Felipe went to the bar and tore a slip of paper off a pad with the club's raised letterhead. "Can I borrow your pen?" he asked with another smile. Samuel hesitated momentarily but quickly handed the writing instrument to him. Felipe scribbled the number. "Writes nice," Felipe said and went to hand it back, but dropped it in Samuel's glass and grinned, reaching for the fob in his pocket and dangling it in front of him. "I wondered how long it would be before you did something stupid. Do you know this only cost me seventy-five dollars? It's quite remarkable. It vibrates when it detects a transmitter or even hidden cameras. I carry it all the time, including at all of our previous meetings. I even have interceptors on my phones," Felipe said and saw Samuel nervously glance at the exit. "I told the staff I wasn't to be bothered. Nobody is coming to your rescue Sammy."

In the alley, Randall opened a small carton of milk and bent down, trying to entice the cat to emerge from behind a garbage can. "Here you go. Come on buddy," Randall whispered and carefully tore the carton's top half away. He glanced over his shoulder at the annoying trickle of water from a rainspout and returned his attention to the feline as he edged closer. "This milk is better than that shitty water you've probably been drinking. Got some canned food too," he said and withdrew the tin from his pocket. Randall peeled back the lid and used a stick to scoop it out onto a discarded pizza box. "Liver and beef feast. Smells great," he said as the cat inched towards him with its nose sniffing. "Bet your name is Shadow. Dark as the ace of spades, aren't you?" he said, setting the milk beside the food and happily watched as the ravenous animal began to eat. Suddenly, the cat looked up, past Randall's shoulder and bolted away.

"I... I don't know what you're talking about... look, just give me the contract and I'll sign it," Samuel said and swallowed hard.

Felipe shook his head and began to laugh as he wrapped his arm around Samuel and led him to the treadmill. "Let me tell you a little story, Sammy. When I was in my teens, I knew my mother wanted to have another child. I'm not stupid. I knew I would have to eventually share the family fortune with a sibling, so I arranged for my father to have an accident," he said and loosened Samuel's tie. "Walking the streets can be dangerous Sammy. There are a lot of sick people in the world. Sick enough to remove a man's testicles. Dear old dad recovered, but he was never quite the same and oddly enough, the criminals were never caught. Do you understand?" he asked with an ice-cold glare. "You know, I once read an article about you in the paper about your rise as a prisoner of war to a successful businessman. It must have been hell to walk all those countless miles to the camp. I understand many men dropped dead from exhaustion, but you managed to hang on. It said you used to sing God Save the Queen to keep up morale, even after they beat you."

Samuel used all his might to stop from shaking and leaned heavily against his cane for stability. "You only want my team out of stupid, childish revenge! You didn't have the talent for God's sake! I can't help it that Carmen won't allow any more teams!" Samuel said trembling, trying to resist Felipe as the Spaniard forced him onto the treadmill. "Your greed is a sickness... sometimes I wonder if you had Vincenzo and his father killed to gain control of the series," he blurted.

Felipe remained stone-faced, holding Samuel in place and turning on the treadmill. "Everyone that works for me must exercise Sammy. Sentir la vida! That means feeling alive," Felipe said with fiery eyes and stroked his Vandyke beard. "You've let yourself go Sammy. I run ten miles per day. Take a good look at yourself, that is what death looks like," he said, forcing Samuel's head to the mirror and increasing the machine's speed. "Just like business, always start out low Sammy and work your way up," he said as the old man laboured to keep pace.

"I... I can't... my health... please," Samuel managed to whisper, his face becoming flushed.

"You haven't told anyone about our little secret, have you Sammy?" Felipe asked and raised the speed again.

"No... no," Samuel replied gasping as he desperately shook his head and felt a tingling in his arms.

"Partners should never lie to each other. You wouldn't lie to me, would you Sammy?" Felipe asked and turned the speed up yet another notch.

"No... no," Samuel said, his legs melting to rubber as he became dizzy and struggled to inhale. His terrified eyes returned to the door, hoping for an intervention from Gwen and Randall.

"Waiting for someone Sammy? Who gave you the transmitter? The police?"

"I just wanted Randall to drive... that's all... I want to keep my team," Samuel whimpered, slurring his words as perspiration dripped from his tortured face.

Chapter Thirteen

"I'm sorry, but that is not an option!" Felipe shouted. "Grange might be good, but not quite good enough! It won't do me much good when he crashes on the first lap like he did at the test session, will it?" he yelled, but quickly composed himself. "Now, did you tell the police?" Felipe asked and switched the speed to its highest power. Samuel mumbled, his thighs tightening and cramping as he neared unconsciousness. "I was going to be reasonable with you today. I was going to tell you that in exchange for the debt, you could just give me the team, but you betrayed me, didn't you Sammy?" Felipe said as Samuel weakened, flinching and fighting the urge to gag. "Who gave you the pen?" Felipe questioned. Samuel's hands began to slip and Felipe switched the treadmill off. The old man dropped to his knees with his fingers still clinging, but Felipe forced him to stand again. "Karl wasn't supposed to kill you, but I will!" Felipe whispered in his ear as Samuel gurgled. "Just tell me who gave you the transmitter!"

"I... I bought it... I wanted to... to get you to admit to buying the debt... I was going to use it to get you to leave me alone," Samuel said, barely audible as his vision doubled.

Felipe stared at him, weighing Samuel's words. "You're used to torture Sammy. How do I know you're telling me the truth?"

"I'll sign... I'll sign," Samuel said, his voice trailing off as the veins in his head bulged. Suddenly, Felipe released him and Samuel collapsed. The old man coughed and wheezed, trying to fill his burning lungs as he writhed on the floor.

Felipe withdrew Samuel's pen from the glass and scribbled on the pad. "It still works," he said flippantly, sticking it in Samuel's hand and producing the contract. "Sign it!" Felipe ordered, but Samuel's eyes rolled back and his body relaxed.

Randall moaned and awakened when he felt the tickle of whiskers against his face. His eyes looked into the stray cat's before the feline resumed eating. Randall lugged himself up and instantly felt the stifling pain in his shoulder. He staggered a few feet and used the brick wall for support as he stumbled out of the alley. Pedestrians gave him odd stares and scolding comments concerning employment and alcohol as he tried to run, but fell to the wet sidewalk and hauled himself up again. Randall finally made it back to the car, fumbled to open his door and froze. Gwen was slumped over the wheel with the transmitter in her lap. "Jesus, no," he whispered and hurriedly climbed in. His shaking hands pulled her back to discover a trickle of blood from a gash on the side of her head. He desperately felt for a pulse.

Chapter Fourteen

Braedon's Ferrari rumbled past the Waterloo Grove Men's Club and followed the busy street to a hospital. There were several, mobile television trucks out front and other members of the press were milling about, but his attention focused on a pregnant woman being helped from her car by the nervous husband near the emergency room entrance.

Braedon felt a chill rocket through his body as he sped up and turned onto another road. He parked in a no parking zone at the rear of the building, stepped out and hurried to an open door where the laundry staff were working. "You're not allowed in here," a surprised woman said, but another employee whispered to her as the others exchanged excited murmurs about the world champion.

Braedon withdrew his wallet and firmly slapped some bills on a table. "I'm here to see Teresa Legaro, but I don't want to be bothered. Could somebody please show me how to get to her room?"

Minutes later, Braedon fleetly climbed the steps of the stairwell and opened a door, leading to a ward. He took a deep breath, nervously checked his inside breast pocket and shielded his face as he whisked through the corridor, but found two police officers stationed at the nurse's desk. One officer elbowed the other when he recognized Braedon and indicated to a newspaper on the counter with the bold headline, 'Teresa Legaro Azzopardi Victim Of Random Shooting'. Beneath was a photograph of her and another of Braedon with its own by-line reading, 'New Widow Seen At Club Ruse With World Champion'. "Can I get you to sign an autograph for my boy?" the first officer asked and held out the newspaper.

"I'm here to see Mrs. Azzopardi," Braedon said, quickly signing the newsprint as his eyes avoided the article.

"She's not supposed to have any visitors," the second officer said. "Security reasons Mr. Stirling."

Chapter Fourteen

"Please tell her I'm here," Braedon said and stepped closer to them. "There's some tickets to the next British Grand Prix in it for you. I just want to see how she's doing, that's all. I have something for her... something she's expecting."

The officers eyed one another before the first policeman motioned for the nurse to make the call. "We do have to search you Mr. Stirling," the officer said reluctantly. Braedon felt his heart skip a beat and a surge of adrenaline course throughout his body.

"I don't the think the world champion is a threat," the second officer said and winked with a toothy smile. "Provided those tickets are the fancy kind. You know, in one of those VIP boxes?"

"Food and liquor as well," Braedon said with a relieved smile as the nurse hung up the phone.

"Go ahead. Last door on your left," the nurse said. Braedon nodded his appreciation to them and calmly strolled away.

"Lucky bugger. I wouldn't mind laying the sausage to a grieving supermodel," the first officer whispered to his partner and both chuckled.

Braedon placed his hand on the doorknob and hesitated. He could feel himself getting warmer and he opened a button on his shirt. Finally, he opened the door as the strong scent of flowers greeted his olfactory senses. Teresa sat by the window, surrounded by dozens of bouquets, get-well cards, teddy bears, balloons and various, morning newspaper editions. Teresa's shoulder was bandaged and she wore a bland hospital gown. "No flowers?" she said disinterestedly.

"How are you?" he said, gently closing the door.

Teresa sat forward, watching the throng of reporters. "I remember the first time I saw my picture in the paper... it was when I was in the high school Christmas pageant... the next time was after I moved to Miami and was arrested for fucking the mayor's brother, but he paid well," she said and glanced at him. "Do you have it?" she said and reached for a nail file.

Braedon removed a check from inside his jacket and a contract, showed it to her and tucked them away again. "If I divorce Lisa, what are the chances we could get back together?" he said, sitting on the edge of the bed.

"Anyone who tries to kill me is hardly worthy of my love. Besides, I know you. You'd only do it to save your wallet," she said and continued filing her nails.

"I swear to God I didn't shoot you, Teresa," he said and blessed himself.

"You still go to church, don't you?" she asked and he nodded. "What do you like best about it?" she said softly and studied the crucifix over her bed.

Braedon debated whether to answer, but saw the esoteric look in her eyes and thought for a moment. "I guess... I guess I liked the peace... the feeling of being secure from what was outside the doors... I wanted to forget all of the hatred," he replied, slightly embarrassed, but his face rapidly soured and he stared at his hand with the tattoo. "But then you remember why you had it in the first place."

Teresa's eyes slowly moved to his and she smiled. "What you said about being secure... I used to feel the same way... but men have a funny way of changing that... even men of the cloth," she whispered as her gaze returned to Christ. "But I'm fighting back. I've got all the ammunition I need now," she said, rubbing her stomach. "And the tape. I have two aces and I intend to use them if I have to."

"Have you ever considered the damage to your own career if you release that tape?" he asked and padded his sweaty face with his handkerchief despite the air-conditioning.

"It would be worth it to get what I want... and see you publicly humiliated," she said, returning her attention to the press again.

"Maybe I don't care what the public thinks," he said and stood with his hands in his pockets.

"You're wife did," she said with an evil simper.

"I suppose you're proud of yourself for ruining my marriage?" he said as his jaw tightened.

"As a matter of fact, I am, but you did your share. I wonder what the great Mrs. Stirling will think of all this?" she said with a laugh and threw a newspaper at him.

"Have you spoken to the press yet?" he inquired full of fear as he cleaned up the scattered papers.

"No... but I will if you screw me around," she said and reached for her nail polish.

"What about your baby? Our baby?"

"This little angel is money in the bank," she said, patting herself again. "I'm sure any lawyer worth his salt will be happy to tell me that no signed agreement with you will stand up in court after he or she is born. Something they call duress. Are you familiar with that term?"

"You're going to come after me for financial gain in the future, aren't you?" he said, slowly moving towards her.

"Did you really believe I wouldn't? You know you're going to have to pay up, so you may as well get used to it," she said and blew on one of her nails.

"I'll want to see the blood test results to see if it's mine," he said with simmering anger.

Chapter Fourteen

"Fine. Now give me the check and I'll sign the papers," she said, holding her hand out.

"You've got it all figured out, haven't you?" he replied with flaring eyes.

"It certainly seems that way. Now, if you don't mind, I'd like to get some rest," she said, still waiting with an outstretched hand.

Braedon reached inside his jacket and retrieved a plastic bag. "Do you know what this is?" he asked, removing the home pregnancy test and holding it up so she could see. "I want you to take it... now."

Teresa chuckled and said, "Go to hell." Braedon checked over his shoulder and eyed the bathroom. In an instant, he grabbed her arm and covered her mouth with his hand. Teresa tried to scream as she struggled to break free from his grip, but his hands were too powerful. Braedon dragged her towards the bathroom as her legs kicked wildly.

He latched her hair with his free hand and pulled her head back, her terrified eyes pleaded with his. "Listen to me you whore, you're taking this test! Now!" he said, forcing her onto the toilet seat before closing the door and withdrawing a roll of duct tape from his jacket. Teresa continued to wriggle, but stopped as he dug his nails further into her scalp. Using his teeth, he tore off a long strip of tape and covered her trembling mouth. Silenced, he tore off another piece and imprisoned her hands behind her back. Subdued, Teresa relented as he pushed her gown up past her waist, exposing her mound. Braedon expeditiously removed the package from the bag with quaking hands, ripped open the box and withdrew the test strip as his eyes slowly dropped to between her legs. "Do it!" he whispered, prying her thighs apart with his knee and holding the strip beneath her as Teresa violently shook her head through muffled cries.

Braedon pinched her nostrils closed. Teresa's face quickly reddened, her wide eyes beginning to roll back and her limbs starting to convulse. "I should kill you... you bitch!" he whispered through clenched teeth as the veins in his neck bulged with anger. Her trickle of urine brought him back to reality. He released his grip and positioned the test strip between her legs.

The stick moistened, he carefully placed it on the basin counter and turned to her. Life was returning to Teresa as her nostrils flared, sucking in as much oxygen as possible. Slowly her eyes opened and she stared at him with a blank expression. "If it's positive... my life's over anyway," he said casually and caressed her face. "I'm... I'm sorry... I had to do it... you have to understand Teresa... it was the only way... you should feel lucky," he said as his glazed eyes became hypnotized by the window blinds' cord swaying in the breeze. "I can kill... I almost did when I was only ten... slit an old man's throat in an alley... Protestant bastard... it can be done and you never get caught... I don't care what you do with that tape... my marriage is finished," he whispered and snapped out of his trance.

Her breathing composed, she leaned back, totally exhausted as Braedon checked his watch. He picked up the test stick and examined the results. "Sweet Jesus," he whispered to himself and hid the stick in his jacket. He stumbled slightly and sat, balancing himself on the edge of the tub and burying his head in his hands as Teresa watched him, completely terrified. Suddenly, he stood and unwrapped her hands. "Scream if you want... it doesn't matter now," he said and gently removed the tape over her mouth. She gasped for air with teary eyes. He quickly gathered the pregnancy packaging, crumpled the tape into a sticky ball and placed the items in his pocket. Braedon removed the check and contract and shredded them in front of her face before hurrying out the door.

Braedon marched down the hallway, a grin breaking across his face. "See you at the race," the first officer remarked and handed Braedon a slip of paper. "That's our telephone number for when you get those tickets." The world champion didn't break stride as he snatched the paper and nodded his approval.

"By the way, we're very sorry about Mr. Jenkins," the second officer said. "Bloody shame having a stroke." Braedon froze and turned back to them, completely shocked as the paper slipped from his hand.

The bloodstained gauze flew from Gwen's hand into a wastebasket as she leaned against the lockers in a posh, private changing room at Silverstone. "Can I please have one of your cigarettes?" she asked.

Surprised by her request, Randall reached into his denim coat and handed her the wrinkled packet as he zipped up his racing uniform. "Fine time to start a stupid habit after a slight concussion," he said and lit the smoke for her. "Maybe you should have stayed overnight, like the doc said."

"And this isn't the time for you to start telling me what to do," she barked and inhaled deeply.

"A little on the rag aren't we?" he asked and tucked Jessica's charred picture beneath his racing overalls. "Call your mother or something."

"What is that supposed to mean?" she replied and coughed.

"It might take your mind off being a bitch... although she was one herself," he said and pulled on his shoes.

"How would you know? You never even met my parents," she said angrily and accidentally burned her finger with the cigarette.

"They couldn't be bothered to come to our wedding, and I sure as hell wasn't going to spend all that coin to fly to France for Christ's sake," he

CHAPTER FOURTEEN

said, attaching the Velcro straps on his footwear. "Christ! They didn't even come when Jess was born!"

Gwen wanted to retaliate, but thought better of it and took another, long drag. "Look, I know you're nervous about competing against Braedon, but I'm not the enemy! Maybe *you* should have a cigarette!"

"I'm trying to quit, remember?" he shouted, but suddenly calmed himself. "Look, I'm nervous and you're a bitch. Okay? Can we just move on now?" he said and stood. "I still say you should be in the hospital."

"Why, because I'm a woman? You had a concussion and you didn't stay!"

"There's that feminist shit again. Jesus! What are you, bipolar or something? All it means is you're as stubborn as I am," he said and felt his sore shoulder. "Damn fuckers must have clubbed me with a baseball bat."

She stared at him for a moment and crushed out the tobacco on the floor. "Sit down and turn around," she said. Randall obliged and Gwen began to massage his throbbing shoulders.

"Arguing like this is just like being married again, eh?" he said, feeling an erection starting, but suddenly forgot about it and winced as her fingers worked harder.

"Don't remind me," she replied and grinned, noticing the expansion between his legs.

Randall's gaze shifted out the window and down to the two, Jenkins' racers on the starting grid amidst the crew. "So fast they're unnatural," he said and focused on the Hispania Gold tobacco emblems on the rear wings. "Wonder how many people died at the expense of that company... wonder if *I'm* going to die at the expense of that company," he said matter-of-factly. "What the hell was Jenkins doing on a treadmill anyway?" he asked rhetorically.

"It's all over the news that he had a stroke," she said and looked to the muted television in the corner, showing a reporter in front of the hospital and a graphic informing viewers about Teresa and Samuel being patients in the same building. "Obviously Suarez forced him to do it. I didn't get a recording of their conversation. I think maybe Suarez found the bug, which means he knows someone's watching him," Gwen said, suddenly feeling dizzy and probing the bump on her head. "I remember you leaving the car and then all of a sudden, my door was opened and I got hit," she said and checked her wound for blood.

"I didn't see shit either except that goddamned cat," he said and hauled himself up. "Whoever fucked us over is sending another warning that we're not needed. Not sure why they don't just whack our asses. They had the chance."

"Well we can't question Suarez because he'll just deny any wrongdoing, and we might tip him off by identifying ourselves. If he gets a lawyer, the press will find out and then there goes our cover. Besides, there were no witnesses and Jenkins is in a coma," she said disgruntled and poured herself a cup of water from the sink. "I'd just like to know if Jenkins signed the team over to Suarez before the stroke," she said and swallowed a few pills.

"I don't see the spic here so I don't think he did, but who takes control of the team now?" he said with a heavy sigh and she shrugged. "This is just fucking great, isn't it? All we have so far is a list of suspects that we can't question and a concussion for both for us," he said and splashed some cold water over his unshaven face. "Dumb fucks in your government ain't making this any easier by gagging us."

"If push comes to shove, I can always haul Suarez in regarding the Russian mafia. Who knows? He might get scared and spill his guts, but I doubt it. He knows I wouldn't have any proof. As usual, we can only wait and see what happens," she said and noticed the angst upon his face as he searched the grandstands. "And yes, my people are out there watching your back."

"So now who do you think iced Vince?" he asked, continuing to survey the grounds.

"At this point Braedon," she said with uncertainty. "Like you said, he wants to remain champion and Vincenzo was a threat. And maybe Braedon was having an affair with Teresa, which would explain why she's not talking to the press or the police about who shot her. Braedon had motive. All that stuff between Jenkins, Suarez, Carmen and the mob seems like a red herring to me. You?" she asked and rested her pounding head against the lockers again.

"Jenkins is our man," he said confidently with his hands on his hips, admiring his uniform in a mirror.

"You've got to be kidding," she said with a hearty laugh. "The man's a vegetable now, and the doctors don't think he'll ever be able to talk or walk again."

"Makes sense to me. He creates this phoney extortion shit, which is why you can't trace the money, then ices Vincenzo to collect eight million on the insurance. Who knows, maybe Teresa was in on it too. She's going to cash a fat check for four million from Vincenzo's policy," he said and began loosening his neck muscles.

"You're forgetting that Vince was worth more to both of them if he remained alive."

Chapter Fourteen

"Been thinking about that. What if Vince didn't keep winning? It happens to every driver," he said, but wasn't convinced by his own words, "but then again maybe it is the spic."

She scoffed. "You really don't have a clue, do you?"

"It's possible," he said defensively. "He would have access to Jenkins' stationary to write the letters. Maybe he knew the old man would have to borrow from the mob. Maybe Suarez and the mob are in on it together?"

"Okay, and how does the Rabbit fit in?" she said, enjoying his theorizing and watching an hare bounce along on the other side of the fence across the track as an eagle circled overhead, waiting for a chance to kill.

"Well... maybe Suarez hired him because... well, maybe the mob capped the Rabbit because... maybe I haven't got a fucking clue," he said and surrendered with his hands. "What about Carmen then Sherlock?"

"If Vincenzo's father's plane crash could be traced to Carmen, I'd say we could pursue it, but that doesn't seem to be the case. Face it Randall, everything we have is circumstantial and the only evidence we do have is a rifle with the Rabbit's prints, and he's dead," she said with a worried expression.

"Maybe whoever's responsible has nothing to do with the team because all three times we were attacked, it happened away from the track," he said and began exercising his fingers by bending them gently backward. "Like we said, only Jenkins, Carmen and Hesse know who we are, so it has to be one of them then."

"What about your last test session? Are you saying it *was* an accident?" she asked full of doubt.

"It could have been... fuck. I don't know," he said impatiently. "All I do know is I got a one race contract and I'm going to do it... and if I get smoked for whatever reason... at least I bought it doing what I love... I think," he said with an awkward smile. "And then you don't have to worry about the divorce papers."

"Don't talk like that!" she suddenly snapped and lunged at him, slamming him against the lockers, the metal sound echoing. "It's not funny and I don't want you pushing it out there!" Gwen promptly realized her actions were excessive and revealing so she stepped back. For an instant, their eyes remained locked and they both felt the urge to embrace, but a huge boom of thunder awoke them from their temporary trance.

Randall's eyes slowly moved to the window where tiny drops of rain began streaking the glass. "Goddamn weather... clouds keep following me," he said dumbly. "Ah... um... how... how's Jess today?" he asked, trying to change the course of the conversation as they checked their emotions.

"Fine... fine.... ah... Peter's looking after her," she replied uneasily and pushed back a strand of her hair from her suddenly hot face.

"I think the nanny would be better than the meatball," he said, straightening his collar.

"Don't call him that, and while you're at it, stop calling me split lips! You can think whatever you want, but I'm the one who makes the decisions when it comes to my... our daughter!" she said tersely, and checked her watch when she found nothing else to say. "Come on, we're late!"

"You're beautiful when you're angry," he said with a grin, satisfied she couldn't hide her affection for him.

Randall followed her down some steps, through a short corridor to the exit leading to the pits as he spied the threatening sky. "Reminds me of my racing debut in the cart my dad bought me. Sure was fucking cold that morning," he said with a nervous laugh. "Even remember what I had for breakfast, a bagel, yoghurt and some fruit. Was the only shit I could keep down," he said and snuck a peek to see if his hands were shaking, "And all my old man was worried about was that I didn't make a fool out of him. Whoever said be careful what you wish for... hell, they weren't kidding," he said, unwillingly looking at the racers as they drew closer.

"Oh, I almost forgot... I have something for you," she said and timidly withdrew a pink, baby bracelet with Jessica's name. "Remember this? I thought you might like it for good luck. I want you to have it."

Randall's face softened as he stared at the tiny token in his scarred palm and tucked it into his pocket. "Thanks," he said quietly, suddenly disconcerted by the tender moment and trying to mask his fallibility. "Um... by the way, what are you going to say if you're asked about your head?"

"I'll tell them you hit me," she said with a smile. They were both startled when they heard someone coming up behind them.

"Good morning," Ichiro said happily and bowed, causing his blonde hair to bounce. "I have your helmet Randall. You can have it designed any way you want," he said and pushed his glasses upward with a beaming smile. "It is good to see you on time."

"Fear breeds punctuality," Randall replied, running his fingers through his messy hair.

"You do not seem the type," Ichiro said, noticing the tremor in Randall's hands when he handed him the plain white helmet.

"That's how drivers stay alive," Randall countered, examining the headgear.

"My parents taught me there are three marks of existence; pain, impermanence and egolessness. Accept that and you will be a better

Chapter Fourteen

racer," Ichiro said assuredly, but his mood rapidly became more sombre. "But they also told me it is impossible to make a permanent relationship with anything."

"Like Vince?" Randall said and Ichiro simply nodded. "Was he ever scared?"

"Nobody noticed, but I did," Ichiro said proudly. "When you are entrusted with a man's life, you get to know his secrets."

"What secrets?" Gwen asked innocently as she wrapped her arm around Randall's waist for the benefit of anyone watching.

The question caught Ichiro off guard and he eyed her with suspicion. "I am not sure what you mean."

Randall winked and gave him a shot in the arm. "You know, boy talk. When I raced against Vincenzo he fucked every pit bunny he saw."

Ichiro gave an embarrassed chuckle and adjusted his blue rims again. "I would not know anything about that."

"Sounds like you didn't like the horny fucker," Randall said and spat through the fence onto the track.

"His name was Azzopardi... Vincenzo Azzopardi!" Ichiro said too harshly. "The racing surface is sacred ground! Please do not defile it!" he said and stormed off.

"Hey?" Randall said. Ichiro stopped and turned to him. "Sorry about what happened to Jenkins. You sure we should go through with this session? I mean, he's lying in a hospital bed and barely fucking alive."

"He would want us to continue," Ichiro said and hurried away.

"Ichiro?" Randall said, the engineer reluctantly stopping again. "Just out of curiosity, who's the boss now?"

"Do not worry, Samuel told me he offered you a one race contract," Ichiro replied and quickly went into the garage before Randall could question him further.

"Strange fucking cat he is," Randall said, circling his finger in the air by his head to indicate mental problems.

"I wonder what else Jenkins told him," Gwen said and rubbed her aching forehead. "Maybe Ichiro knows who we are and what we're doing."

"Guess we're going to find out," Randall said and saw the frown upon her face. "What's wrong?"

"What you said about Vincenzo and women... was I your first?" she said shyly. "I know I asked you that when we first met and you said I was but... be honest.... was I?"

"What the hell are you asking me that for now?" he said, completely uncomfortable.

"Was I?"

Randall couldn't help being hypnotized by her inviting, brown eyes as she pleaded silently for the truth. "It was before the bastard was killed. Was thirteen. Stole the money out of his wallet and went downtown. Us guys always used to watch the hookers, especially this strawberry blonde with big... you know," he said and demonstrated with his hands. "She was the first... he never found out, but he knew I took the cash. That was a session I'll never forget... couldn't walk for a week," he said and forced a laugh, hoping to erase her anguish.

"You never asked me but... you were my first," she said quietly. "I just thought you should know that."

"Are we going to do this thing or not?" Braedon's voice barked. Randall and Gwen turned to the champion, wearing his racing togs and meandering towards them. "Come on superstar. Let's see what you've got in traffic."

Ichiro quickly emerged from the garage and clapped his hands together until the crew hushed. "I... I just wanted to say I know we all feel badly about Samuel... but we do have a job to do," he said nervously. "I would like this test to be as close to race conditions as possible... so keep it between the ditches as Samuel would say," he said and laughed stupidly, but soon stopped when nobody else did and referred to his clipboard. He shuffled some papers and one of his comic books fell out. He hurriedly gathered it up. "Um... to start off, we are going to have a ten lap stint. This is going to be an equal affair, so both drivers will do the usual standing start, side by side on the grid," Ichiro said and looked to Randall. "I want you to practise a pit stop. I will tell you when over the radio. I do not want you thinking about anything else but driving. That goes for you too Braedon. And Randall, the car has been set up the way you requested for the first session. If it begins to rain harder, then we will switch to wets," he said, looking skyward as tiny raindrops pelted his glasses. "Good luck, gentlemen," he added, wiping them against his team shirt and hurrying back into the garage.

"Just a minute Ichiro," Braedon said and pointed at him. "I'd like to know who put you in charge."

"It is written in my contract with Samuel... if he is unable to attend, I am the one who shall run the team," Ichiro replied awkwardly and disappeared into the building.

"Imagine that, Samuel gives control of the team to him. The same people that almost killed him in a POW camp," Braedon said with a bewildered shake of his head.

"It ain't so strange. You're an asshole, but you still manage to drive a car," Randall said. Braedon glared at him before angrily snatching his fireproof balaclava and helmet from one of the mechanics.

CHAPTER FOURTEEN

"Time to turn up the heat and see if the potato-head is our man," Randall whispered to Gwen.

"You keep acting like that and it'll be a full fledged barbecue," she said and patted his backside.

"That's the idea," Randall said with a wink and sauntered to his racer.

"Good luck," she said. Randall merely waved at her over his shoulder.

"Sorry about what happened to Teresa," Randall said casually to Braedon after the crew were out of earshot. "I figured you'd be concerned since you were probably fucking her," Randall said and elbowed him. "Is she as good as I think she is?"

"Hey rookie, I don't know where you're getting your information, but it's wrong," Braedon said, trying to remain cool, but was clearly blushing.

"I suppose then that the two of you weren't together last night," Randall said and pulled on his balaclava.

"We happened to be at the same club and frankly, I don't have to answer to you," Braedon said and wrenched on his helmet.

"What about your wife? Do you know who she's fucking, because it obviously ain't you?" Randall said and wriggled on his headgear. Braedon clenched his fists and was contemplating striking Randall, but decided against it. "I wouldn't take a swing at me potato-head or you'll be driving with your fucking feet," Randall said, eyeing his curled fists.

Braedon grinned and spied the dark clouds. "Do you know what it takes to be a great driver?"

"Tell me, oh great one," Randall replied sarcastically.

"A great driver, like me, is one that wins when he's supposed to and still does when he isn't supposed to," Braedon said, pulling on his gloves and eying him from head to toe. "You can do neither."

"I guess I'm just more style than substance," Randall shot back and held one finger to his jaw, pretending to remember. "Seems to me though Mr. IRA that your record in the rain ain't so fucking shit hot, whereas I was the goddamn king of the wet," he said and leaned closer to Braedon. "But I'll let you in on a little secret that even a spud-eating fuck like you can understand, in the dry the car shouts what's wrong with it. In the wet, it whispers. Rain is the great equalizer pal."

"When I was driving in Formula 3000, my team-mate had the same kind of dangerous attitude that you have. It was in Austria that he raced his last race. Poor fellow tried to intimidate me on the track in these same kinds of conditions," Braedon said and barely motioned to the sky. "I gave him a little tap to remind him of who the boss was and he hit the wall head-on. Shattered both femurs. He was too scared to drive after that," he deliberately whispered and slapped Randall on the back, "and he was the supposed 'king of the wet' too," he said and flipped Randall the finger before climbing into the cockpit.

Inside the garage, Ichiro was perplexed by the champion's rude gesture. "What in the world could Randall have said that caused that?"

"Try being married to him," Gwen replied and sat beside him.

"It must be nice to have someone," he said solemnly and grabbed a headset, instantly regretting his remark.

"You don't you have a girlfriend?" she asked, pretending to be surprised.

"I... I used to," he said, avoiding her eyes and fiddling with a computer monitor.

"What happened?"

"She was not faithful," he replied shamefully without looking.

"I hope you punched him out," she said with a chuckle, trying to lighten the atmosphere.

Ichiro glanced at her before returning his attention to the computer. "I could not... it was Azzopardi."

Gwen hoped her stunned expression wasn't obvious as she scrambled for something to say. "I'm... I'm sorry that happened... did Vincenzo know that you knew about it?"

Ichiro took a few seconds and debated whether to answer. "We never spoke about it, but I think he did... I do not even think his wife knew," he said and adjusted his radio.

"You must really hate him," she said, anxious for his response.

"Everyone has good in them... there really is not any bad people... Azzopardi just made a mistake," Ichiro said and donned his headset. "It is time for work."

Both Randall and Braedon were nestled tight within their cockpits and the engines were fired. The crews backed away as Randall glanced at Braedon, but the world champion just stared straight ahead. "Composure in the cockpit, but chaos on the outside. Ten laps to separate the men from the boys," Randall said happily and tightened his visor.

"Keep your eyes on the lights," Ichiro's voice said via the radio. The racers' power plants sprang to life, the revs beginning to rise and the gears were engaged. The starting gantry of lights began to blink off.

Randall felt the rush of adrenaline as his heart rate doubled. "Time for a pissing contest."

"Remember, the first rule of racing is to not take out your team-mate," Ichiro said.

"Wrong Itchy. The first and *only* rule is to beat your team-mate," Randall said to himself.

Chapter Fourteen

The lights turned off and the duo blasted away in a cloud of dust. Braedon immediately chopped left in front of Randall as the cars hurtled towards the right-hander at Copse. Randall swept directly behind, hoping for a quick slipstream to pass. Not enough track. Not enough time.

Braedon led around Copse and headed for Maggotts with Randall in tow. The world champion gave a quick glance in his mirrors, watching Randall dicing left and right, looking for a place to stick his nose as the two machines followed the trail of pavement, exiting Chapel.

Randall slammed into seventh gear, maximizing nineteen thousand RPM, glued to the back of Braedon as they flashed down the Hangar Straight in a blur of colour. Randall could feel the draft working as his racer began to buffet, his hands clenching the wheel. "Don't mirror him... don't mirror him... you'll make the same mistakes... might lose air," Randall grunted, despite the violent ride.

Braedon checked his mirror again. Randall was so close he could only see the impetuous Canadian's rear wing. The sweeping right-hander at Stowe's Corner was rapidly converging as Braedon swung further to the left, preparing for the turn. In an instant, Randall was alongside him. "A little game of chicken! Going to out brake me?" Randall said. The novice squeezed left, causing Braedon to steer to the border where the road met the grass. Braedon's right front tyre and Randall's left front nearly touched as Braedon shot an anxious glance at him. Randall forced Braedon off line and the world champion slowed too late, scorching his brakes as Randall swept into the lead. "Text book!" Randall yelled gleefully.

"Bastard!" Braedon screamed inside his helmet.

In the garage, Ichiro watched the speed warriors on the monitor without expression. "I guess he's no fluke," Gwen said proudly.

"Wait for it," Ichiro said with a knowing smile.

Randall geared down approaching the slow left at Club Corner and checked his mirrors, but couldn't find Braedon. Suddenly, the champ was on his left and Braedon stood on the brakes for a split second, smoke trailing from the melting rubber. Braedon slipped to the inside, cut to the right, across Randall's path and nearly sliced off his front wing. Randall watched helplessly as Braedon up-shifted and stretched the distance between them, heading for the Abbey Curve. "Damnit! Fucking rookie mistake!" Randall yelled.

High in the corner of the grandstand, past the Woodcote Curve, a shadowy figure hurriedly leapt two steps at a time, heading for the top. A silver case dangled from the person's right hand, occasionally banging into the seats during the ascent. Their breathing was laboured with each furious step until finally, the stranger arrived at the top row. Hands clumsily unsnapped the case.

Braedon wove through the tricky curves at Priory and Luffield, his helmet slanting left and right, diving into the corners. A hasty view through his left mirror revealed Randall lagging a hundred yards behind. A grin broke across Braedon's face and he geared up, heading for the long, sweeping asphalt that would take him to the start/finish line.

"You're trying too hard!" Randall scolded himself as he struggled with low down force through Priory. "Back end has to sit down! Too much oversteer!" he said, shifting into seventh as he rocketed along the straight. In a mere second, he was closing in on Braedon's black ribbons of rubber, but wasn't near enough to catch the draft and remained behind him as both started the curve at Copse for a second time.

"Patience, Randall. Nobody ever won a race on the first lap," Ichiro said calmly into his mike.

"This thing handles like a pig!" Randall's voice crackled over the radio.

"You are the one that wanted low drag. It is the first day of school Randall. This should teach you that balance is needed, which means you have to listen to me. Tell me what is happening," Ichiro said as Gwen listened in.

"I'm driving the fucking car!"

"I need to know how the car is handling so we can make adjustments," Ichiro said, watching Randall's racer squirm under braking as he drove through Stowe's Corner.

"This thing is fishtailing all over the goddamned place!"

"You are not getting enough power down in the corners, that is also why you are sliding," Ichiro said and scribbled in his notepad.

"I'm not a fucking idiot! Leave me alone!"

"Something tells me he's going to be difficult to work with," Gwen said to Ichiro, slightly embarrassed.

"That makes him like every other driver," Ichiro replied with his eyes glued to the monitor.

Randall ripped the radio cord from its jack. "Got to brake earlier or later!" he said as he sped towards the Abbey Curve.

Braedon geared down approaching Abbey and casually checked his mirror. His heart skipped a beat and he winced, waiting for the impact. Randall's car was barrelling towards him as a plume of smoke billowed from the rear tyres. Randall suddenly bolted to the inside, bounced over the saw tooth curbs and back onto the track. Braedon scrubbed off speed to avoid a collision and watched Randall resume the lead.

In the grandstand, cross hairs focused on Randall's car as it exited Luffield. The Jenkins' racer swung wide to the left, using all available road to gain a faster entry into the straight, leading to the start/finish line. Suddenly, the stranger spotted two of Gwen's men in the adjacent grandstand and quickly began packing the gear.

Randall drove with his mirrors, closely surveying Braedon slipping under his gearbox. Braedon yawed to the right and Randall followed, cutting him off. The world champion bolted to the left to slingshot past as Randall allowed him the space. Both racers flashed across the start/finish line in a dead heat. Another game of chicken. Copse was closing in and one of them would have to cede their position. Suddenly, Braedon ducked in behind again and deliberately tapped Randall's rear. Randall's machine bobbled wildly from side to side, but he maintained control as Braedon took advantage of the momentary tank-slapper and shot through on the inside, barely a foot ahead. Randall backed out of the gas and promptly fell in behind again as Braedon locked up his tyres. The Irishman ran out of track, veering over the curb and onto the grass. The racer spun wickedly and nearly overturned, but came to a stop in the gravel trap in a massive cloud of dust. Braedon smashed the wheel with his fist and angrily unbelted himself.

Randall slowed, hit the accelerator and performed a perfect, smoke filled, three-sixty. He drove back to the scene of the accident and stopped as Braedon marched out of the haze towards him. Randall unhooked the wheel, released his belts, stepped out of the cockpit and pulled off his helmet. "I bet that was a real neck-stretcher, eh? Fuck that was cool. You okay?"

Braedon ripped off his helmet and balaclava. "Are you out of your mind?"

"What's your problem?"

"You nearly killed me!" Braedon said, throwing aside his headgear.

"What? You're the one who kissed my ass! I'm lucky I'm not splattered all over this fucking track!" Randall shouted, gesturing to the road.

Braedon pointed a threatening finger. "You don't belong here!"

"You're just pissed because I passed you! Twice!"

Braedon waved him off and walked away. "Go back to Canada and stick to hockey!"

Randall grabbed his arm and spun him around. "You arrogant little shit, you can hate Vincenzo and dick his wife, but you're not going to fuck with me!" Randall said. Braedon went to swing at him, but Randall grabbed his fist in midair and delivered a heavy blow to his stomach. Braedon doubled over and dropped to one knee, gasping for wind. "Stick to fighting on the track," Randall said and strolled away.

Ichiro, Gwen and a medical team pulled up in a van and quickly stepped out. "Is he okay?" Ichiro asked, running towards Braedon.

"I think he's got food poisoning," Randall replied and sat on the chassis of his car.

Confused, Ichiro and the medical crew looked to Braedon. "Do you need a doctor?" Ichiro inquired.

Braedon caught his breath, peeled off his gloves and slapped them into Ichiro's hands. "Find yourself another driver! I quit!" he said and stormed off.

"What? You can't do that!" Ichiro said and chased after him.

"I'm out! The man is too dangerous! It's not worth my life to play wet nurse to some rookie!" Braedon said, motioning to Randall.

"But you have a contract," Ichiro said worriedly. "It is better to be part of a group than an individual."

"Oh cut the Buddhist bullshit Ichiro! My contract is with Samuel, not you!" Braedon said and marched away.

"No, it is not... it is with me now," Ichiro said nervously with his head cowed.

All eyes turned to Ichiro as Braedon pivoted. "What do you mean?"

"It is doubtful Samuel will come back to lead us... we can only hope he lives now... and I own the team if he is unable to operate it," Ichiro said quietly and saw his explanation wasn't adequate as everyone watched in stunned silence and waited for him to continue. "Samuel's late wife Aki... she... she is my grandmother... Aki had a baby out of wedlock before she met Samuel... she was raped... that baby was my mother," he said, brimming with shame. "Samuel could not have children of his own... he always took care of me... like a son."

The information was soaking in as Randall and Gwen glanced at one another while the others whispered their disbelief. "I don't care! I quit!" Braedon said and hurried away as a clap of thunder echoed, followed by a heavy downpour.

"Holy shit! The plot thickens," Randall whispered to Gwen. Her cell phone suddenly rang and she discreetly moved further away from the others.

"Yes? Where? Did you get them?" she asked excitedly, but her enthusiasm abruptly diminished. "Damn. Okay," she said, hanging up and seeing tufts of bloody fur blow past her feet.

"What was that all about?" Randall asked, appearing from behind.

"There was someone in the grandstand... but they got away," she said angrily. She turned to face him and rubbed her sore forehead. "I think *I* need a drink," she added and saw the eagle flying above her with the dead hare in its talons.

Chapter Fifteen

A banderillero, carrying a banderilla in each hand, ran towards the charging bull at an angle and thrust the colourfully decorated, barbed darts into its shoulders. The beast temporarily staggered and stumbled away, its neck muscles further weakened. Julius Carmen grimaced as he padded his moist forehead with a handkerchief and felt the heat evaporating his energy. "You don't wave your handkerchief until the toro is dead," Felipe said happily, enthralled with the event. "My father took me to only one bullfight when I was a boy. It was the first time for both of us. He cried because the beast was dead... but I cried because it was alive. I always wanted to be a matador, but he thought bullfighting was too cruel."

"It is. I prefer the Russian ballet," Julius replied as his green eyes spied the burning sun. "You didn't fly me all the way to Spain to watch a bullfight. I have to get back, so what did you want?"

"Ole!" Felipe shouted joyously with the spectators as he watched the matador gracefully sidestep the rampaging animal. "Bullfighting is all about avoiding a brutal confrontation using intelligence, grace and elegance.... just like your beloved ballet," Felipe said, demonstrating with his hands. "The relationship between the matador and the toro is based upon distance, but the bullfighter is supposed to be the creator and master. The beast will always attack and the matador enhances the danger with each pass, getting closer and closer," Felipe said with a menacing look and slowly turned to Julius. "Which one are you, the matador or the bull?"

"I think I'd rather be the matador," Julius said, completely perplexed and running his fingers through his sweaty, blonde hair. "What does that have to do with anything?" he asked, growing impatient.

"I'm just like the toro. I keep charging until I win, no matter what the cost," Felipe said as a small bead of perspiration dripped from his Vandyke. "I want you to expand the number of teams in the series."

"You're in no position to demand anything. We have been through this before. Besides, legally, the other teams have a say and they always vote no, and will continue to do so, even if I wanted to add more," Julius said sternly as the matador drew his cape over the charging bull's head.

"You must have heard that Ichiro Tanaka is now in control of Team Jenkins," Felipe said and showed him a newspaper clipping stating the fact. "I only found out about it myself this morning," he said as the bull spun and lunged again.

"So?" Julius said as the matador barely stepped aside, much to the delight of the fans, followed by another chorus of *ole*.

"I believe as the sponsor, I would also make a good team owner... and driver of course," Felipe said as the matador prepared his killing sword.

"You can do whatever you want. That's between you and Ichiro," Julius said as the stricken bull lumbered a few feet and stopped.

"There is no way Ichiro will sell to me... or any other team," Felipe said, the matador extending his arm and aiming his espada at the wavering, maddened taurine monster. "And even if you did expand the number of teams, it would be years before I could get a share of the television revenues."

"That's business," Julius replied matter-of-factly and couldn't help but watch as the matador lowered his cape, the bull's exhausted head cowing to expose the vulnerable spot behind the shoulders, anticipating the death stroke to its heart. "Your reputation prevents you from realizing your dreams, and that's nobody's fault but your own."

"I... we, have a problem," Felipe said, trying to mask the sting of Julius' words as the matador ran towards the bull.

"Which is?" Julius replied, the matador's sword bouncing off the animal and skipping across the sand as the crowd roared their contempt and hurled cushions.

"What if I told you that Samuel was helping to finance his team with money from illegitimate sources?" Felipe asked as the matador grabbed the sword and tried again, but the weapon glanced off the beast once more, further exasperating the crowd.

"How do you know this?" Julius said, barely interested as the matador withdrew another sword with a cross on the end and stabbed the toro's head. The beast listed slightly and collapsed, but continued moving as the spectators lusted for the coup de grace.

"Because Samuel told me. He came to me as a friend to ask for my help. That's why he was at the men's club with me before he had the stroke," Felipe replied as the bullfighter's aide was about to thrust a dagger into the bull's brain, but the beast suddenly lurched forward, one horn penetrating the matador's throat and exiting the back of his neck. The crowd rose to their feet in a collective scream as the bull thrashed its head wildly, the bullfighter instantly killed. "If news of Samuel's indiscretion

Chapter Fifteen

was made public, imagine what your... our sport would suffer. The damage could be irreparable to all of us," Felipe said as Julius watched the mayhem.

"You've always been too dramatic," Julius said with a carefree laugh. "The only harm will be to Samuel. Besides, I'm sure quite a bit of *your* fortune is not exactly aboveboard," Julius added as the bullfighter's aide tried to help the matador.

"That is one thing you and I have in common," Felipe said, placing one hand on his shoulder.

"You and I share nothing," Julius snapped, moving further away before fanning himself with his hat and shaking his head with disgust at the scene below. "I do not enjoy barbarous sport."

"Bullfighting is not a competition, it's an art. It's all about fluidity... just like money," Felipe said as he rubbed his fingertips together. "You're a hypocrite Julius. You hunt, don't you?"

"I eat what I kill. I do not murder for the sake of death or money," Julius barked as the matador was placed upon a gurney.

"Really? That's odd," Felipe said condescendingly. "I met a man in Sweden who told me he used to work for the KGB... and you were his boss," he said as Julius' confidence vanished. "Let's stop playing games. I want you to disallow Team Jenkins from participating. Force Ichiro to sell the team. I'll buy it and change the name."

"I'm not responsible for the actions of a former subordinate. I have to leave," Julius replied nervously and went to walk away, but Felipe stopped him.

"Did you know that the matador's traje de luces, his suit of lights with all that beautiful gold decoration is hand-made and takes six people a month to make?" Felipe asked and lit a cigar. "All that hard work and all that training for a man to become a matador... gone in a mere second by a more powerful force," he said, snapping his fingers.

Julius fully understood the meaning of Felipe's words and grinned. "Let me tell *you* a little story. There was a man from Moscow who fell in love with a beautiful woman and married her. They were together for about two years and had a baby. He worked in the Politburo and was always eager to please... too eager," Julius said and bent down, moving his lips closer to Felipe's ear. "He never saw it coming and to this day, they still haven't found his body. He was a spy from Israel... but my sister found another love," Julius whispered with steely eyes. "The matador's cunning will always win over brute force."

"You are in the Plaza de Toros, Julius," Felipe said unaffected. "You're in the bullring and there's no way out but to accept my terms. I want the team, and you are going to help me get it," Felipe continued as he pretended to tease him with an imaginary cape. "Unless of course, like the toro, you prefer to die fighting rather than running."

"I *am* the bull Felipe," Julius said through gritted teeth, "and you'll find more anger in me than that twelve hundred pound beast!" he said and gestured to the animal.

"That bull is dead, and it will be a cold day in hell when a Spaniard loses to a communist," Felipe said with a chuckle and stroked his beard.

"I've always admired your fierce patriotism, but it can be blinding. There's nothing I hate more than meetings that don't produce results and cheap threats Felipe. You've wasted enough of my time," Julius said and sauntered off.

"Julius? I never play my best hand until the end," Felipe said, withdrawing an envelope and waving it at him. "Money can buy a man's soul... and Mr. Vladin was happy to sell," Felipe said as Julius' face drained of colour, his legs becoming wobbly. "I have it in writing that he not only worked with you at the KGB, but still works for you and how Samuel was given the money. But don't expect Vladin to stick around. I would imagine he's already changed his name and moved to a place where you will never find him," Felipe said as Julius found himself sitting again. "I don't care if you knew about the money to Samuel or the reasons. Actually, I don't think you did know because a billionaire doesn't need a paltry two million in interest... unless it's a means of entertainment," Felipe said with a broad smile and indicated to the chaos in the bullring. "It's not what I think that should concern you, but what everyone else will, and it just might be enough to ruin your empire and send you to court... even a Russian court, and no amount of money and bribery can change that."

"You bastard," Julius said, barely audible as a wall of panic enveloped his being and he felt a storm of nausea brewing.

"You see Julius, when it comes to business, I have to know what skeletons are in my enemies closets," Felipe said, wrapping his arm around him and puffing on his cigar. "So, how do we get Ichiro out of the picture my friend?" Felipe said and slapped him hard on the back. "I'll tell you how... by eliminating his best asset."

Ichiro sat at his natty desk in a small, modest office with only one decoration on the wall, his framed certificate from the Tokyo Polytechnic University, indicating first in his class. There were several, neatly stacked boxes on the floor, thoughtfully packed with the contents of his desk and a filing cabinet in the corner, resting on a dolly.

CHAPTER FIFTEEN

The window behind him offered a foggy vista of an industrial park and the Team Jenkins signage at the end of the lane, leading to the offices, factory and wind tunnel.

Ichiro thought for a moment, opened a drawer and retrieved a bottle of Scotch and a faded shot glass from Las Vegas. He filled the glass and raised it, staring at a photograph of his parents, posing soberly beside his father's fishing boat. Ichiro drank and a slow grin broke across his face as he sat back with his feet atop the desk and buffed his glasses with a Kleenex. "I see you're getting ready to move into Samuel's office," Braedon's voice asked. Ichiro quickly removed his feet, stood, bowed and sat down again with his back perfectly straight. He suddenly remembered the bottle and went to put it away, but the world champion waved him off. "I just came from the hospital. There's no change in Samuel's condition. I sure could use one of those," Braedon said and sat across from him. "I'm going to miss celebrating with champagne in the victory lane with Samuel," he said as Ichiro wiped the glass with another Kleenex, poured and handed it to him.

"Sorry, it is the only glass I have," Ichiro said nervously. He picked up a pencil and began tapping it.

Braedon sipped the whiskey. "It's not Irish, but it's better than nothing," he said and studied Ichiro's parents. "Your mother doesn't look very happy."

"She never was... it was an arranged marriage," Ichiro said as he tapped the pencil harder. "She wanted to be a career woman, but Japanese society was not yet progressive enough."

"My father hated the fact that my mother worked," Braedon said as his eyes drifted off, remembering. He finished the drink. "Do you realize that's the first time you ever told me anything about your family?"

"We should have got to know each other better," Ichiro said and poured Braedon another shot when he held the glass out for a refill.

"It's funny, I always thought I was more like a son to Samuel," Braedon said as he studied the golden liquid in the glass. "He practically raised me after my father died, but I guess it just goes to show you that you never know, do you?" he said, glaring at Ichiro.

"Samuel... Samuel paid my way through university. I never saw him until I applied for this job," Ichiro said, hoping to demonstrate he wasn't favoured over Braedon. "I will take care of *him* now, but I would say you are more of a son to Samuel than I am," he said and started packing another box.

"I didn't inherit the team, did I?" Braedon said bluntly and downed the Scotch before bowing his head. "I'm sorry. I shouldn't have said that... and I'm sorry I quit like that yesterday... I never thought I'd reach a point in my career where I had to ask for my job back," he said with an apologetic chuckle as he stood, put down the glass and went to the window with his hands in his pockets. "Owners have always courted me... the only time I ever saw myself pleading for a ride, would be in the twilight of my career... but then again, I'd always figured I would retire while I was still on top of my game... too many athletes hang on for too long... or return from retirement... I want to be remembered as the consummate champion... but I guess all that changed because of one moment of poor judgment," he said and glanced over his shoulder to measure Ichiro's reaction.

"There is no shame to admit that you might be jealous of Randall," Ichiro said, sitting rigid, fearing an outburst.

"You may be right," the champion replied softly and watched as a young couple jogged by. "I... I've been having some trouble at home."

"How is Mrs. Stirling?" Ichiro said, staring at his mother's picture.

"We ah... we're having some problems... I don't think it's going to last," Braedon said, thoroughly embarrassed and watching as the joggers disappeared down the misty avenue.

"Who is she?" Ichiro asked without looking as he continued emptying the desk drawers and found a photograph of his pretty, former girlfriend.

"Why do you automatically assume it was me?" Braedon said and looked at the window's reflection to see Ichiro's facial expression.

Ichiro pushed back his glasses, studying another picture of himself, his girlfriend and Vincenzo at a party. "It is always the men."

Braedon could feel the anger swirling inside himself, but he remained calm. "You're wrong. She was the one cheating," Braedon said and caught a brief glimpse of a jet lifting through the haze. "So... ready for Montreal?"

"We are leaving tomorrow morning," Ichiro said and tossed the photos of his girlfriend into the wastebasket. "I want to finish the move before I leave."

"I don't want to take any more of your time then," Braedon said politely and strolled to the door, depressed Ichiro was letting him go. "I guess Randall will be making the trip."

"Most definitely. I do not believe his full potential has been reached. He could be a real diamond in the rough, as they say," Ichiro said merrily and suddenly remembered his framed certificate on the wall.

Braedon pursed his lips and took the comment as a calculated shot to his ego. "There is such a thing as luck," Braedon countered.

"Randall is not a technical driver, but he does make things happen as opposed to waiting, and that can be a very good thing," Ichiro said as he carefully placed the certificate inside a box.

CHAPTER FIFTEEN

"There's another term for it Ichiro, reckless!" Braedon snipped. "The man almost got me killed!"

"He was racing. You must give him some credit. He has not driven one of these machines before, and I think he did very well," Ichiro said and saw there was enough Scotch remaining for one more drink. He waved the bottle at him, but Braedon shook his head and Ichiro went to fill the glass for himself.

"You think he's better than me, don't you?" Braedon blurted, grabbing Ichiro's hand and preventing him from pouring.

"You are the world champion. How could he be better?" Ichiro said, totally surprised by Braedon's actions and waiting for his release.

"Then cancel his deal!" Braedon said and squeezed Ichiro's hand harder until the bottle shattered.

"It is *my* team now. If I want Randall to stay, he will," Ichiro replied angrily as the blood curled around his fingers.

Braedon held his hands up to relent and hurried to offer him the box of Kleenex. "I'm sorry... I'm not questioning your judgment... it's just that I don't think you're decision is based on sound advice and personal experience."

"Why are you here Braedon?" Ichiro said and padded the blood from his hand.

"I lost my temper at the test session... what I said was wrong and... and I still want to drive," Braedon said quietly.

"You said you quit. There were witnesses. A verbal commitment is as binding as a written statement," Ichiro replied laconically and meticulously picked up the shards of glass before placing them in a wastebasket, some of the blood from his hand spilling onto Vincenzo's photograph and obliterating his face. .

Braedon breathed through his nose, struggling to maintain his demeanour, thinking Ichiro was purposely being difficult to gauge his remorse. "I know I was wrong... it was the heat of the moment."

"I expect better behaviour from a professional driver, especially from the man who holds the crown jewel of racing. A champion should act like one," Ichiro said firmly and winced, watching his cut bleed.

Braedon felt his body temperature rising, his rage ready to fulminate. His mind boiled as he fought to keep his true feelings silent. "You're right... I acted stupidly."

"Please tell me why I should take you back," Ichiro said and wrapped a Kleenex around his finger.

Braedon snickered, stunned Ichiro even asked. "Aside from the fact that I'm the best, you need me. Without Vincenzo, I'm the only one who can deliver another title," he stated arrogantly.

251

"You never thought much about Vincenzo's ability. Why the sudden admiration for him?" Ichiro said as the tissue turned red.

"I always said he was talented, but he wasted it. Some men drive from the heart, but he drove for the glory and that's why I didn't like him," Braedon said and looked at Ichiro's wound. "Maybe you should get it stitched."

"I know you cheated with his wife," Ichiro said with piercing eyes as a pallor enveloped Braedon's face. The world champion's anger vanished, replaced with dread. "I believe trust is the foundation of a successful team. I hope you have not lied about anything else."

Braedon was trapped and realized he had to come clean. "Who told you? Her?" he whispered.

"Actually, it was Vincenzo. He suspected all along. He was drunk after the victory in San Marino and he said too much."

Braedon's knees gave way and he sat. "Why... why didn't he say anything?"

"I do not know why he did not tell you. I thought it was because he was ashamed. Embarrassed maybe. Like any man... he had an ego, and it is a fragile thing," Ichiro said, glancing at his former girlfriend's picture.

A myriad of questions and thoughts traversed through Braedon's brain as he nodded. Finally, he whispered, "does anybody else know?"

"I don't think so," Ichiro replied with a shrug.

"How did Vincenzo find out?" Braedon said, completely flummoxed.

"Women are not the only sex to have intuition. He never told me how he knew, but he said he had proof. The only question is, what happens now with your personal life? A champion needs a sound heart and mind," Ichiro said, animating with his hands.

"I settled things. It's going to remain quiet... I promise," Braedon said with begging eyes.

"I hope so. If this got out, it would ruin our team. We do not need that kind of press," Ichiro said and slid a newspaper towards him with Braedon and Teresa's picture on the front page.

"You have my word," Braedon said humbly and offered his handshake. "Just take me back... please Ichiro."

"If you come back, I want you to have that removed," Ichiro said, frowning at the tattoo on Braedon's hand. "It is a team, not a political forum. There is no place for symbols of violence."

Braedon slowly withdrew his hand as his eyes squinted. "Who the hell do you think you are?"

"Fine," Ichiro said curtly, stood and bowed. "I am sorry Stirling. We will find another driver for Montreal."

Chapter Fifteen

The world champion was shocked, his mouth dropping open as reality took hold. "You've made a terrible mistake! Any team will sign me! I'll see you in court... *Mr. Tanaka!*" he said and marched for the door as the phone rang.

Ichiro picked it up. "Yes?" he said, his eyes widening and he slowly sank down into his chair. "What... when? I see... thank you," he said as the receiver fell from his hand. "Braedon?"

The champion stopped in the hall and smirked, knowing Ichiro was about to take him back. "What?" Braedon asked impatiently as he waited in the doorway.

Ichiro removed his glasses as his eyes filled. "I thought you would like to know... Mr. Jenkins... Samuel is dead."

Chapter Sixteen

"This place is so alive, isn't it? God, I've always wanted to see this," Gwen said happily, strolling with Randall along one of the cobblestone streets of Old Montreal. Randall just kept his head down with his shoulders hunched. "What's wrong?" she asked.

"Oh... just thinking about Jenkins buying the farm," he said with a light smile. "I kind of liked the old guy. Admired his guts... and he believed in me."

"What's done is done," she said casually and continued soaking in the ambience.

"Doesn't it even bother you?" he asked with surprise. "The man had a tough life."

"We all will. You know as well as I do that police officers can't get too emotional, and he's one less suspect to worry about, I hope," she said, staring in awe at the 18th and 19th century, grey stone buildings. "It's like a giant objet d'art," she said and unconsciously took his hand as she studied the guidebook in the other. Taken aback, Randall could only glance at their interlocked fingers, her soft skin and subtle perfume, causing his heart to stir. "It says here, Montreal is the second largest, French speaking city in the world and over three hundred years old. There's over thirty museums too," she said excitedly.

Randall watched the people enjoying the sunny afternoon, taking in the picturesque network of towers, stores, hotels and restaurants. "Is this a murder investigation or a fucking sightseeing tour?" he said sarcastically, still jolted by her touch. "Actually, it's nice nobody knows who I am yet. Once we do the press conference, look out. Won't be able to have a piss without answering a question."

"We can talk about that later tonight with Ichiro," she said and withdrew her camera as he bemoaned the loss of her hand in his. "I told you we should have come here on our honeymoon."

"Niagara Falls wasn't good enough for you, eh split lips?" he replied as his head swivelled when several, beautiful women walked by. "Maybe the meatball will bring you here when you get hitched in September."

"I asked you not to call him that!" she said overly defensive and checked her anger. "Look, we have a full weekend of work ahead of us and this is the only time we have to take a break. Besides, a little culture might be good for you," she said and snapped a few pictures.

"I'll never be more than I am," he replied and sank into a chair outside a cafe with an umbrella.

"What's your problem?" she said and slid into the seat across from him.

"I think we should be discussing the case, that's all. We owe it to Jenkins," he said as a petite waitress with a skimpy skirt and a tight T-shirt advertising the Canadian Grand Prix appeared. "Just a coffee," he said.

"A glass of white wine please," Gwen said and turned to Randall. "I know you're nervous about racing again, but maybe you *should* have a drink. One isn't going to kill you."

"I don't want booze. Got to keep my wits. Heat from the fucking engine is the least kind that can burn your ass... the press... the fans... they'll eat you alive. Racing is a deadly serious sport Gwen. Add murder to the mix and the whole thing is fucking downright lethal," he said and looked at the majestic, gothic, Notre-Dame Basilica looming in the distance. "Sure wish I had some faith now," he said and shook his head clear. "Your folks drag you to church?"

"I wanted to go," she replied half-interested and examined the menu.

"Old lady made me go. Guess she was looking for forgiveness," he said as he continued staring at the lavish structure. "Always wondered why she didn't stop him, you know? She must have been as scared shitless of the fucker as I was," he said and retrieved a packet of cigarettes from the pocket of his denim jacket. "She used to hold my hand while she prayed. Had a short attention span so I just stared at the stained glass... the paintings... statues... all that gold carving and shit... never knew who to pray to... nobody was listening anyway," he said with a chuckle and stuffed a smoke in his mouth, but didn't light it.

"I used to love going," she said as her mind wandered, the church's bells beginning to ring. "Have you ever heard a piece of music that was so beautiful it gave you goose bumps? I remember listening and trembling... it could make me cry. I always did when the choir sang," she said, still lost in memories, but soon realized she was too melancholy and cleared her throat. "Look, the reason I wanted to take a walk was to get you to relax and not think about the case... or your childhood," she said with a disappointed sigh.

"Do yourself a favour and stop caring, okay?" he snapped as the waitress returned with their drinks.

"Then stop talking about it," she replied and lightly tapped his glass. "Cheers."

"Doesn't your past haunt the fuck out of you?" he asked and blew the steam off his coffee.

"Only when you keep bringing it up," she said and sipped her wine and her nose wrinkled. "French it isn't."

"How's Jess?" he asked when a father with a stroller went by.

"She's fine. I sent her to my mother's and gave the nanny a few days off. Peter is in New York on business," she said and removed her sunglasses.

"How's the kid's future supposed to be stable when she's all over the place?" he grumbled and stirred in some sugar.

Gwen popped a few pills and took a healthy drink. "You're giving me headache," she said with a hint of anger.

Randall stared at her for a few seconds and debated whether to continue the line of conversation. "I'm just tired. Didn't sleep a goddamn wink on the plane. Kept having those same fucking nightmares about the asshole sitting up in the casket," he said and realized he was still ruining her enthusiasm. The baby in the stroller began to cry and the father picked her up. "I just miss Jess... think about her every day," he said with an awkward smile.

A serious look enveloped her face and she looked away. "I've made a decision... about you and Jessica... if something happens to me... I want my mother to take care of her."

The comment stifled his brain and he scrambled for a reply. "Why?" he heard himself ask.

"I think she would be better off. You have to agree with me," she said shyly, reaching across the table and taking his hand. "I want you to promise that if that happens, you leave her alone."

Randall quickly retracted his hand. "Fuck you," he whispered.

"I know this upsets you, but if you think about it, really think about it, you'll see that I'm right," she said and tried to smile. "I know you want what's best for her. She's used to my mother and living in France. Taking her away will only create unwanted stress, and she has enough of that."

"How come you assume I can't be a good father to her, uh?" he practically shouted. "What gives you the fucking right to keep passing judgment on me? I know I fucked up her life!"

"Keep your voice down," she commanded as several other patrons looked over. "It was just a suggestion. All I ask is that you think about it."

Chapter Sixteen

Randall waited until his wrath subsided and nodded to himself. "Give me the fucking divorce papers," he said and gestured to her purse. "Got a pen?"

"I... I don't have them with me," she replied, shocked at his request.

"I'm surprised you don't have them shoved up your pussy just in case," he said and took a sip of his coffee.

Gwen ignored the statement and waited for a moment, knowing it was best she change the subject. "So, what do you think about Jenkins in regards to the case?"

"I don't want to talk about this right now," he barked and dug through his pockets for a match.

"Work before pleasure," she said with a forced laugh. "The autopsy revealed nothing foreign in Jenkins' body. He simply had a stroke, but I think Suarez probably helped, don't you?" she said as he opened her guidebook.

"Maybe you and the meatball can take a romantic stroll along the wharf," he said, flipping through the pages.

A calculated sigh to maintain her temper. "It's too bad Jenkins requested an immediate cremation without a service. It would have been interesting to see who showed up at his funeral. What do you think about Ichiro?"

"Oh I know, you and the meatball can take a carriage ride. See?" he said and showed her a photograph in the book of a young couple embracing behind the driver.

Another deep sigh and Gwen pursed her lips before continuing. "Ichiro wasn't a suspect before, but I think he is now. You said he knew Vincenzo was fooling around with his girlfriend, and I don't think we should tell him who we are."

"You guys can go to the casino too and have even more fucking money," he said and turned another page. "Then you can go over to Ile Notre Dame and see where my stupid ass got wiped out in a racing car."

Gwen massaged her forehead and sipped her wine, struggling to remain patient. "Of course, maybe Ichiro already knows. Jenkins left him the team. It sounds like they were pretty close, like a father and son," she said, but suddenly regretted her words.

Randall raised his eyebrows. "I wouldn't know anything about that."

"Can you stop being so selfish for a minute and talk about this case for a bit? You can complain later!" she said and snatched the book out of his hand.

"What's to discuss?" he said and kicked his feet up onto the other chair, her glare causing him to surrender with his hands. "Okay, okay. The problem is, your stupid government and the fucking blue bloods won't let us do any real detective work. All we have is guessing, and I'm sick of it."

"Why do you resent people with money?" she asked just as a Rolls Royce drove past.

"Because I don't have any," he replied sardonically and gave a frustrated sigh; "We can take Jenkins off the list, now that he's a crispy critter. What about Braedon?" he said and was about to strike a match, but decided against it.

"Still has motive," she said, happy he was finally conversing about the investigation. "He wants to be the champion again and might have been having an affair with Teresa," she said, opening a button on her blouse and letting the breeze cool her warm skin. "Maybe Teresa had Vincenzo killed for the insurance and if she was fooling around with Braedon, that's another motive. And don't forget she probably isn't too thrilled that Vincenzo stopped her line of credit at the casino."

"And then there's Julius," he said, completely uninterested. "And he and Friedrich are the only ones who know who we are," he said in a monotone voice, imitating hers as he tried not to look at her breasts and donned his sunglasses. "He's majority shareholder now that both Azzopardis are dead."

"It seems too obvious. It could be Friedrich. He did try and start his own series but Vincenzo blew him off," she said, not appreciating his boredom. "It could be Ichiro too. It's a long shot, but he knew he would inherit the team and maybe by sending the letters, he figured it would happen sooner," she said and took another drink.

"Hey, a better long shot would be Lisa Stirling if she knew about the affair. You know, hell hath no fury? I was married to you so I know all about that. Maybe she's the one that took a shot at Teresa," he said, not believing his own words, his eyes locked onto Gwen's breasts as he felt a tingling between his legs. "Or maybe it was the big, bad wolf?" he said sarcastically.

"That leaves Felipe. We know he wants the team and wants to drive. He probably wouldn't know Ichiro would take over though," she said, flapping her blouse to cool herself further and giving Randall a glance of her lacy bra. "Or maybe it's none of them and just some crazy person."

"How many fucking times do we have to go over this? The letters were on Jenkins' stationary so it's likely someone involved with the sport. Somebody hired the Rabbit and… and… fuck! I don't know!" he said and forced himself to stop gawking at her. "All we do know is people keep trying to scare us off for Christ's sake, and maybe we should listen to them! Fuck! I told you we shouldn't have talked about this," he said, fanning himself with the menu and feeling the weight of her stare. "I know, I know," he said, waving her off. "I just have to continue being a target and wait for something to happen. Hell of a dumb way to catch a killer," he said as a gust of wind blew some bits of paper onto the table. A chuckle. "Remember that night when we sat out on Hess Street in Hamilton in the middle of winter?" he said. She couldn't help but smile. "Damn near froze our asses off. I think my drink was frozen."

"I knew right then and there you were afraid of long lasting relationships."

"Then why did you marry me?" he asked with a frown.

"Because she loved you. It's a funny thing for women. My mother loved my father so much she put up with way too much. He cheated on her, drank until he passed out and even used to tell me he was sorry he had me... and he was a rabbi," a vaguely familiar voice announced. Startled, Randall and Gwen looked up to find Candice Goldenstein standing before them, dressed in a pair of cut-off denims, a revealing halter-top, and carrying a letter size, leather case. "May I?" she asked, pulling the chair out from under Randall's feet and sitting before he could answer. "Nice," she said, pointing at his cowboy boots. "I used to wear them when I lived in Israel. I stopped because too many Palestinians thought I was an American. Like being a Jew wasn't bad enough," she said with a dumb laugh.

"What... what are you doing here?" he said, totally disconcerted.

"The race, remember?" she said with a flirtatious smile, swinging the case onto the table and nearly knocking over his coffee. "Good to see you again, Randall," she said and looked to Gwen. "I wish I could say the same for you. My mother always told me not to trust men like him, but then again, I'll do anything for a story," she said and waved to the waitress. "Bottled water, please," she said and offered a giggle. "Trying to watch the old waistline."

"We were just leaving," Gwen said curtly and began gathering her things.

"I didn't print that piece I did on you Randall. The editor didn't like it. He didn't see any relevance to the story. Sorry. He's a sexist pig anyway. He hates the fact that I'm a women covering a male dominated sport," Candice said as Gwen took Randall's hand.

"He's a smart man," Randall said and stood.

"It sounds like you're a chauvinist too," Candice said as the waitress arrived with her drink. "So, have you heard who is taking Vincenzo's ride?"

"Ain't got a clue," he replied and handed the waitress a few bills. "Got to go."

"That's it? We share a bed in Milan, I don't see you for a week, and then by chance find you in Montreal, and then you split?" she said, playing with the straw in her bottle.

"Stop following him and stay away if you know what's good for you," Gwen said and put on her sunglasses. "Get your own man... if you can."

Candice sarcastically mimicked a cat's claw and hissed. "How about telling me what you guys are doing here?"

They started to walk away. "Just taking in the race before heading back home," Randall said.

Candice's eyes iced and a devilish simper came over her face. "Are you a contender or a pretender?"

"What?" he said without breaking stride.

"I think you should sit down... Officer Grange," Candice said. Her words echoed inside Randall and Gwen's minds and they exchanged a brief glance. A coy grin from Candice. "An actor you're not. I know you're a cop."

"So... I changed careers," he replied with a shrug, but was visibly shaken.

"What is a police officer doing in Milan for Vincenzo Azzopardi's funeral?" Candice said as she teased her cheek with the straw.

"He told you before, Vincenzo was a friend of ours," Gwen said, masking her dread much better than Randall.

Candice took a soothing sip of the chilled water. "Do you think your accident at Silverstone was deliberate or just a mechanical failure?" she asked and held up his coffee cup. "Need something stronger than this now?" she asked playfully.

"How did you know I was a flatfoot?" he said, full of suspicion.

"Beat cop? I don't think so. More like a top-notch homicide detective that angered a few too many people and ended up on the streets again," she replied and sighed heavily in a condescending manner. "Frankly, I'm a little insulted Randall. I'm a reporter remember? Any first year journalism student could dig that up. I made a few calls and a nice young man named Tony D'Angelo helped me out."

"Booger?" he said with surprise, but gained his composure. "I mean Tony... he wouldn't tell you anything."

Gwen leaned closer to Candice. "I don't know what kind of game you're playing, but if you keep it up, you just might find yourself in jail."

"Have you ever heard about freedom of the press? I hope that wasn't a threat because I have some very interesting evidence," she said unconcerned and took a long sip from her bottle. She smacked her lips together, exhaled with satisfaction and emptied her case, various photographs spilling onto the table; Randall and Gwen on top of the hill at

CHAPTER SIXTEEN

Vincenzo's funeral, speaking to Jenkins after the service, Randall lifting Vincenzo's coffin lid, Randall conversing with Braedon at the first test session and the subsequent accident, Randall and Braedon at the second session and Randall, Gwen, Julius and Friedrich at the pool in Milan. "It was way to easy to get past the security, but at the last testing session, I almost got caught. These big bones sure can move when they have to," she said with a laugh and snorted. "You can keep those. I have another set safely locked away. It should make one heck of a story, don't you think?" she said and mimed her own headline. "I can see it now, reporter of the year. That Pulitzer might be closer than I thought."

Gwen quickly stuffed the photos back into the case, fearful that someone might catch a glimpse. "What else do you know?" she asked quietly.

"That you're not his wife, at least not now," she said, examining one of the pictures. "You used to be a cop too, but moved back to France and took a job with the DST. My uncle the publisher has a lot of contacts all over the world and really did a great job of helping me out, don't you think?" Candice said and drained her bottle, her eyes trained on Gwen.

Gwen waited for her to continue, but realized Candice was waiting for confirmation of her theory. "Go on," she said with a grin.

"I also know that Braedon and Randall have something in common, in principle anyway. I'm pretty sure he was having an affair with Teresa Legaro. A limo driver took Braedon to her place in Italy. He was working for me," she said and loudly sucked the last few drops from her water bottle. "I think there's more to Vincenzo's death than meets the eye. As crazy as it sounds, I think he was murdered and that's why Randall is driving again. Both of you are working on this investigation together. Maybe Jenkins' death and Teresa's shooting are a part of it too," she said and sat back with crossed arms, proud of her conjecture.

Gwen whistled and clapped sarcastically. "Encore! Encore! That's quite a story. Would you like to hear the facts?" she said, Candice clearly concerned her theory was incorrect. "You're right, Randall and I used to be married. We went to the funeral because we both knew Vincenzo very well. We were good friends at one time. I was a cop with Randall in Hamilton, but I left the force and moved back to France to raise our handicapped daughter," she said and motioned to her leather case. "As for your photos, Randall wanted to see Vincenzo's face one last time. As for Braedon messing around with Teresa, who knows? He was probably just paying his respects in private without the whole world watching," Gwen said confidently.

"What about Teresa getting shot after she was seen with Braedon at that club?" Candice asked, her eyes locked with Gwen's in a staring contest.

"I don't know. Maybe they are having an affair, but who cares? And as for Randall driving the car, he asked Jenkins for a chance despite my concerns," she said and took Randall by the hand again. "I think Randall performed pretty well and he's contracted to race this weekend. End of story. Boring but true," Gwen said and wrapped her arm around Randall's waist.

Candice stared at them, searching for any signal of an untruth. None was forthcoming. "So, are you still married?"

"We're trying to work it out," Gwen said and raised her wedding finger as proof. "Haven't you ever been in love, but had problems?"

"No... I guess... maybe," Candice replied, thoroughly embarrassed but quickly recovering. "It sounds too neat to me."

"The truth always does. Look, I still want to race and I believe I'm good enough. I'm taking advantage of an opportunity. I don't want any regrets and that's all there is to it," Randall said as the convincing news deflated Candice. "Listen, if it makes you feel any better, I'm having a press conference tomorrow to announce all this with Ichiro Tanaka. You probably already know he's taking over the team. I'll let you have the first question. Hell, I'll even give you the rights to the story. Okay?"

"Promise?" she said, the idea lifting her spirits.

He extended his hand. "I promise."

She accepted the handshake then Randall and Gwen meandered away. "I'll definitely see you tomorrow... but you might not see me," she said to herself with a grin and watched them disappear around the corner.

Teresa sat in the messy, dim living room of her palatial mansion, surrounded by flickering candles and the soft glow of the television. She took another hit of cocaine straight from the small, cellophane bag on the table, cluttered with empty fast food containers and bottles of alcohol. She gazed at the full moon through the open sliding doors, watching it eerily disappear behind black clouds and reappear again.

She lazily tiled her head to the television, the tape of Braedon and her making love. "When she's dead... we can be together forever. You don't love her anyway... I'm doing you a favour," she whispered, a sinister smile coming across her face as she slid her fingers beneath her panties and began to masturbate. Eyes closing, she laid her head back and moaned, listening to the pleasurable sighs emitting from the tape. Eyes open again they found their way to a photograph of Vincenzo in full racing garb, hanging askew on the wall. "I don't miss you... and I never loved you,"

CHAPTER SIXTEEN

she said and giggled. "You were just like all the rest. I always got what I wanted with these," she said and quickly flashed her breasts at him. "I even fucked my ninth grade teacher to pass English."

Teresa stumbled to her feet and inched closer to the picture. "But what am I supposed to do now? What about money? You always cared more about your fame than me! You deserve what you got!" she groused and saw her reflection in the glass, but didn't notice the distorted silhouette of someone standing behind her. Teresa lifted her hand, felt her drawn face and touched the dark circles beneath her weary eyes. "I was never voted beauty queen... all that nigger blood!" she shouted and ripped the photograph off the wall and threw it, smashing it on the floor. She stepped across the shards and cut her feet, but she didn't feel it as a violent gust of wind swept the floor length curtains, her black, silk peignoir rippling. "Vincenzo?" she whispered fearfully as she edged towards the doors, leading to a stone pathway. Full of trepidation, Teresa slowly stepped onto the ornate patio with its massive garden and held onto a white, wrought iron chair for support. She became hypnotized, looking down at the splendid valley, the lights of Milan twinkling in the distance. A click. Teresa wheeled around to find someone standing in the shadows. "Who's there?" she said, cautiously retreating as her eyes peered into the darkness to discover a man's outline coming towards her. "Vincenzo?" she asked with a disbelieving frown and violently shook her head. "No! You're dead!" she yelled and ran down the embankment, glancing over her shoulder as the intruder gave chase. She felt the branches lacerating her face and she tripped and fell to her knees. Another look. He was getting closer. Teresa desperately crawled into the bush and covered her mouth with trembling hands, her breathing intensified. She heard the sound of crunching twigs and her terrified eyes caught a glimpse of his shoes as they walked by. Teresa waited for a few moments and slowly stood. After looking carefully in all directions, she inched out of the bush and went to take a step, but a nylon rope suddenly wrapped around her neck and a hand covered her mouth.

"You're dead," a man's deep, Australian voice said as she was released. "Our mutual friend told you I was good, eh," he said with a hearty laugh. "It's okay Mrs. Azzopardi... I mean, Miss Legaro. It's me, Jack."

Teresa studied him, an imposing man with slicked red hair, dressed in a blue silk suit as he flashed her a dazzling smile with perfect teeth. "You... you don't look like what I thought," she said, fighting to catch her breath and rubbing her throat.

Jack saw the blood on her feet, picked her up and carried her up the hill. "That's what they all say," he said and sat her in a chair. He took a seat beside her. Instantly, he retrieved an elastic band and started playing with it. "Keeps me from smoking," he said, slightly abashed.

"Can... can I get you a drink?" she asked nervously, still trying to recover from the chase.

"No thanks, love. If I were you, I'd keep that security system on at all times. I even gave you a head start. Now, down to business then, eh?" he said and expertly wrapped the elastic around his fingers with the same hand.

"One million, right?" she asked, entranced by his dexterity.

A nod. "And another million when it's done," he said as he watched a spider spinning a web near the sliding doors.

"How... how will you do it," she inquired and swallowed hard.

"You don't want to know that, love. Best you don't in case they ever ask. Know what I mean?" he replied with another, wide smile.

"Will she... will she feel it?" Teresa questioned with a whisper and felt a chill rifle through her body.

"Only if you want her too," he said with a laugh.

"It's not funny!" she barked and stood.

"Sorry love. Don't get asked that question much," he said and watched as she began to pace, leaving a tiny trail of blood as she went. "It's okay to be nervous. Everyone always is."

"Don't you even want to know why?" she said and continued pacing and began biting her nails.

Jack eyed her, frequently catching a glimpse of her body whenever she passed by the light. "None of my business, really," he said and licked his lips.

"Guess!" Teresa said angrily.

"Okay... you're shagging her husband?" he said with a shrug.

Teresa stopped and turned to him. "Why do you say that?"

Another shrug. "I saw the papers. How's your shoulder?"

"Uh?" she said, lost in thought and resumed her march.

"You got hit. You know, shot," he said and pointed at her wound.

"How good are you?" she asked worriedly.

Jack flicked the elastic at the spider and hit it dead on, the insect vanishing, leaving a neat space where it had been. "It's easier with a gun," he said with a grin.

Impressed, Teresa sat down again without taking her eyes off the web. "Tell me about yourself."

"Not much to say, really. Normal parents. Middle class in Brisbane. Just liked killing. Could have been a cop, but there was more money as a merc," he said and found another elastic band.

"Merc?"

Chapter Sixteen

"Mercenary. You know, hired gun. Like in the old west," he said and pretended to draw a pistol from a holster.

"Doesn't it bother you? Don't you see their faces?"

"Get used to it. Just business. It's nothing personal," he said as his cheerful face promptly hardened and he rubbed his fingertips together indicating money. "Have you got it?"

"It's in the house... where do you want me to send the rest?" she asked as she watched his acrobatic fingers begin playing with the elastic again.

Jack slid a piece of paper to her. "Deposit it in that account the next day."

"Did anyone... you know... did anyone ever not pay you?" she said and studied the note.

A broad smile as his eyes moved to the spider web. "Yeah... but he's dead."

Teresa suddenly stood and crossed her arms. "I... I've changed my mind," she said, his grin promptly disappearing. "I don't want her dead... I want him dead."

A slight look of concern and an unsure chuckle. "You want me to pop the world champion, love?"

"I'll double it to four million," she said and his eyes lit up. "But I want you to do it when he's on the track in Montreal. I don't care whether it's during practice, qualifying or the race. Just do it."

Jack rose to his feet and stared at the moon. "I don't know about that. It's a hell of a risk. A lot of people around. Too much light."

"You're supposed to be the best! If you want the money you'll do it!" she said angrily as he shot her a serious glance.

"Eight million," he said and returned his gaze to the moon.

"Deal," she said without hesitation. "I'll be there to see it."

"You got that much money lying around, love?"

"Don't worry. I'll be getting a lot very shortly," she said and strolled towards the house. "By the way, have you ever killed someone in a speeding car?"

"Once."

"I'll want to see the bullet before you do it."

"Why?" he asked, thoroughly puzzled.

"I want to stick it up my pussy so he'll know what he's going to miss," she said with conviction. "I want him to smell me when he dies."

A raised eyebrow and another smile. "That's a new one, but okay," he said as he looked between her legs. "I need one more thing," he added, loosened his tie and unzipped his fly.

Teresa smiled knowingly and disrobed before strutting inside as Jack happily followed.

Inside the darkened, open-air building, Randall waited until some other patrons wandered through the near-blinding light of an exit. "What the fuck did you do that for?" Randall asked incredulously, watching Ichiro approach an incense burner as Gwen pulled on Randall's arm to hold him back physically and emotionally.

"This is a temple. You must behave calmly and respectfully," Ichiro said as he tossed a coin in the offering box before saying a short prayer. "I am sure you do not act this way when you go to your church," he said and breathed deeply, the rich smell of wood delighting his senses.

"I don't go," Randall said and went to say something else, but Ichiro wheeled to face him.

"Do you believe in your God?" Ichiro asked with a serious expression.

"What the hell has that got to do with anything?" Randall said.

"Did your parents believe?" Ichiro questioned and took a step closer.

"Not that it's any of your fucking business, but yes. My old man had more faith than my old lady and she was damn near Mother Teresa when it came to God, but he was the biggest asshole sinner of them all," Randall said, glaring at him. "So what's your fucking point?"

"My father was a Buddhist and my mother followed the Shinto faith. They both introduced me to their beliefs, but eventually, all spiritual journeys must be experienced alone," Ichiro said and put a hand on Randall's shoulder. "Perhaps you have not searched hard enough for your answers," he said and lit a bundle of incense.

"There's only one answer I need right now and that is, why the hell isn't Braedon driving? For Christ sake, I need him out there! Team-mates are supposed to watch each other's back!" Randall said as Ichiro waved his hand to extinguish the flame and dropped the bundle into the burner.

"I cannot allow him to drive. Even as a child, I kept my word," Ichiro said and began fanning the smoke towards his face.

"This ain't the playground!" Randall barked as Gwen stepped forward and brushed him aside with her copy of the Montreal Botanical Garden booklet.

"Randall told me you don't practice Buddhism," Gwen said and dropped a coin in the offering box as Randall rolled his eyes.

"I do not normally, but I still turn to Buddhism and Shinto when in need," Ichiro replied as he closed his eyes and continued waving the smoke towards himself.

"What is it you need?" Gwen asked.

"I want the smoke to clear my head so I can make sound business decisions," Ichiro replied.

Chapter Sixteen

"You're going to need a fucking volcano for that!" Randall said with a laugh and began pacing. "Firing the world champion was not a great idea! What the hell were you thinking?"

"It was a personal matter between Braedon and I," Ichiro said and sauntered away. Randall and Gwen followed.

"Look, I agreed to drive because Braedon was part of the team," Randall said as Ichiro neared a wooden Torii, painted orange and black, leading to a Shinto shrine.

Ichiro eyed the two, stone guardian dogs on either side of the entrance. "I will find a replacement before this weekend's race. There are many men that will be happy to fill the seat." Gwen took a ladle at the purification fountain and washed both hands as Ichiro watched. She cupped the water into her mouth, rinsed and spat beside the fountain. "Very impressive. Have you been to Japan?" Ichiro asked curiously.

"Once. It was before Randall and I were married. My father took us there on a vacation," she replied as Ichiro looked to Randall.

"I got pissed on Saki once. Who fucking cares? What are you going to do about Braedon?" he snarled. Ichiro performed the same cleansing ritual before proceeding to the main hall with Gwen and Randall in tow. Ichiro threw a coin in the offering box, bowed deeply twice, clapped twice, bowed deeply once more and prayed for a few seconds. "Now what the hell are you praying for, the latest edition of Superman?" Randall said and snatched the comic book from Ichiro's back pocket.

"Actually, I was praying for the both of you... that you will find Vincenzo's killer," Ichiro said as Randall and Gwen stared at him, completely dumbfounded. "Samuel told me everything about you and the investigation. I knew about the letters he was getting that asked for money."

"Why didn't you say anything before?" Gwen asked suspiciously as Randall handed Ichiro the comic book.

"It was none of my business, but now that I am the new owner, it is," Ichiro said and strolled towards an Omikuji dangling fortune telling strips of paper. "Tell me, will the two of you get back together again?"

The question temporarily stunned Randall and Gwen. "We... we're just partners on this thing... friends... nothing more."

"Those are nice words, but words will not keep you company in your old age. You cannot hug them. You cannot kiss them good night and you cannot tell them you love them. I see the way you look at each other. For people who sleuth for a living, you are not too adept at solving the mysteries of your own hearts," Ichiro said and plucked a fortune as Randall and Gwen exchanged an abashed glance, both feeling the blood rushing to their faces. "It seems to me Randall, that you are more scared of your feelings for her than you are of driving a racecar," Ichiro said and read the fortune. "Daikichi. Great good luck," he added with a smile.

"Look, all I'm here to do is help on the case and that's all. We ain't getting back together again," Randall said, thoroughly flustered and turned to Gwen. "Right?" She nodded, avoiding Randall's stare.

"Fine, but do not try and tell me that if you continue to perform as well as you have in the test sessions, that you would decline the opportunity to race on a full time basis. I would hazard to guess that police work does not pay as well. Besides, racing is about more than money, glamour and technology. It is about passion, and I think you have it whether you want it or not," Ichiro said and sat on a wooden bench.

"What matters most at this time is getting Braedon back on the team," Gwen said and sat beside him.

"Why? Is he a suspect?" Ichiro asked and tucked the fortune in his pocket.

"To be honest, everyone is. If need be, we can force you to take Braedon back," Gwen warned.

"I sincerely doubt the DST will want to pick up his expenses, never mind the lawsuit I would file for interference when this affair is finished," Ichiro said and folded his arms.

"Whatever personal problems you and Braedon are having, forget them. Sometimes we all have to swallow our pride," Randall said, haphazardly yanking a fortune and feeling the piercing slice of a paper cut.

"I saw a side of Braedon I did not care for and I will never allow a driver to dictate terms. Frankly, it was the best thing that could have happened. I will barely be able to meet the payroll as it is," Ichiro said and started to march off.

"You know another team will snap him up and Braedon will go out of his way to make you look like a fool," Randall said, chasing after him and sucking the blood from his finger as Gwen remained on the bench and withdrew her cell phone.

"But I have you," Ichiro answered with another smile and leaned closer to him. "Now tell me, what is the reason you cannot get back together with Gwen, despite the fact that you obviously still love her?"

"Why is this so important to you?" Randall said, struggling to mask his embarrassment and wiping his bleeding finger against his jeans.

"Because if you are driving for me, I need to know what I am dealing with. If a man's head is not in his work, it means there is a woman to distract him."

"I can walk and chew gum at the same time," Randall said as Ichiro meandered towards a stage for Japanese dancing.

Chapter Sixteen

"There comes a moment when you have to look beyond your own selfish reasons and see that the best answer on the stage of life is the one you have always feared the most... the truth," Ichiro said as his hands gently rubbed the smooth wood of the railing.

"Hey man, my life's already a fucking movie, it's not even half over and I'm ready to walk out on it," Randall said matter-of-factly. "So don't lay all that Confucius shit on me."

"Confucius is Chinese," Ichiro said, pushing up his glasses and continuing to walk.

"Were you pissed enough at Vincenzo for banging your chick that you had him capped?" Randall inquired, freezing Ichiro in his tracks.

"I did not have him killed and I resent you asking me!" Ichiro replied as he stormed for the exit.

Randall caught up to him and spun him around. "Look pal, you're up to your elbows in this shit. Those letters Jenkins got were on team stationary. Only so many people would have access to that."

"I worked hard to get where I am! I would not throw it all away because of jealousy!" Ichiro said as a bead of sweat suddenly appeared and rolled down the bridge of his nose.

"So you *were* jealous."

"Of course. Any man would be," Ichiro said and lowered his head as his voice dampened. "I loved her... I wanted to marry her... she was the only one I would ever spend my life with."

Randall slowly looked to Gwen, strolling towards them. "I know the feeling... but who knows, maybe it's not too late for both of us?"

Ichiro shook his head. "No... she found another. Besides, after Vincenzo, she was no longer pure."

"Fuck man. We're all as pure as the driven slush. You'll find someone," Randall said and slapped him on the back.

"Call Braedon and tell him he's back on the team," Gwen said sternly, handing Ichiro the phone.

"I cannot," Ichiro said before bowing and hurrying off.

"I did a little research Ichiro. I found out your father died from what the Japanese call karoshi," she said and glanced at Randall. "Death from overwork."

"So?" Ichiro said without breaking stride.

"The official cause of death was a heart attack, wasn't it?" she asked and referred to her notes. "That was just six years ago... and you were there."

Ichiro stopped and turned back to them. "All he knew was to work. We went out on the boat... he said he wasn't feeling well... he collapsed... and died," he said mournfully.

Gwen studied her notes again. "Seems there was a witness nearby who said you pushed him."

"He fell! I was trying to help him!" Ichiro said and began shaking.

"It says here your father drowned and that his body was never found. Even your mother said the two of you didn't see eye to eye because you wanted to live more of a western lifestyle," Gwen said and flipped her pad closed. "The case could be reopened and there's always the possibility you might be charged. It could drag on for years. You'd have to leave the team, especially if you're held on suspicion."

"Apparently, killing gets easier the second time around," Randall said casually to Gwen.

"Who told you all this?" Ichiro asked, bubbling with rage.

"You'd be amazed at how fast we can find information. The DST has a lot of friends in law enforcement," she replied. Ichiro finally held out his hand for the telephone. He dialled and marched away.

"We'll see you back at the hotel to discuss the press conference," Gwen said to Ichiro and massaged her head.

"You play dirty pool, split lips," Randall said with a smirk.

"I had to do something," she said and put her pad away. "We haven't got a lot of time."

"What about the press conference tomorrow? What do we say about *us*? If Candice can dig it up, anyone can," he said and popped a cigarette in his mouth, but didn't light it.

"Don't worry about her. If she makes any trouble, she'll disappear until this is over. If anyone else asks, you *were* a cop and I used to be. As for me, we're divorced, but best of friends and we had a daughter together. It'll fly," she said confidently and reached for her medicine but saw he wasn't convinced. "We are friends... aren't we?"

"According to Ichiro, we should be a lot more," he said bashfully.

"Well, we never will be," she said with conviction and realized her words were too harsh. "Are we friends?"

"We are," he said with an earnest nod, but was visibly disappointed. "What if someone finds out you're with the DST? And what about the meatball? What if someone gets to him?" he asked, withdrawing his matches as she scowled.

"Stop calling him that! I've already got a cover story and Peter knows about it. The agency will deny I work for them. As far as anyone is concerned, I'm a stay-at-home mom living off my family's money," she said and swallowed a few pills.

Randall chuckled. "Well, most of it's true."

"What is that supposed to mean?" she asked with her hands on her hips.

Chapter Sixteen

"Jesus! You live in fucking Buckingham Palace thanks to dear old dad, don't you?"

"You're not doing this to me again. I refuse to be dragged into another pointless debate about how poor you were, and still are," she said and slung her purse over her shoulder. "I'm not going to apologize for having money."

Randall wanted to retaliate, but took a breath and looked to Ichiro. "This thing's turning into a fucking carnival. So Miss Marple, think he's still a suspect?"

"I didn't think so, but now I'm not so sure," she replied as Randall lit a match, but she blew it out. "You've come this far, don't ruin it now."

"You're pushing it, split lips," he said with a frustrated sigh. "If Braedon's involved, you do realize you're inviting the wolf back into the chicken coop."

"That's the whole idea," she said, removing the fortune paper from his denim pocket and reading it. She reluctantly handed it to him.

Randall examined the message and frowned. "Da... daikyo? What the hell does that mean?"

"Great bad luck," she replied and tried to smile. "But if you tie it around a tree branch, you can stop it."

"Fuck that," he said and tossed it to the floor. The breeze picked it up and swept it away.

Lisa's lavender, silk scarf fluttered as she performed the *plie* action, her hand grasping the barre, running alongside a mirrored wall. Damon, a forty-year-old English choreographer with a scruffy beard, glasses and a well-worn sweater knotted around his thin neck, leaned back in his creaking chair on the hardwood floor, smoking a filterless cigarette. "There is immediate devastating dance for the principle ballerina in Sleeping Beauty," he said and drew heavily on the tobacco. "Love it. Easy to understand, a happy ending and well-known music. It's what gave the Royal Ballet its name. Great for the kids. How is the baby by the way?"

"What are you trying to say?" Lisa asked, continuing to bend her knees as brilliant rays of sunshine suddenly flooded the room.

"I just want to make sure you're ready, that's all. It's been a while," he said as he longingly admired her form, not noticing someone's shadow, listening outside the marbled glass of the door.

"Why did you give me the lead without an audition?" she asked and stole a glance at him.

A boyish smile. "Because you're talented," he replied with a shrug.

"What's the real reason?"

Damon shifted in his seat, crossed his legs and put his hands behind his head. "How about dinner tonight?"

"You know I can't," she said and commenced with the *tendue* exercise.

"You're getting a divorce. Why not?" he asked casually and lit another cigarette.

"We can't be together again," she said sadly as her feet pointed and stretched.

"I was there for you when he was never around... and I'm here for you now that's he gone... I would think that would be worth something to you," Damon said and sat at an old piano. The smoke dangling from his teeth, he began to play the theme from Love Story.

"A bit dramatic, wouldn't you say?" she said with a laugh and pushed aside a wisp of her red hair.

"At least I got you to smile," he said playfully.

"You always could," Lisa said and began the *ports de bras* as she moved her body through a series of back bends.

Damon suddenly stopped playing, a serious expression upon his face as the ash fell from his cigarette and fell between the keys. "Does he know?" he asked quietly.

Lisa ceased her exercises and gazed out the window. "No... and I don't think I'll ever tell him."

"He's my son, not Braedon's... you said he never wanted children... we can be together for real this time," Damon said with pleading eyes.

"I can't," she whispered full of shame.

Damon abruptly slammed the piano closed making the keys echo. "It's not fair Lisa! I'm the one who loves you! He's never loved you!" he shouted, but quickly lowered his voice. "I... I'm sorry."

She slowly turned from the window with a heartbroken smile. "But I love *him*," she said softly as they heard someone outside the door cough. Damon returned to playing the piano and Lisa resumed her stretching.

Braedon opened the door and strolled inside, holding a bouquet of roses. "May I cut in?" he said sarcastically just as the sun hid behind the clouds again, casting the room darker.

Damon rolled his eyes to himself and stood, forcing a smile. "Nice to see you again Braedon," he said, shaking the champion's hand and feeling Braedon's deliberately tight grip before turning back to Lisa. "I'm taking five," he said slightly panicked, and rushed out of the room.

"What are you doing here?" Lisa questioned and continued warming up as Braedon closed the door.

"Do you remember I picked that rose out of the garden outside the dance where we met and gave it to you? You're as beautiful now as you were then," he said and held out the flowers.

Chapter Sixteen

"Keep them. If you think I'm coming back, I'm not," Lisa said tersely and performed the *ronds de jambe a terre* to loosen her hips.

"I didn't know you were going to dance again," he said and awkwardly set the bouquet aside on the windowsill. "Where are you staying now?"

"I rented a flat downtown," she said without looking at him.

"I want... I'd like to see my son, *our* son," he said with a raised eyebrow and started to take off his coat.

"Don't bother, you're not staying."

Braedon pulled his jacket back on and gestured to the roses. "Shouldn't you put those in water?"

"Keep them. Better yet, give them to Teresa," she replied and began the grand battements, moving one leg in a semi-circle on the floor.

"That's what I would like to speak to you about," he said quietly. "I'm not going to lie to you anymore Lisa."

She shrugged away his honesty. "That's a switch."

"I saw her for about a year... but it's over now," he said and sat in the chair with his fingers interlocked. "She... she was the only one I ever... it will never happen again. I promise."

"Who else knows?"

"Samuel did... that's it," Braedon said regretfully and hung his head.

"I should have known. You two were as thick as thieves," she responded and began kicking her legs.

"What can I do to make it better?"

A brief chuckle. "Believe me, absolutely nothing," she said, slightly winded and reaching for a towel.

"I have to leave for Montreal in a little while," he announced, looking at his watch. "I'd like you to come with me."

Lisa waved. "Bye."

Braedon felt the nausea brewing in his stomach and struggled to hang on. "Teresa isn't pregnant," he said, shaking his head.

"Is that supposed to make everything okay again?" she said and drank from a water bottle?

"No," he responded sheepishly. "She lied to us Lisa. She was trying to break us up."

"She succeeded."

"It doesn't have to be like this... we can work things out," he pleaded and went to her.

"How Braedon? I can't trust you anymore! You made a fool out of me! I don't think I can forgive that!" she shouted and threw the towel away.

He bowed his head, trying to demonstrate his remorse. "What can I do to convince you?"

Lisa searched for the right words and went to light a cigarette, but thought better of it and simply stared at the flickering flame of the match. "Raising our child together is obviously the best choice... but I have no guarantee you won't do it again... you've ruined my trust... my self-esteem," she said and shook out the match as she studied herself in a floor length mirror. "I know I'm thought of as the *plain-Jane* in racing... all those beautiful wives and girlfriends... I tried to pretend it didn't bother her... but it does... I guess I'm not surprised by what you did... you're all surrounded by them... but you still betrayed me and staying with you would be a constant struggle to trust you... I can't live that way... always wondering."

"I'm trying Lisa... and all I can give you is my word," he said with a hint of anger and eyed her thin frame and drawn complexion. "You've lost some weight."

"I haven't slept much," she said, touching the velvet of a rose pedal.

"I hope you're not purging again," he said and edged towards her. "I don't want to visit you in the hospital like before and see you hooked up to an intravenous. Are you still taking the anti-inflammatory drugs?"

Lisa turned to him, her eyes beginning to water. "What about *her*?" she asked softly.

"She won't make trouble," Braedon said and took her hand as he knelt to one knee. "I promise. Please come back."

"What about the tape? If she's as evil as you say, she'll probably sell it to the highest bidder. I won't stand for that kind of public humiliation Braedon," she said and wiped away a tear with a trembling hand.

"I can't promise that she won't... I told her I didn't care what she did with it... but I do. We'll deal with that if it happens... all I care about is you and me and our son," he said, kissing her hand and pressing his cheek to it.

"I want things to be different... I want to have more children... and I want you stop giving money to the IRA... please," she said, spying the Provo tattoo and cupped his chin, forcing him to look up at her. "If you want us to be together, you'll do it."

Braedon took a moment to suppress his wrath as heat enveloped his face. "What about my racing?"

"I know you love it. Do it as long as you want," she said as Braedon embraced her, his head resting against her stomach as she stroked his hair. "I have a confession," she said.

"What is it?" he said, barely interested as he felt the burden of his uncertain marriage melt away.

"Teresa... I was the one who shot her," she said. Braedon's eyes slowly found hers. "I love you so much."

Chapter Sixteen

"I love you too," he said and buried his head against her midriff once more as a sinister smile broke across his face. "And you'll never leave me because I know I am not the father of our baby," he said and gave her a chilling stare as Lisa began to shake. Braedon stood and held her overly tight. "Now we both have insurance against each other... forever."

"To the eternity of woman," Felipe shouted over the blasting music and toasted Julius' glass as they sat in the wash of strobe lights, inside the VIP lounge of a strip club in Montreal. On the floor in front of them, an exotic dancer writhed on a leopard skin rug and peeled off her petite panties as Friedrich stood outside the one-way glass, looking thoroughly uncomfortable. "Your man needs to get laid," Felipe said, glancing at the German.

"I think it's the wrong type of club for him," Julius said, wearing a fake beard. His eyes couldn't help but ogle the stripper's taut behind.

"Don't underestimate Friedrich," Felipe said as the stripper crawled towards him. "You never knew it, but he tried to get me to sponsor a team when he was hoping to get a new series off the ground. He might have succeeded if Vincenzo had agreed to race in his league."

"What other secrets do you know?" Julius asked as the ice cubes in his drink danced with the deep base of the thundering sound system.

Felipe simply flipped his eyebrows at him with an evil grin before leering at the young dancer inching closer. "It was quite clever of you to request a deaf stripper. Business and pleasure at the same time," Felipe added blithely.

"How are you going to do it?" Julius said and gulped his vodka, letting it burn his throat.

"Do what?" Felipe replied and spread his legs, inviting her near.

"Eliminate Ichiro's best asset," Julius replied and topped up his drink from a full bottle.

"That's my problem so don't worry about it," Felipe said and rubbed his Vandyke beard as the dancer's fingers slid up his thighs.

"I cannot be a part of it," Julius said and smiled upon seeing Friedrich step back from a stripper trying to solicit him.

"You're in no position to dictate anything," Felipe said and stuffed a few bills between the girl's legs. "Relax Julius, the night is on me," he said as the stripper sat in his lap and forced his head between her false breasts.

"Do you remember a few years ago when that Belgian diplomat dropped dead in London?" Julius asked and downed another shot.

"Vaguely," Felipe said as the stripper slipped her hand inside his trousers.

"It was the tip of an umbrella laced with ricin. It was my idea. I signed the papers," Julius said and pretended to slash his own throat. "He was dead in under a minute."

"I don't scare easily," Felipe countered as the dancer teased the tip of his penis with her tongue.

"Anything can happen to anyone at any time."

"Like the way the Azzopardis died? Tell me you didn't have anything to do with that," Felipe said and spun the stripper around. "It ensured your monopoly of the series."

Julius grinned, stood and wandered to the windows to watch the large crowd of men cheer the dancer on the main stage. "What are you going to do about this Randall Grange?"

"Let him run," Felipe said with a heavy sigh as he pushed his manhood into her vagina from behind. "Maybe he is a diamond in the rough, but I doubt it. I'll see to it that he and Braedon don't finish the race, then Alberto takes a ride and so do I," he said happily and mimed driving a racecar.

"You think you can just remove Ichiro's drivers and take over his team? I don't believe it will be that easy," Julius said as the stripper stared at him, sensuously licking her lips.

"Sammy was on the edge financially and that means Ichiro is too. Trust me, without the world champion and his new boy wonder, he'll be happy to sell," Felipe replied and imitated a bird of prey with his fingers as talons. "Just like a vulture, waiting to swoop in for the pickings."

"Don't you think it's going to look just a little suspicious? How much bad luck is believable for Team Jenkins?" Julius wondered as the dancer sucked her finger while continuing to gaze at him.

"You worry too much," Felipe said and shook his head, the sweat flying from his face.

"Are you going to the press conference?"

"No. Let Ichiro have his glory for a little while," Felipe said and pumped harder as the stripper's flesh rippled. "I haven't even spoken to him yet, but I will. Trust me."

"What do you know about Grange anyway?" Julius asked suspiciously.

"He's a loser from the Atlantics. He's a Canadian and used to drive with Vincenzo," Felipe said as he slapped her on the bottom with each stroke and inserted the tip of his beer bottle into her backside.

"Is that it?"

Felipe's eyes slowly moved to Julius and he smiled. "He's a cop and his supposed wife is a DST agent, although they *were* married at one time. I'm sure you had your people check it out."

Chapter Sixteen

"Why do you think they're posing as driver and wife?" Julius asked and sat again.

"I'm not really sure. I was hoping you would know," Felipe replied, positioning the stripper's head between his legs and rammed his penis into her warm mouth.

Julius watched as she greedily slurped Felipe's erection. "Having any kind of sex with her is dangerous... you never know what might happen."

"I've had every STD there is, except the big one, but that's the price of admission," Felipe answered as Julius signed something to the girl. Her teeth suddenly clamped onto Felipe's penis. He yelped and tried to get away, but to no avail. "Get this bitch off of me!" he managed to whisper through gritted teeth.

"You don't know what real power is Felipe," Julius said and drank directly from the bottle. "Why didn't you tell me about Grange?"

"I... I thought you knew," Felipe cried as her teeth split his delicate foreskin.

"What are they doing here?" Julius said and signed again, the stripper increasing her grip.

"I don't know!" Felipe whimpered as his fingers dug through the arm of the leather chair.

"Power is having more than one option. Your wife owns fifty-one percent of Hispania Gold, but everyone has their price... and so does she," Julius said, eyeing Felipe's blood oozing from the corners of her mouth.

"What the hell are you talking about?" Felipe said breathlessly and winced as he struggled to escape, but she bit harder.

"I liked the old ways of Russia, but capitalism is much more fun. Money can buy anything... even your wife. I made her an offer, but it's conditional upon you," Julius said and grabbed Felipe's hair. He pulled his head back, "You see, I have a theory. I think you had Vincenzo and Samuel killed to take over the team, but that doesn't matter to me. We all do what we have to and I don't care what you do with Ichiro and the team, but if you mention Mr. Vladin or I to anyone, you'll be picking tobacco again faster than it would take to kill you," Julius said as he signed again and the stripper released him. Julius handed her a wad of bills, slapped her bottom and she casually strolled away as he emptied the bottle of vodka into Felipe's aching crotch. "Maybe the green snake will make you feel better. Do svidAniya," he said with a wink and meandered out of the room as Felipe slumped down into his seat, squirming in pain.

"I can't wait all day," the taxi driver grumbled with a thick, French accent and glanced at Randall sitting in the back of the cab with his hand on the door handle, his eyes transfixed upon something in the distance. "Well?" the cabby bellowed.

Randall awoke from his temporary stupor, withdrew his wallet and handed him some bills. "Here's an extra twenty. Stay here. I'll be back in a few minutes," Randall said and bolted from the car.

The cabby stuffed the money into his breast pocket and resumed devouring a thick, sloppy sandwich. "You're the boss," he said with a careless shrug as brown lettuce dangled from the corner of his mouth.

Randall took a few, guarded steps and stopped at a set of iron gates, banging in the wind. Despite the blue, sunny sky, he shivered, digging his hands into his pockets as he pushed his way through and anxiously followed the dirt pathway up a hill.

At the top, he froze and gazed upon the dozens of headstones, old and new. Slowly, he strolled along, eyeing freshly placed flowers and squinted, trying to read antiquated lettering. His attention focused on the many trees as the branches and leaves rustled, causing a sudden, noisy departure of birds. He watched the wave of wings as they swept to-and-fro until finally, they landed further ahead. Randall's eyes lit up when he saw a crooked tombstone with the name John Green etched in faded marble.

Randall's heart began to pound and a profound sadness engulfed him as he inched closer. He stooped to touch the cold, smooth structure and felt an odd warmth before awkwardly sitting on the grass. "Hey, Dad... it's nice to finally visit you here," he whispered and withdrew a small flask from inside his denim coat, along with two shot glasses. He poured into both and set one in front of the marker. "To your memory," he said and tapped the other glass before downing the liquor. "Got to tell you, Mom always missed you... I never got the chance... too young... but I wish I'd gotten to know you... see what kind of a guy you were... and see what kind of a man I am," he said with a sigh and retrieved a cigarette. "I'm a cop... used to be good... the best actually... but I kind of fucked up in an car accident... guess you know all about that... only I was the one that was drunk... you should know they jailed the dick who did it to you... got two years... joke uh?" he said and lit the cigarette. "So... Mom told me you were a steelworker... shit job I guess, but it put food on the table... thanks for that... well, I guess you can tell I ain't the perfect son... drink too much," he said with a brief chuckle and waved the bottle. "Caused me to fuck up Jessica's life... that's my daughter... Gwen... our marriage ended because of it... me... but I still love her... hard to let go even after time's gone by... makes you wonder what might have been," he said and pulled his collar up after a gust of wind. "Now I'm working on this case... was anyway... scared... in over my head, you know? I should have walked away when she said I could... should just be walking the beat and then go

Chapter Sixteen

home to a fucking shit apartment and a cat, but it's home... it's where I belong," he said and nodded to convince himself. "Goddamned strange how I used to dream about a chance like this... but it's fucking terrifying when you take a good hard-ass look at yourself and your worth... your ability. I could be one of those losers that's scared of success... at least the criminals know what they want," he said as he scratched his stubble and his unkempt hair. "Always ignored the theory... might be time to admit the asshole is to blame... even Mom... sorry... guess I should have jumped off the fucking bridge... the piece of shit Lunder would be alive... Gwen could get married again... and Vincenzo's death wouldn't matter... ain't no shame in giving up to fear... nobody going to be hurt," he said as he studied another monument atop a fresh grave. "Except maybe me if I keep going... but I wanted out... fuck... maybe I do want to stick around, but there ain't no moral cause here... don't owe anybody anything... and what if I got one in the head, Dad? Not much fucking honour when you're dead because you ain't around to appreciate it," he said and coughed before taking another, long drag. "But what if I wasn't capped? What about the ex and the kid?" he said, fumbling for his wallet and holding out a picture of Gwen, Jessica and himself. "Look good, don't they? Ah shit, doing both of them a favour by leaving... might have been done in anyway... not enough experience... rusty as hell... that'd be worse than a bullet," he said and tucked the picture away. "Press would hound the fuck out of Gwen... and my grave would say I died of goddamned stupidity... fucked up and died on the first lap," he said and ran his finger along the rough engraving of the headstone. "Nobody remembers the heroes as much as the fucking fools who thought they were *somebody*... a dead racecar driver... scolded for trying to fulfil a dream and solve a murder... you might think I'm a coward, Dad, but... but I'm actually protecting them."

Randall pulled some weeds away, spat on them and used them to clean the marble. "Death has a presence, doesn't it? Can taste it... smell it," he said and dug his fingers into the crusty earth. "You wouldn't have liked him... can still smell the ground the day we buried the fuck... wet... was thawing... slippery... clouds seemed darker that day... rolled faster... hanging lower," he said and spied the sky. "Even remember the smell of the casket... pine... creaking when they put it in the hole... worms... kept wriggling even after they were cut by the shovels... Mom held my hand... she had a look like the rest of the world should have stopped what they were doing," he said and examined the dirt under his fingernails. "Realized right then and there I had to become a man quicker than most... accept the harsh rules of life and death... but she didn't shed a tear... fucking idiot priest sounded like a record... dumb shit told me to take care of her, like I fucking wouldn't... asshole," Randall said. He drank directly from the bottle while staring at a crucifix on another tomb. "After everybody was gone, we just stood there staring at the coffin like we were waiting for something to happen... for God himself to show up... it's so fucking final, isn't it? Tried to imagine what it was like to be dead... boxed in for eternity... cramped... silence would be deafening," he said just as a bird chirped. "Fucking black... unless you believe... I don't anymore... but if there is... maybe you can come down and see me sometime... get to know each other," he said with a slight smile and dragged himself up before checking his watch. "Almost nine. Gwen thinks I'm waiting for her in my room... supposed to go to the track for a press conference... didn't even leave her a note... call her later when I'm back home," he said sheepishly, avoiding looking at the marker. "Been good talking to you pop... if you know what I've done... and what they don't know about... please don't judge me, okay? See you later," he said and turned to walk away, but found Gwen waiting for him.

"I haven't gone back to see my father since we buried him... I guess I still haven't forgiven him," she said and stepped closer to Randall. "I knew you'd come here sooner or later, but this is getting tired Randall. You can only punish yourself so much before the damage is beyond repair."

"I can't do it... I can't drive. It's over for me," he said and brushed past her.

"What about Jessica? What am I supposed to tell her? She asks me about you sometimes... and I tell her you were a brave man... a good man. When you used to read her Cinderella every night... she was too young to understand, but to this day it's her favourite... *I* read it to her every night," she said and looked off. "Do I tell her that her father was a quitter? That he was so absorbed with self-pity that he just gave up? It's a hard thing to tell a girl who will never walk again," she said. He wheeled around to confront her.

"I have enough fucking guilt without you laying more on me so just say it, okay?" he shouted.

"What?"

"Say what you've always wanted to but never had the goddamned guts!" he yelled and grabbed her by the collar.

"What? That you screwed up! You did! You wrecked our marriage! You ruined your daughter's life and I'll always hate you for that! All right? Is that what you needed to hear?" she shouted and shoved him away. "But there's nothing to be done about it! Nobody can change it! And I can't believe you'd come this far, only to walk away, again!"

"What the fuck do you want me to do?" he yelled and hurled the bottle, smashing it against the ground.

Chapter Sixteen

"Finish what you started for once!" she said and massaged her head. "The only one living in the past is you!"

Randall gave her a long, hard look. "It's where I should be... because there's nothing in the future... no... I can't... I'm sorry," he said, dropping the cigarette and crushing it out with his cowboy boot.

"Then you tell her," she said and motioned to Jessica, struggling to wheel her chair along the path. "You can walk away from me... but can you do it to her?"

Randall's energy drained and he felt his legs give way and he stumbled slightly. His face contorted and he didn't notice he was suddenly crying. "Why... why did you bring her here?" he managed to whisper as his voice broke, his lips pursing together to fight back the emotion.

"I thought you should see her again... just in case... you know... something happens to you... or me," she said with a reddened face, but she quickly scowled. "But now you're quitting."

Randall finally pried his eyes away from his daughter and focused on Gwen, but he didn't have any words. Overwhelmed, he looked to Jessica again with wonderment. "Can I tell her I love her... can I hold her?" he whispered shyly as he gasped for breath. Gwen nodded as Randall ran to Jessica, but he promptly stopped, thoroughly terrified.

Gwen knelt down beside Jessica and wrapped her arm around the child. "I have something to tell you Jessica... this is Randall... he's your..."

"I'm an old friend of your mom," Randall interrupted as Jessica's angelic face promptly became confused. "It... it's nice to meet you," he said with a breaking voice.

"Hello," Jessica's soft voice said as she leaned forward and held out her arms, inviting his embrace. Randall slowly bent down, picked her up and quietly began to weep as Gwen looked away, hiding her own emotion.

Chapter Seventeen

"Tell me, what happens to the team should you decide to retire... or God forbid, something happens to you?" Felipe questioned as he casually finished searching the other rooms inside Ichiro's trailer, heavily decorated with Japanese swords. He clandestinely checked his radio receiver inside his jacket pocket to ensure the room was clean of transmitters and dropped into a chair while Ichiro stood by the door, hoping he would leave.

"The team would dissolve. I do not want any other person to own it. I want it to be Samuel's, even in death," Ichiro replied and opened the door, anticipating Felipe's departure.

"Very noble, but stupid. I think you should change the name to Team Tanaka," Felipe said and ran his fingers along the blunt edge of a sword displayed on a coffee table.

"No. The name must stay the same to honour him," Ichiro said and closed the door, realizing Felipe wasn't going anywhere.

"If you had decided to change the name, would you have told me?"

"Why?" Ichiro replied with a frown.

Felipe abruptly bolted out of the chair and confronted him. "Because you've made me look like a fool! Just when were you planning on talking to me about the future of the team and my money?" Felipe shouted, but quickly lowered his tone. "You do know that I pay the bills," Felipe said with a cool smile as Ichiro remained silent and crossed his arms. "Aren't you going to offer me a drink?" Felipe asked.

"I am sorry, but I do not have time. The press conference is in thirty minutes," Ichiro said, nervously checking his watch. "Could you please leave?"

Felipe nodded and buttoned his jacket. "I admire a man dedicated to his work," he said, but suddenly slapped Ichiro across the face. "The last time a former employee of mine told me what to do, he got a bullet in the head! Sit down!" Felipe commanded. Ichiro sank into the chair. "Now listen to me you slant-eyed, little bastard, you should have consulted me about Grange. I had to read about it in the paper!" Felipe said furiously and angrily knocked over a lamp, smashing it to the floor.

Chapter Seventeen

"Our contract clearly states Team Jenkins picks the driver," Ichiro said and bent down to gather the broken pieces of the light, but Felipe stepped on his fingers.

"My contract was with the old man, but he's dead!" Felipe said and kicked Ichiro in the buttocks, making him fall over.

Ichiro quickly rose to his feet, his body tightening and muscles pulsating to retaliate as he spied one of the swords beside him. "Violence is not necessary. I have never struck another human being in my life and I am not about to start," he said and motioned to the door. "Good day, sir."

Felipe wrapped his arm around him and escorted him to a wall with some photographs. "Look, I know you're having financial problems and I want to help."

"You caused Samuel's stroke and I know you want the team, but it is not for sale," Ichiro said, his eyes dancing as he waited for another physical assault.

"Is that why you won't sell to me, because you think I was too hard on the old man?" Felipe said with a laugh.

"Samuel was decent and he deserved better than what you did to him. You caused him great stress... and I can never forgive that," Ichiro said, shaking his head.

Felipe waited for a few moments and pointed. "Is that your mother? How's she doing?" Felipe asked condescendingly, staring at an old picture of a Japanese woman. "We're all getting older, aren't we? She must miss your father. All the time you spend away from her would be hard on her too."

"I have to go," Ichiro said quietly, recognizing the implicit threat.

Felipe retrieved his cell phone and handed it to him. "A man should call his mother every day, and if she doesn't answer, well, you start to wonder if something bad might have happened. It's only human nature, but things usually turn out to be fine."

Incredulous, Ichiro stared at him for a few seconds. "What have you done?" he whispered with a quaking voice.

"She stays alive as long as you do what I say. I want Grange, *Officer* Grange and Braedon to both have an accident, the kind that ends a career... and a life. Some kind of mechanical problem that can be blamed on a design flaw or a faulty part, I don't care. And then you sell me the team at a price I offer," Felipe said snapped the phone closed.

In a flash, Ichiro removed one of the swords and held it to Felipe's chin. "You can only push a man so far," he said and barely moved the weapon across Felipe's Vandyke, making a few hairs fall, but the Spaniard didn't flinch.

"Only a coward makes threats. I'd have more respect for you if you did it," Felipe said and pushed his chin harder against the blade, causing a trickle of blood. "I'm waiting," Felipe said. Ichiro shook with anger and slowly lowered the sword as Felipe wiped the blood away with his Spanish-flag-coloured handkerchief. "And if you're thinking of telling Grange or his wife, or anybody else for that matter, then you just signed your mother's death warrant," Felipe said and shattered the photograph with his fist. "And I promise you it will be slow and painful."

"You are an evil ... evil man," Ichiro whispered with watery eyes as Felipe wandered to the door.

"No... you're just weak," Felipe said with a grin, leaving the door open after he strolled out. Ichiro began to shake uncontrollably as he stumbled and collapsed to the floor, his eyes glued to his mother's broken picture, hanging askew on the wall.

Randall checked his hands to discover they were trembling and felt the thumping of his heart as he sat alone on the ground with his back against a wall. The sun warmed his cleanly shaven face and his hair was neatly combed. His wide eyes soaked in the atmosphere; individual garages, each stall depicting every team in the series, brightly clad team members with their distinctive colours unloading equipment, others wheeling toolboxes and carts with various car parts, rows of transport trucks and hospitality trailers enveloped by a sea of reporters and photographers.

He focused on a young boy, holding his father's hand as they wandered through the bustling paddock, both in awe. "There you are! I've been looking all over for you," Gwen said breathlessly and fanned herself with her hand. "Where have you been? I have some amazing news."

Disinterested, his head remained in the clouds as he continued staring at the boy and his father. "Goddamn there's something magical about a race weekend... sun seems brighter," he said as his eyes sparkled. "It's the anticipation... is the most exciting thing... I remember walking through the paddock in the Atlantics and all those kids with their dads... could see the bond between them... somehow changed them... like they were the same age... a passion," he said and smiled. "Can still see their faces light up and force their dads to walk faster after they heard an engine fire... I was jealous of that," he said and finally looked up at her. "I wonder what Jessica would think of all this?"

"We can talk about that later," she said impatiently and withdrew a piece of paper. "I have some information about the Cayman account. It's been traced to Braedon, and the money has since been withdrawn and wired to banks all over the world. It took a while, but we got it!" she said excitedly.

Chapter Seventeen

The announcement stirred Randall from his trance and he hauled himself up. "Are you sure?" he asked and dusted off his behind.

"Positive," she said and happily waved the photocopy in the air. "I have his signature. It's airtight."

"I'll be goddamned. Congratulations," he said and shook her hand. "I knew it was that son-of-a-bitch. But why would he be dumb enough to put the coin in a bank that would give up his name?"

"He wasn't. The bank rejected the warrant so we hacked into their computer system and found it ourselves," she said as her face dimmed. "There'll be hell to pay for that, but we'll take care of it. The DST is working on the cover story as we speak."

"So now what?"

"You don't have to race. I'll arrest him and take him in for questioning," she said and hugged him. "Isn't that great?" Randall nodded, but was clearly deflated. "What's wrong?" she asked.

"I think you should let him play his hand," he said with a shrug. "That's all. Maybe he's got an accomplice... maybe there's a few... don't show your cards until you know all the facts."

"Randall, he had access to the team's stationary. I have his signature on a bank account in the Cayman Islands. He's our man and once I tag him, he'll start talking about any possible accomplices. I'm sure he had something to do with the people shooting at us. He must have figured out who we were," she said and offered him a warm smile. "Look, I know you want to race, but it's too dangerous."

"Then arrest him and I can drive knowing my ass is dead only if I fuck it up. Okay?"

"I don't think you should do it," she said and put the missive away.

"You don't have a say. Fuck! In a few minutes the whole goddamned world will know who I am. I get to live my dream... and you're not going to ruin that for me!" he said and marched off.

"It's not about the racing... it's about Jessica, isn't it? You don't want to let go of her... or me," she said and followed him.

"The only reason you brought Jess here was to get me to follow through with this. You used her as emotional blackmail... just to solve this fucking case," he said with disgust. "And now you're taking her away from me for a second time."

"That's ridiculous! If you're so dedicated, then why did you tell her that you were just a friend of mine?" she said and clamped his arm. "You didn't have the courage to tell her the truth!"

"Not telling her was the bravest fucking thing I've ever done!"

"You didn't say two words to her in the car or at the hotel!" Gwen said and released him.

"It's going to take time for Christ's sake! I... I wanted to earn her trust... be her friend before I could be her father... again," he said and searched for something else to say. "And by the way, it wasn't too fucking smart for you to bring her in the first place. Whoever did shoot at us might have tried again with Jess in the car."

"Don't make assumptions!" she barked and slammed him against the wall outside the press conference building. "I had my people in a car behind us!"

"What the hell are you so mad about?" he said, taken aback and surrendering with his hands.

"I hate disrespect! When I started on the force in Paris, there were only two other women! The uniforms were uncomfortable because they were made for men! They didn't bother having ones made for us because they didn't think we would last!" she said with clenched fists and felt the veins in her neck bulging as Randall stared in disbelief, listening to her diatribe. "Well, I'm still here! And I'm sick and tired of people wondering about my ability, and I don't need you questioning my skills! Save that for yourself!" she said and went to storm off, but he grabbed her arm and swung her around.

"I know why you're so pissed split lips, you're afraid of what you feel!" he said angrily. "Why don't you just admit that you still love me?"

The truth pierced her and she laughed mockingly. "Every time you open that mouth of yours, it proves I was right to leave you," she replied and tried to escape, but he forced her back again.

"Just say it and we'll move on!"

"You've lost your mind," she countered with a chuckle and was restrained once more.

"Say it," Randall said, his eyes locked with hers.

"No!" she said tersely.

"Then tell me you don't love me," he whispered. "Before I invest more time with my daughter... because if it's all been for nothing... it'll destroy me."

"Stop being so dramatic," she said with a careless wave of her hand.

"I mean it Gwen... I'm so close to the fucking edge it ain't going to take a lot... I can't play this game, if that's what it is, especially with Jessica," he said with a sober expression. "Just tell me the truth... do you love me or not?"

Gwen hesitated, debating what her response should be, stymied under the weight of his hopeful stare. "I'm sorry Randall... I don't love you," she said quietly just as a door burst open.

Chapter Seventeen

Ichiro stood in the doorway and tapped his watch. "Where have you been?" he asked sharply. "It is almost time. I have your uniform," he said and eagerly gestured for Randall to follow.

"Randall, listen to me," Gwen pleaded, but he shoved past her.

Randall looked over his shoulder at her after Ichiro disappeared inside. "I can't believe you used me like that... used her like that," he said with a shake of his head. "Our kid ain't a fucking pawn!"

"Will you please listen to me?" she begged and scrambled for her pills. "I don't care if you race. Go ahead. If someone brings up the fact you're a cop, just agree and I'll make the arrest during the press conference if I have to... but I didn't mean to hurt you... I really didn't."

"Fuck you, split lips... just fuck you," he said and kicked the door closed behind him.

Gwen remained there, his words echoing through her mind. "I do love you... and that's why I can't tell you," she whispered.

Randall hurriedly began to disrobe, watching Ichiro begin pacing after peeking through another door to discover the pressroom filling up. "Stop that, you're making me nervous. Just do what we said over dinner last night and it'll be fine. Read your fucking comic books or something," Randall said and pulled off his jeans.

"Do you know I never once used foul language? My parents told me it showed ignorance and a lack of respect for others, as well as myself," he said and pushed his blue rims further up his nose, sweat stinging his eyes. "I expect more from a policeman."

"Who gives a shit what you think? Look bub, I say what I feel and that's all there is to it," Randall replied and finally stripped down to his underwear. "My culture is full of cursing and I'm the goddamned poster boy."

"As a member of my team, I do not like to hear obscenities," he said and checked his bleached blonde hair in the mirror before dusting some dandruff off his shoulders.

"There's an even bigger obscenity, it's called life," Randall said and ripped away the cellophane holding his uniform. "Remember, the guy that was fucking your girlfriend, the one who was killed?"

A deep breath from Ichiro. "I take it your romance with Gwen is not working very well," he said and straightened his team shirt.

"It's none of your fucking business," Randall answered and stepped into his overalls.

"What do you think is the problem?" Ichiro asked and studied his reflection for any imperfections.

Randall zipped up his suit, but caught his finger, the pain shooting through his hand. "Goddamnit! Hey Itchy, listen. I've screwed over a hundred women. That's right, I've been keeping score," he said, jamming his feet into his fireproof shoes as Ichiro raised a shocked eyebrow. "And the only thing I've learned is that they're all fucked... but not as much as me. Now shut the hell up and let's get this over with."

"Please Randall, please do not swear in front of me," Ichiro asked and bowed. "I like you... it would mean a lot to me."

Randall waited for a moment and nodded his compliance. Ichiro bowed again just as Braedon promptly appeared through the backdoor, clothed in his racing garb. "Sorry I'm late. First time ever," Braedon said slightly winded. He looked to Randall and offered his hand. "No hard feelings. Welcome aboard."

Randall returned the gesture, albeit suspiciously. "Thanks, but I'm not going to be your Svengali out there. I'm in it to win."

Braedon smiled and slapped him on the back. "Spoken like a true team-mate. I like confidence, even if it is misplaced," he said as Randall spat in his hands and smoothed back his hair.

"Why were you late?" Ichiro inquired as the din of voices grew louder from within the pressroom.

"I... I was signing autographs," the champion replied bewildered and shook the cramps out of his writing hand. "It's good for the team."

"Did you bring a note?" Randall said sarcastically and stood.

"How many do you sign a day?" Ichiro demanded as he readied his clipboard and gave Randall a disapproving glance.

Braedon frowned and shrugged. "I don't know... it depends on where I am. Sometimes hundreds, I guess. Why?"

"From now on, you do not sign any unless I say so. We should be paid for that. You work for me and I am entitled to compensation," Ichiro said with his hand on the knob. "Ready?"

"Wait a minute!" Braedon said as Ichiro turned back to him. "What's this *we* business? I'm not about to start taking orders!"

"And the next time I see you, I want that tattoo removed. Cover it with your sleeve for now," Ichiro said to Braedon. "If you disagree, tell me now and you can leave, but it is obvious that we both need each other. If you say no, then you can wait until next season to drive," he said, giving Randall a nervous glance as he waited for the answer.

Braedon reluctantly acquiesced, angrily tugging at the arm of his uniform. Ichiro bowed and opened the door. "It's like Pearl Harbour all over again, isn't it? Come on superstar," Randall said and invited him to walk out first.

"I'm going to make a fool out of you," Braedon said, giving himself a cursory once-over in the mirror.

Chapter Seventeen

"Good luck out there," Randall replied, pretending to scratch his forehead with his finger, but was actually flipping Braedon the bird as he marched out of the room. "Make a fool out of me? Shit... don't worry, I can do that by myself," he whispered and closed his eyes. "Please Vince... help me to not fuck up," he said, looking to the ceiling. Randall slowly strolled into the pressroom and instantly squinted upon seeing the blinding barrage of flashing cameras.

Ichiro led Randall and Braedon to a long table with three chairs, besieged by a network of lights and audio equipment. There was more continuous clicking of flashing cameras and a deluge of whispers. Ichiro took the middle chair and was joined by Randall on his right and Braedon on his left. Randall's throat dried immediately and he reached for a pitcher of water, but accidentally knocked it over, soaking a nearby pile of press releases. There were a few giggles and a loud snicker from Braedon as more cameras popped.

Ichiro covered the microphone in front of him and leaned towards Randall. "Relax. All this is, is twenty second sound bytes that we have all heard a thousand times before," Ichiro whispered.

"I've never screwed up at a press briefing so watch me and you might learn something. You're just another mouthpiece for the team so deliver your lines," Braedon chimed in, smiling broadly for the media.

Ichiro removed a piece of paper from his pocket, sat closer to the desk and clasped his hands, ready to address the audience. "Ladies and gentlemen, I would like to thank you for coming this afternoon and to remind you that this press conference will be kept civil," he said, reading from the note. "We will not entertain questions about Samuel or Vincenzo. As you know, our team has suffered a great tragedy in both men. Samuel was one of the great pioneers of racing and we will miss him dearly. I owe my career and everything I have to Samuel... he was more than an owner... he was a true friend," Ichiro said with a weakened voice and took a moment to compose himself. "But we will continue in Samuel's tradition and as the new owner, I will strive to maintain his level of excellence and hard work. We will do this with a dedicated team and of course, the world champion, Braedon Stirling," Ichiro said and began to clap. Randall and the room joined in. Braedon tipped his imaginary hat and nodded his appreciation to Ichiro before casually pouring himself a glass of water while looking at Randall to silently demonstrate how it was done. The subtle message was noticed by the press and there were more pictures snapped. "Now, on my right, is a man some of you may remember. He raced in the Atlantic Series some years ago and recently tested with Team Jenkins at Silverstone. Samuel and I saw great promise in him and I welcome him to the team. Ladies and gentlemen, I am proud to announce we have signed Mr. Randall Grange," Ichiro said and motioned for Randall to say something as there was another round of applause, led by Gwen, standing at the back of the room.

Randall cleared his throat and inched closer to the mike. "Thank you," he said, his voice too loud as it boomed over the sound system, causing him to jump. "Thank you very much," he continued with restraint. "I... I'd like to say a special thanks to Mr. Jenkins, God rest his soul, and Mr. Tanaka for giving me this opportunity... and to Braedon for all his support... and I look forward to the challenge," he said with a nervous smile as reporters scribbled down Randall's comments.

"We will take a few questions now," Ichiro said and neatly folded his opening remarks.

The room instantaneously erupted with a spate of queries, but Candice Goldenstein merely waited until Randall's eyes found her and he nodded. "Candice Goldenstein, Open Wheel," she shouted over the others. "Mr. Grange, having driven in the Atlantic Series, what makes you think you're qualified to drive in this series?" she asked with a smirk. "I mean, I love movies and I was an extra once, but I'll never win an Oscar," she added and the room filled with laughter.

Randall studied her with contempt and searched the crowd for Gwen who was already moving quickly towards Candice. "To be perfectly frank with you Miss Holstein... I mean, Miss Goldenstein," Randall said. The crowd laughed again and Candice scowled. "It doesn't take years of experience to figure out if a man has speed. Either you have it or you don't and nobody cares if you cross the line backwards, just as long as you cross it. Hell, you can ask Mr. Stirling, the test at Silverstone was very successful," he said, glancing at Braedon as Ichiro winced.

Another reporter stepped forward. "Chad Furrows, Toronto Star. There are two types of competitors, Mr. Grange, those that drive from the inside out, and those from the outside in. Which one would you classify yourself as?"

Randall paused for a few moments. "If you're asking me if I'm doing this for the fame, the glamour, the women and all that sort of thing, I'm not. That's a dangerous way to drive because you're focus is wrong. So, I guess that makes me an inside out kind of guy," he said, his answer immediately gaining respect.

"Roger Pack, Montreal Gazette," a man said, feverishly waving to Randall. "How do you feel about replacing the legendary Vincenzo Azzopardi?"

"First of all, that's a damn stupid question. Nobody will ever fill his shoes, and I'm not even going to try. Vincenzo was an old friend. As a matter of fact, he saved my life in Toronto during a race," Randall replied,

Chapter Seventeen

becoming more at ease as Braedon was clearly agitated, Randall was coveting all the attention.

"Can you tell us about that?" the Gazette reporter asked as everyone awaited the story with their writing instruments poised.

"No. You people can do your own homework. Look it up," Randall said and took a long drink.

"Well, I did my homework Mr. Grange... and I discovered that you were a police officer," Candice yelled over the others, enjoying the sudden stares of her colleagues as the room grew deathly silent. Ichiro sank a little lower in his seat as Braedon looked fearfully at Randall. Gwen waited behind Candice with a tiny syringe in her hand, in case she needed to stop her.

"Yeah... I used to be a cop, but I still wanted to race," Randall said and took another drink. "And I used to be married. She's still a cop in France, but we're trying to work it out... we have a daughter," he said and withdrew Jessica's tattered photograph as Gwen watched anxiously. "The rest of you don't have to dig anything up... I'll tell you about it... I got us in a car accident and my kid can't walk now... it was my fault... and there isn't a day that goes by that I don't wish it was me that was in that chair," he said and drew a deep breath. "So I'm going to race again to earn my family's respect... and love... and get my life back in order again... and I'd appreciate it if you didn't bug me about that... please respect our privacy and I won't be answering any more questions about it."

It took several seconds for the substance of Randall's words to permeate the room as Candice stared at him, still weighing the validity of his statement. "How do you feel about your newest team-mate Braedon?" Candice asked.

"I... I think he's a fine addition to the team," Braedon responded, fighting to recover from Randall's stunning admission. "All drivers are cut from the same cloth... only some are smoother than others," he said and deliberately stole a look at Randall. "I'll still be champion come the end of the season," he said confidently with a forced, cocksure smile as everyone looked to Randall for a reply.

"Well, he's probably right in that he will be champion again and it's expected. That's great for me because there's no pressure. If I out perform him like I did at Silverstone, then we'll see what he's made of," Randall said with a polite smile to the Irishman. The press core clearly enjoyed the exchange and hastily wrote their notes as the flashbulbs clicked.

"John Drake, ESPN. Mr. Tanaka, what do make of this friendly rivalry?"

"They say the most important part of the car is the nut that holds the steering wheel," Ichiro said, making a few people laugh. "I think we have two. Braedon's smooth driving and Randall's raw talent should make things even more exciting. We saw something in Randall we liked," he said and glanced at him. "My mother... she used to say controlled aggressiveness is the key to success," he said, suddenly becoming overwhelmed at the thought of her and Felipe's warning. Ichiro hastily reached for a glass of water and drained it as everyone watched in confusion. "Randall... Randall's talent is refreshing... and... and the pundits say racing has become nothing more than a parade of usual characters after the first lap. Mr. Grange's participation will change that perception. I guarantee it. A few more questions and then that will be all," he said curtly.

Another reporter shouted above the frenzy. "Tyler Patterson, CBC. Mr. Tanaka, no doubt the tragic death of Vincenzo has cast a gloom over this race weekend, but how will you and Team Jenkins overcome this?"

Ichiro took a few seconds to answer, searching for something profound to say. "In racing nothing is easy... it is a calculated risk and Vincenzo knew that, as we all do," he said as Randall noticed his name scribbled on the back of one of the press releases and pulled it out of the stack. Glued on letters, clipped from a newspaper read, *'I know who you are... officer. Ten million pounds or Braedon dies! The account awaits.'* "We will miss him dearly, but we do have a job to do and we shall proceed. It is what he would want. One more question," Ichiro said as the press shouted. Randall hastily folded the letter and slowly raised his eyes; optics so luminous only silhouettes could be seen, shadowy figures milling just a few feet in front. He tried to find Gwen off to the side, but the flashing cameras made her impossible to discern.

"Jeffrey Login, Hamilton Spectator. Randall, can you tell us what the biggest difference is for you between driving an Atlantic car and one of these cars?" the reporter asked.   Randall   remained entranced by the overpowering brightness. Ichiro elbowed Randall back to reality. "Sorry... um... well... obviously theses machines are much more powerful... and they brake quite a bit faster... but I guess the level of competition is the biggest thing... everyone here is capable of winning," he said.

Ichiro promptly stood. "That is all for now. Thank you for coming," he said and motioned his drivers to the back room as the reporters continued to yell more questions. Randall tucked the letter inside his trouser pocket and scurried off followed by Braedon and Ichiro. Once in the changing room, Ichiro closed the door and angrily pointed at them. "I will not tolerate that kind of verbal jousting in front of the press! We are

Chapter Seventeen

supposed to be a team, not a dichotomy!" he yelled and realized he was losing his composure as Randall and Braedon stared at him, completely puzzled.

"What's your problem?" Randall asked and unzipped his uniform.

"Nothing... nothing is the matter," Ichiro said calmly, but was patently worried about Felipe's earlier threat. "I am sorry for shouting," he said and hurried out the door.

"I'd scream too if I hired a rookie like you," Braedon said and scoffed at Randall.

"Does that fucking arrogance of yours ever take a break?" Randall asked and stepped out of his suit.

"So *you* were a police officer," Braedon said mockingly, but was equally suspicious as he leaned against the wall.

"Nothing gets by you, eh?" Randall replied sarcastically and flung his overalls aside.

"What was that like, pretending to be a big man?" Braedon asked with disdain.

"Boring, like this conversation," Randall said and wormed into his jeans.

"I hate cops... they all think they're above the law," Braedon said as his eyes glazed over. "The bastards used to harass me even as a kid... we'd throw rocks at them, but they used guns... I saw a few friends die at the hands of them."

"Well, that's a real tearjerker, but who gives a fuck?" Randall said and threw on his shirt.

Braedon heaved with anger and stepped closer to him. "You're out of your league here boy, and I'm going to send you back home to write parking tickets like the meter maid you are!"

Randall waved at the air and whistled. "Phew! Talk about an asshole with teeth. Hey potato-head, try a mint," he said and pulled on his denim coat.

"No wonder your daughter's in a wheelchair, look at her father," Braedon said and went to walk away, but Randall knocked him to the floor and stepped on his throat while twisting the champion's hand.

"You mention my kid again and I'll pull your fucking arm out of its socket. Be hard to drive looking like a slot machine. Got it, moron?" Randall said as he released him.

Braedon battled to his feet and grinned. "Drivers like me have respect for the dangers, but guys like you spin out and dust themselves off. You're going home in a body bag, mate," he said and whisked out the door.

Randall stood there, found his cigarettes and lit one just as Gwen hurried in through another door.

"You handled the press well," she said with a light smile, trying to soften their previous exchange and opened the door a crack to see Braedon greet Lisa with a kiss, ignoring autograph hounds as they went. "I'll arrest him tonight. I'm going to need the time to brief the locals and Ichiro anyway."

Randall withdrew the threatening note and casually handed it to her without looking as he blew a smoke circle. "I don't think so Miss-Can't-Be-Wrong," he said matter-of-factly.

Chapter Eighteen

"Right over there," the bartender said and pointed. Randall clumsily dragged himself off his stool. He staggered through the smoky pool hall, excusing himself as he bumped into several customers and dug his hands into his pockets, searching for some change until he found the money and dropped the coins into the cigarette machine.

"I think I've said this before, but I thought you gave them up," Gwen's voice said as Randall retrieved the smokes. He brushed her aside and stumbled back to his stool. "I had quite a time trying to find you," she said and followed him. "But then I realized you'd probably go to the seediest place within walking distance of the hotel," she added with a chuckle.

"Good work detective," he said too loudly and clapped sarcastically before downing another shot of Tequila. "The old man used to take me to dives all the time because he was too fucking lazy to take me anywhere else. I'm surprised your blue blood would come in here. This place sure ain't the Le Sainte," he said with a snooty, French accent.

"Do you think getting drunk the night before you qualify a racecar is a good idea?" she said and sat on the stool next to him.

"She'll have a Shirley Temple," Randall said sarcastically to the barkeep and laughed stupidly as he motioned for another shot. "Leave the bottle, bud."

"White wine," she said to the bartender and suddenly realized. "Wait a minute. How do you know about Le Sainte?"

"Nothing," he grumbled and poured himself another.

"Le Sainte is in Paris. It's an exclusive club. How did you know about that?" she asked in astonishment.

Randall exhaled heavily as his blurry eyes focused on the rows of bottles. "I followed you there," he said under his breath, thoroughly encumbered. "I saved my money like a goddamned kid with a paper route and flew to Paris and tracked you down a few months after you left... didn't have the fucking guts to let you see me... just hung around for a few days like some stupid, lovesick schoolboy," he said as the warmth of embarrassment engulfed his face. "I just remember you going into that club... my clothes weren't good enough for me to get in... so I just packed up my shit and went home," he said and drank again.

Randall's catharsis was overwhelming as she could only stare at him, completely dumbfounded. "I'm not sure how to say this so I'll just say it... I think we should try again," she said bashfully.

"Try what?" he replied and belched as he filled his glass, spilling most of it.

She cleared her throat. "Us."

Randall laughed again and chased the liquor with a long gulp of his beer. "You'd have been a better comedian than a cop," he said and winced as the Tequila caused him to shiver.

"I've been thinking about it... and well... what have we got to lose? At least we'll know we gave it one more chance," she said with a frustrated sigh.

"I want to play pool," he abruptly announced, grabbing the bottle and wandering to a table.

"I'm serious," she said and joined him in the adjacent room.

"Look split lips, I'm already on the case so you don't have to fish me in again," he said, mimicking a sportsman reeling in the big one, before fighting to stuff some quarters into the coin slot.

"What is it going to take to convince you?" she asked as he retrieved a cue from the rack.

"Nothing. I don't mind being used... just tell me up front," he said as he eyed the stick to gauge its quality.

"I'm not using you. I really believe we need to try again," she said, suppressing her temper.

"Tell you what," he said gamesomely and handed the cue to her. "If you win, we try again... if I win... we don't," he said and noisily racked the balls.

"Randall, I'm not going to bet our future on a game of pool," she said and placed the stick on the table before finding her pills.

"You break," he said and chalked the cue.

"I'm not doing this," she replied with a roll of her eyes and crossed her arms.

Randall thought for a moment and shrugged. "Okay, I'll break," he said and launched the cue with a thunderous crack, the balls rocketing around the table until one fell in a pocket.

"Why are you drinking?" she asked, sitting on the table's edge and swallowing a few tablets. "Are you scared?"

CHAPTER EIGHTEEN

"Why do you take drugs? Shit. Racing ain't for the gutless... and I'm running a little short. Of course I'm fucking scared. I don't want to look like a goddamned goof," he said and aimed.

"Why haven't you asked me to see Jessica again? She's at the hotel with... with Peter," she said nervously.

"The meatball? You brought him to Montreal? Jesus," he said with an incredulous shake of his head and successfully made the shot.

"Why won't you see your daughter?"

Randall wavered on his feet as his eyes drifted off. "I never want to see her again," he whispered and struggled to concentrate on the game.

"Why not?" Gwen said, utterly stunned.

"I'll never earn her love... I don't deserve it... and that's why we can't try again... because I'd have to see what I did to her every day... every fucking day... and I can't handle that," he said, withdrawing Jessica's faded picture and sliding it across the worn felt towards Gwen without looking. "Keep it... you and I are finished... all of us are."

"Maybe I was wrong to leave you," she said, lost in thought, running her finger over the smooth photograph. "Maybe I didn't try hard enough."

"No... you tried enough. You were right... you're always fucking right," he said and dropped another ball with tremendous force to emphasize his point.

Gwen looked away, gathered her thoughts and took a sip of her wine. "What do you think about the note?" she said, promptly professional.

The quick change of gears momentarily left Randall at a loss, but he was relieved. "I... I think whoever sent it was in the room, and it clears Braedon."

"Does it? Maybe he wrote it to throw us off," she said and slumped into a nearby bistro chair.

"Maybe... and just maybe someone's trying to frame him with the Cayman account," he said, blowing a few smoke circles and chalking his cue again.

"I thought of that and that's why I've assigned a security detail to him around the clock. He doesn't know about it of course," she said and studied a filthy photograph of Jacques Villeneuve, hanging crooked on a wall with most of the drywall showing.

"Then again, why would anybody set him up?" he wondered, the ash from his smoke falling onto the felt. He rubbed it into the material until it blended in with the other stains.

"Like anybody else, he's bound to have enemies. There may be some we don't even know about," she said, taking another drink as she continued to stare at the Canadian champion.

"Well, if it ain't someone connected to the team, how in the hell do they know who I am?" he said and readied for another shot.

Gwen contemplated the possibilities and shrugged to herself. "I guess we have to tell Braedon about the note, and Ichiro too, but nobody else. If Braedon's innocent, we can't let the man drive."

"There is a way to ensure his well-being and let him drive at the same time," Randall said and sank another ball.

"I know, catch the killer before the race," she said and waved him off.

"That would be nice, but not likely. I suggest that Braedon and I switch helmets," he said as she backed up, the cue coming close while Randall took aim. "Only Braedon and Ichiro would know. We can get around the crew and the press."

"It's a good idea, but I don't know about that," she said, pushing the stick aside, causing him to miss.

"Just tell them about the note for Christ's sake. We're not getting anywhere; so creating a little tension might reveal the truth. Look, you brought me here to help. It's the only way to catch the killer when he shows his hand," he said and handed her the cue.

"You're not much good to me dead," she said with a warm smile. "I'd rather have you around... to enjoy your daughter... and me," she said and angled the cue.

"It ain't going to happen," he said, more interested in her behind and feeling his manhood expand as she bent over the table.

"I'll make you a deal. If I go along with this crazy idea about the helmets, you have to promise to give us another chance... one chance, that's all I'm asking you for... for me and for Jessica," she said and sank the ball.

"I could pack up and go home now, you know," he said, watching her brush away her silky black hair.

"I know, but you won't because you're a good cop and there's a good man inside of you. I should know, I knew him once... and I want him back. I know he's scared, but have a little faith in him... I do," she said and dropped several more balls.

"What if I mess up again?" he said quietly.

"You won't," she replied and continued her gaming success.

"No... I can't," he said as Gwen ran the table and won the match, much to his amazement. "Jesus! Where the hell did you learn to play like that?"

"I started playing after we broke up. I used to like hanging out in a lot of places like this... they reminded me of you. I even won a few tournaments. I used to pretend the balls were yours," she said with a sly grin. "Never missed."

Chapter Eighteen

Randall tucked the bottle of Tequila inside his coat and crushed out his smoke on the floor with his cowboy boots. "Nice game. Later," he said casually and meandered away, but Gwen grabbed him by the collar and spun him around.

"Aren't you forgetting something?" she asked and backed him up to the table's edge.

"What?"

"I won the game. Don't welch on your bet. We have to try again," she said and gestured to him and herself. "Our relationship, remember?"

"No way, split lips," he said and started to walk off, but she expertly tripped him and pushed him onto the pool table. Gwen leaned a cue across his throat as she straddled his body.

"Are you going to welch on the bet?" she asked and pressed the wood harder to his neck.

"No," he managed to squeak out and snuck a peek at her braless chest.

More pressure. "How about now?" she said with an evil smile as Randall shook his head to deny her. "Give in yet?" she asked again, pushing her full weight across his throat until Randall capitulated with his hands. Gwen removed the cue. Their eyes locked and she kissed him on the mouth as his arms slowly embraced her. "I knew you'd see it my way. Now come on, we have to meet Ichiro and Braedon for dinner," she whispered as he pulled her close again.

Randall pulled his denim collar up and fought to light a cigarette against a warm wind sweeping in off the St. Lawrence. He leaned against the railing of the dinner cruise ship and studied the socialites and tourists inside the cabin as a musical duet performed a romantic song. His eyes drifted skyward to the myriad of stars, the sound of lapping waves against the hull providing a natural soundtrack. "Smoking again, uh?" Gwen said, appearing from the shadows, dressed in a pantsuit.

"We're not even back together yet and you're nagging me," he said and purposely drew heavily on the tobacco. "Isn't it time for a pill, split lips?"

"It's nice to see you dressed up for this," she said sarcastically and stood at the railing, watching the soft, neon glow of the Montreal skyline. "I asked you to wear something decent tonight."

"Nag, nag, nag," he replied, rolling his eyes and tapping the ash into the river. "Have you told them yet?"

"No. I want you to be in there when I do," she said and turned to face him. "Randall, I... I think we have to talk about a few things first," she said awkwardly, her warm face relieved after a light, cool spray sprinkled from below.

Randall continued staring at the shore. "Sex, right? We don't have to do anything until we know for sure if it's going to work out."

"How did you know I was going to say that?" she said and laughed in amazement.

"You're like any other woman. You use sex as a weapon. It's the ultimate prize. Don't mow the lawn and no blowjob for you," he said, impersonating a female's voice.

"I see we have a lot of work to do," she said with a sigh and glanced over her shoulder at the waiters beginning to serve. "We better get in there."

"I ain't hungry," he said, spitting some bits of tobacco and giving her a sideways glance. "I don't think I should see Jessica either. No sense breaking her heart... or mine if it doesn't work," he said and looked her over. "You look good by the way."

"Thanks and... well, I agree with you about Jessica," she said, promptly self-conscious about her appearance.

"What about the meatball? What are you going to tell him?" Randall said and reluctantly looked down at the rushing water.

"For the last time, his name is Peter!" she said with a touch of anger and checked her temper. "I'll just tell him the truth. He probably watched the press conference anyway. He'll understand," she said and noticed Randall's face becoming worried. "What's wrong?"

"Water ain't my favourite thing, thanks to dear old dad. Prick once pushed me out of a rowboat... I felt sorry for the fish," he said with a blush. "Hook in the mouth and all that... struggling to breathe... started crying so he pushed me... I still don't know how to swim," he said with an embarrassed chuckle.

Gwen covered his hand with hers. "How *do* we try again, Randall?" she asked with sincerity.

"I don't know... one day at a time, I guess," he replied, flicking his cigarette into the water as an accordion player began to perform, causing him to scowl and ruining the tender moment. "Christ, I hate that music," he snarled.

Gwen giggled, remembering. "I never told you, but my parents made me take accordion lessons for years. I even sliced my own fingers so I wouldn't have to play it, even though I was pretty good," she said with a smile. "After my father went to prison, I used to visit him and play. I felt stupid, but I knew he liked it. It was his favourite instrument," she said, suddenly aware she was talking too much and took a few tablets.

"Come on, dinner's waiting and it's time to raise a little hell," he said after a few ungainly moments and led her into the cabin.

Chapter Eighteen

"Shall we get down to business?" Ichiro asked nervously as Randall and Gwen took their seats at the table.

"I don't really see what there is to discuss," Braedon said, his face a pale shade of green. "As long as Randall is relegated to blocking for me and staying out of my way, I think we'll have a podium on Sunday."

Gwen eyed Randall, hoping he wouldn't respond too harshly. "Ichiro, I'll do whatever you ask me to do," Randall said in a monotone voice.

Ichiro was lost in thought and finally realized Randall was speaking to him. "Oh... there are no team orders... just do not run into each other," Ichiro said as he began to fidget with his napkin.

Braedon impatiently checked his watch and stifled the urge to vomit. "If things are fine, then why the hell are we having dinner? I could be with my wife!" he said and hurried to swallow a Gravol.

"I... I never tried hard enough to understand my mother... to see things from her perspective," Ichiro said, his voice quivering and staring off into space, drawing odd stares from the rest. "It... it is important to spend time together and learn about one another. I am not very good with people skills... and it has stopped me from having friends. I want that to change. You and Randall do not even know each other and I think it is imperative that the two of you get familiar... that we all do. It can only help the team," Ichiro said and continued wringing the cloth.

"Is there something wrong, Ichiro?" Gwen asked.

"No... everything is fine," Ichiro replied and took a long sip of his water.

"Can someone please tell me what she's doing here?" Braedon said, gesturing to Gwen without looking.

"Her name is Gwen," Randall shot back and grinned. "Feeling a wee bit seasick, Braedon? Hard to believe someone who drives for a living can't take a little back and forth action," he said and tilted playfully in his seat.

Braedon brought a handkerchief to his mouth and gagged. "Why did you tell me she was your wife, but at the press conference, you told everyone you're trying to work things out?" Braedon asked, replete with suspicion.

"I love her... and I want her back... I told you she was my wife... but I knew some fucking reporter would find out, so I told the truth," Randall said with his head down and giving Braedon a cold stare. "And it would do your physical health a lot of good to remember it's none of your goddamned business. Sorry Ichiro, but I think there's more to come," Randall said casually, regarding the use of his language.

Braedon scoffed. "It's easy to talk tough at the dinner table, it's another thing on the track."

"You're the one that went off the road at Silverstone," Randall said as he reached for a bun. "Nothing like food sloshing around in your stomach to make a meal more interesting, eh champ? Hope there's no icebergs out there. Might have to break out the life jackets," he said sardonically with a wink.

Braedon glared at him, stood and threw his napkin on the table. "I've had enough of this!"

"Sit down, Braedon," Gwen said in a threatening tone and clandestinely presented her DST identification to him. "This is official police business."

"I don't take orders from a woman, especially a woman cop," Braedon said with disdain and went to walk away, but Randall hooked his leg with his cowboy boot and tripped him back into the seat.

"Just sit there, potato-head, keep your fucking hole shut and listen," Randall whispered as he noisily chewed his bun. "Lay it on him," Randall said to Gwen.

Gwen withdrew a folded piece of paper and slid it across the table to the champion. Braedon opened it and read. His worried eyes slowly looked up. "What's going on here?" he said as Ichiro unwillingly read the menacing letter and cringed.

"Randall received that today at the press conference. Vincenzo was murdered. Someone shot him. Team Jenkins has been getting these letters for a while, threatening to kill Vincenzo. Samuel knew about it and so does Ichiro," Gwen said quietly as Randall spread a huge amount of butter on the other half of his bun to deliberately rile Braedon.

"And it looks like you're next," Randall said cheerfully with a mouthful. "Gwen and I are working on this thing undercover, and we had to finally tell you for obvious reasons," he said and washed the bread down with his water. "So, your ass stays off the track and I use your helmet. Hopefully, the killer antes up this weekend and we catch them before they succeed. We're nearly the same height and weight. Nobody will notice."

"I'll notice and so will the entire world because you're not as good as me! It's ludicrous!" Braedon said as his face turned greener when the boat rocked slightly.

"As opposed to taking a bullet in the head or Christ knows what else?" Randall said and proceeded to take Braedon's bun to further annoy him.

"How do you know it would be a bullet?" Braedon asked as his stomach churned, watching Randall tear apart the bread.

"We don't, but it happened before and it could happen again," Gwen reasoned, her mind full of mistrust, thanks to Braedon's strange reaction.

Chapter Eighteen

"I... I have to agree with Braedon," Ichiro said anxiously. "No offence Randall, but if Braedon takes the pole, which he probably will, second row at the least, I do not know if you are ready for that kind of pressure."

"And what if you make a mistake? It goes on my driving record, not yours. Meanwhile, I perform my usual excellence and you get all the glory!" Braedon said through gritted teeth.

"What the fuck is wrong with you guys? Just how big is that ego of yours Braedon?" Randall asked in bewilderment. "It's a wonder you can get your fucking helmet on. We're talking about your life here and we're trying to save it!"

"I'll take my chances," Braedon said matter-of-factly and turned to Ichiro. "We don't have to listen to this. Think of the embarrassment for me and the team when they drop the rag and he parks it in the fence!"

"I *have* had the pole position before superstar," Randall said, overly defensive.

"You don't understand rookie. The boys we're up against are the best in the world! You can't drive with your mirrors for the whole race!" Braedon said too loudly, garnering some stares from a few of the other patrons.

"Don't worry, I won't ruin your reputation," Randall said snidely and purposely jammed too much bread in his mouth.

"Talk about ego problems," Braedon said and looked at Gwen. "I'm not going to throw away my career because of an amateur and you can't force me," he said as he gazed out the windows and focused on Ile Notre-Dame, the island location of the race. "I was in my first fight when I was five and I've never backed away from one, and I'm not about to start now," he said to Randall with conviction.

"Hey pal, this ain't the streets of Belfast when you were a kid, this is the real fucking deal here and somebody wants you dead," Randall said and wiped his mouth with his sleeve.

"I'm not missing a race because of some maniac who may or may not try and kill me," Braedon said and buttoned his jacket, preparing to leave. "The odds are in my favour."

Full of doubt, Randall and Gwen stole a glance at one another. "I think there's something you're not telling us," Gwen said to the champion as Ichiro continued to sweat, his eyes darting around the room.

"Like?" Braedon replied unconcerned as he pushed his chair back.

Gwen produced another slip of paper and handed it to Braedon. "Can you explain how your name got on a Cayman Island bank account with the money Samuel paid to stop the first threat?"

Shocked, Ichiro couldn't help but bring his hand up to cover his mouth and Braedon was temporarily stymied. He quickly recovered, recognized the insinuation, smiled and offered his hands. "If you're implying I had anything to do with Vincenzo's death, then cuff me right now. Otherwise, keep your lame threats to yourself. I have no idea how that happened. That account doesn't belong to me. Obviously, someone is trying to frame me," he said confidently.

"Listen to me you pompous shit, the only reason your precious ass isn't in jail is because we're willing to give you the benefit of the doubt about the Cayman bank account... for now," Randall said and dusted the crumbs in front of him towards Braedon. "So I'd cooperate if I were you."

"Is there anybody you can think of that would set you up?" Gwen inquired and withdrew her pen and pad.

"There is one person... but I don't know how she could have done it," Braedon answered, avoiding everyone's eyes.

"She? You mean Teresa?" Gwen said and scribbled in her notebook.

Braedon was shell-shocked. "How did you know?"

"There's always been rumours about the two of you," Randall chimed in and gave him a friendly elbow. "You get seasick when you were doing her? Bet she's a screamer."

"Tell me about it," Gwen said to Braedon after giving Randall a reproachful glance.

Braedon scratched at his tattoo and lowered his voice. "We had a relationship... she had video of us... she threatened to show it to the press if I didn't give her money... a lot of money... I refused... and then she told me she was pregnant... I didn't believe her... I'm not proud of what I did, but I forced her to take a test," he said sadly.

"And is she?" Gwen asked with a raised eyebrow.

"No... but that doesn't explain who killed Vincenzo... I mean, we were seeing each other long before it happened," Braedon said, reaching for his water to soothe his cotton-dry mouth after preventing another gag.

"Did you shoot her?" Gwen asked, pen ready.

Braedon vehemently shook his head. "Absolutely not! I did give her a lift after we met at a club in London, but I didn't shoot her! I don't know who did! God! I have enough problems!" he said, protecting Lisa from certain prosecution.

"Did your wife know you were plugging her?" Randall asked as he perused the menu.

Braedon's ire swallowed his being as he struggled to keep calm. "No! And I don't like your choice of words!"

"Oh, I see," Randall said, pretending to care. "Well, how about banging? Or how about fucking? Screwing? It's all the same bud, and you're no better than the rest of us so you can stop with the high horse shit."

Chapter Eighteen

"So... so what happens now?" Ichiro said, stopping the staring contest between Randall and Braedon.

Gwen flipped her pad closed. "I'm sorry Braedon, I can't let you drive."

Braedon immediately stood and pointed a warning finger at her. "You'll be hearing from my lawyer!" he said.

"I'm sure I will... you're under arrest," Gwen said, just as a fireworks display began off in the distance. She gestured to two men, dressed in suits, waiting by the door. "Those gentlemen are with the Montreal police. We can do this quietly or you can make a scene. It's up to you," she said as Ichiro's mouth dropped open in disbelief.

Randall grinned and looked to Braedon. "Isn't she great? God, I love it when she does that," he said sarcastically. "Better than sex."

Chapter Nineteen

"Here pussy, pussy, pussy. Hey, little man in the boat. Want to smoke my rod?" the young inmate said and withdrew his stiffened penis as Randall and Gwen strolled down a hall with jail cells on either side, the stench of urine, cigarettes and sperm hanging thick in the air. "Look at this snake, girl, you won't have to eat for days," the prisoner said laughing and pushing his member between the bars.

In a flash, Randall grabbed the man's penis and twisted it. "What are you in for asshole, besides having a small dick?" Randall whispered.

The inmate struggled to escape, but Randall's grip was too hard. "I... I stole a car," he managed to say through clenched teeth as he stood on his toes.

"Randall!" Gwen barked. "Let him go!"

"Apologize to the nice lady," Randall whispered and squeezed harder. "Or I'll rip your cock off and shove it down your throat."

"Sorry... I'm sorry," the prisoner said. Randall released him, causing the whimpering youngster to curl into a ball on the floor. "Learn some fucking manners you piece of shit," Randall said and spat on him.

Gwen yanked Randall by the arm and hurried him along. "What do you think you're doing? And don't tell me you're protecting my honour again!"

Randall pulled his arm away from her grasp. "I hate these fucking animals! Bunch of goddamn trash!"

"They have rights," she said as they continued further down the corridor.

"These fucks gave them up when they walked in here. You've been off the streets for too long," he said and wiped some saliva from his mouth. "You're a victim of your own success."

"If it wasn't for me, you'd be in with those animals back in Hamilton. We do things my way and that means by the book. This isn't our jail," she said and opened a door, leading to several rooms. Randall threw his arms up to surrender and retrieved his cigarettes as he looked through the two-way mirror.

CHAPTER NINETEEN

Inside a tiny room, Braedon's eyes were swollen from a lack of sleep and dilated from the single bulb hanging above. He kept his shaking hands in his lap and looked around the cold, concrete enclosure with its typically sterile, police interrogation accoutrements; a minuscule camera in one corner of the ceiling, a desk with a pitcher of water and a glass, a pad and pen and an ashtray. There was another chair and a mirror nearly covering one wall. "Well, he looks pretty fucking scared so he's prime. Make them wait and their nerves always begin to unravel. You can't hold him though. Forty-eight hours at the most," Randall said and searched himself for a light. "Any mouthpiece will have him out of there in a minute and he knows it. That's why he waived his rights."

"But like you said, create a little tension and he might crack," she said. She withdrew a piece of paper from her purse and reluctantly handed it to him with a sober expression. "I ah... I got the lab results from your accident at Silverstone. Inconclusive. I also had them expedite the analysis of the note from the press conference. No prints. Nothing."

"Jesus Christ! Is the nutty fucking professor working for you guys?" he said in frustration, lighting the smoke and stifling a yawn. "Alright, it's time to play good cop, bad cop."

"Maybe you should go back to the hotel and get some rest. I can handle this," she said and fixed her hair into a ponytail.

"And miss out on the fun? No fucking way, split lips," he answered and checked his watch. 10 p.m.

"How are you going to drive when you're asleep?" she said and perused herself in a compact mirror.

"I have to be in on this. I'll be okay," he said and shook his head clear. "I want to see superstar fold like a fucking deck chair. I'll have that potato-head begging for his mother by the time I'm done."

"Take it easy Randall. I don't need any more headaches," she said and found her pills.

"Hey, if you ain't got the stomach for this shit, then maybe you should go polish your gun or something and leave it to me," he said. Gwen started to giggle and tried to stop, but soon found herself laughing. "What the fuck is so funny?" he asked.

"What you just said. It reminded me of my first interrogation. I was so scared I threw up on the suspect," she said and finally calmed down.

"Were they guilty?"

"First degree murder," she replied with a nod and buttoned her jacket.

"Then who cares?" he said and blew some smoke rings. "My first time they tried to charge me with police brutality. The fuck was hanging cats around the city, so I decided to use my belt and hang him to see how he liked it. That's how I got Spart. Was almost his last victim."

"What happened?"

"Put me behind a desk for a while," he said with a shrug.

"I meant him."

"Oh, he confessed. Found him strung up in his cell. Killed himself. Boo-hoo uh? That's what I call ironic justice. Best fucking outcome to a case I ever had," he said happily.

Gwen shuddered at the thought and felt a shiver run through her body. "Okay. Let's do this," she said, reaching for the knob. "Who knows, if we get lucky, you might not have to drive at all tomorrow," she said and swallowed her medication.

"Hit the jackpot, eh? Catch a killer and I still get to race," he said and cracked his knuckles.

Gwen smiled. "Your incredible disregard for your own safety never ceases to amaze me... or your ego. Come on."

"If he's guilty, it'll be hard to break him. The guy's used to incredible pressure," Randall said as she opened the door.

"We'll see," she said and took the seat opposite Braedon as Randall leaned against the wall. "Are you sure you want to waive your right to an attorney?" she asked the champion.

"I didn't do anything so I have nothing to worry about," Braedon replied confidently and proudly displayed his tattoo. "I had this done when I was nine years old. All the other kids cried and some even ran, but not me... I've been through this before."

"We just want to ask you a few questions," Randall said in a friendly manner.

"Why did you have Vincenzo killed?" Gwen said and picked up the pen.

"I didn't," Braedon answered with a smile and locked his fingers together.

"Who did you hire?" she quickly asked.

Braedon's fists tightened and his face flushed, but he managed to grin. "I didn't."

Gwen leaned across the table and pointed a finger, mere inches away from his panicked face. "You are a liar!"

"I didn't have anything to do with any of this. You're wasting your time," Braedon said and eased back in the chair.

"He might be telling the truth," Randall said to Gwen.

Gwen swiped the ashtray off the table, smashing it against the wall. "Oh bullshit!" she shouted. Randall raised his eyebrows, not used to hearing her curse. "This arrogant asshole is as guilty as hell!" she said, glaring at Braedon. "I want some answers and I want them now, or I swear you'll be in prison for the rest of your life!"

Chapter Nineteen

Braedon remained unaffected with his hands behind his head. "I'm innocent."

"Do you think your affair with Teresa has anything to do with why Vincenzo was murdered?" Randall said as he pushed aside the broken pieces of the ashtray with his cowboy boot.

Braedon shrugged. "I don't think so. I really can't say."

"That's not what Teresa says," Gwen said, even though she was blatantly lying to try and solicit a confession. "She says the two of you hired a hit man to kill Vincenzo so you could be together."

"That's not true, and I know what you're trying to do," Braedon said with a chuckle, casually rising to his feet and giving them a half-hearted salute. "I've had enough of this."

"Sit down!" Gwen shouted. "Or I leak everything to the press, including your affair with Teresa. Innocent or not, your career would be over," she added. Braedon slowly sank into the chair.

"If you weren't involved, why would Teresa lie?" Randall asked and flicked his ash on the floor.

Braedon reached for the pitcher of water, but Randall quickly poured a glass for him. The world champion drank loudly, his arid, constricted throat finally relieved. "I... I admit I had an affair with Teresa, but we didn't kill him... I'm not even sure Vincenzo knew what was going on... maybe she had him killed, but I didn't."

Gwen pushed the pad of paper and pen towards Braedon. "I'm going to make this simple for you, just write down who is involved and why."

Promptly stolid, Braedon stared at the paper for a few moments and brushed them away. "I can't write what I don't know."

She pushed the paper back in front of him and clicked the pen. "Do it!" she yelled.

Braedon's lip curled with rage as his eyes flickered. "Go to hell!"

Gwen broke into a smile and sighed heavily. "Listen to me and listen carefully. Cooperating will make things worth your while. Judges and juries have a tendency to be lenient when an accessory is helpful."

"She's right you know," Randall said as he dropped the cigarette on the floor and stepped on it.

"We know your wife took a shot at Teresa, and I'll bet Lisa's hip deep in all of this too," Gwen said and gestured with her head. "We have her in the other room."

"Lisa has nothing to do with any of this!" Braedon replied anxiously.

"Did Lisa shoot Teresa?" Gwen asked as Braedon looked away. "Answer me!" she shouted, but the champion simply stared into space. After a few moments, Gwen stood and started for the door. "Once we take her written statement, we'll be back and then that's your last chance to come clean so I would think about that very hard if I were you," she explained and strolled out the door with Randall.

Outside the room, Gwen and Randall studied Braedon, the champion well aware he was being watched. "What do you think?" Randall asked and withdrew another cigarette.

"He knows something... I can feel it," she replied with steely eyes. "You?"

Randall scratched his stubble and stretched. "I ain't sure. How fast can we get a lie detector test?"

"He'd never agree to that, especially without a lawyer. You want to be the bad guy this time around," she said, motioning to the closed door leading to Lisa.

"It's what I do best," he answered with a wink and opened the door.

Lisa sat there completely terrified, nervously wringing her hands. "What's going on?" she asked softly.

"Keep your fucking mouth shut until you're asked a question," Randall yelled and slammed the door, causing a rush of air across their faces. The abrasive beginning even caught Gwen off guard as she propped herself against the wall with crossed arms. Randall stood directly behind Lisa, resting one foot on the rung of her chair. Lisa's eyes shifted side to side, trying to locate his exact location. "We just had a chat with your husband. He said the two of you were in on Vincenzo's murder and hired the assassin."

"What?" she said incredulously, pivoting in her seat to face him.

"Turn around!" Randall shouted as Lisa began to sob, her quivering body slowly returning to its original position.

"Are you protecting Braedon? Because if you are, you'll go down with him," Gwen said and slid a box of Kleenex towards her. Mortified, Lisa just shook her head, denying Gwen's suggestion. "Lisa, we know you shot Teresa. Tell us the whole story and I promise you that I'll do everything I can for you," Gwen said with sincerity.

"What's going to happen to me?" Lisa asked with a trembling voice.

Randall leaned over her shoulder. "A lot of bad shit, and you can forget about seeing your kid again and kicking up your heels unless you come clean," he said in a menacing tone.

"I admit I shot her," Lisa said. Randall and Gwen glanced at each other, satisfied their intuition was correct. "But I swear to you I didn't have anything to do with Vincenzo."

"What about Braedon? Did he tell you anything?" Gwen inquired and sat beside her.

"No," Lisa whispered.

Chapter Nineteen

"Does Braedon know that you tried to kill Teresa?" Randall asked and purposely blew some smoke in her face.

"I didn't try to kill her... I just wanted to scare her," Lisa answered, dabbing her eyes.

"I said does Braedon know what you did?" Randall shouted and kicked her chair, startling Lisa.

"Yes!" Lisa replied and buried her head in her hands.

"How did you know he was having an affair with Teresa?" Gwen said and placed a gentle hand on her shoulder.

"I found a tape of them... I still love him... I know it's wrong after what he did to me... she was ruining my marriage," Lisa said, feeling the smooth diamonds of her wedding ring.

"I suppose you don't know anything about the millions of dollars deposited in a Cayman bank account under Braedon's name," Randall said and shoved the photocopy of the report in her face.

The announcement stupefied Lisa. "What? I... I don't know anything about that. Braedon's always handled the money... he just gives me a monthly allowance."

"I figured you'd say that," Randall replied with mock disgust. "Did you know Braedon had Vincenzo killed?"

"No! I... I didn't know Vincenzo was... I thought it was an accident... Braedon never said anything," she replied and began to cry harder.

Randall and Gwen glanced at one another again. "We'll be back," Randall whispered in her ear. "And think about this while we're gone, think about what they'll do to a woman like you in prison. All prim and proper. They'll fucking eat you alive. Better get used to the taste of dirty pussy," he said and hurried out the door, followed by Gwen.

"One of them is lying, or they both are," Gwen said as she massaged her forehead.

"I think she's innocent," Randall said, watching Lisa through the mirror as she continued sobbing.

"Actually, so do I."

"Now what?" he asked, resting his head against the door and closing his weary eyes with the cigarette dangling from his mouth.

"Let's try him one more time," she said, opening the door to Braedon's room. Randall and Gwen resumed their previous positions. "Okay Braedon," Gwen said tiredly. "What do you say?"

Braedon gave them a long, contemplative look, turned the pad around with a few lines scribbled on it and slid it across the table towards her. "I confess," he replied quietly, totally ashamed. The redaction caused Gwen and Randall to stare dumbly at one another, shocked at the sudden revelation.

Chapter Twenty

Ecstasy, coursing through the rivers of his body as Randall continued kissing Gwen while they fumbled to undress one another. He soon found himself exploring her magnificent body and tasting her sweetness, his tongue between her silky legs as she moaned, her body writhing. Gwen straddled him and shuddered upon climax, her eyes locked with his. Randall watched as she gyrated, throwing her head back making her black strands fell over her soft shoulders, her luscious breasts heaving with each thrust of her hips.

Randall opened his eyes and smiled, sitting in the cockpit of the racer, wearing Braedon's helmet and staring at its reflection in the left side mirror as reality grabbed hold. "Two thousand kilos of down force... could drive this fucker upside down... maybe I haven't earned the right to be here... and maybe I should feel guilty that so many guys more talented than me are never going to get their chance... maybe potato-head is right... maybe I am a fucking amateur," he lamented and shook his head clear. "But this ain't about racing... ain't about being an adrenaline junkie... it's about murder. Besides, I feel lucky... da... daikichi, great good luck," he said awkwardly. "Ain't nothing bad going to happen," he said and felt his wedding ring beneath his racing glove.

The firing of the engine jolted Randall from his introspection. A quick glance at his surroundings in the pit lane revealed that all heads were turned to him. He looked left, past the fence to the long grandstand where he sensed each pair of eyes were focused squarely upon him. Randall stared straight ahead but could see Gwen and Jessica off to the side, waiting anxiously just inside the garage area. "Thank Christ this is only practice," he said and carefully rolled away as Jessica waved earnestly at him.

The car surged, but didn't go full throttle as Randall's finger pressed the pit lane speed limiter. "Wrap your fucking head around this," he said to himself. "Forget all the what ifs and maybes. You're in the office and

Chapter Twenty

it's time to go to work," he said and caressed the wheel. "Okay baby... Itchy set you up with little down force... suits my style and he says it's the best setting for this place. I'm going to be tough on your brakes, but forgiving on your tyres... deal? Don't let me down."

Randall crossed the white line at the end of the pit lane and shifted up, heading for the tricky, second gear, forty mile per hour Senna Hairpin; a slow left, followed by a tight, winding right that led onto a short straight. "Feels good, but it's early... don't get too confident, even though the tyres are up to temperature... ain't used to tyre warmers, weren't allowed in the Atlantic's... and don't stand on the power too soon, might spin or worse," he said to himself as the racer rapidly approached the Senna turn. Randall slightly touched the brakes. "Brakes. Carbon discs that can heat to thirteen hundred degrees Fahrenheit... brakes that can stop me faster than it can accelerate," he said with wonderment.

Randall worked another flowing series of chicanes before rocketing down the long, one hundred eighty mile per hour straight. He could see the packed grandstands at the extremely tight, thirty-five mile per hour right-hander at L'Epingle. His foot pushed the brake pedal, but there was no friction. A slight sense of panic. Randall coolly downshifted to bleed off the speed. The throttle was stuck. "This can't be happening! Fucking helpless! Riding a goddamned bullet and I'm just a passenger!" he told himself in disbelief. He considered deliberately spinning the car to scrub off the intense velocity, but he was travelling one hundred yards per second. The racer might flip and it would surely result in a catastrophic crash. In an instant he wondered what Gwen and Jessica were thinking as they watched him pilot a broken missile.

The grandstands were ever closer and he thought he could actually see the eyes of a few, worried fans. The machine flew off the pavement and into the gravel trap, but he was still carrying far too much speed. "Going to die," he whispered calmly as he released the wheel, anticipating the tumultuous collision. "Fucking nightmare," he mumbled as the blurry outline of a man in a dark suit came into focus. Randall's smiling stepfather stood there at the railing with his arms outstretched, ready to embrace him in death.

"Jesus!" Randall screamed and sat bolt upright on the couch in the Team Jenkins trailer. Regaining his faculties, he felt his heart pounding beneath his soaked clothes as sweat dripped off his forehead. "Jesus," he whispered again and leaned back, holding his clammy face as Gwen scurried into the trailer upon hearing him shout.

"Are you okay?" she asked and sat beside him.

Randall finally caught his breath and sat forward, his trembling hands wiping away the perspiration. "Just a bad dream."

"What was it about?" she said and rubbed his back.

"Nothing... can't really remember... you get them?"

"Yes... I keep having the same one... there's a fire and I can't get to Jessica... I wake up crying every time," she said and closed her eyes tight, trying to forget.

"You look like you didn't sleep much either. I couldn't stop thinking about the case... and not fucking up too much," he said with a nervous smile.

"Maybe you should have stayed with Jessica and I in my hotel room last night," she said and pushed aside the remaining hair from his brow.

"I always wanted to be left alone the night before getting behind the wheel... besides, we made a deal, no Jessica... and no sleeping together just yet," he said sadly and dragged himself up. "How is she by the way?"

"Fine."

"Did... did she ask about me?" he inquired without looking at her, full of hope but apprehensive about the answer.

"No," she said regrettably.

Randall simply nodded, trying to demonstrate that her response didn't bother him, but it clearly did as he struggled for something to say. "The plan the same for today?"

"Yes! How many times do we have to go over this?" she said, promptly testy but soon relenting with an apologetic smile. "I'm sorry. My nerves are a little shot and my head is killing me," she said and withdrew her tablets. "I'm worried about you... I've never stopped since we separated... and I've lost a lot of sleep over you."

"Don't," he said and turned up the air-conditioning. "It doesn't suit you."

"What do you mean?" she said, slightly offended at his curt reply.

"Nothing... I guarantee everything will be fine today. Vincenzo's triggerman is probably a million miles away from here anyway," he replied and ran his fingers over the satin surface of the exact replica of Braedon's helmet he would wear as his face grew concerned. "But... if not... then by pretending to be Braedon, I might draw him out... which means Braedon really is innocent after all, but I doubt it... I guess I still need to be a target to know for sure."

"Are you willing to bet your life on that?" she said and reluctantly extended her hand to see if he would make the wager.

"Absolutely. That Irish fuck is guilty and his accomplice is lying on a beach in the middle of fucking nowhere right now, but sooner or later superstar will crack and spill his guts and then we nail his sharp shooting friend," he said and held up a hand to stop her from interjecting. "And yes, I know that doesn't explain the Rabbit. Look, Braedon's just trying to

Chapter Twenty

throw us off like he did by writing the note at the press conference," he replied with conviction and gladly shook her hand. "It's a bet. You're going to owe me one hell of a nice dinner after we get the prick to talk and get all the answers."

"What if he *is* innocent?" she asked fearfully. "His confession pointed out that he was receiving threatening letters to open the account."

"Letters that he didn't keep because he didn't want his wife to find them, yet he keeps a video of him and Teresa fucking," he scoffed.

"But what if he *is* innocent?"

"Well... if he isn't guilty... then we detained him for his own safety and... and the assassin is still out there," he said as she stared at him with anguished eyes. "And yes, I'm fucking scared shitless... have been every day of my life," he said shyly.

"But why would an assassin kill Vincenzo if Braedon didn't put the money into the assassin's account, an account with Braedon's name on it? Shouldn't the triggerman's name be on that account?" she asked and began to pace, anxious to hear Randall's explanation.

"Well... maybe Braedon didn't pay up and now he's the target... or maybe Braedon was going to pay him later... or from another bank we don't know about. Maybe Braedon opened the Cayman account to make it seem obvious in case he got caught so it *would* throw us off the trail. Someone had to sign for it and no assassin I've ever heard of would do it. Just a red herring," he said with a carefree wave. "And Braedon telling us that someone threatened to kill his family if he didn't agree to sign his name on the Cayman account seems too fucking neat to me," he said and peered out the window.

"That's a lot of maybes... although it is hard to believe he flew all the way to the Cayman Islands just to write his signature without knowing who was forcing him to. That's an odd thing for a man who grew up in Belfast and supports the IRA," she said, sitting on the armrest of the couch, lost in thought.

"Then again... threatening to kill your wife and kid can make a man do anything," Randall said, suddenly replete with doubt as he studied his faded photograph of Jessica.

"Then why didn't he tell Lisa about it?" she said and stopped pacing.

"Maybe he didn't want to worry her," he said and tucked the picture in the pocket of his denim jacket.

"He's not the type. If he's telling the truth, he should have gone to the police," she said and checked her revolver.

"He said he was told not to, and if you're terrified enough, you probably wouldn't," he said, watching her load a magazine with a snap.

"What about the press?" he asked, looking out the window again and noticing a television crew unloading equipment.

"I gave Ichiro a brief statement to give them about you. He told them that you badly sprained your hand and would miss the entire weekend, and that he's only going with Braedon as a driver," she said and hid her weapon under her trouser leg before examining the helmet. "The visor is impenetrable and the helmet itself is bullet-proof. You already have your vest," she said soberly.

"That protects me... what about the rest of the car?" he asked jokingly.

"I have my people posted all over the grounds. I have them dressed as track marshals, vendors, paramedics, fans, reporters, you name it, so if anybody makes a move, we'll see it," she said confidently.

"Your people don't exactly give me a lot of confidence," he said and lit a cigarette.

"They're trying! We're all trying!" she shouted. "We're not all as perfect as you!"

Randall decided to ignore her outburst, knowing her emotions were running high. "What does Itchy have to say about all this?" he said and greedily drank from a water bottle.

"He was as jittery as he was at dinner, especially after I told him we were holding Braedon. There's something he's not telling us, but he's not giving it up," she said and finally downed her medication with a drink of his water.

"How is the world champion holding up?" he asked, but not really interested.

"He passed a lie detector test, but he's starting to talk about getting a lawyer so he must be worried... guilty or innocent," she replied and winced at the bitter taste of the pills. "Maybe we're concentrating on Braedon too much and somebody truly is trying to frame him. I'm still not sure about Suarez and Carmen. Friedrich and Ichiro too for that matter. I've even wondered if Lisa hired the hit on Vincenzo to get back at Teresa," she said, her head clouded with the possibilities.

"Why? Teresa probably didn't love Vincenzo and wouldn't care anyway. The bitch is a gold digger," he said as she checked her watch.

"We have to get moving. Wrap your wrist," she said and handed him an elastic cloth for sprains. "You better change into your uniform in the garage. The crew doesn't even know it's you and all radio contact will be done through Ichiro and I. Only Samuel was allowed to talk to Braedon on the radio so nobody will suspect. All set?" she asked, adjusting her tight jeans before putting on her sunglasses and stuffing Braedon's helmet into a gym bag.

CHAPTER TWENTY

Randall hesitated and gave her a sideways glance. "We don't have shit, do we? All we got is a German rifle with no prints and Braedon's name on a bank account... fucking inconclusive as usual. Think we could get a conviction that?" he asked worriedly.

"Not likely. If we make too many waves then the whole world finds out what's going on and Braedon clams up if he knows anything. His lawyer would make sure of that. They'd win the battle in the court of public opinion too and then Vincenzo's murder never gets solved," she replied with a frustrated sigh.

"Fucking eggshells," he said and crushed out his cigarette with a long face.

"What's wrong?"

"Ever since I was little... I always dreamed about being one of the best driver's in the world... everyone would know my name... I finally have a chance to prove it, but nobody out there will know it's me," he said sheepishly.

"What matters more, your ego or justice?" she asked as she opened the trailer door.

"A little bit of both," he replied and took a deep breath. "Alright, let's do it," he said, admiring her shapely behind and supple breasts beneath a Team Jenkins T-shirt as he went to follow her out, but she suddenly stopped.

"Your nightmare... what was it about?" she asked quietly without facing him.

"I told you, nothing."

"You were going to die... in the car... weren't you?" she said, lowering her head.

"It was just a dream Gwen," he said and placed a comforting hand on her shoulder.

"I know... but sometimes dreams can come true," she said as her frightened voice trailed off and she opened the door where they were instantly met by Candice Goldenstein.

"Well, well, well, if it isn't Ken and Barbie," Candice said sarcastically and readied her pen and pad. "You promised me a story Grange."

"After that shit you pulled at the press conference, forget it," Randall said and hurried Gwen along.

Candice waved a press release in the air. "Sprained, left wrist, uh?" she asked doubtfully as a sudden wind picked up.

"Too much of this," Randall said and pretended to masturbate.

"How did it happen?" Candice questioned and scribbled some notes.

"He fell," Gwen said brusquely.

"Doing what?" Candice asked and followed.

Randall turned to face her and leaned closer. "If you must know, we were fucking in the shower and I slipped."

"Can I print that?" Candice said gleefully as she wiped aside her windblown hair.

"I don't give a shit. Hell, if I had photos I'd give them to you," Randall said and meandered away with Gwen's hand in his.

"My mother used to tell me the more outrageous the lie, the more it will be believed... that doesn't cut it with me," Candice said and eyed the gym bag in Gwen's hand. "Packing up and leaving town?"

"We'll stick around and see if Randall's hand gets any better," Gwen said as she strolled into the garage area.

"Might be tough sledding out there today," Candice said and looked skyward. "That wind will be blowing pretty good down the straights."

"Lucky I don't have to deal with it then," Randall said and slipped inside the door.

Brimming with suspicion, Candice grinned at him. "The wind was always the hardest thing about shooting in the military... but I was still the best."

His interest and memory piqued, Randall glanced at her over his shoulder. "That's right, you had to serve in the Israeli army. How come you were such a good shot?"

"My uncle was in the Special Forces and told me stories about how great a marksman he was," she said proudly and deliberately adjusted her healthy cleavage. "Especially when he went rabbit hunting."

"What's he doing now?" he asked, trying to sound disinterested, but his heart skipped a beat upon hearing the revelation.

"I don't know. We haven't heard from him in a long time. He could be dead for all I know. He just kind of faded away," she said and tried to look past him into the garage. "Where is Braedon? I'd like to get a few minutes with him," she said and stood on her toes, struggling to see, but Randall blocked her path.

"Press ain't allowed in here. Lots of technical secrets and Braedon wants to be left alone," he said and went to close the door, but Candice jammed her foot in the way.

"You still owe me that story," she said with a sly smile.

"You'll get it... but it's a yawn," he said and disappeared inside.

"Murder's never boring," she whispered happily to herself and wandered off.

Inside the garage area, Randall immediately grabbed Gwen and whisked her away from the busy crew. "Why did they call Rabowitz the rabbit?"

Gwen shrugged. "I've heard a few theories. His name sounds like a rabbit. One is he liked to eat them, but more than likely it was because he made fast work of his target. Why?"

"Big tits just told me her uncle was in the Israeli special forces and liked to hunt Bugs Bunny."

Gwen was astounded by the bulletin and thought for a few seconds. "Maybe you should make a move on her. You know, win her confidence over a few drinks and see what she says."

"*Now* you want me to fuck her?"

"I didn't say that! Flirt with her until you get some information," Gwen said as the sound of an approaching scooter was heard. "Or you could just threaten her like you do with all your other suspects."

"Me?" he asked sardonically. "I'm against violence," he said as they turned to find Alberto Americo, wearing his racing togs and staring at them as he stopped the scooter. Instantly, a flock of reporters surrounded him, but Alberto stepped off the bike, pushed them aside and ogled Gwen from head to toe.

"Randall Grange. Nice to meet you," Randall said and offered his hand.

Alberto snubbed him and ran his fingers through his perfect hair without taking his eyes off Gwen. "Have we met?" he asked in a sensual tone.

Gwen laughed and wrapped her arm around Randall's waist. "That's original. I'm his wife."

Alberto took her hand and kissed it while leering at her. "Pity. I guess some people will settle for anything," he said and glanced at Randall with contempt. "I've seen you race. I used to drive like that when I started racing... when I was ten. You don't belong here," he said and returned his ravenous stare to Gwen. "When you want a real man, both on and off the track, let me know," he added and strolled back to the scooter.

"Don't," she whispered to Randall, but it was too late.

Randall grabbed Alberto by the arm and punched him squarely in the mouth with his right hand, sending him and the motorized bike crashing to the ground. Randall waved a naughty finger at him; the Spaniard feeling his sore jaw as the reporters quickly snapped pictures. "You should always wear your helmet," he said.

"What was that about violence?" Gwen whispered to Randall.

"So this is my new driver?" Felipe said, appearing from within the crowd and helping Alberto to his feet. "It seems you act like you drive Mr. Grange and that kind of attitude can get a man hurt."

"Somebody ought to teach that boy some manners," Randall said and realized the disapproving press were anxiously awaiting his next move.

Randall slowly offered his hand to Alberto again. "Listen man... I'm sorry. Square?" he said, but Alberto quickly pivoted and stormed off.

Embarrassed, Randall stood there for a second before walking briskly into the garage as Felipe followed him. "It's just as well your wrist is sprained. Canadian trash will never sit behind the wheel of one of my cars," Felipe grumbled and motioned to the crew. "Get out and close the door," he commanded as the reporters clamoured to take some final photographs.

"Your cars? Got news for you, wetback, it ain't your team and Ichiro chooses the ride," Randall countered after the mechanics departed.

Felipe grinned and stroked his Vandyke. "Wetbacks are Mexican which proves your ignorance. That really amazes me since your former wife is a DST agent. I'm surprised you didn't educate this rube," he said to Gwen as she debated whether to confirm Felipe's assertion of her true identity. "As the primary sponsor of this team, it is my responsibility and my right to know who will be driving. So," Felipe said, sitting on a workbench and crossing his arms. "What is an agent of France doing here with a common police officer?"

"I have no idea what you're talking about. Randall and I *are* in law enforcement but we're here to further his driving career and that's all," Gwen said, remarkably believable as Ichiro emerged through another door.

Felipe began to laugh and clapped his hands. "Wonderful performance. I love the theatre... especially tragedy. If that is what you want me to believe, then so be it. All I care about is right there," he said and pointed to the two racers. "Ichiro, let him drive when his wrist is better. The proof is in the pudding as they say," he said and ordered Ichiro to follow him with his finger.

Outside the garage door, Felipe's face falsely lit up as the press converged again beyond the roped off area. "Remember what I told you. Grange and Stirling are going to have an accident or your mother does," Felipe whispered with a broad smile to greet the fourth estate's photographers.

"I will not do it," Ichiro whispered with a defiant shake of his head.

"I figured you would say something stupid like that. I guess their lives are worth more than your old lady's," Felipe said with a smile and withdrew a piece of paper. "Ending notes are so sad. I hear they're quite a new custom in Japanese society. It's such a shame parents must write down their true feelings for their children instead of telling them how they feel when they were alive. Your mother has beautiful handwriting," he said casually as Ichiro stood firm. "I once saw a man lose his fingers at one of our tobacco farms," he said and reached into his jacket pocket and withdrew his Spanish-coloured handkerchief. He unwrapped it to disclose a human thumb. "It will be hard for your mother to play the piano now. That is her favourite instrument, correct?" he asked, much to Ichiro's horror.

"You... you are lying," Ichiro said and tried to feign a smile for the press and felt hot sweat rolling down his jaw.

"When your mother wrote the letter, she did it in her living room. It has nice straw-matted floors. The paper was from a purple notebook. My my, she cried a lot as she was writing it. She kept talking about how she never said she loved you, just that she liked you. Strange how your people cannot say the words that matter most," Felipe said as the familiar details anguished Ichiro's face.

"Lies! Nothing but lies!" Ichiro whispered through gritted teeth.

Felipe opened the missive. "She says your father was greedy. She says she loves you dearly and wants to be with you forever and see you have grandchildren. To see your kindness, a kindness handed down to you by her father," Felipe said as Ichiro's eyes began to water. "'I want you to understand that when I spent my time drawing, listening to music or going to the mountains, it is to confirm my bond with you. To reflect on my life and understand what it means to be me'," Felipe quoted. He folded the letter before handing it to Ichiro. "Keep it. It's all you will have to remember her by."

"Please... do not hurt her anymore... I will do whatever you say," Ichiro whispered and hung his head as Felipe slapped him on the back.

"Don't look so sad, soon all your problems will be mine and you'll be working for me. Remember, I don't want the hassle of Braedon's contract so make sure he never gets the chance to come back. Most of all, if Grange drives this weekend, I want him to suffer. After the race, you and I will sit down over a nice glass of Saki and sign the contract selling me the team," Felipe said and breathed deep with satisfaction. "Just think, Ichiro, in two weeks Alberto Americo and I will be the new drivers. Exciting, isn't it?" he said and waded into the throng of reporters.

Stunned, Ichiro stood there for a few seconds before staggering into the garage and slamming the door. "Go home Randall! I do not want you to drive!" Ichiro remarked angrily.

Randall and Gwen looked at each other in bewilderment. "If there's something you need to tell us, now would be the time," Gwen said and put her arm around Ichiro, but he hurried away from her and tried to busy himself with one of the monitors. "What's wrong Ichiro?" she asked.

Ichiro spun around to face Randall. "I am upset with you Randall, that's all! What do you think you are doing? You do not strike another driver in full view!"

"Just defending the honour of my wife," Randall replied, still shaking the pain away from his fist.

"There is enough attention upon us without you adding to it!" Ichiro snapped and scurried into a private changing room, but they followed.

Randall paused to cool his temper. "Look, everything will be okay. I won't make a fool out of you or Braedon. I know what's at stake."

"Do you?" Ichiro barked and pointed to the tobacco livery on Braedon's uniform hanging on a rack. "Do you know what that costs Hispania Gold? Mr. Suarez pays fifteen million a season! Behaving like some petulant bully in the school yard will not help my sponsors, nor the image of my team!"

Randall debated whether to counter but decided against it. "Sorry."

Ichiro's eyes wandered into space and his body slumped onto a stool. "My mother... I... I remember she used to make paper animals for me when I got sick... she was always there for me," he said and realized they were staring at him. "She... she is very ill... that is all... I am just worried about her... I apologize for yelling," Ichiro said, promptly calm and coerced a half-smile as the memories soothed his frayed nerves. "But Randall, I really do think you should go home... I... I do not want you here."

"You don't have a choice," Randall said and unwrapped the uniform.

"Please leave!" Ichiro said and tried to stop him from undressing.

"What's the real reason you don't want him to race?" Gwen asked and held Ichiro back.

"I... I do not want him to get hurt! It is very dangerous!" Ichiro replied and marched out of the room.

"Get changed," Gwen said to Randall and chased after Ichiro. "Ichiro, there's something you're not telling me. Please, just let me know what it is and I promise you everything will be fine."

Ichiro fought with his conscience as he dug his hands into his pockets and felt the note Felipe had given him. "Nothing... nothing is wrong. I cannot be held responsible for Randall's well-being," he said and consulted his watch. "The track is green in ten minutes," he said with a bow and went to walk away, but stopped. "What is going to happen to Braedon?"

"You know I can't talk to you about that right now, but I'd say his driving days are over. You don't say anything to anyone. Understand?" she said and rubbed her pounding forehead.

"Is there any chance he will drive this weekend?" Ichiro asked with his back to her.

"No. Why?" she replied as Ichiro merely bowed again and returned to his monitors.

"Itchy's pretty uptight... just like me, I guess," Randall said as Gwen entered the changing room again.

"I've got a bad feeling about today... Ichiro knows something's going to happen," she said and gazed into Randall's eyes. Her hands slowly caressed his face and she gently kissed his mouth. "Listen to me, be careful, okay? Maybe you should say a prayer or something," she said anxiously.

"Prick never listened anyway," he said and eyed the ceiling. "No problems," he said confidently and slipped into the racing overalls. "Piece of cake. I know you got my ass covered."

"Are... are you sure you want to go through with this?" she said nervously.

"Split lips, we've been over this shit a hundred times," he said, zipping up the suit and pulling on his shoes, balaclava and finally Braedon's helmet. He playfully opened and closed the visor. "It's alright? Alright," he said jokingly.

"Don't," she pleaded and embraced him. Randall felt her breathing become laboured and heard her sniffle.

"Hey, hey, hey. It's okay," he said and stroked her velvet hair. "I'm too fucking mean to die," he said and forced her to look up at him. "Don't go soft on me now. It'll be okay. I promise."

Gwen managed a simple nod and straightened herself. "Okay... you're right," she said and kissed him again. "Remember, you have two women that want to get to know you again... you'd better be back," she said with a warning finger and disappeared around the corner. Randall took a moment to gather his thoughts and held out his hands. Trembling badly. He sheepishly looked skyward. "Ain't done this in a while... hope you're watching for once," he said and blessed himself before closing the visor. He entered the garage again, stepped over the chassis and slid into the cramped cockpit as Ichiro quickly appeared and knelt down.

"I am going to be your fuel man today," Ichiro said as he began bucking Randall in.

"Why?" Randall replied, instantly suspicious.

"I want you to practice a few pit stops during this practice session. Later we will concentrate on the car set-up for tomorrow's qualifying. I would think your standing starts are fairly good thanks to your days in the Atlantic series," Ichiro said and continued attaching the belts. "I need you out there as much as possible."

"Ichiro, where's the regular fuel man?" Randall asked and caught his breath as the restraints were tightened.

"He is down with the flu. The car is trimmed out the way you like but remember, the series banned traction control this year so when this car starts to go loose, it is all up to you. Just go out, get in a few laps and come in for a pit stop because you have never done one of those in one of these cars. After that we will make any adjustments you want. Understand?" Ichiro said and rushed away despite Randall holding up a finger to stop him. Ichiro opened the garage door, the mechanics flooded in and the engine was cranked, creating a loud, reverberating drone. "Watch out for Alberto. After striking him, Team Jenkins is a prime target," Ichiro said quietly into his radio headset as the mechanics removed the tyre warmers.

Soon, engines were fired all along the garage area as the filled grandstands erupted into a massive cheer. Randall waited as a few of the mechanics waved the press out of the way before he carefully exited the garage onto the pit lane. There was another, instantaneous uproar of cheers from the fans as some waved their Irish and British flags upon seeing Braedon's racer. Randall checked his mirrors to discover Alberto falling in line directly behind him. "Oh shit," he whispered to himself.

Randall crossed the white line demarcating the racing surface from the pit lane and up-shifted. Alberto followed, the nose of the Spaniard tucked under Randall's gearbox. Randall suddenly downshifted and swung left as Alberto passed him, heading for turn one. Once Alberto was in front, Randall throttled upward and tailed him.

Alberto veered left for the turn as Randall nudged his backend, causing the Spaniard's head to lunge forward and tap the steering wheel. "Just a little brake test... asshole," Randall whispered to himself and rocketed out of sight.

"Do not poke an already angry tiger!" Ichiro's voice crackled over the radio. "When you come in for the practice pit stop, we will check the nose."

"Going to pile on the coals chief!" Randall responded, exhilarated by speed.

"Easy! Do not cook the tyres. We are going to need that set. Remember, you're supposed to be Braedon and he would never do that," Ichiro said.

Randall slid through a fast chicane and flashed down the straight, his hands fighting the car all the way. "I could use a little more rear wing. Lots of dust. Slippery."

"Once there is some rubber down, it will come alive," Ichiro said.

"I think I could use a set of scrubs," Randall said as the car shimmied.

"Fine, fine. We will take care of that after a pit stop. I want you to come in at the end of the next lap," Ichiro said.

Gwen jumped two stairs at a time and finally made it to the top of the garage building. She scrutinized the right side of the grandstands opposite

Chapter Twenty

the pit lane with a pair of binoculars and gingerly moved further to the right to a grassy area on the other side of the track where a few track marshals with headsets stood at the fence. Her heart skipped a beat upon seeing a red-bearded man, wearing sunglasses and a baseball cap, carrying a silver briefcase, approaching about twenty yards behind. The individual suddenly stopped, knelt down beside a tree and opened the case. "Unit seven, Evans here! Check out possible suspect in your grid. No visible ID. Close to the fence, opposite pit entrance. Red beard. Baseball hat. Silver case!" she said and changed the frequency on the radio, clipped to her jeans. "Randall, stay out of the pit lane! I repeat, stay out of the pit lane! Copy!" she said anxiously as the intruder retrieved items from the case, but the shadowy, long grass prevented her from distinguishing what the person was building. Frequently, the man would look up, check in all directions and hastily resume his task.

"Damnit!" Gwen said as her fingers fumbled to change the frequency again. "Ichiro! Keep Randall out of the pits!" she yelled into her headset mike. Gwen waited for a moment but heard no reply. "Ichiro, answer me!" she bellowed. Nothing. The racket of cars screaming out of pit lane forced her to cup her ear to try and hear if any response was forthcoming as she lunged for the stairs.

Randall entered the final, long straight, ending with a severe right and left chicane that headed towards the start/finish line or a left lane into the pits. "In this time for a pit stop," Ichiro said calmly through the radio.

"Got it," Randall replied as his head buffeted with the wind.

"Remember the pit lane speed limit," Ichiro added.

Swiftly descending the stairs, Gwen searched for the bearded man, but suddenly couldn't find him. She was more alarmed that the two track officials were no longer at their post as she continued to scramble down the aluminium steps. Gwen finally reached the bottom and ran as fast as she could towards the direction Randall was coming from.

The bearded man held a long instrument at his side as he leisurely moved closer to the fence. The suspect leaned against the wire barrier and positioned himself so he could see the approaching racers from his left and raised a long, narrow, black tubular device.

Gwen frantically ran towards Randall, waving her arms, hoping he would see her just as the bearded man was suddenly tackled to the ground by two agents. She breathed a heavy sigh of relief and dropped to one knee as her trembling fingers reached for the radio, toggle switch. "All clear... thanks guys," she said breathlessly, sensing someone was watching her and slowly looked to her right. Gwen frowned, thinking she saw Teresa near a fence, but the woman quickly melted into the myriad of fans.

Randall's car sputtered, maintaining the speed limit as he neared his pit spot. Perfect. The nose of the car barely touched the lollipop man as the machine was quickly raised off the ground. Four tyres were expertly removed and new ones attached while Ichiro rammed in the fuel nozzle. Randall kept his foot on the throttle to keep the car from stalling as the engine screamed. The jacks were removed and the car slammed against the pavement, literally sucking the air out of Randall's lungs. Ichiro yanked the hose away, but some of the fuel spilled, splashing the chassis and cockpit. A static spark instantly ignited the racer into an impenetrable wall of flames.

The spectators reacted with a collective gasp and immediately stood. Gwen snapped her head around upon hearing the commotion and instinctively knew something was terribly wrong and she started running for the pit lane.

Hell on earth. Surreal. Randall could feel the incredible heat and saw his gloves ablaze as they inherently fought to unbuckle. The drink tube bubbled and dissolved away in a flash. Through the raging firestorm, he could see an extinguisher attached to the leg of a ghostly crewmember, fervently trying to rip the canister from its holster.

Bedlam. Ichiro was pushed to the ground as members of the crew doused him with foam. Other crews joined in the effort, but the machine was unapproachable as the heat rippled the paint and began to melt the sponsorship decals. Despite their fire suits, nobody could get close to the inferno as Gwen watched in horror. "Get him out! Get him out!" she screamed, tears welling in her eyes.

Randall could smell the styptic smoke and the intoxicating odour of burning fuel, carbon fibre and plastic. The view through his visor was strange; images distorted and stretched in an ocean of flames as the balaclava was beginning to sear into his face, but no screams emitted from his parched lips. Eyes half closed, he thought he saw the silhouette of Gwen and remembered Jessica's photograph in his pocket. One last burst of adrenaline and Randall's hands ripped away the belts. He hauled himself out of the fire-ravaged seat as the flames licked his uniform and he stumbled over the chassis, emerging from the firestorm to the applause of the fans. Crewmembers quickly extinguished him and both he and Ichiro were assisted into the garage, quickly followed by Gwen as the press converged. Trying to maintain the facade that Randall was Braedon, she leaned towards Ichiro. "Get everybody out!" she whispered. Ichiro waved the mechanics away and closed the doors. Randall waited until they were gone before removing his helmet and peeling off the balaclava, revealing bits of the material scorched into his flesh. He instantly splashed cold

Chapter Twenty

water from the sink over his blistering face. "Are you okay?" Gwen asked worriedly, but Randall ignored her and slammed Ichiro against the wall.

"You fucking son-of-a-bitch! You cut that fuel line!" Randall shouted and rammed Ichiro again.

"Randall! Stop it!" Gwen said and tried to pull him off.

"I did not do it!" Ichiro said as Randall finally released him.

"Telling me the regular fuel man is down with the flu was fucking bullshit!" Randall barked and studied his burned hands. "Jesus Christ! Look at this! I look like a fucking well-done steak!"

"It might have been a faulty line... or maybe someone did cut it, but I did not!" Ichiro said adamantly, clearly shaken by the trauma and sitting on a stool, fighting to catch his breath.

"Everybody calm down!" Gwen said as her radio beeped. "Yes!" She answered impatiently. "What? I'll be right there," she said excitedly and hurriedly turned the device off. "Get changed Randall. Ichiro, tell the press Braedon has second and third degree burns. Tell them that he has already left the building and that he won't be racing this weekend."

"What the hell is going on?" Randall said and lit a cigarette with tender hands as Gwen escorted him into the change room.

"Maybe, just maybe, I think we've got our assassin," she said with a hopeful smile.

Chapter Twenty-One

A rented, brown sedan turned off the highway onto a narrow, gravel road as dust kicked up behind the vehicle despite a gentle, spotty rain. The canopy of foliage caused the sun to flicker through the windshield as the car travelled deeper into the woods until the sound of civilization vanished, replaced by the chirping of birds and the frequent snapping of twigs beneath the tyres.

The car stopped and Gwen stepped out from behind the wheel as Randall climbed out of the passenger side and opened the back door. He aided Jack out of the seat, his hands handcuffed behind his back. Uneasy, Randall looked to Gwen who motioned him to escort Jack to a nearby tree. Gwen sat on the hood of the car, the warmth of the hood pleasing to her bottom in the cool, forest air. "What are you going to do, kill me?" Jack said with a carefree smile just as there was a flash of lightning, followed by distant thunder.

"I just wanted to chat with you in private," Gwen said and swallowed some pills. "My father always said be direct, so here it is, who hired you?"

"Sorry love, I can't tell you that. It would breach client confidentiality," Jack said gamesomely with officialese and studied Randall's face. "You've been in the sun too long mate," Jack said and watched as Randall lit a cigarette. "Can I have one of those? Now all I need is a blindfold," he said sarcastically as Randall placed the smoke in Jack's mouth and lit another for himself.

"Why would an assassin wear a fake beard, have false press corps identification and carry a telephoto lens which is actually a high powered rifle to the Canadian Grand Prix?" she asked rhetorically.

"I didn't know a DST agent would be there with her goons," he promptly answered sardonically and squinted as the smoke wafted over his eyes, his nimble hands secretly working to loosen the handcuffs.

CHAPTER TWENTY-ONE

"You can do better than that Jack. I did a little checking on you... Mr. Fletcher. You've been an assassin since you left the Australian Special Forces," she said and unbuttoned her coat. "Why did you kill Vincenzo Azzopardi and Benny Rabowitz?"

"I didn't," Jack answered with a shake of his head. "I've heard about Rabowitz but never knew he actually existed. He's dead?"

"Who was your target today?" Gwen asked as Jack managed to free one hand.

"Can't tell you," Jack said with another grin.

In a flash, Gwen withdrew her gun from beneath her coat and fired, blowing out Jack's right knee. Randall jumped, startled at the sound as a rain of birds launched from the trees. Jack collapsed, writhing on the ground in agony. "Who was your target today?" she asked calmly.

"You fucking bitch!" Jack screamed, bits of bone and flesh splattered across his trousers. "Fuck you!"

Randall edged towards her. "What the hell are you doing?" he whispered.

"I've had to do this kind of thing many times, but I don't like it," she said quietly, slightly offended as Jack brought his free hand into view to stem the flow of blood from his wound. "See Randall? You never know with these types, but don't worry, I have the authority and if it makes you feel any better, we'll say he lunged at us," she said and kissed Randall before sliding off the hood. Gwen strolled over to Jack and stepped on his injured knee, causing him to emit another hair-raising scream. "Who was your target today Jack? Did you send the note at the press conference? Are you threatening Braedon's family?"

"Fuck off!" Jack said, spit spraying from his trembling mouth.

Gwen took a moment, nodded to herself and chuckled. "Once again Randall, in my world, I have to deal with these people all the time and they're a lot tougher to crack than some street thug," she said and promptly turned back to Jack and shot out his other knee as Randall cringed in horror and looked away. "Listen to me, Jack," she said softly and bent down to speak to him. "You see this man here with me? I love him and when somebody messes with that, I get very, very angry. You're going to spend the rest of your life in prison anyway so why don't I make things easier for you and kill you now because apparently, you're not going to help us," she said and jammed the revolver against his temple.

"Teresa! Teresa Legaro! She gave me four million... I'd get another four million when the job was done... she wanted Braedon killed on the track," he said sobbing. "Please... please don't kill me."

"Very good, Jack. Where is she now?" she said and brushed aside his red hair with the tip of the barrel.

"I... I don't know," Jack cried. Gwen fired at his left foot, disintegrating his shoe as several toes flew off. "Goddamnit! I don't know!" he yelled.

"Why did you kill Benny and Vincenzo?" she asked as Jack squirmed in a pool of blood.

"I... I didn't... you have to believe me," Jack whimpered as she fired again, blasting away his right foot. "God... I didn't kill them... I didn't," he moaned, his eyes suddenly rolled back and he slipped into unconsciousness.

Gwen took a moment to reflect. "I believe him," she said to Randall. "You?"

"Holy fuck!" Randall said and drew harder on his tobacco with a shaking hand. "Shouldn't... shouldn't we call an ambulance or something?"

Gwen pivoted and fired directly at Jack's heart. His body heaved and relaxed with a death rattle. "One less piece of human trash to worry about," she said, dialling her cell phone and waiting. "It's me, Gaudet. Tell Interpol to put out an A.P.B. on Teresa Legaro. Start at the airport and have some people waiting in Milan in case she gets by us. I'll call you in a while," she said and hung up.

"Jesus... why the fuck did you kill him?" Randall said and stumbled to support himself against the car.

"Mr. Fletcher knew he was going to die. It's part of the risk of what he does... or did, I should say. This isn't the streets of Hamilton, Randall. We play for keeps in the intelligence community... and I'm sorry you had to see it," she said and gave him a comforting pat on the shoulder.

"I never killed a man that didn't deserve it," he said as his eyes drifted off.

"Are you saying he didn't? Would you like to take a look at his rap sheet?" she said, producing a piece of paper and reading from it. "Jack Fletcher killed over thirty people. One time he mowed down three kids and their parents in a restaurant because the father was the mark. Every police organization in the world has a warrant out for his arrest."

"You can't be judge and jury," he said and spied a flock of birds returning to perch on a high branch.

"Are you listening to yourself? Since when did you become so pious? The difference is, I have the moral and legal authority and you didn't when it came to Lunder!" she said, patently insulted.

"You're right... but I expected more from you, I guess," he said and flicked the cigarette away.

Chapter Twenty-One

"You expect too much," she said unemotionally and stepped on the tobacco. "What are you trying to do, start a fire? Don't you care about anything?"

Randall shook his head clear of the paradox. "What about Braedon?"

"We'll hold him until we know for sure what's going on. As for Lisa, she's suffered enough with him. I'll see to it she's released."

"What about all the others?" he asked, withdrawing another cigarette.

"It's not my problem anymore," she said and retrieved her car keys.

"What? We still don't have Benny or Vincenzo's killer," he said with a frown.

"I'm going to have the DST put the ten million the note asked for in the Cayman account, and they can wait and see what happens. If it's withdrawn, Braedon is innocent, and if he's an accomplice, he'll talk pretty quick. He isn't going to take the rap alone," she said sombrely. "I've had enough of this."

"Why not trace all the other accounts with the twenty million Samuel paid?" he asked, struggling to pry his eyes from Jack's lifeless body.

"It will take too long to hack into their computers. The DST can get away with breaking into one account, but not a dozen," she said as her face softened. "The truth is... I don't want you to have another accident like today... it scared the hell out of me... because... because I do love you," she said and passionately kissed him again as their eyes locked. Randall's hands soon removed her jacket and popped the buttons on her blouse. He buried his face in her breasts until Gwen pushed him to the leaf-carpeted floor and started to undress him. "I've been dreaming about this for so long... I know it's wrong, but I always imagined you instead of... of him," she whispered and wrapped her warm, wet lips around his manhood. Randall's fingers ran through her hair as she worked him faster and faster, the rain falling harder, leaving cold, blotchy marks on his burning skin. He pulled her off and turned her on her back as he mauled away her jeans and panties. Randall quickly entered her, Gwen's head rolling in ecstasy as her legs clamped around his waist. "I love you," she whispered with each thrust of his hips. He felt his thighs numbing with the oncoming climax but he suddenly dismounted. "What's wrong?" she asked completely bewildered.

"Um... qualifying tomorrow, remember? I ah... I need my legs. Should never have sex before getting behind the wheel," he said nervously and rapidly began to dress.

"Didn't you hear what I said? I'm having the money put into the account. You don't have to race! You don't have to do anything but be with me!" she said with an astonished laugh and playfully tried to pull him back down, but he resisted, a solemn look upon his face.

"It sounds stupid... but I used to have this wallpaper in my room with racing cars on it... was one of the few nice things he did for me... I used to stare at them when he was... I used to dream about being them... being the champion," he whispered with a distant stare. "Let me finish this thing Gwen... I want to race... it's my last chance to actually live the dream... and who knows, the killer might try again," he said and threw on his jacket.

"The killer won't try again because they're getting the money!" she said angrily, but she soon became saddened. "It's... it's me, isn't it? You don't want me."

"Christ, are you kidding? I've always wanted you... but this isn't the right time," he said, gesturing to Jack. "We have to finish this case."

"What if you get hurt or killed whether the assassin shows up or not?" she said with pleading eyes.

"For fuck sakes, I know what's involved and the risks! My life is my responsibility and only mine," he stated, pointing at himself, but quickly checked his temper. "If anything, you helped saved me from myself and now I can pay you back by helping you out."

"We haven't achieved anything! You know as well as I do that the case was cold after forty-eight hours!" she said curtly and started to dress. "And that's why I'm telling them to deposit the money!"

"I have a hunch, okay?"

"Instincts don't get convictions, only facts do," she countered and zipped up her jeans.

"We just have to be in the right place at the right time."

"And you're the bait," she said with an incredulous shake of her head.

"Can't fish without it," he said with a simper. "So, are you with me?"

Gwen avoided his stare and gazed at the sheeting rain, its sound amplified against the leaves. After almost a minute she slowly looked to him. "No... I'm taking Jessica home tomorrow... with or without you."

"You can't do that... what... what about the investigation?" he said, completely astounded.

"I've decided to call my superiors and have them assign somebody else. I'll give them the file... circumstantial as it is," she said and finished dressing before opening the trunk and removing a shovel.

"You were going to kill him all along, weren't you?" he said in disbelief as a shiver rippled through his body.

"I did what I was told to do. Like any assassin, Jack had too many secrets that could embarrass a lot of people, including governments, governments that are trying to do a lot of good in this world," she said and began digging. "Go and race Randall. Everyone thinks Braedon has burns

Chapter Twenty-One

anyway... be yourself or be him... it doesn't matter. It's up to Ichiro. I'll wait for you in France."

"My mother... she made me throw dirt on his casket as a show of respect... I never forgave her for that," he whispered to himself as he closed his eyes.

"What?" she said, thinking she heard him say something.

Randall regained control of his emotions. "I need you with me... you know I don't work and play well with others," he said, trying to lighten the mood.

"I can't be a part of this... seeing you get hurt... or worse... I can't handle it anymore," she said and began lifting the mounds of wet earth.

"And I can't believe you'd come this far in your career and then piss it all away because you've suddenly turned into... into a real split lips... a goddamned pussy!" he said, fully exasperated, but she kept digging. "What about Peter? He'll fight for what he wants, and he *wants* you."

"I don't love him," she replied, apace with the spade.

"You said you did."

"I thought I did," she responded and stopped working with a demoralized smile, slowly melting away under the weight of the naked truth. "I guess I do... but not as much as I love you," she said abashedly.

"I don't even know him, but I do know this much... he's a better man than I am... and he'll make a better father," he said reluctantly.

"If you don't love me... just say so," she said, terrified to hear the answer.

"This has to stop Gwen... this back and forth that we're both guilty of... don't you think things are moving too fast?" he said and edged towards her.

"I guess that says it all," she said mawkishly.

"I never said I didn't love you," he parried with a blatant sense of panic. "But I'm not sure it would be better... I mean, what if it doesn't work out, for whatever reason... can you live with the fact that you and Jessica lost a chance for happiness and security with Peter?"

Gwen held up a demurring hand and pressed a finger to his lips. "It's okay Randall... would you like to say goodbye to Jessica before we go?"

Randall's throat tightened. "No... no I'd better not."

"I'm never going to see you again, am I?" she asked with watering eyes. "You're just too damn scared to try again... well I'm scared too!"

Randall struggled to maintain his composure and looked to the road. "I'll ah... I'll hitch a ride back," he said as they stood there in the rain, staring at one another.

"Careful," she whispered and resumed digging. Randall waited, hoping she would have something else to say but after a few moments, he wandered off. Gwen waited until he disappeared down the path before the shovel slipped from her hands. She began to cry, dropping to her knees, embraced herself and rocked with her head down, Jack's eyes oddly staring at her.

Chapter Twenty-Two

Felipe's brown eyes gazed out the lavish, hotel suite window at the glittering lights of Montreal. "The first time I ever tasted a man was in a place like this. He was one of my father's young and upcoming managers. He had flown in for a meeting in the Philippines. I didn't like him, but I knew what he was and I used it against him," Felipe said and sipped at his glass of champagne as he secretly checked his radio receiver to ensure there wasn't a transmitter in the room. "Once this is done, if you tell anyone, just remember, we can always find her again... and you," he said and turned to Ichiro. Wearing nothing but a partly open, velvet robe, Felipe offered him a gold pen with a sparkle in his eyes and a smirk upon his face. Behind him on the king-sized bed, Alberto was sprawled naked, reading a men's magazine. "I think you'll find it is a fair and reasonable price," Felipe said.

Ichiro hesitated, but finally took the writing instrument and bent down to sign the contract. The ball of the pen against the paper, he glanced up. "My mother... I want to speak with her," he said quietly.

"As soon as you sign," Felipe said with another smile and dangled his cell phone by its aerial as Ichiro continued to wait. "What is more important, owning the team or the well-being of your mother?" Felipe asked impatiently, but Ichiro remained stone faced. "You know, I've always been fascinated by pain and death. Tell me Ichiro, what is the worst memory about your mother?"

"When my father died... seeing her suffer like that... she did not speak for weeks," Ichiro whispered as the painful recollection stirred his heart. Alberto chuckled with a sarcastic roll of his eyes.

"I promise you that she will suffer a great deal more if you don't do as I say," Felipe said and gestured for him to sign.

Ichiro quickly scribbled his name and slammed the pen down. "I want to speak to her. Now!" he said. Felipe handed him the phone and Ichiro hastily dialled. After a few moments, his mother answered and Ichiro went to say something but Felipe snatched the phone away. "Talk to her on your own dime," he said and strolled to the bar. "We should toast our agreement," he said, filling his glass again and two others. He offered one to Ichiro but was refused. "You did a great job by spilling the fuel on Braedon. It was very convincing, especially when you caught fire too," Felipe said and laughed, as did Alberto.

"You must have done very much evil in another life... a demon has possessed you," Ichiro said, beginning to tremble. "I would like to go now," he said with a bow and turned for the door.

"Is Braedon or Randall driving tomorrow?" Felipe asked and sat on the bed, his hand stroking Alberto's back.

"I... I doubt it," Ichiro said with his hand on the knob.

"I've changed my mind. Let them race if they want to. Alberto will win anyway and two weeks from now, he and I will be the new drivers so it doesn't matter," Felipe said happily and playfully slapped Alberto's bottom.

"But Braedon has a contract... and Alberto does with another team," Ichiro said as he tried not look at Alberto's erection.

"Money can buy anything Ichiro," Felipe said and waved the contract at him. "And don't forget, you still work for me." Ichiro was about to say something, but merely bowed again and closed the door behind him.

"You trust him? If he stays working as a race engineer, he could sabotage us," Alberto asked and downed his champagne. "The only accident I ever had was because of one of those Asian drivers."

"Of course I don't trust him. As soon as I have my dessert, I will see to it his mother has an accident," Felipe said and slowly poured his drink over Alberto's crotch, the cold liquid causing the young Spaniard to flinch.

"There's something I need to tell you about Grange and his wife," Alberto said, but his eyes suddenly widened, looking past Felipe's shoulder. Felipe turned and in an instant, a sword decapitated him. Alberto watched in horror as Felipe's head rolled to a stop on the bed, its mouth agape and eyes shocked. Felipe's body remained sitting upright, its fingers continuing to wriggle until finally, the torso fell off the bed. Alberto scrambled to his knees just as another slice of the weapon sheared away his penis. Alberto writhed in agony as the sword was plunged in and out of his stomach in a flash. Alberto clutched the wound and slumped face first into the bloody sheet.

The contract was removed from Felipe's hand, followed by the sound of feet padding across the carpet and the door gently clicking closed.

Chapter Twenty-Two

The Air France jet soared through the cumulus during its ascent and as it cleared the fog, the aircraft levelled off above a crimson bed of clouds, the first, brilliant twinkle of stars visible in the navy-blue heavens.

Gwen stared out the window and stole a glance at her sleeping daughter beside her in the first-class compartment. Gwen's attention shifted to a young couple situated across from her, holding hands and kissing before giggling. A quiet ping and the seatbelt sign turned off. She immediately stood and started for the gantry and as she hurried along, she suddenly became cognizant of all the couples, young and old. "A large glass of white wine please," Gwen said anxiously to the steward.

"We'll be serving drinks shortly," he replied curtly and resumed his duties. Gwen was about to argue the point but simply nodded and nervously made her way back to her seat.

"What's wrong?" Jessica asked as she rubbed her tired eyes.

"Nothing. I just had to go use the bathroom," Gwen said and took her seat.

"It would be fun to be out there," Jessica said and pointed to the carpet of sparkling clouds. "Looks like candyfloss."

"You'd get a cavity," Gwen said with a motherly smile and searched her purse for her pills.

"I wouldn't eat all of it," Jessica said with an overly dramatic shake of her head.

"Don't be silly," Gwen said and swallowed some pills.

A heavy sigh from Jessica and she played with her tongue. "When will we be home?"

"In a little while. Stop that," Gwen said, slightly impatiently and took Jessica's fingers away from her mouth.

"Where's Peter?" Jessica asked, although not really interested as she fiddled with the tray in the seat before her.

Gwen snapped the tray closed again. "He's in Tampa again... I think... it doesn't matter, we'll see him in a few days," Gwen said tersely, withdrawing some crayons and a colouring book. She placed them before Jessica and massaged her forehead.

"How come you get so many headaches?"

"Because you keep asking me questions! Please be quiet and do some colouring," Gwen barked just as the steward appeared. "I'll have a white wine please and she'll have an apple juice." The steward retrieved the drinks from his cart and wandered off.

"I need a straw," Jessica groaned.

"Drink it like a grown-up," Gwen said and took a healthy swig of her wine. Jessica went to have a sip, but some turbulence caused her to spill the juice down her front. Gwen grabbed the bottle away from her and angrily dabbed at her daughter's dress with a Kleenex. "Behave! It's time you started acting like a little lady and not a baby!" she said too loudly, a few passengers glancing over.

"Is he going to be my father?" Jessica asked and cringed, afraid she might be castigated again.

Gwen stared at Jessica. Her eyes softened and she gazed out the window again. "Maybe... I'm not sure."

"If you marry him, that means you're supposed to love him, right?" Jessica said and drew a heart with an arrow through it.

"Yes... I think so," Gwen whispered, lost in thought.

"Do you love him?" Jessica questioned innocently and began colouring the heart red.

"Yes I do... but maybe not enough."

Jessica frowned at the puzzling response and continued colouring, her tongue sticking out the corner of her mouth. "I look like him," she said matter-of-factly.

"You don't look like Peter," Gwen said, still preoccupied with the view.

"Not Peter, that man you said was your friend at the cemetery," Jessica said, her attention riveted upon her work of art.

Gwen turned to her daughter with a stunned expression. "Why do you say that?"

Jessica playfully poked at her nose. "He has the same kind of nose as me," she said and giggled.

It took a few moments for Jessica's words to sink in before Gwen could speak again. "Did... did you like him?"

A shrug. "I guess. He's cute," Jessica said and smiled as she turned away, obviously embarrassed. "I saw him before," she said and returned to her crayons.

"You did?" Gwen said incredulously.

"He's been in some of my dreams," Jessica said casually and started drawing a car.

"Are they bad dreams?"

"No. We're always in this. See?" Jessica said and held up her crude depiction of a vehicle. "Do you ever dream about him?"

A chill enveloped Gwen's body as she was mesmerized by her offspring's comments. Another distant gaze as Gwen's eyes drifted off. "All the time... every night ever since we... we," Gwen said and promptly came back to reality. "You're only five years old... when did you start having these dreams?"

CHAPTER TWENTY-TWO

"I don't know," Jessica replied with an unconcerned shrug and continued drawing as Gwen watched in astonishment. "Mom, was I born this way or did something to happen?"

Gwen's eyes began to fill and she privately debated whether to tell her the truth. "My God... what am I doing? What am I doing?" Gwen whispered to herself in disbelief with a shake of her head. "I'll be right back," she said and quickly stood.

"Where are you going?" Jessica asked, but her mother was rushing for the cockpit.

"You're not allowed in there! It's locked," a stewardess said and blocked Gwen's path.

Gwen withdrew her identification. "DST," she said and pushed the stewardess aside, the commotion causing one of the pilots to open the door. Gwen held up her credentials. "I have the authority. Turn the plane around. We're going back to Montreal," she said sternly just as her cell phone rang. She answered it. "Yes? Randall?" she said, happily surprised. "I was just about to... what? When? Both of them? Did they remove the bodies? Damn. Who's in charge?" she asked and scrambled to write down the name. "Where are you now? Where? What are you doing there? No, no that's good actually. I'll meet you there," she said and hurriedly tucked the phone away. "I'm not going to tell you again! Turn the plane around! Official French Government business!" she said and handed him a piece of paper. "That's the number of my superior. Radio him to verify it," she said. The pilot adjusted his headset mike to make the inquiry.

Randall sat on the steps of the altar, an unlit cigarette dangling from one corner of his mouth and staring at the three, large ceiling windows as the natural light streamed inside. His eyes fell to the gilt and blue designs, intricate painting, carving and the ornate structure surrounding him. One of the doors to the Notre Dame Bascillica opened and Gwen's shoes echoed as she entered. "We will go to the House of the Lord, and now we have set foot within your gates," Randall said with priestly officialese, watching as she meandered towards him. "If there is a God... I don't think he likes all this expensive shit in his name while most of the world is fucking crazy."

"It's almost five a.m. How did you get in here?" Gwen said and blessed herself before taking a seat in one of the pews.

"I pounded on the rectory door until one of the priests answered... told him I was a cop looking for some guidance so he let me in," Randall said and lowered his head. "I didn't bother to post a time yesterday... think I would have been pretty good in the single lap qualifying... Ichiro's pretty pissed... just couldn't bring myself to do it... not scared... I drove this track in the Atlantics," he said overly defensively and stole a glance at her. "I guess it's not the same without you around... pulling for me... protecting me," he said with a slight smile.

"Then what are you doing here?" she asked and indicated to their heavenly surroundings.

"I wanted to have a chat with the invisible man," he said, lighting the tobacco and snapping the lighter closed, the metallic clank reverberating throughout. "We still have some issues."

"I know... that's one of the reasons I came back," she said bashfully.

"I'm talking about Him," Randall said, motioning to the ceiling and taking a long drag of the smoke. "Ever wonder what the fuck the point in living is if you can't remember it when you're dead? Not that I'd want to... makes me wonder why He put me through all that shit."

"Maybe it was a test," she said with a shrug.

"Bullshit. That's all these fucked religious types say when things go wrong. It's an easy way of explaining something that can't be," he said with disdain and shook his head. "My mother used to say He never gives us more than we can handle... well I've had more than enough," he said, withdrawing his wallet and thumbing through the various, tattered cards until he found a laminated picture of Jesus. "I've had this as long as I can remember... my mother gave it to me. I used to put it under my pillow... and when things were happening with him... I used to close my eyes and hope Jesus would stop it... but he never did," he continued and flipped open his lighter again. "So I've come to a conclusion... God doesn't exist or he doesn't care... either way I say fuck you." He lit the picture. The plastic took a moment to catch but finally began to melt as the paper inside curled into black ash.

"Are you sure that's a smart thing to do, especially in here?" she said and strolled towards him.

"I wish He *would* do something... at least it would prove the son-of-a-bitch cares," Randall said, entranced by the smouldering paper.

"Where's all this coming from?" she said and sat on the steps beside him.

"He was only ten... that kid with Lunder... only ten years old... Booger told me... he was only ten for fuck sakes... killed himself... in the foster home," Randall said and hauled himself up, transfixed upon the crucifix. "There are no happy endings."

"I'm so sorry Randall... Tony shouldn't have said anything until you were back in Hamilton."

Chapter Twenty-Two

"I called him to check on Spart and he told me... what the fuck did that kid ever do to deserve that?" Randall yelled to the crucifix and angrily flicked his cigarette at it. "Where the hell were you, uh?"

"I don't know what to tell you... just that things happen for a reason," she said quietly.

"Fuck that! How the hell would you know? You're a princess sitting in your goddamn ivory tower," he shouted.

"I know you're upset, but life isn't any easier for me!"

"The only time you get your hands dirty is when you cap somebody like Jack! Even then you didn't flinch!" he said with disgust.

"How dare you?" she said and bolted to her feet. "How do you know how I feel? You don't think stuff like that doesn't keep me up at night?" she said and shoved him. "Why do you think I get these damn headaches? Why do you think I have insomnia?"

Randall's eyes began to fill, his knees buckled and he stumbled to support himself on a bench. "I want to believe... I have to hate Him... I have to blame Him... because if He doesn't exist... then that means there is no fucking meaning to anything... it means that kid... and Jessica... even me... just bad fucking luck... like rolling the dice," he whispered with a breaking voice and wiped his eyes. "And that's even fucking worse to think about."

Randall's weakness alleviated her ire and she sat next to him, wanting to put her arm around his shoulder, but didn't. "Well... maybe there is some justice. Suarez and Americo weren't exactly the salt of the earth."

"Pretty fucking gruesome, eh? I think we're dealing with a fucking psychopath, split lips," he said, regaining his composure and sparking another cigarette.

"I spoke to the investigating officer. His name is Gallant. He's going to keep it quiet for as long as he can. Alberto's team owner has been told and they're not racing out of respect. The press is being told they simply withdrew. Gallant also gave me this," she said, retrieving a sheet of paper and handing it to him. Randall opened the document and read. *'Got the money. Another twenty million pounds before the end of lap one or another dies.'* "The original was stuffed into Alberto's mouth along with his manhood. Obviously, we're not paying it," she said and rubbed her aching forehead. "Since we deposited the money the last time and it was withdrawn, that means Braedon is innocent and he was in custody when Suarez and Americo were killed. He wouldn't take the fall by himself if he had an accomplice. I'm going to release him after the race tomorrow."

Randall leaned forward and reached into his back pocket. He withdrew a newspaper clipping and showed her the photograph of him punching Alberto. "I wish I hadn't hit the poor son-of-a-bitch," he said, crumpling the paper and throwing it aside. "Do you know who withdrew the money?"

A sad shake of her head. "No... but it's early. We're working on it and if it goes nowhere, I'm probably out of a job. It was my idea. I do have some news though. Candice's uncle is not the Rabbit. Interpol tracked him down and informed us he's been dead for two years."

"Anything at the crime scene?"

"Nothing. No prints or video and nobody saw anything," she said and found her pills. "The maid found the bodies. The do not disturb sign wasn't on the door."

"At least we can forget about Felipe as a suspect."

"Ichiro doesn't know yet," she said and closed her eyes and raised her head to the windows, the warmth basking her face. "Want to go with me to tell him and see how he reacts after I have a little chat with Carmen?"

"Maybe Ichiro already knows."

"He did have motive the way Felipe was trying to take over, but was it enough?" she said and ran her fingers along the cool, marble steps. "He doesn't seem the type."

"They never do."

"One of those swords Ichiro has could easily have been the weapon. I think we should confront him," she said as Randall turned her wrist and checked the time.

"I say you don't tell him."

"Okay. Now what?" she asked, slightly puzzled.

"We move our asses. Ichiro said he was packing up this morning before the race... and well... I don't want some other driver killed because... because I didn't have the guts to drive," he said with a heavy sigh. "Somebody has to be the target while you're looking for the hit man."

"So you still want to go through with this?" she asked incredulously.

"Do you?"

"I guess... and I think it takes a lot of courage to do what you're doing," she said with a warm smile and stood, as did Randall. "Jessica... she thinks you look like her... she has dreams about you."

"She does?" he asked, pleasantly surprised.

"Strange. She was too young to remember the accident... I've never told her what happened... maybe you should," she said and swallowed her medication.

"I... I don't know about that," he said, promptly nervous.

"Randall, I came back for two reasons... one to finish what I started with this case but most importantly, to force you to try again with us."

"And how are you going to force me?" he said with a guarded chuckle.

Chapter Twenty-Two

Gwen brushed aside her hair and removed a small, gold crucifix from around her neck. She closed his hand over it. "After I tell you what I happened just after the plane landed last night... you might want to stick around," she said as Randall went to open his hand, but she tightened her grip. "Promise me we'll try again."

"I need to hear the deal first," he said with a sideways laugh to ease his anxiety.

"Jessica... I don't know how it happened... she didn't even realize... I wouldn't have believed it if I hadn't seen it myself... she moved her legs for an instant."

Randall felt an overwhelming frailty and found himself leaning against a pew. "What?" he whispered totally stunned and fighting back his emotion.

"She told me that she gets a tingling in her feet sometimes and that it's happening more and more," Gwen said as a tear rolled down her soft cheek. "I told her to tell me when it happens again. As soon as we get back to France, I'm taking her to the doctor."

"She might walk again?" he said excitedly.

"I don't want to think about that... I don't want to raise her hopes... or ours," she said and forced a light smile. "That's worth another try at us, isn't it?"

Randall waited several moments before finally nodding and embracing her. He stepped back and studied the crucifix in his hand. "Why this?"

"I was in Iran... they figured I was a spy... tortured me... raped me... for a month... I needed a miracle... there was a woman in the next cell they accused of the same thing... she was an aid worker... she gave it to me," Gwen said and eyed the crucifix. "When I was scared I'd squeeze it so tight it dug into my skin... but they finally released me... it saved my sanity... it reminds me to never give up," she said and placed it around his neck. "Jessica isn't giving up... I'm not giving up and neither should you... I'll be outside," she said knowingly and lightly caressed his face.

Randall waited until she was gone before sheepishly glancing at the ceiling again. "Okay old man... here's the deal... thanks for the hope with my baby... you make her walk again and I don't give a shit... I mean, I don't care what you do to me... I can't change... you made me what I am," he said and hesitated in the deafening silence, "I do love Gwen... and I know I should give it another shot... I mean, I will give it another shot... but you have to promise me Jessica walks," he said and slowly knelt down to show respect. "We got a deal?" he asked just as a brilliant ray of sunshine suddenly beamed through the windows, illuminating the altar for an instant. Randall felt the hairs on his neck rise and he nodded before examining the crucifix Gwen had given him. "I'll take that as a yes," he said and turned for the door.

"The answer is no," Julius said as he stepped into the Sikorsky helicopter, followed by Friedrich, who reluctantly climbed in the back.

"Why not?" Gwen asked as Julius sat in the pilot's seat and buckled himself in.

"Braedon and Randall failed to qualify. If you don't qualify, you don't race. It's as simple as that," Julius replied and started the engine.

"Where are you going? The weather is getting bad," Gwen said, the rotors slowly starting to turn as she watched a sailboat knife through the choppy water of the Saint Lawrence River, its canvass rigid and bowed with the stiff wind. It whisked towards the marina near the Gilles Villeneuve Circuit where a coterie of crafts were anchored in a tabular array, bobbing beneath a rapidly approaching boreal, black morning sky. Despite the inclement weather, the inhabitants of the vessels happily went about their leisure, satisfied to be a part of the forthcoming racing spectacle.

"A little sightseeing," Julius answered and put on a headset. "I always rent one of these things the morning of the race and take a look around."

Gwen jumped in just as Julius purposely lifted off the ground at a steep angle. "Where did you learn to fly?" she asked and quickly fastened her belts.

"The KGB can teach a person a lot of things," Julius said as the helicopter flew over the deserted facility. "I used to pilot a gunship like this in Chechnya. I loved firing rockets at those Muslim bastards," he said while Friedrich suddenly began to gag. He reached for a bag inside his jacket as Julius started to laugh. "Poor Friedrich. I make him go on these flights all the time, but he still gets sick. Don't worry my friend, I'll make a man out of you yet."

"You should be careful," Friedrich managed to mumble. "You can't fly like this. It's too dangerous."

Julius waved away Friedrich's concern and nudged Gwen. "Friedrich loves rules. He won't even have sex until he's married," Julius said with a chuckle.

"I want Randall in the race today," she said as Julius deliberately flew sideways, causing Friedrich to heave again.

"It wouldn't be fair to the other teams," Julius said and steered the helicopter into a dive.

"I don't care. It's part of my investigation," Gwen replied and withdrew her pen and pad.

Chapter Twenty-Two

"What's the point? Braedon can't compete because of burns and Randall has a sprained wrist. Besides, our doctor didn't give either of them medical clearance to race."

"The DST supersedes your medical staff," Gwen said as she handed Friedrich a Kleenex to wipe his sweaty brow.

"Why does Randall need to race?" Julius asked and forced the helicopter to climb rapidly.

"I'm not at liberty to say," Gwen said as Friedrich closed his eyes and held his mouth.

"I don't suppose you know the real reason Alberto America's team isn't racing?" Julius asked, full of suspicion.

"They're not? That's news to me," Gwen fibbed, but was convincing. "So, do I have your blessing to have Randall behind the wheel? Of course, I realize he would have to start at the back of the grid."

"I've been very patient with you," Julius said to her. "I've kept your investigation a secret and I've tried to cooperate," he said as the helicopter flew over a rowing basin. "But my patience is running out."

"You still haven't answered my question," she said and checked her watch.

"Why do you even bother to ask for my permission when you're going to do what you want anyway?" Julius replied as the helicopter passed over a small, man-made lake and swimming beach.

"I need to know your answer because everything I do goes into a report," she said and scribbled in her pad.

"Did you know Sikorsky was Ukrainian? Brilliant man. He was from Kiev. He was born May 25th, 1889. He studied Leonardo Da Vinci's drawings of a helicopter and used to read Jules Verne," Julius said as he swung the machine low over the casino. "Great men have vision and take chances when other people will not, but don't feel bad, we do have something in common, *Mrs. Grange*. We both like to hunt people. Only you do it for a pay check and I do it for sport," Julius said with a wink.

"What is that supposed to mean?" she asked.

"The best game in the world is a human being... they're smarter than animals when they're being chased," Julius said as his eyes glazed over. "And they'll do anything to get away... no matter how fast they're going."

Julius' words chilled her blood and she avoided his sudden stare. "Are you going to make me force you to let Randall drive?"

A hearty laugh from Julius as he let go of the cyclic control stick and the collective control stick. "I'd rather die before I let an egomaniac of a woman tell me what to do," he said casually, the machine beginning to fall as Friedrich promptly reached for his bag again. "I'm telling you that

Randall is not driving today and if you disagree, we're all dead in just a few seconds," he said with a smile. "So, what's it going to be?"

Gwen took a moment before suddenly striking Julius in the side of the head, causing the Russian to slump forward. She quickly yanked him out of the seat and took over the controls. "I hate a backseat driver," she said as Julius moaned, fighting to stay conscious. "I learned a lot of things in the DST too. Randall is driving... it's as simple as that," she added sardonically as Friedrich grinned.

Chapter Twenty-Three

Randall sat in the cockpit of the racer, last on the grid, wearing Braedon's helmet with the visor closed and smiling to himself. "My life was like a dream... just waiting to wake up from the nightmare," he whispered to himself as he noticed the press mingling amongst the other cars. "You're a hell of a long way from the Skyway Bridge kid... trying to kill your stupid ass... self-pity's a good thing, until it's the only thing," he said with a self-affirming nod. "It's good to be alive... going to survive this thing," he said as he watched Ichiro and the crew making last minute preparations.

Randall retrieved his tattered photograph of Jessica and studied it. "Looking forward to spending time with you baby... you and your mom," he said and tucked the picture away again.

He focused on the concrete walls of death along the main straight and closed his eyes. "Don't worry about gaining at the start... can't win it at the first corner, but you can sure as hell lose it," he said. "Just maintain your position... overdrive the car and there's going to be a shitload of trouble... racing's about driving on the edge... got to remember the machine is delicate... like an icicle...breaks fucking easy if you put a wheel wrong... these things are a living, breathing thoroughbred... beast has to be controlled or it's going to ruin your day," he said as his fingers stroked the wheel. "Didn't walk the circuit this morning for good luck like I used to... last time I didn't... damned near burned to death... ah, just stupid, fucking superstition."

His eyes still shut; Randall could feel every bump in the road and held his breath as he imagined the car circumnavigating the traffic as the racer slid through the turns. "Got to slam the throttle... in the rain I got to stay fast so I don't start hydroplaning... remember, you're king of the wet... king of the wet," he said as his voice trailed off with another confident nod.

"Ichiro said you're not giving any interviews before the race, Braedon," Candice said loudly so as to be heard through his helmet. She appeared at the nose of the car, noisily chewing her bubble gum. She popped a bubble, the gum sticking to her face and she grinned. "I once drove in a stock car race at one of those powder-puff derbies. I didn't finish and my dreams of a racing career ended right there," she said with a laugh. "Some of those girls could really drive though. Maybe even good enough to compete at this level, but racing is still a sexist sport, don't you think," she said with her pen ready, but Randall merely shook his head to deny her. "Not talking, uh? By the way, why are you in the cockpit so early?" she asked suspiciously and checked her watch. "It's not technicians only for another two minutes," she said as Randall waved her away. Candice happily withdrew a folded piece of paper and gave it to him. Randall's gloved hands held her fingers for a moment, his hidden eyes examining her psoriasis-covered skin. "Sorry about my ugly hands. I have a skin condition. It's hereditary. It comes and goes," she said with a smile. Randall released her and opened the missive. It read, *'I know it's you, Randall. Have a good run. You still owe me that story... if you survive.'* Randall's heart skipped a beat as he watched her playfully wiggle her fingers to say goodbye and hurry to another car, further up the grid.

"Gwen? You sure Candice checks out?" Randall asked via the radio as he stared at the gladiators; veterans wearing mirrored sunglasses despite the overcast day, a few jocular while conversing with crews and some alone, others fidgeting and tense.

Gwen hurried up the last few steps to her lookout position above the pit lane building, close to where the racers make a last right and left before finishing the lap. "Positive? Why?" she replied breathlessly as the wind whipped her hair.

"Nothing. You sound like you did on our honeymoon," he said sarcastically. "Listen, I was thinking, since we're giving me and you another shot, where are we going to live?"

"France, of course," she said, running for the cover of a makeshift tent. She set her binoculars down beside several, small television screens revealing different locations throughout the circuit.

"Why can't we stay in Hamilton?"

"Are you kidding? I can't walk away from the DST," she said and withdrew her medication.

"Why should I quit the force here?"

"I thought you'd pursue racing again. You once told me that Europe is the best place for that," she said and swallowed a couple of pills.

"What... what if I don't... what the hell am I supposed to do in France?"

Chapter Twenty-Three

"I can get you hooked up with a police job. Don't worry," she said and put an elastic band around her hair.

"I want to stay in Canada. I don't give a shit about France. I hate those frogs... except you."

Gwen slowly sat on the edge of the railing, a serious expression upon her face. "I just assumed you would come back with me."

"Did you tell Peter yet?"

"No... I will after the race. He's here, you know. Flew in last night on business," she said, withdrawing the engagement ring as a distant boom of thunder rumbled. "He proposed to me in the pouring rain at a cafe in Nice... even then it didn't feel right."

"Then why did you say yes?"

"I don't know... Jessica needed a father... I was tired of being lonely... and I guess I convinced myself that if I tried hard enough, I could love him... the way I love you," she said and stuffed the ring in her pocket again.

"Remember when I asked you to marry me?" he said with a laugh. Gwen giggled and her face lightened. "I had to do it over the police radio because I thought you'd say no," he said and hesitated. "Hey Gwen? I... I um... just wanted to say thanks for thinking I could help you with all this... it means a lot."

Gwen focused her field glasses on Randall's racer directly below her. "You're welcome," she said softly.

Randall strained his neck to look up at her. "I wish you could be down here with me... you know... a good luck kiss... but I know you can't... I mean, why would you be locking lips with Braedon?" he said with an anxious chuckle. "It's going to sound dumb but... I used to wonder how my life was going to end... if it was going to hurt... if I could handle it with dignity... or even if I was going to care," he said quietly. "Well... none of it matters now... because I do love you... and I'm glad we're going to try again... and... and well... thanks for believing in me."

Gwen swallowed hard and lowered the binoculars. "You're welcome... and I love you too," she whispered and blew him a kiss as he gave her the thumbs up. "What do you say I buy you a drink after the race?" she said, fighting emotion.

"You got a deal," his voice crackled over the radio. "Could sure use a smoke."

"After it's over, I just might have one with you," she said.

"Kind of scared," he said with a forced laugh. "Ever been so scared that... that you think you might not make it?" he asked reluctantly.

"Just once... after the accident with Jessica... you were unconscious for a few hours and we weren't sure you would come out of it... that was the most frightened I've ever been," she said as her eyes drifted off. "Even though I was mad as hell at you... I prayed you would survive... and that's how I know there's a God."

A few moments of silence. "How is she today?"

"Good. She wants to go home," Gwen said and noticed a jet slicing through the clouds.

"Gwen... just in case... I... I don't want no service... I want it done quick... you know, cremation... make me a crispy critter split lips," he with a chuckle, but was soon serious again. "I've written it all down... it's with my photograph of Jessica under my uniform... okay? Promise me."

Gwen hesitated and considered the tragic possibility as her throat tightened. "You better come back to me Grange... but okay... I promise."

"I'd better go... we'll talk soon," he said quietly after an alarm sounded, indicating only the technicians were allowed on the grid.

"I know you're going to be busy so I won't speak to you unless I have to. You be a racer and I'll be a cop," she said, trying to ease the sombre mood. "I have my people covering you."

"Hey?" he asked.

"Yes?"

"I think I might like it in France," he said quietly. "As long as I'm with you and Jess."

"Good luck," Gwen said, her eyes beginning to water as her finger released the radio button. She stood at the building's edge and stared at Randall as she blessed herself. "Please watch over him... make him be careful... because I know he won't ask for help," she said and looked skyward. "And give me the guidance to protect him before they... please... please help me catch them," she whispered as something suddenly caught her attention out the corner of her eye and she turned. "What are you doing here?" Gwen said with surprise, her face quickly becoming fearful as her eyes gradually lowered.

The sky had darkened considerably over the circuit and the nearby water was churning a violent, blue-green. Rumblings of thunder reverberated ever closer and a slight wind began to pick up with the spit of intermittent rain. The full grandstands were abuzz with excitement and laughter as umbrellas bent and broke in the gusty air. Legions of fans continued pouring into the aisles, headed for their seats despite the optical illusion that not one more soul could be squeezed in. Team and driver banners stood erect in the stiffening breeze as sections rose to their feet and sat again, simulating waves.

Chapter Twenty-Three

The neophytes of racing watched in wondrous silence, captivated and giddy to be a part of the magic and familial, liturgical pageant of elite racing. A blast of thunder, and a torrential downpour began.

"Fuck! Any rubber that was laid down is going to be washed away," Randall said via his radio.

"Just do not lock them up," Ichiro said, kneeling next to the car as the crew quickly gathered their things.

"Christ... what if I do and go off at the first turn?" Randall said worriedly. "I did that in my very first race."

Ichiro smiled nervously, recognizing the usual pre-race jitters. "You and I are very much alike. My father wanted me to be a fisherman like him, but my mother encouraged me to do what I wanted. Your life may never be the same after today. I bet this is what you have always wanted, Randall."

"You're right. Who knows, if this goes well, I might make a comeback in racing with Team Jenkins?" Randall said, thrilled at the prospect.

"Got a drip back here," one of the crewmembers announced anxiously.

Randall watched through his mirror as Ichiro quickly ran to the back of the car. "It is just a little oil overflow. It will burn off," Ichiro said unconcerned. "Remember Randall, we are doing two pit stops today," Ichiro whispered so the crew couldn't hear and gestured for them to crank the engine. The racer roared to life, as did the others, filling the air with the hair-raising din of ferocious horsepower as the fans applauded and cheered. Ichiro wiped away the moisture from his glasses and offered his hand. "Good luck, my friend."

Randall shook Ichiro's hand. "Go read your comic books," Randall said sardonically. "Hey Ichiro?"

"Yes?" Ichiro replied and zipped up his jacket as the rain fell harder.

"Where's Felipe? I figured that asshole... sorry, I thought he would be here pushing you around."

Ichiro shifted on his feet and covered his soaked head with his clipboard. "I... I do not know. It is strange... he is not here and nor is Alberto Americo's team."

"You know, I was thinking. Remember how Samuel used to tap the front of the cars with his cane for good luck? You should do something like that... use one of them swords you got. Press would love that shit," Randall said with a chuckle, but was eager for Ichiro's reaction and closely monitored his body language.

"It may not be necessary," Ichiro responded with a stiff smile. "I am thinking of selling the team after this weekend... but I am sure another team would give you a chance," he said and bowed awkwardly before running to his pit lane station.

The news took a second to process in Randall's brain, but he promptly shook his head clear. "Forget it. Just man and machine now," he said to himself and watched the gantry of lights blink off and the cars depart on the formation lap.

Small, rooster tails of spray emitted from the rear tyres of Randall's car as the racer followed the others. Condensation was already beginning to form on the inside of his visor and he slightly opened it to moderate the temperature, the air refreshing against his hot skin. His eyes lifted towards the heavens. The outline of the sun was barely discernible for a brief moment until low, dark clouds rapidly covered it again.

Randall glanced at the pavement beside him and saw the tiny ripples of windswept water. "Fucking ride is going to be a bitch... someone's going to need a doctor by the end... hope it ain't me."

"How are you?" Ichiro asked over the radio.

"Ready to get into the fray," Randall replied, watching the drenched fans waving madly as the field passed.

"Remember, Braedon is a clever driver, so do not do anything reckless," Ichiro said.

"Ah shit," Randall mumbled, not realizing his finger was still depressing the radio button.

"What is it?" Ichiro asked with concern.

"One too many coffees," Randall said, slightly embarrassed.

"I am sure this has happened to you in your career. Do what any driver does," Ichiro whispered, equally uncomfortable.

Randall tried to suppress the impulse but to no avail. Soon, there was a pleasant warmth between his legs, followed by the distress of the moisture cooling. He suddenly felt his heart rate skyrocket and his thighs beginning to numb. "Damnit, Randall! I know it's been a while but stuff your balls back down your fucking throat!" he whispered to himself and loosened his grip on the wheel. "Don't hold it too tight! Remember, it's an egg. Easy does it," he said as some of the cars swayed side to side to, the rookie drivers desperately trying to heat their tyres, but Randall knew the exercise was pointless as the rain was too strong. "Nervous boys out here today," he said and geared up, but could go no further, the racer already twitchy on the soaked track. "Last fucking starting position... never had to begin here... kind of relieved though... leader gets his ass bothered all the time... all I got to do is try and pass.... shouldn't be that hard... the old man's cars are famous for their grunt," he said and listened to the note of the engine. It was reassuringly metronomic.

Chapter Twenty-Three

Randall's eyes shifted outside the cockpit and he found himself searching for possible locations from which a bullet could come. "If you're out there... going to take a shot at one of the slower sections or when I'm at full tilt? If it's coming... it's supposed to come before the end of the first lap," he said, scrutinizing every track marshal as he passed. "Wearing a bullet-proof vest and helmet... maybe they hit a tire? Stop it!" he shouted to himself. "Block that shit out! Concentrate goddamnit! Once you start with bad thoughts, you're a fucking accident waiting to happen! No room in the attic for doubt!" he said and tapped his head.

The parade of machinery exited L'Epingle, travelling down the long straight, leading to the final chicane before the grid. Randall wiped the droplets off his visor, but the moisture quickly reappeared, the ghostly vehicles ahead slipping in and out of the low, lingering spray. A red flash. Randall checked his electronics indicating the oil gauge. "Fuck! Got a problem here!" Randall said, lighting up the radio.

"Telemetry says there is nothing wrong," Ichiro's replied.

"Do you want me to come in?" Randall asked.

"No! No, stay out there," Ichiro said adamantly. "If it becomes serious, then we will bring you in."

Randall suddenly found himself gearing down as the pack of racers began to take their grid positions. The rain was now torrid. "Should red flag this fucking race!" he said to himself. "At least start under the pace of the safety car and go single file... not fucking likely... goddamned stewards always want to give the fans what they paid for... a fucking accident."

Randall carefully eased his machine into the last position and caught a glimpse of the flashing lights atop the safety car several hundred feet behind him. Aside from the heavy rain, he could see the gigantic heat haze hovering above the racers in front as the engines were already beginning to boil. He looked to the anxious crowd, gazing down upon the warriors before the fight. Many held plastic cups of beer to toast, offering a chalice to the their heroes of racing. Time seemed to slow. Every second a minute. The fans. Standing. Cheering. Screaming. Randall didn't realize the tears slipping from his wide eyes. Tears of pure excitement, pride and utmost fear. "No turning back... you'd be proud of me, Dad... hope you're watching Mom," he whispered as he watched the row of red starting lights come on as his piercing, salty, sweat-stung eyes stared straight ahead beneath the snow white balaclava, his peripheral vision heightened, as were all his senses. "Get in the zone... get in the zone," he chanted and gazed upon the formation of cars before him, the cool, indomitable rain splashing against the warm pavement, creating a flagitious fog. "Looks like a fucking medieval battlefield," he said and stole a glance at the shoal of humanity in the grandstands. "Perhaps the

Lord will do a miracle for us. 'For it makes no difference to him how many enemy troops there are...' 1Samuel, fourteen, six," he whispered as the row of red starting lights began to blink on.

Four. Three. Two. A sudden, unified, rising, ear-splitting scream from the mendicant power plants, aching to be unleashed. One. All lit. "Let's fucking do it!" Randall yelled inside his helmet. The lights blinked off and the field launched off the grid in a fantastic display of waterworks and thunderous racket.

Randall rocketed towards the back of the car in front and made a daring manoeuvre on the inside. He could see the other competitors playing it safe as they veered to the outside of the track, trying to avoid some standing water. A millisecond to decide whether to follow the conservative route. The racer in Randall promptly emerged. He kept his foot on the tank and torpedoed through, creating a wall of wash, temporarily obliterating his car. Through the sheen of blur, he saw brief bursts of smoke to his right as tyres braked heavily, evaporating the moisture beneath the rubber as the jousting continued. He passed six cars but the turn was rapidly approaching. His foot touched the brake and the racer immediately started to fishtail. "Fast hands! Fast hands!" he said to himself as his racer quickly recovered and fell into line at the apex. Fifteenth place. A cursory check of his mirrors revealed two cars bumping and helplessly driving into each other and onto the slick grass where they broke off their rear wings against the tyre barriers.

A cataclysm of imposing, swirling spray. Randall could barely see the rain light of the vehicle ahead of him and pulled to the outside in the hope of better vision. Unexpectedly, there was another racer mere inches away. Randall swung hard to the left, narrowly missing a collision. The Jenkins' machine slammed the brakes and slid, shooting up the inside of three more racers, entering a quick left and right before a fast straight. Randall knew it wasn't skill but plain, dumb luck. "Twelfth place! You are doing great!" Ichiro shouted excitedly over the radio.

"She's a slippery creature in a straight line so I can take a few more!" Randall said anxiously.

"One at a time," Ichiro said.

Randall shifted to sixth, the car rapidly gaining on eleventh place until he caught the draft, instantly unstable with the dirty air. Close. So close Randall could see the bolts on the rear wing. The jettison of water emitting from the car ahead missed Randall's head because of the vacuum and showered harmlessly over the back of his car. He steered hard right, now commensurate to the man beside him.

The slowest part of the course. A severe, first gear right-hander, leading to the fastest straight. Again Randall braked late and easily took eleventh position much to the loud delight of the packed grandstands across the track.

Oil light. He noticed the beacon of distress on the computerized dash just as he was throttling into top gear. "Oil warning again!" Randall announced.

"There is no sense bringing you in. If it is terminal there is not much we can do anyway," Ichiro said.

A gloved hand wrapped around a trigger. The rifle's sights clearly focused on Randall as he raced towards the final chicane before the start/finish line.

Randall's heart quickened. "Supposed to happen before the end of lap one," he said casually to himself. "Let's play a little chicken!"

Randall wasn't sure what exactly occurred, but he thought he saw the left, front tyre disintegrate. Instinctively, he held the steering wheel with all his strength and tried to veer in the direction of the skid. His foot depressed the brake but it was useless, the racer beginning to spin out of control as he released the wheel to protect his wrists. "Fuck! Going to be bad!" he said to himself.

The Jenkins' machine careened into the left retaining wall with a tremendous crash as car parts were flung high into the air. Randall closed his eyes. "Hope you got him Gwen... remember me... it's okay," he whispered calmly as the car spun back onto the pavement. It slammed into the wall separating the pit lane from the circuit with a savage impact, causing the entire car to shatter in an instant.

Ugly. Some fans turned away. It was difficult to distinguish what was left of the vehicle. Hundreds of pieces scattered astride the grass and slick road. Some were still waffling in the air before gravity sucked them back to earth in a gentle shower of carbon fibre, aluminium, steel and plastic. The emergency crews hesitated, for they couldn't tell where the cockpit came to rest amidst the brutal carnage. It was discovered at the base of the fence next to the grandstand. In an eerie hush, some macabre spectators stood and craned their necks to see.

Randall remained strapped in the seat, only a shell of the chassis intact. His posture was strangely peaceful, sitting upright with his legs slightly bent and his arms resting at his sides. The red flag flew to stop the race and an ambulance hastened to the scene. The medical crew leapt from their vehicles and scrambled towards Randall. The visor was gently raised. A collective shock. It wasn't Braedon. No pulse.

Gwen managed to lift herself to one knee, but collapsed again. She noticed the blood dripping from a huge laceration over her left eye. Mustering strength, she stumbled to her feet and leaned heavily against the wall. After catching her breath, through bloodied eyes she peered over the edge and saw the activity surrounding Randall. "No," she said mournfully and staggered towards the stairs, but pain caused her to double over and fall. "All units... I... I want the medical crew to keep this quiet," she said breathlessly, looking down at her red-stained hands and realizing she had been shot in the stomach. Her memory was jogged. There was a brief struggle with her masked assailant before a silencer's bullet shredded her abdomen. Her radio headset was gone and so was her weapon. Gwen fought losing consciousness and clung to the railing as she slowly descended the steps.

Ichiro ran as fast as he could to the hospital building behind the pit lane. Reporters were already crowding him, snapping photographs and yelling questions. "Let me through!" he yelled as race officials tried to clear a path. A race against time. A race against death. The doors flew open and the principals rushed inside. "Does anybody know anything?" Ichiro asked with moistening eyes. Silence. Everyone looked to a closed door with a small window, but nobody wanted to get too close as the race chaplain stood nearby.

Gwen limped into the hospital, trying to conceal her injury beneath her closed jacket, but blood was oozing through. She pushed her way past the reporters shouting questions about the condition of Braedon as cameras flashed while security struggled to keep the press at bay. Gwen managed to slip through the doors and was about to be collared, but Ichiro nodded his approval as he suddenly realized she was wounded. "Get a doctor for her right away!" he shouted.

"How is he?" she asked, clutching her stomach.

Ichiro took her by the arm. "Help me here!" he requested of the others and she was aided to a chair.

"I said how is he?" she queried again impatiently, the doctor appeared and peeled off his latex gloves with the chaplain behind him as Gwen battled to her feet with the help of Ichiro.

"Who are you?" the physician asked and looked to Ichiro.

"She is... she is with me," Ichiro replied with a breaking voice.

"We did all we could," the doctor said quietly.

Gwen wasn't sure she heard him correctly and took a painful step forward as she felt a tinge of dizziness. "What?"

"He's gone. We couldn't save him," the doctor answered calmly.

"What...? He... he's dead?" she said, totally shocked and beginning to falter as Ichiro wrapped his arm around her. Still not able to comprehend the news, Gwen stared dumbly as a gurney was wheeled towards her.

"We have to get you checked out," the doctor said and extended his arm to her.

Chapter Twenty-Three

"I want to see him!" she shouted, beginning to weep. The doctor nodded and went to aid her onto the gurney, but she pushed it aside and staggered into the room.

Gwen stood and stared at the bestial site. Randall's lifeless eyes were half-open. Nature responded timely and gently. Her gaze shifted to the window where the rain suddenly stopped. A powerful glimmer of munificent sunlight pierced through the dark clouds and shone through the blinds, illuminating his monochrome, gilt body. After a few moments, she leaned over and held him close, trying to capture some of his spirit before it evaporated. She caressed his cheek and kissed him with trembling lips. "I'm sorry Randall... I'm so sorry," she whispered as the doctor entered.

"Miss Gaudet?" he said softly.

"It's Mrs. Grange... Mrs. Randall Grange," she replied, grief beginning to overwhelm her as she slipped her hand beneath Randall's uniform and withdrew the photograph of Jessica and Randall's will. "I'm sorry Jessica," she whispered and carefully placed the picture of her daughter in Randall's hand before closing his still-warm fingers over it.

"We really do need to take care of your injuries," the doctor said. Losing strength, she tried to resist, but he forced her onto the gurney and motioned for the medical entourage to remove Randall from the room. "Please don't go Randall... I don't want you to go," she cried as she grasped his other hand. "I love you... I do," she whispered as her eyes rolled back and she slipped into unconsciousness.

Chapter Twenty-Four

Hands held *Open Wheel Magazine*. Inside, *The Racing Soap Opera* was the bold headline. *Vincenzo Azzopardi Died From Suspension Failure* read the first caption. The second article displayed a photograph of Ichiro and the accompanying by-line stated *Tanaka Sells, Says So Long To Racing*. Beside that, another piece declared *Braedon Stirling Retires Post Montreal Grand Prix Due To Injuries - Divorces Wife*. Below, another paragraph revealed *Teresa Legaro Azzopardi Indicted For Tax Evasion - Still In Hiding*. *Friedrich Hesse Takes Command Of Series - Julius Carmen Sells Shares - Suspected Of Links to Organized Crime* was the next titbit with a photo of the Russian being escorted into court. The penultimate copy read *Felipe Suarez & Alberto Americo Found Murdered - Investigation Continues*. The final story related *Rookie Randall Grange Disappears From Racing As Fast As He Appeared*. The entire piece was authored by Candice Goldenstein.

"Here you are sir," the woman's voice said as a full-bearded Braedon Stirling set the newspaper aside.

After a simple nod to her, he accepted the briefcase and placed it on the desk. A quick pop of the buttons and he slowly opened it, his eyes widening. "Thank you," he said, quickly closing the case and donning his dark sunglasses. He hurried to the exit and casually checked in all directions.

Braedon stepped out of the Grand Cayman Sun Bank into the staggering humidity, his lungs suddenly heavy and his skin instantly damp beneath his smartly pressed, summery, light shirt. "My life begins now," he whispered cheerfully, his nostrils filling with the delightful scent of the ocean.

Strolling along the steamy street in George Town, Braedon stared at the translucent, turquoise water gently washing over the coral reef and spied the rays of brilliant sunlight streaming down through fluorescent holes

Chapter Twenty-Four

amidst the dirty blue clouds. He fished through his walking shorts, found the keys to his rented BMW and unlocked the door.

Flinching at the hot leather sticking to his legs, he immediately turned the air-conditioning on and found himself focused upon the briefcase. He opened it and grinned at the numerous, neatly tied bundles of money. "Not bad for a kid who used to give his newspaper money to the IRA," he said happily.

A quick squeal of the tyres and he drove off, but he didn't notice a black Porsche with tinted windows pull away from the curb and follow.

Braedon nonchalantly checked his rear-view mirror and raised a curious eyebrow at the exotic automobile directly behind him. Just to be safe, he slammed the BMW into fifth and accelerated around a corner, but the Porsche gave chase as the world champion's adrenaline skyrocketed. Someone had finally found him.

Braedon kicked the wheel and rounded another turn; the tyres bawling as he narrowly missed a streetlight. The Porsche rapidly gained on the BMW, dodging left and right before tagging the rear bumper. Braedon started to fishtail but quickly recovered. The duet roared down another street, dust flying and motors sharply gearing down as they made a sudden left, causing the pedestrians to scramble for safety.

The Porsche pulled alongside and rammed into Braedon's right door. The BMW veered off the road and back on again. A frenetic pace at nearly one hundred miles per hour as Braedon steered onto the busy, but slow moving West Bay Road, routing through the touristy Seven Mile Beach section. The Porsche was closing in. People stopped and stared at the unbidden duo as they raced past tawdry shops and restaurants towards the affluent, colonial neighbourhoods.

The Porsche swung into the oncoming lane and was door-to-door with Braedon again, but another vehicle was driving straight towards it. The Porsche slammed its tired brakes while simultaneously the emergency brake was lifted. The Porsche lunged forward and drove hard to the right, tucking in behind Braedon once more.

The dexterous world champion suddenly turned right into an alley, but the Porsche couldn't stop in time and flew by, coming to a screeching halt. It backed up in a cloud of smoke and followed.

Braedon's trail saw him smash through metal garbage containers and scrap the brick walls as sparks showered in the dimly lit corridor. The BMW temporarily left the ground with the tiny hills and vales, constantly crashing against the wet pavement. The whoops and hollers from the taxed engines bounced and echoed off the high walls around the town centre. Blinding slivers of daylight flashed by as each vehicle raced past the various, crossing alleys. A mere foot on either side of the cars was the only distance between sleek, polished steel and the damp, unforgiving barrier.

Sunlight. The BMW exited the alley and rammed over the curb as it angled left. The Porsche followed but spun. Traffic was rapidly converging upon the Porsche and there was no time to right the car. It geared into reverse and the stressed engine was maximized, manoeuvring backwards through the maze of vehicles. The Porsche teetered on swerving out of control as the automobile rocked side to side. Finally, it created enough distance and performed a perfect power spin without losing momentum.

Braedon stole a look through the rear-view mirror to discover the Porsche was gone. A smile of relief broke across his face. He slowed the car and exhaled happily as he signalled a left hand turn to get back onto West Bay Road.

Braedon heard it first before he felt it, the gut wrenching sound of steel against steel as the Porsche T-boned the BMW and pushed it along the road in a blur of speed. Braedon frantically tried to steer away and eventually broke free and drove off as fast as he could. The Porsche straightened and bashed a wall, but managed to maintain the chase.

Braedon's eyes focused on the mirror again as he angrily pushed the BMW to its limit. Nary a second. When he turned his attention back to the road, he crushed the brakes, the tyres screaming mournfully while skidding helplessly to avoid a mother and daughter. The BMW began to spin as Braedon let go of the wheel and ducked. The car slid beneath a transport and the roof was sheared off before hitting the curb where it flipped over twice and came to a smouldering wreck upside down.

Braedon was barely discernable amongst the mangled metal and steam as his fingers scratched at the pavement, a deep gouge in his arm dribbling blood over his Provo tattoo. A steady stream of petrol splashed against the ground, pooling and trickling towards Braedon as he fought to wriggle free through the passenger side window. His face was bloodied with shards of the windshield peppered into his skin as his eyes blinked frantically to try and focus on the silhouette strolling towards him.

"I... I'm sorry... I am... I'm sorry," Braedon managed to whisper breathlessly and began weeping, blood oozing from his mouth and nose as the fuel continued to soak his body. A gloved hand reached inside the car and removed the briefcase, followed by the sound of shoes hurrying away. "Please... please don't leave me," Braedon cried just as the BMW caught fire. The world champion began screaming, but his voice faded as the vehicle became engulfed in flames and finally exploded.

The gloved hand carried the briefcase down a plush corridor of the hotel and silently inserted the room key. Inside, it was dark, the curtains

CHAPTER TWENTY-FOUR

swaying gently with the incoming breeze from the balcony. The briefcase was set down on a nearby table and the silhouette of someone wandered to the sliding doors, gazing upon the sinking red sun, partially obscured by rolling storm clouds.

Hands poured a glass full of wine and carried it outside to the long balcony, overlooking the dazzling, emerald water. There were two lounges and a midsize, marble statue of Chief Morgan.

"I see the pirates still come to the Cayman Islands," a man's voice said.

The silhouette on the balcony quickly pivoted and stepped into the dim light. Sarah Lynn, despite fading facial scars beneath her makeup, was a breathtaking beauty, long blonde hair, blue eyes, sharp features and a tight pair of jeans with a flimsy blouse. "Who the hell are you?" she asked with concern, trying to see in the murkiness and saw a glimmer of something metallic.

The lights suddenly turned on, revealing the massive, luxurious suite, decorated in light pastels with a distinctive Caribbean flair of art and rattan furnishings. There was an opulent bar with stools and rows of liquors. Silence, save the whirring ceiling fan, the crashing surf and the occasional, frolicking voice wafting in from the beach. "Are those the same gloves you wore to pull the trigger when you killed Vincenzo?" Randall said and limped closer with the aid of a steel cane.

"Get out or I'll call the police!" Sarah shouted.

Randall meandered to the bar and tossed a few ice cubes into a glass. "They're already here... Sarah Lynn," he said mockingly and poured a healthy amount of bourbon. "Cheers," he said, raising the glass and drinking half the contents before awkwardly sitting on a stool. Sarah ran for the door, but Randall quickly withdrew his pistol. "I'll put one in the back of your fucking head. Don't matter much to me," he said, making Sarah freeze. He lit a cigarette and spied the briefcase. "Looks like a tidy sum. You must be worth about thirty million... would pay for that voice change and the plastic surgery you got. That's why your prints don't match." Perplexed, Sarah slowly edged towards the balcony, but stopped when he waved the gun at her. "That's far enough, unless you plan on jumping, in which case, be my guest," he said sarcastically.

A moment of uncertainty until Sarah's eyes suddenly iced and she grinned. "Medial frontal lobe injury," she said with officialese. "I always tried to think right after... but I never could," she said and sat on the couch with her wine.

"Where is he?" Randall asked and took another gulp.

"Frying nicely in his BMW. He was going to take it all while I was away getting my make over," Sarah said with a brush of hand against her face. She emptied her wine and held it up. "May I?" she said, motioning to the bottle on the bar. Randall gave it to her and she filled her glass as he watched closely to ensure she didn't make a move. Sarah sat back and took another sip. "It's a lot of money. Perhaps we could make some kind of arrangement," she said gamesomely.

"The only thing I ever did was take a little dope from the evidence room and that was a mistake," he said and blew a perfect smoke circle. "I actually cried when I took the oath... it meant something to me... and it still does."

"Pity," she said with a sigh. "So, how did you know?" she asked playfully.

Randall withdrew some folded papers from inside his denim jacket. "She's been dead for over a year. I checked. No calls ever made to her. I knew that for a while. I just wanted to see how far you'd go."

"A slight oversight," Sarah said with a carefree shrug and a chilling smile.

"Those are the ones that usually get you caught," he said matter-of-factly as a distant rumble of thunder was heard and Sarah grimaced from a sudden pain in her head. Randall reached into his pocket and found a bottle of pills. "Aspirin uh? It's really Haldol," he said and tossed them to her. "They obviously don't work... split lips," he said as his face soured.

Gwen smiled again and washed the medication down with her wine. "Let me guess, you found those papers when you were in my study at my house in France," she said and Randall nodded. "You're supposed to be dead. Am I talking to a ghost?" she asked ironically.

"Almost. I damn near did die. The doctor was in on it. The vest under my uniform wouldn't let you hear my heart," he said and crushed out his smoke before lighting another. "The cane is only temporary, no thanks to you."

"I guess you want to know why," she said and crossed her legs.

"Where's Jess?" he said with concern.

"I put her up for adoption. You might not think so, but I knew it would be too traumatic for her after my change. Besides, she would have given me away being seen with her," she said casually.

Randall stared at her in disbelief for a few seconds. "Jesus... you really are a psychopath... a fucking monster," he whispered.

Gwen suddenly hurled the glass past him where it smashed against the wall. "I'm a victim! You made me what I am!" she yelled. "If you weren't drunk, the accident would never have happened!"

"You could have got some help for Christ's sake!"

"I tried!" she screamed, but was soon eerily calm again. "I realized I couldn't change... so I just told them what they wanted to hear," she said with a grin. "I'm a respected member of the DST. I wasn't going to throw it all away because my ex-husband was responsible... the French government is taking away our family estate because of my father! I'll have nothing and I deserve more... financially more and I had the means to do it," she said with a menacing face.

"How?" he simply asked, but couldn't stand to look at her.

Another heavy sigh and she drank directly from the bottle. "It all started by accident," she said with a laugh. "The DST had got word that Vincenzo was in the market for an assassin. He wanted Braedon dead for screwing Teresa. He wanted it to happen on the track. We knew the Rabbit was the trigger. I told Braedon about it... greed is an amazing thing, isn't it?" she said happily. "I had a plan and Braedon went along with it. That's why his name is on the account."

"Did you fuck him?" Randall asked, seething with anger.

Another wide smile. "Naturally, but I was going to kill him anyway eventually," she said unconcerned.

"Why me? Revenge?"

"I needed to keep the game going. You know, raise the stakes," she said and pointed to his cigarettes. "Can I have one?"

Randall lit one and gave it to her. "I was expendable... you wanted a target to get more money," he said rhetorically.

"Oh, don't look so surprised. You said you had it figured out long ago," she said and drew heavily on the tobacco.

"You cut the fuel line, didn't you?"

"I had to keep the threat alive. I also had Braedon chase us that day in the black BMW. Thank goodness he's a bad shot. And he arranged for us to get shot at in the motel," she said with a hearty chuckle. "I even hit you from behind in the alley and gave myself a pretty good bruising."

"So you shot yourself in Montreal?"

Gwen raised the bottle. "It was convincing, wasn't it?" she replied proudly. "A fan did get up to my position, but I made him leave."

"You trained in sharp shooting with the DST, didn't you? You forced the Rabbit to drink and helped him over the balcony," he said, eyeing the patio as the rain began to lash inside. "What about Felipe and Alberto?"

"Now that was fun. I borrowed one of Ichiro's swords. Remember Alberto thought he knew me? We had met in Monaco last year and I couldn't take the chance that he would cause trouble," she said and closed her eyes, refreshed by the cool air across her face. "I did society a favour anyway."

"What about my accident at Silverstone?"

"Pure coincidence," she said and started laughing again.

Randall removed a tape recorder from his pocket and clicked it off. "You're under arrest Gwen... but you already know your rights, don't you?"

Gwen laughed harder and set the wine down with a bang. "Don't be so serious. Look, if it makes you feel any better. I really was starting to fall in love with you again," she said, her voice trailing off. "But then I would remember what you did to me... to my baby," she said angrily.

"Stand up please," he said and withdrew a pair of handcuffs.

Gwen's face hardened. "You're going to have to kill me Randall. Otherwise, I walk out of here. That tape is inadmissible and you know it. You have no jurisdiction here."

Randall produced a small, plastic folder and flipped it open. "I do now... the DST was very interested in my theory even before you asked them for the money to put into the account. I'm a special agent for them, and since you're one of their former employees and a French citizen, I can haul you in."

Gwen's smirk vanished just as a huge strike of lightning doused the power. In an instant, she bolted for the balcony and leapt off, but Randall managed to grab her arm and she dangled twenty floors up. Her face softened as she closed her eyes again. "I love the ocean... my father used to take us... I can still see the water sparkling... it went on forever... I can smell the sand," she whispered and slowly opened her eyes. "Let me go, Randall... please... I want to rest... I want to be free now."

Randall struggled to heave her back over the rail, but couldn't as his game leg began to ache and buckle. "Hang on!" he said through gritted teeth as his hands began to moisten with the rain.

She began to weep. "I did love you... I always have," she said, her eyes locked with his.

"Don't... please, Gwen," he said as his grip loosened. "Give me your other hand!"

"I'm sorry, Randall... I hope there's a heaven... for both of us... take care of her," she said with a warm smile and released him. He watched in horror as her serene eyes faded, her white blouse flapping with the wind until finally, she disappeared into the arms of death.

Chapter Twenty-Five

"Don't do it sir," Tony said anxiously, peering over the railing of the Skyway Bridge. "Please wait until help arrives."
Randall craned his neck and looked skyward, his delicate balance wavering. It was a clear night. Stars were visible, a rarity since the steel companies' plumes of smoke usually obliterated any signs of celestial bodies. The wind was picking up and for a split second, Randall thought he felt the bridge move. Impossible. It must be an optical illusion, thanks to the barely visible clouds passing fleetly overhead. He could hear the sound of water far below, crashing against the steel structure.
"I hate the night," Randall said. "Fear... I guess... terrified to go to bed because my brain takes over... thinking about how screwed up things are... with me... with the world," he said and gazed into the black abyss. "Every time I make an arrest... I lose a little more faith in humanity... and sometimes I used to drink myself into oblivion just so I could close my eyes, if only for a few hours... but that kind of life leads to an early grave... so I stopped. Think about what you're doing," Randall said. No answer. He stepped off of the ledge with one foot, clung to a girder with both hands and searched the darkness again. "Can you hear me son?" he asked, his voice echoing off of the dizzying network of beams and rivets.
"Just leave me alone!" a young man's reply bellowed from below. He was close but invisible.
"All I want to do is to talk to you. What's your name?" Randall said and withdrew a cigarette.
"Tom," the frightened voice reluctantly said.
"Tom, my name is Randall. How old are you?" Randall said, cupping his hands to the lighter.
"Fifteen."
"Tell me about your problem," Randall said and leaned against the steel frame.
"Fuck of a lot you care!" the angry teen shot back with a hint of tears.

Randall meticulously planted a foot on a descending beam and lowered the rest of his body. A sudden whip of bone chilling air howled through the labyrinth of construction and dissipated, but not before relieving Randall of his policeman's cap. He watched it sail and disappear into the inky darkness. "Believe it or not, I do care. I want to help you, Tom," he said, his eyes scanning the murkiness for movement.

"You're just saying that because you're a cop!"

"What could be so bad that you want to kill yourself?" Randall said, the cigarette hanging from his mouth.

A few moments of silence. "I... I can't talk about it... I don't want to talk about it! Just leave me alone!"

"Try me."

"No... you'll send me to jail! And I'm not going back there! Ever!" the youngster shouted.

"If there's a valid reason, I promise you that won't happen. Tell me what you did. I can help you," Randall said and lowered himself to another beam.

"I think... I think I killed him," the boy blurted and began to whimper. "I didn't mean to... I just wanted to... I didn't mean to," Tom said, his voice fading with the breeze and the sound of heavy traffic.

"Who do you think you killed?" Randall asked quietly and looked up to find Tony leaning over the railing, listening intently.

More crying. Sobs wafting upward. "My dad... I pushed him and he fell... hit his head against the couch... he was bleeding... wasn't breathing... I didn't mean it."

"Why did you push him?"

"I can't," Tom replied, patently embarrassed.

"Listen to me Tom... you can tell me. I promise nothing is going to happen to you," Randall said and hurried to turn his shoulder radio off when a dispatcher's voice came on.

"He was... he did things to me... he... I can't!"

Randall's eyes dilated and his heart suddenly pounded harder. "He abused you, didn't he, Tom?" he asked, lowering his voice.

More seconds of shamed silence. "Do you... do you believe in God?"

"Maybe... I guess... yes... it's a work in progress... He and I are going to try and work things out. Do you?"

"I did... but how could there be a God when He lets that kind of shit happen to me?" Tom shouted and began to sob.

"It's okay to be angry with Him, Tom... shows you believe in Him but... but I don't know why stuff like that happens... maybe He doesn't have any control... maybe He isn't supposed to... I know it doesn't make a lot of sense, but we all have to believe in something," Randall said and looked to the heavens again. "There has to be more to life than life itself and death... someone or something watches over how the universe unfolds."

"My dad... he did abuse me," Tom's weakened voice said.

"I know how you're feeling... it happened to me too," Randall said as his eyes glazed.

"You're lying! You're just saying that to get me to stop! It won't work! Leave me alone!"

Randall sank to his knees and leaned against a beam, lost in the torture of his own past. "My father was murdered... when I found out about it... I was devastated... but kind of glad it was finally over," he said as the pigeons fluttered away, leaving a few feathers to float and circle. "I remember the morning that would be my last with him... it was cold... we'd been in a deep freeze for days and it just kept snowing... that morning my mother woke me up and told me to come down for breakfast.... I can remember the hallway and see their separate bedrooms... even the dank smell of the old house," he said as his eyes began to water. "There was nothing special about the breakfast... same old porridge and bacon... was always lots of meat, but it was too expensive for the other families... I'd always trade my roast beef sandwiches at school for peanut butter and jam," he said, recalling with a smile. "The kids figured they were taking advantage of me, but I was smarter... I got their desserts too... at breakfast we didn't talk... never did... old man read the paper while my mom did kitchen duty... I hated eating at the same table with him... he was messy and noisy... made me angry," he said as his lips curled in rage. "He was a butcher... he ate like the animals he killed, but at least they had an excuse... they were animals... sometimes I think he ate like that just to make me mad... but I never said anything because he'd cuff me... or worse," Randall said and sniffed hard. "We didn't even make eye contact that day... the night before I woke up because they were having an argument... always were, but this was bad... I knew why... I saw him stumbling down the hall towards her room... I could smell that disgusting alcohol... I guess she refused him and he hit her... hard," he said and winced at the memory. "That was the only time I was mad at her... if she had let him... he might not have come to me... he left for work... always heard that engine trying to start and that sound... the tyres crunching the packed snow," he said and shivered at the thought. "She tried to talk to me... like it would make up for what was happening to me... maybe she didn't know... maybe she did and was scared... maybe the disgrace was too much... for both of us... I went to school... I'd always pass his shop... sometimes he would wave," Randall said with a faint smile. "He was in the back that day... the closed sign was on the door... I opened it... the knob was dull and sticky from years of his blood-stained hands... I was careful not to make the bell ring above the door... I walked to that filthy leather flap," he said angrily and started trembling. "He was hovering over a fresh kill... it was heavy, but I managed to lift it... he kept it behind the counter... took both hands... I wasn't even shaking... the blast knocked me over... I got up and saw him slumped over the cow... was a tiny bullet hole in his back... smoke coming out of it," he said as the cigarette fell from his hands. "No guilt... no tears... I started to think maybe he wasn't dead... but he was... his blood drained into the grate just like the animals... I threw the gun away and went to school... and that was it... I killed my dad Tom... I never told anybody that... you're the first person," Randall said with a shaking voice.

Above, Tony was shocked and moved by the revelation as several police cars were now approaching. Tony turned and waved them to stay back. "That's a secret between you and me, Tom... okay?" Randall asked trying to maintain composure, but the emotion gave him away.

"You crying?" Tom wondered, starting to believe the disclosure.

"Let me help you... don't make the same mistakes I made, Tom... please," Randall said and peered over the beam's edge to discover Tom, a lanky boy, stepping out from beneath the shadow of another strut. "I spent a lifetime being angry for something that wasn't my fault," he said with a warm smile. "Got to follow your own way and don't punish people who have nothing to do with your grief... there's a lot of messed up people in the world for a lot of different reasons, but we're all equal... you just have to believe in yourself... even if you're the only one," Randall said and extended his hand. Tom went to grab it but a sudden, stiff current of air caused him to lose his balance. Tom fell screaming and vanished into the darkness. A tumultuous splash seconds later. "God!" Randall yelled and without hesitation, jumped from the beam.

The water knifed through his body and he nearly lost consciousness, but the frigid water awakened him. Randall opened his eyes, but could discern nothing in the dead quiet of blackness. He caught a flash of his own bubbles as they glimmered upward. His chest ached; the pressure of the collision had broken his ribs. There wasn't much time. Randall grabbed at the water around him, hoping to catch a piece of Tom. Air was running out. His lungs were ready to explode. Randall kicked his legs and started to the top, all the while his hands feeling for life.

Skin, getting colder but a hint of warmth. Randall took hold of Tom's arm and rushed for the top. Both burst through the water's surface and greedily sucked at the air. Randall cradled the young man in his arms and kept him afloat. "I got you Tom... I got you."

Chapter Twenty-Five

The young man was loaded into the ambulance as Randall watched, huddled beneath a blanket. "I'll visit you tomorrow and we'll talk," Randall said to him with sincerity. There was a nervous but hopeful smile from Tom before the doors closed.

Tony covered Randall with another blanket and offered him a cup of steaming coffee.

"That kid is pretty lucky. Just two broken legs after that fall?" Tony said incredulously as he looked up at the bridge. "I once fell off the garage roof and broke both my arms and legs. I was out cold for two days," he said and realized he was running off at the mouth. "Are you okay, sir?"

"I think so," Randall answered, wincing from his cracked ribs and checked his tattered, moist photograph of Jessica in his breast pocket. "Had my lucky charm with me."

Tony wrapped his arm around him and walked him out of earshot, away from the other officers milling about. "I ah... I heard what you said about your father... it won't go any further."

"I haven't decided what I'm going to do about that," Randall said and lit a cigarette, "Might talk to the Crown, might never say anything."

"The kid did kill his father. The call just came in," Tony hesitated to say. "Poor kid. I hate to think of the shit he's going to have to go through."

Randall raised an eyebrow at Tony's cursing. "An officer shouldn't swear... lets the world know you have no respect for yourself."

"I've been hanging around you too much, sir," Tony said with a smile and watched the ambulance driving away. "I hope he makes it."

"I'll be there for him. In a way he's lucky, he's still young enough to face it and get some help... and not let it ruin the rest of his life," Randall said. "Hiding only makes it worse... for everybody... and sooner or later you have to deal with it."

Tony awkwardly slapped him on the back. "It's been quite a night. What do you say I buy you a drink?"

Randall gave it a long thought, grinned and shook his head. "No, I've had enough of that thanks. I just want to get home to my daughter. Cat's probably wrecked the place too," he said and dropped his smoke on the ground. "Guess I'll quit these things too. Got to stick around for Jess. See you," he said with a wave.

"Don't forget, Wallace wants to see you in the morning. It sounds like you're going back to homicide," Tony called out to him.

Randall stopped and slowly pivoted to face him. "I think I'll keep walking the beat with you. I'd rather deal with the living for a while.

Night Officer D'Angelo," Randall said respectfully with another smile and walked out of the splash of light before blending into the shadows.

A rookie officer promptly appeared at Tony's side, watching Randall's silhouette, the blanket flapping on his back as he walked to an awaiting ambulance. "I saw what that guy did. Jesus, who the hell is he, Superman?" he asked sarcastically.

"Close... booger," Tony replied, picking up Randall's cigarette and popping it in his mouth. He spied the junior cop and focused on Randall again, "Pretty damn close."

The End